DAWN OF THE CHUPACABRA

Chupacabra Series Book IV

Michael Hebler

Night After Night Publications, LLC

For Barbie
(for lending her time, her support, and her home)

CONTENTS

Title Page

Copyright

Dedication

Book IV   1

Chapter I   2

Chapter II   21

Chapter III   36

Chapter IV   54

Chapter V   71

Chapter VI   91

Chapter VII   110

Chapter VIII   133

Chapter IX   148

Chapter X   168

Chapter XI   195

Chapter XII   214

Chapter XIII   224

Chapter XIV   247
Chapter XV   268
Chapter XVI   287
Chapter XVII   307
Chapter XVIII   326
Chapter XIX   346
Chapter XX   362
Chapter XXI   376
Chapter XXII   395
Chapter XXIII   408
Chapter XXIV   432
Chapter XXV   452
Chapter XXVI   478
Book V   491
Acknowledgement   493
Praise For Author   495
Chupacabra Series   497
Books By This Author   499

BOOK IV

Dawn of the Chupacabra

CHAPTER I

It was dawn. Jeremiah awoke and gasped for air as though he had to fight for his share despite the polluted atmosphere being in ample supply. However, just as soon as he inhaled his first breath, his portion was interrupted when a cold, mud-caked hand covered his bearded mouth. It stymied the reek of burnt cottonwood, hickory, and decomposing human flesh with no intention to suffocate.

Jeremiah did not protest. He lay motionless in the mud and allowed his befuddled mind to align with his brutal reality. Remarkable as it was that he had managed to sleep through the night, the larger astonishment was that he had survived to see another new day.

Having proved that he would remain calm, the hand removed itself from Jeremiah's mouth. He breathed his ration of the air that was just as foul and rancorous as it had been seconds before. Even if able to walk out of this forest patch, the rotten odor of corpses would follow him wherever he went as most of the stench had soaked into his full beard. It would not surprise him one bit to find a small tear of flesh burrowing in his thicket.

"He still out there?"

"Suspect so," answered Martin in a dull whisper.

The way Jeremiah figured, suspecting was not the same as knowing. After cowering down in the muck of near-freezing mud, black ash, and congealed blood, he had every right to know the truth of it.

"Did ya look?"

Martin's eyes glanced first at his wounded right leg where he could no longer recognize the light gray coloring of the shredded wool fabric. Not only the trousers, but his bare flesh and exposed chunks of muscle tissue, integrated with the slimy blackness seamlessly. "I tried."

Jeremiah understood. Laying stagnant for days behind the large tree stump they used for a shield was uncomfortable as hell. In attempting to find some relief, Martin shifted his leg. The occurrence happened two days prior and Jeremiah could still hear Martin's outcry of unbearable torture ringing in his ear. If they managed to get out of this alive, Martin most assuredly would need an amputation. Unfortunately, this also meant that Jeremiah would need to be the one who investigated the sniper.

He stretched his good arm across his body and placed pressure on the hole in his arm. A bullet had gone clean through, and the wound hurt like hell when flexed. Applying pressure would lull the pain some as he leaned up high enough to peer over their protective cover. Jeremiah twisted his body into position when the gun that rested on his chest fell into the mud. He had forgotten he put the revolver there for ease of a quick draw. His mind was slipping some.

Keep yer wits, boy.

Jeremiah peered at his friend awkwardly though the voice sounded nothing like Martin. However, he had no trouble identifying whom the voice sounded most like. The inflections and tones had been deep and aggressive like his father's, but the notion that his pa was in these ruins of battle was as preposterous as bringing the dead back to life. The man would be home where he consistently drank and made life intolerable for his wife.

But nobody other than Martin could have spoken words so legibly next to his ear. He asked, "What'd you say?"

"You know I can't look. Not without screamin' like a lame crow."

He must have been hearing things. Jeremiah shook his head as though trying to cast out whatever got stuck inside. Hallucinations would not improve his situation.

He picked up the pistol then, reminded by its heavier weight, knew the weapon was not his own. While hanging onto to his army-issued, Martin kindly relinquished the Smith and Wesson Number Two Revolver he brought from home. He had

4

kept the Remington '58 concealed in the haversack, which he guarded by keeping it strapped securely around his torso and tucked beneath one arm. Foolishly, Jeremiah had lost his weapon during their attempt to retreat from the losing battle of... he thought for a moment and tried to recollect where they were. A mild panic built inside him when he could not recall immediately, but then he muttered, "Newtonia."

"What?" Martin asked.

Martin's inquiry went unanswered. Jeremiah remained focused on collecting the remainder of his scattered memories. Newtonia was what he remembered first. It lies in the Ozarks at the Southwest corner of Missouri. He and Martin were less than fifty miles from their home in the adjoining county of McDonald. They had never been so close to home since enlisting together in the Confederate's Army two years prior. On that day in September of 1862, they had walked right up to Colonel Douglas H. Cooper and requested to join his division. Their voluntary service had transpired almost exactly where they lie now. It was in Newtonia that he and Martin, who was more like the brother he never had rather than a friend, had their first wartime combat, which ended in victory. Now, here they were again, in October of sixty-four, back where they had started after being defeated in the second battle of Newtonia under the command of Major General Price. This action occurred on the twenty-eighth day of October, which meant it was now October thirty-first, and tomorrow would be All Saints' Day. Jeremiah figured there could be no better day to end this standoff by having one of the two opposing sides perish--preferably that Yankee sniper.

Once he cleaned the mud off the pistol as best he could, Jeremiah continued putting pressure on his wound, and then grunted quietly as he resumed peering over the log. The clearing that led to the tree line was no larger than the size of a small home with more black than color between him and the dense woods. It all looked the same as when he last checked. The only difference was that the smoking embers inside the charred and crusted trees extinguished sometime during the night. Despite the decaying odor coming off the thirty-two decomposing corpses that surrounded him--having had time enough to count them all--the whiff of burning hickory returned his mind to memories of home, and his stomach to food, of which they had none. The near freezing conditions, his pains, and famine were all to blame for his weakened state of mind.

Beyond the seared plot of land, the treetop canopy kept what lay beyond shadowed in darkness, concealing the Yankee's position exceptionally well; unless the boy no longer hunkered down in the woods. After three days, he might have forgone his infatuation on killing Jonny Rebs, returning to the nearby road to catch up with his squadron. However, the more likely scenario was that he, too, had fallen asleep. This Yank had been the most tenacious Jeremiah had ever come across, as though he had a vendetta to settle. More than once the boy had tried to sneak up from behind to put bullets in their skulls, but each time, they had been warned by the sound of footsteps squishing in the dense mud. They fired upon the Yank with repeated shots. The blue coat's slow reloading of the 1861 Springfield rifle was no match for either of their pistols when it came to speed. The Yankee retreated into the woods where he could keep an upper hand, and he had stayed put ever since, patiently waiting for an opportunity to be presented.

"He pull out?" Martin asked, desperate for the answer to his prayers.

"Or he ain't waked yet." All his life, Jeremiah never felt shame for being naturally suspicious of everything and everyone. His cynicism had saved him on more than one occasion, and Martin too, when they got into all kinds of trouble as youngsters.

Jeremiah seeped back into his bed of mud. He then picked up where he had left off before falling asleep, and stared at the same dead Confederate that he had fixated on for the last three days. Jeremiah never considered the deceased a friend because he did not know the man well. In fact, as he thought on it, he could not recall the private's name. His comrade had been gunned down by the same Yank that presently had them pinned, but that was not what intrigued Jeremiah about the corpse. A trick was being played on him. Be it his weakened mind, the frigid conditions, the excruciating pain, or any combination of the aforementioned, because, on occasion, he had witnessed the dead man move ever-so-slightly. Martin had not observed any of the incidents in question, or so he had said, and there was no reason for him to lie. Jeremiah feared that seeing things that weren't possible did not bode well.

"Hey, Jerry? I sho' wish we wuz kids ag'in, an' it wuz summer. Remember?"

Jeremiah did remember, very well. They had just reminisced about their childhood yesterday, and the day before that. Martin's mind was slipping too; either that, or he was desperate to pass the time. He could not deny his friend the pleasure of recollection despite the pact they had made to discontinue all unnecessary conversation. Needless talk would not only call the sniper's attention, but the distraction of discourse about better times and places would keep them off their guard. Nevertheless, the days were too distressing to be kept in constant silence.

"Summer's too hot. Spring."

"Okay, spring then. You, me, an' Alice layin' in the warm sun at the watering hole."

Bitterness consumed Jeremiah, but the attack had not come from the wintery air. Though Martin knew damn well that Alice was the subject of considerable soreness, perhaps he did not intend to acknowledge her name. Since joining the army, he had done well limiting mention of her. Jeremiah did recognize how difficult that would be for Martin when pining for her closeness, just as Martin had recognized Jeremiah's deep feelings for his wife. Both had courted their childhood friend for a time, but to this day, Alice never divulged why she had chosen Martin over him to marry. However, she did not need to. Jeremiah knew why. There were two reasons, with money being the first, and Martin having more of it. The Stebbins were well off. He would not consider them rich, but they were one of the wealthiest families to live in the Ozark Mountains. The Stebbins had two slaves: Bonnie and JoJo, where he and his family had none. They also had their Victorian two-story home built and then filled with the same furniture they manufactured; the house where Jeremiah had been raised was nothing more than a log cabin with one adjoining room. The main quarters did not contain anything more than a dining table, some chairs, and a couple of shelves. But the Stebbins hadn't always been so comfortable. Until he and Martin had reached the age of eleven, both families lived a plot apart, but then Werner Stebbins Furniture met with sudden success. Soon after, Martin's pa moved them to a meadow on the opposite side of town. Jeremiah often wondered if they would have still been friends if Martin had never lived just as meagerly. Perhaps it was best he never knew. But if money was not the reason for Alice's decision, then it had to be her fear that the son of a Whiting could not give her children. His ma and pa had struggled to see him into this world and never were able to conceive another, whereas Werner and Betsy Stebbins had successfully born five children, including a set of twins. Jeremiah's ma often referred to him as her miracle, but he never felt so miraculous. Alice would have preferred Martin as her husband for either reason. Jeremiah saw no other explanation for her decision.

"That watering hole saved our lives," added Jeremiah, hiding all animosity.

Martin chuckled some, but not loudly. "Sho' it did... sho' it did."

"Damn near suffocated breathin' in that thick, hot air."

"Alice always says you can cut through it like butter."

He mentioned her again. Jeremiah now was convinced Martin had done so on purpose, but he also knew it was not to wound him. Knowing Martin so well, his partner was under the impression that he would die in this spot.

Jeremiah watched Martin's gaze turn to warm affection as he peered up to the morbid sky. He could only imagine how his friend was thinking of Alice, painting the gray canvas with her long black hair, large brown eyes, and milky white skin; of which Jeremiah had caught glimpses of during their time at the watering hole. He knew how many freckles she had on her face after secretly counting them once she fell asleep sunbathing near his side: twenty-two. Just the thought of her was the cause of his current arousal, and he was not in a position to pleasure himself.

"What I wouldn't give for some of that heat now," continued Martin.

Jeremiah shifted his focus back to the woods. All remained quiet and still. This time, the Billy Yank hadn't tried sneaking up from behind during their conversation. The soldier might have been just as cold, tired, and hungry. Jeremiah doubted that the blue coat had any food on him. The catalyst of this most recent bloodbath had been circumstantial and not planned. All hell broke loose when the two squadrons marched along the road and happened upon each other. However, what the sniper did not share with his marks was the weakening of a severe wound; at least, none that Jeremiah witnessed during their brief encounters. If the kid was injured, he sure as hell did not let it influence his fortitude. The boy had bounded back for his post like a frightened jackrabbit after each failed sneak attack. Jeremiah speculated that comparable grueling conditions should be affecting the Bluecoat as well. It was plausible to consider that, during the night, the Yankee might have traded his station for a hot meal and a warm bed elsewhere. Appearing no older than fourteen years, Billy Boy did not share his and Martin's nineteen years of stamina and knowhow, and would most likely discontinue his stalking for the comforts of home. His lack of resilience was Jeremiah's best hope, but hope was all he had. In truth, there was no way of knowing for certain without putting Martin and himself in eminent danger.

No need to look. He's still out there.

Jeremiah shuddered then glanced in all directions. Again, the harsh voice of his father had spoken as though Jeremiah should be able to feel the warmth of breath against his ear, which he did not. For a moment, he considered that the boy in blue had snuck up from behind to send him over the edge of sanity by mimicking his father.

Mocking laughter followed that thought. *Dunderhead. What fuck all world is you livin' where that Yank knows who yer pa is or what he sounds like?*

Jeremiah covered his ears. Honestly, he did not think it would help block the annoying ridicule, but somehow, it did. He exhaled a frustrated breath then glanced upward towards the sky that continued to seize Martin's attention. Until three days ago, a canopy of trees had kept this area cocooned, but then the explosions of cannon fire annihilated this patch of forest and revealed a dark sky saturated with clouds, smoke, or both. Whichever had dyed the air gray--a color he honored a short time ago--he did not much care for at the moment. Jeremiah would much rather be able to see the golden hues of the sun spread across the atmosphere or, dare he wish, the blue of a vibrant sky. The birds as well, he missed them too. Perhaps they were just as miserable without having the sun to sing to, or maybe the battle had scared them away, never to return. He had not heard a single chirp since bedding down in this clearing.

It happened again! Jeremiah crooked his head after seeing movement out of the corner of his eye.

"There!" He burst in a hard whisper while pointing to the remains that had been the subject of his obsession. But again, the body lies as motionless as a rock, and his friend wasn't buying what he was selling.

Jeremiah did not press the issue. He would never be able to convince Martin without him witnessing the movement for himself. In fact, as he continued to watch the corpse, Jeremiah questioned his sanity. In more than just the voice and the twitching remains, it would seem lunacy was attempting to creep in more stealthily than the sniper. He had to get out of here before he lost all his good sense. "I can't stay another day."

"We could make a try for it."

Jeremiah's initial glance was not to confirm Martin's sincerity but to observe the muddied ribbons of flesh dangling from his buddy's leg.

"You can't walk," he reminded.

"I can crawl."

Jeremiah grimaced and did not bother hiding his true feelings of Martin's affirmation.

He'll only slow you down.

Jeremiah considered the idea a moment before he gave a single nod. There were no other options.

He held out his hand. "Gimme the haversack." Puzzlement spread across Martin's face. "You shouldn' be draggin' nuttin' slowin' ya down."

The argument made sense. Carefully, Martin bent at the waist, and then pulled the haversack's strap over his head, relinquishing it with sustained hesitation. Jeremiah understood Martin's struggle. The bag contained all of his most valued treasures: a pair of socks, extra ammunition, a spherical hand grenade, a detached bayonet, a canteen that was, unfortunately, empty, and the piece-de-resistance, a journal filled with all his thoughts since entering the war, which included love letters to Alice and words of endearment for each member of his extensive family. In exchange, Jeremiah handed Martin a tree branch, which had been lying next to him in the filth.

"For bitin' down on," he explained.

By the look of worry that plagued his face, Martin clearly had not considered the ramifications of this escape. He took the branch but did not clench it between his teeth just yet. He would hold out until it was absolutely necessary.

If the sniper continued lying in wait, he was to their north. Jeremiah glanced in the three remaining directions from which they had to choose. Each had its own benefits and its own disadvantages. East was a clear shot but would take them further from the road. The large log that had protected them would continue to do so until they reached the southern tree line, but that path was laden with corpses that would undoubtedly hinder Martin's movement. Additionally, the body that had been haunting Jeremiah lies south. West appeared to be their most viable option as the only obstruction was a not-so-worrying indent in the ground from a cannonball--the same cannonball that had shredded Martin's leg and left them trapped in their position. Beyond that, the main road rested no more than a thousand feet.

"I don' understand why he don' jus' go an' leave us be. The war's gonna end soon, anyhow. Bastard Blue almost got it won."

"Well, the war's over fer us by the ways I see it."

Martin's look of surprise shocked Jeremiah.

"Whatcha mean?" Martin questioned with trepidation.

Jeremiah hesitated to answer while he studied the friend he knew better than his own mother. Predicting that Martin would object at first, he would come around... hopefully.

"I'm talkin' 'bout desertion."

"A. W. O. L.?!" Martin spouted at full volume, and wide-eyed.

Quickly, Jeremiah slapped his mud-covered hand over Martin's mouth much the same way his friend had done to him earlier. "An' why'd not? The Major General went and lef' us fer dead, didn't he? The army wouldn't know no different." Jeremiah paused, but it became apparent that his friend was not convinced. He needed to strike him with what mattered... his heart. "We could go back home an' be with our families. We could getcha back ta Alice." Jeremiah saw Martin twitch; much like the corpse had. Martin's stern expression relaxed, but only a hair. Jeremiah needed to seal the deal. "She's been waitin' on ya. Besides, we ain't fit fer fightin' no more no how."

That was all. Jeremiah had no more ammo. All he could do now was wait to see if he had hit his target, but when Martin slapped Jeremiah's hand off of his mouth, he knew he had missed his mark even before Martin spat, "I ain't no coward!"

The stern scowl Jeremiah received was difficult to witness. Not only was he accused of being a coward, but a traitor to his country. He had never seen his best friend look upon him with such disdain. It was unbearable how small Martin could make him feel, but in truth, not even God would be able to force him in continuing with this suicidal war. If their situation had been different, Jeremiah most definitely would attempt to argue his point, but this was neither the time nor the place to debate loyalties. This moment was reserved for survival. Jeremiah hung his head in shame and nodded in feigned agreement.

"Yer righ'. It wuz the fatigue talkin', thas all. I didn' mean nuttin' by it. We'll catch up with Price an' regroup."

The sternness behind Martin's glower softened, but it did not make Jeremiah feel any more at ease with his position. Martin hadn't bought a word of it. His friend knew he was being told what he wanted to hear. That was the problem with knowing each other so well. Moreover, knowing Martin the way he did, his best buddy would not remain silent once they fled this forest. Martin was too honorable in that regard. Despite all this knowing and forecasting, Jeremiah felt the need to continue with the charade, "I'll carry ya if ya need me ta."

Martin's judgment stayed firm a second longer until the ridiculous offer formed a grin on his lips--Jeremiah could barely hold up a gun with his wounded arm. With the mood between them lightened, Martin asked, "Which way?"

Having made the decision moments before, Jeremiah motioned west.

Martin chomped down on the tree branch and then inhaled a deep breath before he grabbed his leg by the pant. His face tightened and turned bright red instantly. Muffled groans poured through the small gap between his lips as he dragged one leg over the top of the other then rolled onto his stomach.

Jeremiah watched Martin push past the pain. He greatly admired his buddy's effort but was not blind to the fact that a hasty escape would be impractical. Shelving his concern for a moment, he poked his head over the log in search of any new developments regarding the sniper's position. Still, there was nothing. He sincerely hoped he had miscalculated the Yankee's resilience and that the boy had given up already.

He glanced at Martin, who had pulled out his military-assigned pistol, readied for action. Jeremiah ducked his head below the top of the stump to keep the sniper from seeing him nod a signal to his partner that all was clear.

Martin bit down harder in anticipation of the next wave of pain that would occur when he reached forward. His fingers dug into the sludge as he pulled. Martin dragged his body, inch by inch, and did a remarkable job of deadening his agonizing cries. In fact, the loudest noise came from the release of suction when Martin pulled his hand out of the dense stew.

The time to travel six feet had taken more than a minute, but once Martin cleared the stump, he dipped the first half of his body into the cannonball crater.

Jeremiah kept watch on the sniper's vicinity. All remained quiet and serene, but the voice inside his ear boomed, *don't be a fuckin' Dunderhead!*

I ain't a Dunderhead, Jeremiah argued, just as he did each time his pa would insult him by that name.

Hand over the reins. I'll take it from here, the voice ordered. Jeremiah then slipped his hand into the haversack.

Martin struggled inside the depression. The indent of the hole was a mere quarter foot deep, but it was enough to delay any man weakened by terrible and consistent pain.

A small splash of mud bubbled next to his ear, accompanied by the eruption of a gunshot.

Jeremiah ducked as Martin curled into a ball and protected his head. He peeked back at him through the gap between his crossed arms as Jeremiah pulled the grenade out of the haversack.

Another bullet missed, but like its predecessor, it

was too close for comfort. Being below ground level had a slight advantage, but that benefit would last only a few seconds more.

Jeremiah pulled the pin on the explosive and held it out for his trapped friend to witness. He then motioned for Martin to continue towards the forest. Promptly, his friend turned around to crawl.

As though he bore claws, Martin dug in when the next bullet splattered gooey muck across the right side of his face followed by a larger splash on his left. Martin turned to the object that had not been a bullet, but the grenade. Gaping blankly at his own explosive being used against him, Jeremiah shouted, "I have to. I'm sorry, brother!"

The eruption raised a wall made of mud, smoke, and most unfortunately, Martin. Jeremiah ran through the cloud of carnage, leaping over the crater as gunfire chased after him. The cover was what Jeremiah had needed to make his getaway.

The barrier of disruption had worked just as the voice inside his head had said it would. He broke past the tree line and leaped into the thicket, no longer weighed down by a gimp.

Once the patter of raining debris had settled, and the sniper's footsteps were heard running after his prey, the coast was clear. The corpse, which had only pretended to be a corpse, rose from the ashes. The undead Confederate struggled through the slippery mud but managed to escape while Jeremiah Whiting kept the Union sniper distracted.

He ran the opposite direction.

CHAPTER II

When Martin injured his leg, Jeremiah believed that the fate of his friend had been sealed. Then came three days of wallowing in the mud, and with each new day came reinvigorated astonishment as Martin hung on. What Jeremiah initially thought was a delay of the inevitable became Martin's will to survive. However, the struggle for survival had been Martin's hardship to bear, not Jeremiah's. They shared many things throughout childhood but death would not be included, not if he, the one with the brash voice, had any control over the matter.

"You kilt 'im! My friend!" Jeremiah blamed.

The voice explained, *I did what needed doin'.*

The time had come to cut off the supply of good will that Jeremiah continued to offer his life-sucking friend. For his own survival, the voice could no longer allow Martin to slow him down. Not a day had gone by since the Battle of Newtonia when Jeremiah could have made a run for safety with only a wounded arm. Nothing had been wrong with his legs. The sole reason he had stayed behind was to help a friend; the same friend who would have assuredly reported him to the generals once they reached shelter.

The military was well-known for sending out trackers to reclaim their deserters. Some captors even became household names amongst the soldiers. Both Jeremiah and Martin had participated in one or two weary night conversations where the squadron bad-mouthed those who had fled, while Jeremiah fantasized, in secret, that he would make the attempt one day. The decision was not easy to make while he held these trackers in high regard, but their current situation had made hiding from the army as easy as relaxing on a warm spring day. The battle had provided the perfect cover. The generals would not send anyone to hunt them down because they were surely believed to be dead already, with the word of their demise reaching their loved ones. Unfortunately, Martin couldn't see the grander picture. Should he have listened to Jeremiah's entire plan with an open mind, he, too, could have imagined the joyful tears shed by their families upon their return. They would have been only too surprised by the misinformation of their deaths. Then, once the celebration to end all celebrations settled, their loved ones would aide in keeping their return home silent until the war was over. They would not be as unwavering in their nobility as Martin. Even though the army would not have killed the two soldiers for their crimes, capture still would lead to execution. Hanging a board around their necks that read: A.W.O.L., and then parading them through various towns was the customary punishment. Angry spectators would rejoice when pelting them with eggs, mud, rocks, and then a bullet, while their families suffered just as severely from the harsh and punishing judgments of others. If Martin's stubborn pride had been allowed to get the better of him, those whom they loved would have suffered for their misdeeds. No friend worth a damn should allow him and his family to be humiliated so offensively. That was why Martin Stebbins had no longer been considered a friend at the moment of his death. The voice had suspected that Jeremiah would never gather the gumption to toss the grenade and took over at that moment, but then relinquished control back to Jeremiah; though the voice continued to keep a watchful eye from a safe distance. Jeremiah would need all the help he could get as the sniper hunted him mercilessly.

Jeremiah zigzagged through the brush as the marksman engaged his rifle. He realized his disadvantage knowing that the Yankee's eyes were well adjusted to the darkness, having spent days lurking beneath this umbrella of foliage. His vision struggled to improve; scarcely able to see any object until he came upon it, and nearly stepping into a bush and tripping over a fallen branch more than once. Fortunately, the rugged path he chose had a familiarity.

Another round hummed past his ear. He just could make out the sniper's shadow as he dared to remove his eyes from the jagged terrain when taking a look back. The Yank had paused to take a clear shot.

Jeremiah raced behind the thick trunk of a Scarlet Oak. He listened for Jonny Blue to make his next move, but the soldier did not reposition. He was hunkering down like before. Jeremiah felt as trapped as he had been when in the clearing. He would not allow a repeat the last few days; he couldn't.

The sniper could not have both sidelines of the tree covered. He would need to decide to train his rifle on one or the other. Jeremiah contemplated which side of the tree he should charge around when firing upon the boy; preferably, the direction the sniper did not aim. He took a moment to step into his adversary's boots. Being the hunter instead of the hunted, he would speculate that his prey would continue his momentum, and thereby direct his aim on the west side of the tree. On the other hand, the moment he realized he had lost his target, the sniper would think his opponent had attempted to double back, thus return his rifle to the border of the trunk where his target had disappeared. By those calculations, the sniper's rifle currently rested on the tree's east edge. Jeremiah settled on twisting towards the west. He gripped his pistol firmly with a finger positioned on the trigger. Taking a deep breath, he hoped he was about to make the correct decision when...

Hold it, Dunderhead! Jeremiah paused at the voice's instruction. *You'll git yerself killed. Human nature don't work that way. It's always in threes.*

The voice in his head was right. The sniper would swing his aim back to recheck the side where his prey would have continued. Left, right, left; always in threes. People used it before crossing a busy road, and the military used it in their marching orders. The Jonny would have settled his aim on the west side.

Jeremiah pivoted east and swung his pistol around the trunk, thankful to find that the voice's advice had been good. Needing to readjust his aim, the sniper did not fire instantly, but then, neither did Jeremiah. He pulled the trigger to no result.

A whisk of air heated his cheek as the union bullet sped past. Jeremiah retreated behind the trunk, confused by the misfire.

It's clogged from you droppin' it in the mud, Dunderhead.

"Quit callin' me that," whispered Jeremiah.

However, the voice was correct. Jeremiah tossed the weapon; it was useless, just as useless as the tree. He listened to the approaching footsteps. The boy would know his mark did not have a functioning weapon so no longer needed to hide. Jeremiah high-tailed it.

Despite his eyes having adjusted to the shadows, he did not see the metallic object on the ground until after he accidentally kicked it. The thing clanked against the side of a rock then bounced beneath a thick layer of autumn leaves.

Jeremiah dropped to his knees and rustled through the ground's cover, creating a tide of noise that masked the sniper's rapid advance. Before the object had disappeared, he caught a glimmer of iron, and if the thing was what he thought, taking the time to dig for it would be worth the risk. In the meantime, the slope provided protection by keeping him below the sniper's line of sight.

His hand brushed against the object. Hoping desperately that it was the same pistol he had dropped while in the confusing throes of battle, he wheeled around to the silhouette at the top of the slope and aimed.

Higher, insisted the voice inside his head.

Learning to obey the advice, Jeremiah fired.

The Yank collapsed. His body rolled down the short hill and stopped at the feet of his killer.

Jeremiah gazed at the fresh bullet wound above the kid's right brown eye and thought it was no exaggeration to call this blue coat a "kid." He had miscalculated the sniper's age at fourteen and reconsidered that his last year of life was closer to twelve. Confused, he wondered what kind of grudge a twelve-year-old boy could hold against a couple of Confederates that would make him willing to lie in wait, without food and warmth, for what could have easily led into more days than three.

He was a soldier, like me, the voice explained.

"Yes," agreed Jeremiah. He did not need to know

the details of the Yank's motives. Like any true soldier, he simply had to follow orders with the conviction to kill his enemy.

"That don't make 'im like you. You kilt our ally, not an enemy."

Martin needed to die, and you understand why.

"It was murder."

It was survival or are ya too fuckin' dense-headed ta understand that. Does I need ta get yer fuckin' momma ta explain it to ya, boy?

Jeremiah gazed down at the rifle still clutched in the kid's hand, and then twisted to the iron miracle he held in his own.

That ain't no miracle yer holdin', continued the voice. *Whatchu think, boy, Jesus answered yer prayers? I don't remember you prayin' none. And don't think it a coincidence that this path is lookin' familiar. It's the same path you took to the clearing when ya dropped yer weapon like only a dead soldier would do.*

"But I ain't dead," argued Jeremiah.

Because of me. I brung you this way on purpose, ya Dunderhead. So don't be praisin' God for His help. It was me. I provide somethin' better than miracles.

"What's that?"

Instinct.

"You gots my pa's voice, but you ain't 'im. Who are you?"

What I am is me.

I hate games, Jeremiah thought.

Do I sound like a fuckin' game to you, boy?

"How can you be in my thoughts and make me

do things I don't wanna? Is you another soul?
Maybe a brother that never lef' my ma once you died
in her womb?"

Laughter reverberated inside Jeremiah's head
like an exploding bomb. The voice settled to advise,
*Call me The Soldier, 'cuz I'm your soldier, and the only
God you'll ever need. So as long as you listen to me,
you'll live.*

"What reason I got to trust you?"

A pause. Though only short-lived, Jeremiah felt
The Soldier rummaging through his brain.

'Cuz if you die, I die. You're my survival too.

There weren't any two ways about it; The Soldier
was right. The only way for the voice to survive
was if he lived. Then, like awareness punching him
in the face, Jeremiah shot out of his trance at the
sound of rustling leaves between his feet and the
Yankee. He gawked at the body and waited to see
if this corpse twitched like the other. And as he
continued to stare at the trail of blood between the
boy's eyebrows, Jeremiah had an indescribable urge
to smash the kid's face.

Do it, ordered The Soldier, softly.

Jeremiah raised his boot. He aimed for the bullet
hole and slammed his heel down… again and again.
The boy's skull cracked open. His gray matter oozed
with red blood spilling over the seasoned leaves.

After a brief moment of lost time, Jeremiah
paused, exhausted.

*Don't stop! He's the real murderer. You put the
blame on me fer killin' Martin, but what about this boy?*

He made Martin's escape impossible. Don't that make 'im his real killer?

Gaining a second wind, Jeremiah crashed his boot on the puddle of slimy mush and continued to smoosh it into the ground; once for each day he had been kept trapped in the mud, and then once more for Martin. The Soldier had the right idea. By keeping them incarcerated in the field, the Jonny had weakened them further. The Yank was responsible too.

"Almost there," he had repeated over and over outside his head. In the last twenty or so miles, those two words convinced him to keep moving. Jeremiah couldn't give up before reaching home; he had suffered too much. The cuts on the bottom of his feet and the ache in his wounded arm that gave off heat were doing their damnedest to pull him down, but he trudged on, repeating, "Almost there."

The area around him looked familiar; thicker and fuller than what he remembered, but he was getting closer to home. After killing the boy and then reaching a path in Newton, The Soldier had explained his concerns about traveling on the road. Jeremiah might happen upon a squadron of Yanks, or worse yet, Confederates, who would recognize him. Until he reached home, he was, for all intents and purposes, dead, and Jeremiah needed to maintain that forgery. He agreed with The Soldier's summation and traveled off the road, but not too far off, sticking close enough to use the road as his guide home.

From the woods, Jeremiah happened upon two secluded farmhouses that ultimately saved him from starvation and exhaustion. Once concealed by nightfall, he had crawled into their barns for shelter and food and then slipped away before first light. If it had been peacetime, he might not have gotten away with the encroachment. The animals would not much like the intrusion at such odd hours, informing their owners of the unwelcomed visitor with a chorus of bedlam. However, in wartime, livestock was sparse. Jeremiah had heard that many animals perished during the war; almost as many as humans. Some became casualties of war, but most met with an ax. The food they provided was either used when blocked roads cut off incoming supplies--after stores were destroyed in battle--or as sustenance for passing squadrons. Samaritans who supported "The Cause" (the southern way of life) were expected to give all that they had to offer.

Luckily, the two farms he intruded upon were not entirely devoid of food sources. The first had a cow that supplied milk. Because it was the only cow they had, the family would wake to find her dry, but they would only go without for a day.

You need it more than they do.

His inner voice was right; it was a soldier's entitlement. Although he felt no remorse for taking his share, he did regret having done so without knocking on the front door to inquire about food and shelter. He would have most assuredly received the dweller's kindness, but he also would have defeated the purpose of remaining unseen until he reached home. There was no need to take any unnecessary chances.

The second farm had no cow; however, they did own a female goat, as well as a pen full of chickens. Unfortunately, the malnourished nanny had been empty. After a few hours of sleep in the barn's haystack, Jeremiah snapped the neck of one of the hens then snuck her deep into the woods to cook. Even without any salt or seasoning, the stringy meat had been pleasurable.

Though the perks were small, they did keep him moving until reaching a point where he had to pause. Jeremiah gazed at his surroundings that he now could recognize fully. A half-mile south of where he stood was the watering hole, which meant...

He picked up speed, hobbling while giving more favor to one foot over the other. Two hundred yards more, that was all there should be. He passed around a large oak and caught a glimpse of what he hoped was true, and not his mind playing tricks on him again like with the corpse. Jeremiah rounded another trunk and had sight of a white Victorian house; Martin's home. There was no more "almost". He was there; he made it to safety.

Jeremiah halted just behind the tree line next to the road. Directly across lay the path that lead to the front door, a good five hundred yards ahead. He just could make out several Stebbins family members on the front porch, although he still was too far to make out who was whom. However, there was one he could identify instantly, and she had not always been a Stebbins; she was once a Sampson. He would be able to recognize Alice a mile away. Jeremiah gazed upon her as she rocked back and forth in a chair, unaware that she was being watched. The woeful song '*Lorena*' came to mind. Its haunting lyrics were sung every night at the soldier's camp and instigated his longing for Alice, which they most assuredly did for Martin as well: "*A hundred months have passed, Lorena, since last I held your hand in mine, and felt the pulse beat fast, Lorena, though mine beat faster far than thine.*"

Alice's hands knitted swiftly, perhaps fashioning a scarf or sweater, maybe something for one of the boys. Being that the house contained more Stebbins males than females, it was a safe assumption. Until eleven days prior, no other Stebbins currently served in battle. Martin's two-year junior brother, Alexander, had soldiered for The Cause months back but was now home after shrapnel stabbed through his left eye. Honorably discharged, he walked away from the military with a wooden eye plugged into his vacancy. That was what Martin had read out loud after receiving a newsletter from his mother, Betsy. Despite being proud of his brother's heroic efforts for the South, Martin could not set aside the tremendous guilt he clutched. Alexander's time in the Confederate Army had been remarkably short before injury befell him. He joined the moment their father, Werner, had allowed. Principle for the Southern way of life aside, Alexander mainly wanted to follow in his older brother's footsteps. He even tried to enter the same detail, under Major General Price and General Joseph O. Shelby, but he had been sent to Tennessee instead, where he was wounded at the Battle of Chattanooga henceforth. The letter further stated that the two youngest boys, twins Elias and Silas, were not deterred by their older brother's wounds from wanting to join the effort once reaching Werner's approved age of fifteen. That was one year ago when they were thirteen. They now only had another year to wait, but Jeremiah knew they would never see battle, still convinced this war had neared its end.

He continued to stare, debating whether it was safe to approach. He should be welcomed as they knew him well, but as he began to settle on a decision, it occurred to Jeremiah that all the Stebbinses donned black. They were in mourning.

They already know.

A swelling of anxiety burst in the pit of Jeremiah's stomach.

What the fuck you so nervous 'bout? Ya already suspected they'd been informed.

"An' if they knows it was me?"

I done told you time an' ag'in that it ain't possible. Yer jus' a damn pussy is all. You gots regrets about what we done an' that's what makes you weak. You'll never survive by bein' such a coward all the damn time.

The Soldier was right; eleven days had passed since the Battle of Newtonia, which started fifty miles north. Not only did they receive the word of Martin's death, but his own parents, who were five miles further up the road, would have received the word of their son's passing, too.

Jeremiah examined his condition. He did not think he could make another half day's trek, but should he approach the Stebbinses, he would be at a loss as to what to say about Martin when asked. Seeing them before going home had not been part of his plan, and really, it was only Alice he desired to look upon. Jeremiah also considered what they would think once they discovered that God did not provide the same miracle for their Martin. They could hate him out of jealousy and turn him away, maybe even threaten his life. Though far-fetched, it was possible. However, he did not think they would treat him so cruelly.

What's the worst that could happen?

"Alice hatin' me. That'd be worse."

But it was still better than collapsing in the woods and not being able to climb back to his damaged feet. Should that happen, he would die alone because no one would know to look for him, and his remains would then become a wild animal's next feast, possibly even before his last heartbeat. At the horrendous thought of being fed upon while alive, Jeremiah stepped out of the woods then stood on display from the road. A delay lasting a brief moment had passed before he hobbled onto the lane that led to the Stebbins' front door.

But keep up yer guard.

CHAPTER III

A moment of hesitation had passed quickly before the Stebbinses stirred in a contained commotion upon seeing him stagger up the way. They were scrambling to and fro like frightened rats. The sight gave him reason to pause, as though terrified of him until he recalled his beard. He hadn't had one when he left for war. They could not recognize that it was him, most likely. Jeremiah continued, and the closer he strolled, the better look he had of Alice, Betsy, and the Stebbins's one and only daughter, Penelope, noticing that he had been mistaken about the knitting. Alice had been shucking ears of corn along with the other women.

The mother, Betsy, stood first, and then rushed to the front door and hollered inside. Still too far away, Jeremiah could not ascertain the exact words, only the shrill of Betsy's voice as he approached. If he were to venture a guess, he thought her call sounded an awful lot like Alexander's name.

Jeremiah had neared the half-way point of the walk towards the glorious two-story home before he recalled that it had been ten full years since he and his pa had helped with its erection. Work had taken just north of two months to complete construction on the house, barn--which stood larger by half--outhouse, water well, and kitchen; disconnected from the house but just off the back door. Werner Stebbins had paid him and his pa well, in addition to the many other workers, with money for their efforts, but Jeremiah had rather been paid in livestock and furniture pieces from the Stebbinses budding business at the time. His pa used half the money Werner gave him for the purchase of liquor, which did not help his ma any. Matter of fact, it had only made life harder on her. Nathaniel Whiting was stubborn enough when sober, and when drunk, his pa was an insufferable ass. Not only did his ma have to clean up after him when he puked or failed to reach the privy in time, but he forced himself on top of her every night. The man couldn't be gentle when inebriated; not that he knew how to be gentle when clear-minded either. However, in hindsight, that summer was one of the best summers he recalled.

Lafayette Barlow had been a helper during construction. He was one of Werner's hired woodworkers who had been taken off the furniture line and tasked to the house temporarily. Everyone but Werner had to listen to Lafayette, even his pa, which did not bode well. Lafayette was of mixed race: half white, half black, though to his pa, and some of the others, he was all black. However, nobody could argue Lafayette's skills with oak, walnut, and red cedar. He was a true craftsman. He had even taught the younger builders, including Jeremiah and Martin, a few tricks in the construction of traps for their hunting; something Jeremiah always thought should have been taught to him by his own pa, though he was grateful for the knowhow all the same. Those tips had come in handy a few times during the war. There had been some nights when he and Martin were the only two eating meat for supper. Usually fox or squirrel, which had been captured in a simple snare trap a few yards out from camp. They would then cook it up real quick in hopes of not attracting unwanted attention--much like he did with that chicken the other day. Jeremiah sure did miss Martin that night, just as he was missing him now.

Keep yer head on straight. Stay focused on right now.

It was valid advice from The Soldier and came just as Betsy stepped off the porch while Alice and Penelope hung back. He was so close; not only close to home, but close to people he loved and who loved him in return. No more rifles and grenades and Yankee soldiers. That was all behind him now; sympathy and compassion were what lay ahead.

"Jerry?" She inquired after a moment of stunned silence.

"Yes ma'am," he mumbled through quivering lips. "It sho' is good ta see you. You sho' is a sight for sore eyes."

Without a request or invitation, Jeremiah leaned in for a comforting hug. He did not want to come across less of a man by weeping in front of the ladies, but his tears could not be contained. They flowed on their own, blurring his vision while he tried to gaze upon Alice.

"There, there," calmed Betsy as she patted his back. Jeremiah did not remember ever feeling anything quite as amazing. "It's all okay now. You're back."

After carrying on for what seemed an entirely too short length of time, Jeremiah pulled away then hid his face while he dried his eyes.

"Sorry, ma'am. I did not mean ta be blubberin' all over on ya. I jus' never wuz sho' if I'd be seein' y'all ag'in... and this place. Never ag'in, I thought. But here I am."

"I suspect yer glad to have returned," muttered Alice, most probably just as befuddled on what words to use.

It would be a lie to say Jeremiah had not thought of a similar moment in the last five days. Seeing Alice again had been all he thought about during his trek, and her loveliness did not do his memory of her justice, however, he never did expect to lay eyes upon another blossom of exquisiteness, who stood at Alice's side.

"Penelope? Is that you?" The girl of fourteen nodded sheepishly. "You sho' have grown into a fine woman," but it was Alice who still commanded his attention, "And you ain't changed but fer the best. Prettier than the full moon on a clear night."

"Go heat up water," demanded Betsy to the girls, with more authority behind her voice than Jeremiah remembered ever hearing.

Alice and Penelope entered the house. They held Jeremiah's attention until the shadows inside swallowed them. He then turned to Betsy, who continued staring at him as though she just couldn't believe what her eyes were seeing. Giving her a moment to adjust, Jeremiah gazed across the grounds that he had not seen in two years' time, wondering where the rest of the Stebbinses might be. When he heard Betsy call for Alexander, he admittedly thought that she might be calling for him to gather everyone else, Werner, and the twins, to come rejoice at his arrival, but perhaps he had heard wrong; perhaps she hadn't called for Alex. As he pondered his inquiry, a portion was explained when he glanced across the farm to Elias and Silas tending cattle in a pen where their two slaves, Bonnie and Jimmy "JoJo" were pulling linens off a clothesline. That only left Werner and Alexander unaccounted for. On that thought...

"I sure hate to trouble you, Mrs. Stebbins, but I wuz wonderin' if Werner could give me a lift home? I don't think I could take another step."

He had interrupted Betsy's deep thoughts. Seeing how he babied his injured arm, she placed a hand on top of it gently then opened the front door.

"Come inside. We'll getcha cleaned an' stitched

up before presentin' you to yer momma. We don't wanna be sendin' ya home lookin' like we lugged ya through the mud ta git there."

As much as Jeremiah wanted to get home, Betsy made a solid point. Aside from Alice, she was the one he wanted to see most, and he wanted his ma to be able to recognize her own son. "I'd be extremely grateful, ma'am."

Jeremiah entered the house.

Lovely things decorated the room: brightly colored dresses, hair brushes with silver handles, flashy perfume bottles. The femininity did not make much sense to Jeremiah when there were more men than women living in the house, but he imagined the ladies were more inclined to bathe on a regular basis than the boys.

Using a handheld mirror with stenciled framework, he lifted a straight blade to his chin and scraped off another portion of his beard. Though he would miss the look of masculinity, Jeremiah would not miss the smells embedded in his follicles.

Once clean shaven, he exchanged the mirror and blade for a sponge then took it to his good arm and rubbed up and down lazily; partly because he could not move the hand of his injured arm fast and partly because he was mesmerized by the feminine trinkets and clothing. It had been far too long since he had gazed upon various shades of yellows, pinks, and lavenders. Most of what he'd seen in the last two years was blues, grays, and red... lots and lots of red.

Images of Alice parading in the frilly and ruffled dresses that currently hung in the wardrobe cabinet initiated his current arousal. He glanced at the closed door first to listen for any distinct noises on the other side. Dishes clanked and feet stomped, but clearly, they came from the first floor. Confident that he was alone, Jeremiah reached into the water and voraciously grabbed his johnson then stroked while he stared at the gowns. The blackened water splashed over the top and saturated the floor, but the deed had not lasted more than a minute before the tingling sensation of his nearing climax was interrupted by a courtesy knock at the door, followed by a far too brief delay before it opened.

As though he were drowning, Jeremiah writhed in the tub from the unexpected and embarrassing disruption, but then the door stopped just far enough for a ladies' arm, holding a clean pile of clothes, to squeeze through.

"I was asked ta bring you these," spoke the faceless intruder, however, Jeremiah did not need to look upon Alice to know it was her. Instantly, his embarrassment twisted into joy.

"I can't reach from here 'less I lift from the water. You best bring'um in."

A moment of hesitation had passed before Alice stepped inside. With her eyes deadlocked on the wet floor, she hustled to a nearby chair to set the clothes on its seat.

"I don't look like the same man now do I?"

Alice raced back to the door. Titillated by her discomposure, Jeremiah did not pull his attention off her for a second, nor his hand off his cock. She had been aware of his sinful pleasuring, but in her desperation to flee, Alice stopped unwillingly, very nearly forgetting to mention, "Momma Stebbins will come with more hot water and see to your wounds," then slammed the door behind her.

Betsy was coming. Suddenly, Jeremiah no longer experienced heightened excitement and released his pecker. Completion would wait until he could be alone with his carnal thoughts of Alice once again. Until then, he leaned against the back of the tub and closed his eyes. Envisioning his days in the war would relieve him of any provocation in no time.

Betsy had done an impressive job of cleaning and dressing his wound, but then, she had learned to be handy with ailments and injuries when raising four boys—five if she might consider Jeremiah as one of her own, which he hoped was true. Jeremiah could not remember the last time he felt so fresh and clean all over. The entire process had taken in excess of two hours. Betsy scrubbed him down hard. She even managed to scrape out the years of blood and soil from beneath his fingernails. He could not stop gazing at them in sheer amazement, unable to recall a time when they had ever been so clean, even prior to the war.

Realizing how ridiculous his fascination must look to the other Stebbinses, he set his palms down on top of the table next to his silverware placement. But the moment Jeremiah looked up from his hands to their faces, he knew they did not think him foolish at all; that would require them to look at him. However, they could not do that, except for the twin boys, who stared awestruck.

Jeremiah turned his gaze to Alice, who was making the largest effort to avoid any eye contact. Suddenly, it dawned on him why they were acting so suspiciously: they knew. Alice had told them what she caught him doing in the tub. Still, Jeremiah was not discomforted, only elated that Alice must have concluded that he had been masturbating to thoughts of her. Crooking a smile, he faced forward to see every Stebbins clearly from the head of the table... that was, every Stebbins except for the two, who still had not returned.

"Is it customary for Alex and Werner to work at the factory so late?"

"It happens," stated Betsy coolly from the opposite end of the table.

Bonnie entered through the back door carrying the final addition to the meal prepared from inside the detached kitchen--a basket of warm bread. "Thank you, Bonnie."

The Stebbins's gal had curtseyed before she hurried back outside, most likely returning to the kitchen that sat twenty-five feet off the southwest side of the house. She too had been standoffish towards him, but that was no different than before the war. The feeling was mutual; he never did like Bonnie or her husband, JoJo. Jeremiah believed the Stebbinses spoiled the elderly pair by always doling out gratitude for their services. Hearing "Thank you" and "Please" consistently made a nigger uppity. That went against "The Cause," rendering all he had fought for these past two years to be null and void. If Jeremiah thought it his place to express his discontent, he would have, but he would no more do that than put his feet up on the dinner table. Their property was their property, and not his. He turned his attention back to the subject of those not present.

"They miss suppa often?"

Like a startled deer, Betsy paused, then forced a smile. The rest of the family watched her, just as intrigued by the answer she would give, which eventually did come, "I really don't know what's keepin' them boys," then reached out her hands and demanded the others to join with one stern look.

Each took hold of another's until forming a ring around the table--only closing the circle once Alice allowed hers to be taken by Jeremiah. He could feel the trembling of her nervousness. His excitement grew.

"Dear Heavenly Father, we ask your blessing for this bountiful feast, which we are about to receive, and thank you, oh Lord, for the safe return of one of our soldiers and..." Betsy swallowed hard, "...

longtime friend of this family. In Jesus's name, we pray. Amen."

After every soul had repeated the closing, "Amen," Alice was first to break the ring by pulling her hand away, startling Jeremiah out of the silent conversation he was having with The Soldier after the voice asked, *What's that about?*

What?

You deaf an' blind, Dunderhead? That pause was like the ol' woman was chokin' down her words. Summin' ain't right.

But Jeremiah ignored the unsubstantiated warning. Instead, he concentrated on the magnificent spread and beheld foods he had not seen or smelled for what felt like a lifetime. Jeremiah stared at the chicken in front of him that was ten times more appetizing than the one he cooked two nights prior. The fowl he had eaten had been more out of necessity than desire. He reached for the leg and pulled it clean off, not aware that the others had been waiting for their guest to serve himself first before starting; yet another reason he disliked Bonnie and JoJo. They were not required to serve any meals.

Dinner continued in silence--very different from the meals he had with the Stebbinses in the past-- but Jeremiah did not attempt to analyze their solemnness. He already understood. To dine with him in Martin's absence should be difficult, which amplified the peculiar way they were acting towards him. It had been two hours and no one had yet cornered him into answering a single inquiry regarding Martin's passing. Surely, they would want to know every detail of what happened, and Jeremiah used his time in the tub wisely to concoct a story. He was proud of his simple, yet detailed account: *Martin had stepped on a landmine left during the first battle of Newtonia in '62.* However, Jeremiah began to suspect that no one would hear his premeditated farce because nobody dared to ask.

He turned to his left, hoping to stir a conversation by addressing the only two who appeared to be enamored by his presence, "You boys been helpin' yer momma and poppa good?"

"Sure," spouted Elias.

"What did that ta yer arm?" blurted Silas, always the more curious twin.

It became apparent to everyone at the table that Elias had kicked his brother's leg for being inappropriate--the better mannered of the two. Jeremiah smirked at the notion of normalcy then leaned in close to the boys as though he were about to whisper a secret. He pointed to his right arm, "This here? I wuz shot." The boy's eyes became wild with intrigue. "But that bullet couldn't hurt me none. You know why?" The twins shook their heads, buying every word. "'Cuz what I got in me is so strong, the bullet had ta go aroun' my bones, an' lef' me only with this here flesh wound."

"You'll need that looked at by Doctor Sturgin. It's got infection," interrupted Betsy matter-of-factly.

Jeremiah politely nodded to the matriarch--a

motion to show he understood--while doing his best to hide his disappointment in the woman for murdering the tension of his story. He turned back to the twins.

"We wuz part of Shelby's Iron Brigade..." was all he could get out before Betsy interrupted a second time, knowing he was about to ignore her hint.

"All right boys, ya heard enough war talk at the table. Eat yer supper."

The twins obeyed their momma, and the uncomfortable silence returned. Jeremiah directed his attention over to Alice, caressing her lovely face with his gaze. And looking just as appealing to her side was Penelope.

"Alice? Why ain't you hardly said two words ta me since I come back?" She shrugged, continuing to avoid eyeing anything above his neck. "I reckoned ya'd most intriguingly would'a asked about yer husband."

He had grown tired of the elephant in the room. Jeremiah suspected if Martin were to be brought up, he would need to do the honors. But as each and every Stebbins set down his utensils, as though an ailment had forced them all to lose their appetite at once, Jeremiah thought he might have misjudged his audience's curiosity. Unfortunately, it was too late to turn back. He proceeded, "I wuz with Martin when he wuz killed."

"Please!" Betsy exclaimed with anger in her appeal. "I do not wish to have this conversation at the table."

"I'm sorry, ma'am. I truly am. I wuz jus' wonderin' why no one had yet inquired."

Because they already know the truth.

It ain't possible, he argued as Betsy's glare dug into him. Jeremiah shivered as though a rabbit had run across his grave. He then witnessed a spark of fire ignite in her eyes before she could mask her flinch with "Truth be told, the man who come give us news of Martin's passing already given some details."

See. Like I told you.

Stunned by Betsy's revelation, Jeremiah stared in awed silence while he struggled to gather enough gumption to ask with casual intrigue, "Who wuz it that come with the news?"

He watched Betsy rack her brain before avoiding his question with… "Jus' some man" then diverted her nervous attention to her family and inquired, "Where is yer poppa?" She turned back to Jeremiah and stated, rather fiercely, "He will be beside himself to see you. You wuz always like a son to Werner."

Jeremiah had not heard another word, distracted by his dire need to know the identity of the messenger. "Did this man give a name?"

"Yes," mumbled Betsy then hesitated again. "I reckon so, but it escapes me at the moment."

"Didn't he speak mostly to poppa alone?" Alice added before twisting to Jeremiah and looking him squarely in the eye for the first time since his arrival.

"Yes. You are right. That mus' be why I cannot recall."

"I heard Poppa call him Mister Calvin Hawte, momma," spurted Elias, but his helpfulness was met with an under-the-table kick by Silas.

The name, Calvin Hawte, had been mentioned several times during the outfit's conversations regarding the deserters and the men who hunted them. Calvin was a tracker; not a messenger. Jeremiah would have sworn the air in the room was sucked out as his heart stopped beating. But more than losing his breath, he lost his concentration. He glanced over Betsy's shoulder and focused on the back door.

Get outta there now!

Jeremiah heard The Soldier, but he slowed his decision, inclined to think before reacting.

No wonder yer pa lashed you tons. Ya ain't never learnt ta listen.

The Soldier had his chance of persuasion, now Jeremiah wished to hear from his own head. Reason was dictating that if the Stebbinses knew the truth of Martin's death, they wouldn't be so accommodating. They would not sit at a table with the murderer of their kin, bathe him, and mend his wounds.

Unless they knew the whole truth; every detail of your offense.

How could they? Jeremiah asked. *How could anyone know?*

Why else would the family who once trusted you act so damn peculiar?

It was not a solid point. There could be

any number of reasons why the Stebbinses were uncomfortable in his presence. Tragedy does strange things to people.

Despite The Soldier's protest, Jeremiah reached the conclusion to stay. He had many reasons for his decision, but his primary motivation was to avoid looking guiltier than a whore in church by dashing out the door. Moreover, since neither argument made complete sense, it was better to stay calm and continue as though all was well.

He wiped his mouth then set his napkin on the table. "That sho' wuz a fine meal. An' I mus' come clean that I wuz sayin' a silent prayer fer anythin' but beans." Only Jeremiah chuckled at his ill-timed joke. Feeling the need to explain further, "'Cuz thaz all they serve durin' battles. A winter's worth of beans will do a man fer the res' of his days. If I ain't laid eyes on another one of them grains..." He chuckled again, hoping to get the others involved instead of gawking awkwardly, and then decided to give it up. "I thank you, ma'am. It wuz a fine homecomin' meal."

A polite smile had crinkled across Betsy's face before she stood. The rest of the family rose as though following her lead. Bonnie must have been peering through the door because she sprang inside. The slave stood out of the way until the family departed.

As dinner was over, and he had become presentable, Jeremiah suggested, "'Cuz of the late hour and Werner still ain't arrived, maybe I could borrow a hoss?"

Betsy appeared at a loss for words. Typically, Jeremiah would wonder if her bewilderment was out of concern for her husband's delayed return, but under these peculiar circumstances, he could not be so sure. He was more than curious to hear her response.

"I would take you myself, it's jus' that..." She trailed off, as though he had stumped her without intention. The Soldier was inclined to believe they had caught her in a lie until she continued, "...see, the wagon's with Werner, an' we've gone down to one hoss with the war and all."

She made sense; perfect sense. Jeremiah had seen, firsthand, the sacrifices made when it came to the people's possessions for "The Cause."

"Maybe you would like to stay the night?"

Now she had stumped him. This was not a proposal that would come from someone who was suspicious of him, but as honored as he was by the invitation, the idea of staying away from home for one more night did not settle well.

"I wuz hopin' ta git to my ma an' put an end to her mournin' and such. I'll jus' wait fer Werner."

"Of course." Betsy had smiled before she glanced at Alice, who then quickly added, "We would have loved ta have ya."

It was in that instant when Jeremiah's concern for his ma's burdens were not as crucial as they had been in the previous moment. Alice wanted him present; she had requested it. Suddenly, nothing else mattered.

"I s'pose bein' absent one more night wouldn't do more harm to her sufferin'."

Neither Alice nor Penelope showed any elation of Jeremiah's decision, but Betsy did smile wide enough to bare teeth. This pleasantry was the first sign of any joyousness she had shown towards his company.

She turned to give Bonnie a nod of approval to begin clearing the table and then sauntered into the keeping room. The weight of stress diminished. Jeremiah was now thoroughly convinced that The Soldier had been wrong. The Stebbinses hadn't been aware of his transgressions, and for that, he loved them more. They were a fine family, one that he would wish to become a part of one day. As it so happened, there was an opening.

CHAPTER IV

A few years prior to enlisting, he and Martin stopped playing their favorite childhood game, Knucklebones, to focus their interest on their friend and neighbor, Alice Sampson. Watching Silas and Elias play the game while stretched across the keeping room floor resurrected fond childhood memories for Jeremiah. He had been the better player, which had sent Martin into the occasional tantrum. By the twins' current score, Silas was equally adept at tossing one knucklebone in the air then collecting five more before it hit the ground. Elias was more like his elder brother Martin, not as coordinated and wholly flustered.

Jeremiah remained slouched in the chair while he puffed on one of Werner's pipes rhythmically. For the first time in nearly two years, he was relaxed. As much as he appreciated the recollection of one of his favorite adolescent memories, Jeremiah used his intrigue with the knucklebones game as a distraction. Moments earlier, he had caught himself staring at Betsy on the sofa while she sewed a pair of trousers for either Werner or Alexander—who still had not returned. As he watched her, excitement arose in his pants, recollecting that he had not finished off in the tub or more than a weeks' time for that matter. It had been damn near impossible to have a private moment when traveling with a brigade of men. Even if he could steal away behind a tree for a moment's peace, the constant worry of being shot and killed unexpectedly with his hand wrapped around his pecker did not make it easy to concentrate on Alice and what her lady parts might look like. Although Betsy was very much a woman, he did not want the pleasure of his climax associated with a motherly influence. His reserve was for another.

He withdrew his attention from Betsy, but his arousal would not subside while flashes of Alice continued to penetrate his thoughts. She and Penelope had disappeared some time ago, stating they would check on Bonnie and JoJo before washing up for bed. He had been looking forward to hearing the ladies splash water on themselves from the second level, but they had left through the back door at least twenty minutes ago and still had not returned. He doubted that they were reprimanding their lazy slaves, not with their unabated kindness. In fact, it was more likely that the girls were helping the slaves with their chores.

Curiosity got the better of him suddenly.

"'Scuse me while I answer nature's call," lied Jeremiah as he stood.

Betsy gave a half-hearted nod, which was more than what he got from the boys, and then exited through the back.

The sky went from light blue to dark purple, and although the sun was no longer visible below the horizon, it did still emit some light.

Jeremiah glanced at the nearby outhouse then shifted his attention to the detached kitchen. Lantern light came from its single window and one door, but the two girls should have no business being inside there with Bonnie. He then stretched his focus across the large field towards the barn. Though the structure ought to be vacated, it wasn't. Light peculiarly bled through the cracked double doors. The Soldier suggested, *It could be Werner and Alexander returned.*

He ambled towards the byre as best he could while his bruised feet reminded him of the pain they could cause. Still, his aching dogs howled loud enough to have him nearly reconsider and wait for the men to come to the house, but his vanity was too eager to see the looks on their faces when they saw him alive.

Once close enough, male voices were not what he heard from inside but female. He had been wrong about Werner and Alexander's return. Jeremiah crept closer then perched just outside the door to listen in on Alice and Penelope. The acoustics of the two-story hollow enclosure reverberated every word distinctly. He peeked through the slit of the two large front doors only to discover that the girls were out of his line of sight, stationed on the opposite side of a large hay pile that blocked his view.

"...an' I seen the way he's been lookin' at you," gossiped Penelope. "It ain't righ'."

"It ain't, but he'll be gone by tamorrow. It's jus' one night. I don't want him gettin' any ideas 'bout you though when he gets frustrated with me. Ya rememba what Bridget Gates said about her husband after he come home. She feared for the cows too."

Both girls giggled at the impropriety, which also tempted a smile out of Jeremiah. Once the laughter died, nothing but the sounds of stirring about, busy work of some kind, could be heard. Jeremiah returned to his previous suspicions about them doing the slaves' chores.

"Why'd he have ta come here anyway?"

"You need not worry 'bout Jerry no more. The men oughta be returnin' soon," comforted Alice.

I told you they's knew summin'.

Jeremiah cursed himself for not listening to The Soldier's wisdom the first time. Best he could tell, the Stebbinses were aware that he had absconded. It came to reason why a tracker had delivered news of Martin's passing--he was on the hunt for his deserter.

But how could this Calvin Hawte even have known about Martin? There wun't nuttin' lef' of 'im to discover.

It don't fuckin' matter how, The Soldier blasted. *Whacha need to figure is what else he might know, maybe he knows who kilt 'im too. Did ya think of that, Dunderhead?*

Jeremiah mulled over the point briefly, but then eased his concern once he figured that Calvin could not have known much without a witness, and Jeremiah was confident there had been none. However, what the Stebbinses knew, or didn't know, did not deem it necessary to hide Penelope in the barn. This type of caution was not the action of the misinformed.

"I best get back a'fore suspicions arouse," stated Alice before he heard the smack of the ladies giving each other a quick peck goodnight. Alice sauntered around the haystack then stopped to add, "Bonnie should just be finishin' the dinner chores. I'll send her ta come check on ya soon. G'night."

Alice blew a second kiss, and then headed his way. Jeremiah leaped into the shadows beside the door and kept himself from yelping out loud after something hard and sharp clawed the back of his neck. He twisted around to see what it was but couldn't; not in the darkness. He placed a hand on the weapon-like protrusion and felt a lasso spike fastened to the wall.

The barn door opened. Alice peeked to inspect her surroundings before stepping out. She secured the door behind her then hustled towards the house.

Jeremiah waited. He watched her scamper

across the field as betrayal fed on his anger. He thought to follow her, pin her down, and try to make her talk, but he knew she would refuse. Alice was too strong of character. If he were going to get the answers he so desperately desired, he would need to take them from someone meek and breakable.

Once Alice entered the house through the back door, Jeremiah snuck inside the barn, hoping to frighten Penelope by surprising her. Then, making sure he kept her on edge, he would pressure her for information. This tactic was often used on captors during the war. Surely, it would work even better on a little girl.

Once he had eyes on Penelope, Jeremiah halted. She was dragging a heavy quilt towards a hole in the ground, which he knew to be a storm shelter for tornados and her room for the night, most likely. He did not know why he had not noticed earlier, but she was not only becoming a striking woman, she had become one already. The best Jeremiah could reckon was that she looked more mature when not standing at Alice's side, as she had done all day. Moreover, it was quite remarkable how similar they looked for not being tied by blood.

Penelope dropped the large blanket down the hatch then spun around when she heard Jeremiah's tread. The smile on her face was not meant for him because it vanished the moment she cast eyes upon his face. Though failing, Penelope made her best attempt not to appear terrified by his presence.

Jeremiah stopped, yet unsure as to why. The

Soldier was silent with his advice. She was scared for sure, which was how he thought he wanted her, but was no longer certain. He glanced around the barn in reflection and decided the better strategy might be to calm her and show that he was there only for idle conversation.

"Remember the hay fights all of us would have?" She nodded. He stepped closer. She countered. "Then, you didn't use ta be so scared of me. What changed?" She shrugged. "It ain't jus' you neither. Yer momma and Alice too. Even the twins some."

Penelope added nothing. Jeremiah rested his prodding to finish gazing at the memories, but then his demeanor shifted without warning, and the delicateness of his expression dissipated. Jeremiah's eyes grew wide as they focused upon a wagon... the very wagon Werner was said to be using. It had been sitting here, in the barn, and it was easy to see it had done so all day.

"Where's yer poppa? He far?" Jeremiah inquired calmly, hoping not to reveal that he was wise to their lies, but Penelope knew because her body stiffened as she held her breath. She could hardly shake her head in answering his query. "What's takin' 'em so long? Why's yer momma wantin' me here if she's afraid like you?" She remained as rigid as a board. Jeremiah grabbed her, pulled her close, and then shook her as though he could shake the answers right out of her. "I know'd that Calvin Hawte told yer family summin' 'bout me. What wuz it? Speak up!"

She did, but it was only to gasp suddenly, and Jeremiah understood why. He had felt it as well, and it felt good. The moment she brushed up against his stiffy that song played in his head again, "*A hundred months have passed, Lorena, since last I held your hand in mine, and felt the pulse beat fast, Lorena, though mine beat faster far than thine.*" He did not care if her touching his thing had been an accident, she needed to do it again.

Penelope backed away and gazed at his firm manhood that pushed against the inside of his trousers. Catching herself staring, she jerked her head to the side, embarrassed.

Jeremiah ogled her beauty; her likeness to Alice was uncanny. "*We loved each other then, Lorena, more than we ever dared to tell; and what we might have been, Lorena, had but our lovings prospered well.*"

All the panic, betrayal, and bewilderment had faded. Nothing bitter existed anymore, and nobody else did either. At that moment, they were the only two people left in the entire world.

Jeremiah's calm voice returned as he complimented, "You sho' did change lots since I been gone." Their two-step resumed. "I meant what I said 'bout the fine woman you become. But you know how purty you are, don'cha? Sixteen now, right?"

"Fifteen."

"Really? Well, ain' that summin'?"

Having refused to pull her eyes off Jeremiah's shuffling feet, she found herself backed against the wall. He stopped inches from her lustrous white skin and straight brown hair that begged to be handled. He stroked her long strands and purposely brushed the side of his finger against her neck. Penelope winced, but Jeremiah perceived her reaction as more of a wink, letting him know that she approved of his touch.

He lifted her soft tufts to his nose and breathed the scent of rose from the oils and soaps in the bathing room. Again, she quivered.

"I sho' did miss you," he stated romantically.

The subtle brush against her neck had been a mere taste, and Jeremiah could not contain his appetite for more any longer. He released her hair then laid his full open palm against Penelope's cheek. To Jeremiah's surprise, she jerked away. She wanted to change her mind just as any teasing whore would. He wouldn't allow that.

Jeremiah grabbed Penelope then lifted her into the air. Her petrified barrier shattered, releasing piercing screams and kicking legs. Jeremiah tossed her into the hay then unbuttoned his trousers and pulled out his stiff pecker. He reached beneath Penelope's dress and yanked down her bloomers.

She continued bucking like an untamed mare. He covered her mouth and got his erection into position when her eyes suddenly grew twice their size. Jeremiah could not discern why; he hadn't entered her yet, but then followed her beseeching gaze over his shoulder to find Bonnie standing at the door, beyond frightened. The old woman ran.

"Wait! Git back here, nigger!"

It was just like a Stebbins' slave not to obey, but he had to stop her no matter what. Jeremiah gave chase, but not before taking a corn sickle off the wall next to the doors. He would make her mind and listen, teaching her a long overdue lesson for disobedience.

"Miss Stebbins, ma'am!" Bonnie shrilled over and over as her thin elderly body struggled to run fast, but her voice was just as decrepit as her legs.

Under normal conditions, Jeremiah would have caught up with the woman in no time, but despite his determination, his screaming feet slowed him.

He reached Bonnie and grabbed the back of her wild hair then pulled. She slammed hard onto the ground. Jeremiah hovered over her. She wanted to scream and flail, as though surrounded by a hive of angry bees, but the tip of the sickle he threatened against her throat kept her from budging.

"Nuttin' happened, ya hear?! I didn't have my way with her, so help me, nigger! That's the truth of it!" And it was the truth, but it was only a matter of whether she would believe him that counted. He waited for the gal, who shivered as if lying naked in the snow, to communicate some indication that she understood. After a few seconds of nothing, she gave him want he wanted and nodded in agreement.

Jeremiah felt some relief, but that respite was stolen the instant he heard Penelope cry out.

She was racing for the house.

Jeremiah pushed off Bonnie and ran to stop her

but halted once the slave struggled to her knees and continued to shriek her warnings, "Ma'am! Ma'am!"

"Lyin' nigger bitch!"

At his wits' end, Jeremiah pulled her head back and swiped the curved blade deep across the length of her throat--teaching Bonnie a lesson and shutting her up at the same time. The half-decapitated body tipped forward and slapped the ground.

Penelope tried to steer clear of Jeremiah though she had no other choice but to run in his vicinity as he stood within the shortest path between her and the house. He dropped the sickle next to Bonnie's corpse, grateful he had sense enough to know he might hurt Penelope when he leaped for her. Pain radiated up his feet and through his legs, but it was easy to ignore when distracted with determination.

The girl pitched around for another pass.

Jeremiah countered and appealed, "I ain't tryin' ta hurt ya! All right?"

She would not listen. Penelope zigzagged, but he prevented that effort as he charged closer. In her desperation to increase the distance between them, she switched directions but could not shake his tail. At less than ten feet apart, he knew he could take her on her next jagged maneuver, though wished it would not need to come to that. Grabbing her, tackling her, or hurting her in any way was not necessary. He only needed her to fucking listen to reason.

She'll never listen to ya, The Soldier declared, seemingly out of nowhere.

"I didn't touch you down there, now did I? So there! Nuttin' happened. Right?" But the obstinate girl refused to listen and performed her next charge.

He caught her. Jeremiah covered her mouth as she released a piercing cry. She made him do it; made him be the worst he could be by not minding. He carried her squirming body back towards the barn where he might be able to talk some sense into her without being discovered by the others.

What are ya doin'? She ain't gonna listen, repeated The Soldier.

Shut up! I'll make her believe it wuz all just a misunderstandin'. She'll know when I tell her the devil got inside me, 'cuz she knows I could never commit such terrible actions otherwise.

And he would not be lying. Something had gotten into him.

Was it you? Did you force me on her like ya made me kill her brother?

What the hell you thinkin', boy? You think I wanna be handlin' yer floppy thing?

Jeremiah tried to recall The Soldier's presence but had no recollection. Whatever had possessed him, he had no control over. He supposed it was good Bonnie had interrupted when she did; the only thing that nigger ever did well. Now, he just needed to explain the circumstances to Penelope, but by how the girl was fighting him every step of the way; she would not be easy to convince.

They returned to the barn, and he nearly made it to the doors when Penelope managed to clamp down on the skin between his thumb and forefinger, biting through. Reacting impulsively, he threw the girl against the wall and yelped an excruciating howl. Jeremiah tucked his hand into the shelter of his underarm and spun in circles maniacally. He stomped down hard in a desperate effort to distribute some of the pain back to his feet, but the attempt was futile. Stepping into the light that poured out of the barn doors, he stopped to observe the blood gushing from the bite mark.

"Fuck! Look what ya did! Why'd ya do that?!"

Jeremiah held his hand in front of her half-lit face, but Penelope refused to look. Instead, her perfectly calm glossy expression gazed past him. A swelling of outrage expanded from within at her alleged mockery, but then a trickle sprouted from her mouth. He froze at the sight of blood sliding towards her chin.

"Penny? Penny?!" He shouted, bewildered and panicked. He grabbed and shook her as though she were asleep and needed to be awakened. Her body felt limp in his arms, but Jeremiah continued to keep her upheld like a puppet. "Dear, God! What'd I do? I'm so sorry."

He pulled her close, confused as to how and why this happened until he felt the wetness on the back of her head. He rubbed his fingers together then brought them into the light. Her blood covered his uninjured hand.

Truth struck him like a punch to the gut. Jeremiah began to whisper the word "no" repeatedly, refusing to accept the truth when he reached into the shadows and felt the unintentional weapon: the lasso spike that had scratched his neck earlier. Wet, sticky fluid now saturated the metal rod.

Jeremiah took a moment to comprehend why this was happening to him. He thumbed through the history of his life to find what he had done to justify taking the blame for being the murderer of an innocent fifteen-year-old girl, but Jeremiah found nothing.

He held onto Penelope, not willing to let her go just yet.

Get outta there!

Movement from the corner of his eye turned his head. Someone was coming. The shadowed figure was struggling to reach Bonnie's body. It was JoJo, and Jeremiah had known this before he heard the servant holler for his wife. He would have been in the fields when he heard her cries and was running to her rescue.

Gently, Jeremiah laid Penelope's body on the ground, undecided if he would make a run for it or shut JoJo up permanently.

I told ya to be gone already, prodded The Soldier. *You shoulda listened ta me!*

Not only was he right, but Jeremiah thought there was enough blood on his hands... too much, in fact, for any man no longer at war. However, running was not a viable option either, not with his damaged feet. As he quickly learned, there never was a decision to make because there was no other alternative. JoJo needed to die if Jeremiah were to fabricate a story that explained the deaths. Exasperated, he tried to think but struggled to come up with a plausible tale on the fly. He asked The Soldier for his help, who did not look far for inspiration.

Tell 'em dis… when I was settin' on the privy, doin' my business, I heard Penny screamin'. I come runnin' but so did yer niggas. The intruder I saw kill 'em both. He musta come ta the barn lookin' fer food. He looked like a traitor ta me. I, then, tried to save Penny from him havin' his way with her, but I come too late. He saw me an' knew he needed to end her screamin' a'fore lots more came. Then he run off inta the woods. I didn't chase afta 'cuz I didn't want yer girl ta be alone when she began her journey to God. That's why I'm covered in her blood, you see. She was too pure for horror like that. It's such a shame.

Pinning the murders on a nonexistent marauder who could never be caught and questioned was flawless. Better yet, his attempts at heroics would be revered. Jeremiah suspected he would even be forgiven for his desertion; if not by the law, at least in the eyes of the Stebbinses. These deaths had been his blessing in disguise, but he still had one more killing to commit to making the plan work.

JoJo had nearly reached Bonnie's corpse, as well as the sickle. Beating the slave to the weapon would not be a problem if he could ignore his feet as he charged. However, the chance to attempt The Soldier's plan would never come to light. The strategy failed the moment he saw Betsy step out of the back door to call, "JoJo?! What's wrong?"

Jeremiah was not surprised she had heard him bellowing for Bonnie as he ran from the side fields and past the back of the house. What did come as a surprise was the moonlight that had quickly crept over the area and illuminated him in beams, bright as day.

He pressed against the barn wall, making sure he did not stand in the light drizzling from the barn or descending moon. From inside the shadows, he watched JoJo drop to his knees next to Bonnie and carry on as though it were the end of his world.

Betsy ran too, but not towards JoJo as suspected. She was heading for the barn while calling her daughter's name.

Jeremiah glanced down at the girl's body and noticed that he had laid half of her in the light. It was too late to move her. He needed to do what The Soldier had been telling him to do since dinner: make a run for it.

Hugging the wall, he edged towards the far end of the barn, hoping the structure's shadow would keep him protected from the moonlight. Once on the opposite side, he would run past the house and make a break for the road. The chance of being seen was fifty-fifty, but that was before Betsy cried out and flung her body over Penelope's corpse. The distraction of her grief lessened his risk.

Jeremiah reached the end of the wall and readied himself to scamper towards the woods when the hysterical mother diverted his intention with her banshee-like wail towards the heavens, as though cursing God for allowing such evil into His world.

Now was the time. Jeremiah took off, but this night had been against him from the start. Coming up the long path towards the house were three riders on horseback. His escape was blocked. Panicked, Jeremiah fled towards the house.

CHAPTER V

Jeremiah stormed through the rear door. He startled Alice and the twins, who had been lurking at the back. They leaped but did not run. If they did not fear him, then they had not seen all that transpired. Because of their naivety, he considered letting them be, but then The Soldier ordered him to Take a hostage! Jeremiah understood why. What they did not know now, they would discover soon enough.

He picked up the carving knife that the lazy slave had left on the table.

Alice could not back away fast enough from his reach. Surprisingly, it was easy to push aside all the love he had for her when it came to his survival, but he was not so far gone to hope that this terrible misunderstanding wouldn't escalate.

The twins escaped into the keeping room but did not go a step further. With the knife pressed against Alice's throat, they cowered into a corner, understanding his gesture to mean that he would cut her if they ran for help.

Betsy charged through the dining room like a bull on fire. Even in the dim light, Jeremiah had been able to see the grief and rage in her eyes. He used Alice as a shield from the voracious monster.

"I didn't do it! None of it!" He spouted, knowing they would never believe his innocence, but determined to tell his story. "It was an accident. You gotta listen!"

"I ain't doin' no such thing!"

The thunder of the three galloping horses rumbled through the house until they stopped just outside the front. Werner and Alexander most definitely were two of the riders, but the third rider was a mystery: maybe a neighbor, or possibly his pa.

He leaned over the oil lamp and blew out the flame. The room went dark. He, then, used the hilt of the knife to shatter the front window. Jeremiah repositioned the blade against Alice's throat then shouted, "Keep away! I don't wanna hurt nobody."

"Liar! You already killed my eldest, an' now my youngest!" Betsy yelled loud enough for those outside to hear.

So… they did know about Martin. *But how?* He silently asked The Soldier. If either one of them knew, it would be him.

The Soldier didn't respond; even he did have an answer. However, Jeremiah's private thoughts were betrayed by his expression as Betsy advanced, slow but bold, "Thaz right. We all know'd you killed my boy, an' now my sweet, sweet girl."

"I didn't mean ta. It was a mistake. I swear on my life!"

"Yer life ain't worth spit!"

Jeremiah caught himself backing away from the disturbed woman. He had allowed her commanding fury to cause him to forget about the upper hand he possessed.

"All I want is ta go home."

"You ain't got no more home. Ya think yer folks wancha, knowin' what you done? You brung shame upon their good name, Jerry! Yer pa's ready ta shoot you dead jus' as soon as you set foot on his land. No lie. But he ain't never gonna git the chance."

Though he did not want to, he believed Betsy... every word. If his pa knew the truth, and he surely would if the Stebbinses knew of it, then the only redemption for the Whiting name would be to oversee the justice against their son--and not the law's justice, but his father's.

I told ya ta run.

But where? It dawned on Jeremiah that he had nothing left. No home. No family. Nowhere to go. Tears streamed down his cheeks. However, despite the bleakness of a successful outcome, he refused surrender. Threatening Alice's life with the knife once again, he barked, "Stand the fuck back!" after Betsy advanced another step.

"Jeremiah?" An unfamiliar voice hollered from outside. The third rider was no longer a mystery. His voice was commanding and confident, and belonged to someone who needed no introduction.

Calvin Hawte continued, "Jus' stay calm, boy. There's no need ta hurt any more of these good people."

"Jus' leave me be!"

"I ain't gonna do that," stated Calvin, rather matter-of-factly. "Now, maybe it was all jus' a mistake. I might be able to understand that, but yer holed up in there with the rest of this fella's family. That sure ain't no mistake by my account."

He was good with his words, and Jeremiah felt the need to put a face to the voice of the man he had heard so much about. Using caution, he glanced through the window and spotted him standing next to Werner, however, with the moon behind them, he still could not see Calvin's face. But even more discerning was that it only was the two men. Alexander was nowhere to be seen.

"Go git my gun." He ordered Betsy, surpassing desperation.

"Fuck you!" She screamed, shocking all who was around her.

Jeremiah would never have predicted that was all it would take for The Soldier to claim control. He remembered how the possession felt from days earlier; like he was nearby but watching from the shadows. That sensation had now returned.

Alice's squeal broke apart once the blade severed her cords. He yanked the knife out of the puncture wound, releasing a stream of blood that squirted across the length of the room. Betsy and the twins howled the cries of unrelenting torment as Jeremiah released Alice's body. Before she rested on the floor, he grabbed Betsy as her replacement.

The surmounting chaos inside had brought pounding footsteps to the front door.

"Stay back!" The Soldier demanded and pushed Betsy to the shattered window to demonstrate the knife held against her throat. "I mean it! I'll kill every las' one of 'em, I swear ta God Almighty." He then ordered Betsy to "Tell 'em!"

"He jus' killed Alice. She's dead, Werner!"

Keeping behind Betsy, Jeremiah peeked around to make sure they could observe his sincerity when he explained, "An' it's your fault! Ya made me do it! Tell 'em that too!" But Betsy refused. He dug the blade into her throat deep enough to draw blood. "I said, tell 'em the truth."

"Go ta hell!"

He wanted to do it so very badly; The Soldier wished to see her bloody body drop on top of Alice's, but somehow—someway—Jeremiah was present enough to advise that he soon would not have any Stebbinses left to hide behind if he fed his desire. Instead, The Soldier bashed her head against the window pane.

Calvin attempted to reason. "Jerry? Why don't you let them be and come out and take yer medicine like a man?"

Beads of sweat trickled down The Soldier's face. As much as he did not want to admit it, he was about to lose control of the situation again, and there was still no accounting for Alexander. He glanced at the twins, who remained huddled in the corner. They hung onto one another and tearfully glared at him.

"Elias. Go upstairs an' git my gun."

"No!" Betsy ordered.

Jeremiah twisted her around to make sure Elias got a close look at the blade's tip already dug into his mother's neck.

"Do it now boy, or I'll do yer momma the same I done ta Alice."

Elias released his brother then stood. Silas began to rise too.

"No, Dunderhead! You stay put. Keep yer momma company." The Soldier shifted his attention back to Elias and nodded for him to hurry.

Elias reached the foot of the staircase but paused when The Soldier added, "An' boy, if you do anythin' but git my gun, I'll kill yer momma, yer brother, and then you. Hear me right?"

Elias forced a nod, which more closely resembled a tremble, and then hustled to the upper story.

A shroud of silence fluttered over the room. During the moment's peace, Jeremiah examined The Soldier's rash, and unwarranted, decision to stab his beloved in the throat.

They betrayed us. This family you love so fuckin' much set a trap for you.

That was true. This day had become a trap from the moment he arrived. Thanks to Lafayette, Jeremiah understood a thing or two about them. The Stebbinses had fed him, bathed him, offered him a bed with the intention of never allowing him to leave alive. As soon as they spotted him hobbling up the path, Betsy had leaned into the house and yelled something. He suspected it had been Alexander's name, and he had been correct. She had instructed him to get Werner and Calvin and bring them back. Alexander then snuck away unnoticed while the rest did whatever it took to make sure he stayed put until Alexander returned with his intended. The Soldier had tried to warn him, but Jeremiah allowed himself to be distracted by the past. From this moment forward, he would never disregard The Soldier's good senses again.

Jeremiah left the stage and returned to the auditorium to watch The Soldier perform as needed. His first action was to peer outside and discover the root for the sudden silence.

"You still there, Calvin Hawte?"

A brief pause. "I am."

"An' the others?"

"Here with me. They're just anxious to be with the family you ain't killed yet."

The Soldier peeked past the flapping draperies to see for himself. "Where? I don't see 'em."

Calvin's arm shadow made a beckoning motion. Two other figures stepped into view.

"Why you chasin' me?"

"You killed one of yer own in cold-blood."

"There ain't no way ya coulda know'd that. Who told ya?!"

"Don't matter. You did it."

"Yeah? Did whoever tell ya Martin was dead

anyway? He couldn't run on account of his leg. It got all tore up and infected. He wanted me ta do it! End his sufferin'. So I could escape."

The Soldier heard sniffling next to his ear. His lies had brought the strong-as-iron woman to tears.

"Yer still a deserter," reminded Calvin. "You gotta answer fer that crime too."

"I fought for The Cause! I did my duty!" The Soldier yelled, boiling with rage for the lack of notoriety.

Elias galloped down the steps with the pistol in hand. He paused at the bottom.

The Soldier aligned Betsy in front of him then reached out his free hand. "Give it here."

Fear was what slowed each step Elias took. His hand shook as he held out the gun.

The Soldier grabbed air in anticipation of reclaiming his pistol. The weapon was nearly within reach when Betsy announced, "The devil's gonna come for you, Jeremiah Whiting!"

As though her curse had summoned a demon, the back door crashed open. But it was no evil spirit that demanded his blood; it was JoJo.

Betsy escaped from her confinement as her sickle-wielding servant distracted her captor. She snaked the revolver out of Elias's hand with every intention of spinning around to kill the bastard, but The Soldier jabbed the knife into her back, and the gun dropped from her loosened grip. He swept up the pistol and trained it on the charging slave. JoJo had the sickle raised above his head when a blast of gunpowder stopped him from bringing the tip down into the top of Jeremiah's skull.

Once the slave's body joined the others on the floor, The Soldier expected a moment's peace, but the insurgence continued as quickly as his next breath when Alexander burst into the dining room with guns blazing.

Elias kept low and ran towards his twin while bullets soared in every direction.

The Soldier leaped behind the staircase banister as Elias went down. The boy crashed to the floor inches away from Silas's outstretched hand. Even in the darkness, and with only one good eye, Alexander knew of his fatal mistake because he howled a regretful bereavement.

The Soldier took advantage of Alexander's self-inflicted torment to return fire. He had managed only one shot before splinters exploded off the banister, flanked by gunfire coming through the shattered window. The Soldier dashed up the stairs in retreat.

Calvin charged through the front door as Werner leaped through the window, but then recoiled at the massacre lying at his feet. Calvin paused to get a handle on the situation, knowing Jeremiah was trapped and wouldn't be going anywhere. The delay allowed the father and son a moment to agonize over their losses. Calvin caught a glimpse of the bodies bathing in puddles of blood. Like a ray from heaven, the moonlight that beamed through the window glistened the wetness. The sight was unbearable, even for a military man. As Alexander and Silas mourned over their fallen brother, Werner jolted from his wife's body to dart after her killer in a passion fueled by madness.

"Wait, Werner!" Calvin shouted in vain but then turned to Silas, who appeared to be the most clear-headed of the two, and commanded, "Go hide the horses. Now!"

By his look of befuddlement, Silas did not understand why, but that did not delay his scrambling out the front door.

The Soldier sped to the locked window just beyond the porcelain tub--still filled with the scum-crusted soapy water that the slaves never emptied. He heard Werner approach as his hateful threats traveled down the tapered hallway. "Goddamn you, Jerry! I'm gonna rip ya apart with my hands!"

Once The Soldier heard Werner reach the landing, he darted across the room, then pressed against the wall. The calculation was four against one, and he would not have enough bullets. Until he could escape, he would need to kill as many by hand as possible.

Werner was not being held back by any fear. He did not have an inner soldier of his own to stop him from making a beeline down the open corridor in a rampage.

The Soldier shot a single round at the charging torpedo, who fired back. He then ducked behind the wall.

Werner was struck. The Soldier had glimpsed the man's shoulder thrust back during the flashes of gunpowder. Unfortunately, the injury did not hinder the man.

The Soldier moved to slam the door shut, but his action was too late. Werner kicked in the closing barrier. The powerful thrust sent The Soldier stumbling into the tub where he lost his grip on the gun. Waves of water splashed over the sides and drenched the floor. The Soldier flailed in the restraining tub that stung his eyes with its contaminated water. Then, immediately, he was pulled forward, not able to see Werner reach for his collar. Before The Soldier could feel the pain of the first blow, his head was thrust to the side by the power behind Werner's fist. The livid man repeated his attack again and again without taking a moment to breathe when The Soldier fought back. He reached out, grabbed a fistful of Werner's saturated shirt, and pulled. A loud screech echoed when Werner slipped in the soapy water and fell face first into the tub. Each man struggled to drown the other, which became more of an impossibility once there was more water on the floor than in the tub.

Running footsteps pounded from the hall, heard over the unrelenting battle. The moment they arrived, The Soldier knew he would have no chance of escape if he did not fight dirty. He felt for the hole in Werner's shoulder and then dug his finger inside.

Werner broke their brawl and screamed bloody

murder. He leaned back far enough to escape the reach of The Soldier's fists, but not his feet. The Soldier folded his legs to his chest then stamped Werner in the gut. The force sent the man flailing back into Calvin, who reached the door in the same moment.

His two attackers toppled over each other. The Soldier squirmed to climb out of the tub, but Werner's determination would not be thwarted. He climbed back to his feet faster than his foe.

The Soldier looked for his gun, but the room was too dark, and the sting in his eyes continued to obscure his vision. Then, as though knocked over by a runaway coach, The Soldier was tackled. His feet slipped out from under him and he fell backward, even while Werner kept him locked in a bear-like brace that knocked the wind out of him. Glass shattered, and shards sliced open his face. Next thing The Soldier and Jeremiah both knew, they were looking at the night sky in a moment of weightlessness as they plummeted from the window. The Soldier had them twirled around before they hit the ground.

The sound of a hundred bones breaking would have been shrewder if not for the quick sharp pain The Soldier felt to his abdomen. He reached for the sensitive area and felt the knife-like protrusion inside him. Based on the pain, he knew it was not his own rib, but one of Werner's that stabbed him in the gut. Despite the suffering, The Soldier felt empowered. His instinct to switch places with

Werner in the air had been quick thinking. It could have just as easily been he who fell to the ground back first.

The chasing gunfire was startling but did not come as a surprise. He hadn't forgotten about Calvin, who fired down upon him. Immediately, The Soldier rolled over onto his back with Werner still attached to him like a conjoined offspring. He yowled, suffering from the pain that the binding rib had caused. The pain was intense but not as strong as his will to live.

Werner's body jerked with each bullet that burrowed into him. The Soldier kept patient, waiting for Calvin to run out of ammo, and he did not need to wait long. The tracker left his position at the window. He was coming down.

Though prepared, The Soldier still could not have imagined the torture that would occur when he pushed Werner off, but then he saw the man's bone protruding from his stomach and understood. It had broken off Werner and found its new home inside him. He grabbed the projection gently, to keep it steady, as he rolled onto his side and peered at the barn. Still with blurred vision, he caught a glimpse of a person, no taller than someone in his early teens, leading three horses inside. *Silas.*

The dread of knowing that he would have to ride out of here was as excruciating as the pain he would endure during the escape. Jeremiah had The Soldier peer back towards the road, in hopes of finding another way.

There ain't none. We ain't gonna make it without a hoss, so stop yer damn whimperin'. You never left the war, yer still in it! You do what needs doin' to survive. Ain't ya learned that yet?

Jeremiah did learn, but he didn't see why he couldn't look for another option.

Yer wastin' my time! They're comin' to kill us!

Just minutes ago, Jeremiah had made the promise to listen to The Soldier's every word, and he was intent on keeping that promise. Swallowing the pain that came with each step, he stood back and allowed The Soldier to hustle them towards the barn.

The journey took longer than it should have, but it gave his vision time to return to normal. Regrettably, The Soldier did not feel his situation was any clearer when the moon had yet to expose Calvin's whereabouts. The tracker should have leaped from the house by now to run after him.

He reached the barn doors and glanced back one last time, spotting Calvin finally, with Alexander, which then explained the short delay to regroup. The Soldier suspected it must have taken some convincing on Calvin's part to pull the boy out of his devastated stupor. However, no one could argue that four eyes were better than two.

Or three, thought The Soldier, surprising Jeremiah with a wit of humor about Alexander's wooden eye.

He slunk into the barn. The Soldier was not confident that the men hadn't seen him enter, but even so, it would not take long for them to figure which direction he had gone. He kept a sharp eye out once inside, which proved difficult when all he could think about was yanking out Werner's rib from his bowels. However, that would need to wait until he was out of earshot. Only then could he holler at the top of his lungs from the merciless pain, and not worry about calling attention to himself.

The wagon and three horses were just ahead, not yet put into their stables. Silas had abandoned them in a moment of panic.

He heard me comin'.

An' now he's hidin'. Jeremiah could not have been more relieved by that prospect. He did not want another death.

Maybe he ain't hidin', The Soldier pointed out, not knowing what state of mind the kid would be in after witnessing what he did. He could be cowardly and remain in hiding, or enraged and biding time.

"Silas? Be a good man an' let me take a hoss ta ride on. I swear on my life, I'll never come back."

The Soldier continued deeper into the barn, each step causing him to wince. He clutched the rib bone tighter when out of the corner of his eye he spotted a pitchfork leaning against the wall. He grabbed it.

"We got a deal, Silas?"

Movement stirred near the stables. The Soldier considered it could have been just the horses but knew better than to commit to that conclusion.

"If yous plannin' on a fight, rememba, I've taken on many men at once an' I'm still alive ta tell ya that truth. Yer jus' a weak boy. Ya ain't got a chance. Bes' ta jus' keep yerself hidden."

Footsteps ran closer towards him, but they did not come from Silas; they were outside. The Soldier glanced to the open doors and noticed the trail of blood he had left in his path. An idea sprouted. He looked for an obvious place to hide and spotted the open door of the storm shelter. He rushed towards it to continue his trail, and then closed the doors while he remained above ground.

The Soldier heard a mournful sound come from Alexander just beyond the barn doors. They had discovered Penelope's body, but more importantly, they had arrived. He leaped into the hay pile then buried himself, grateful for the distraction little Penny turned out to be.

He kept watch as they entered and mimicked the same caution he had demonstrated, but then Alexander lost his patience and pushed past Calvin. He had found the trail and followed it to the storm shelter.

The Soldier kept still while they stood less than five feet away, careful not to make a sound. Both men grabbed a handle then yanked the doors open with their weapons trained at the darkness below. Calvin motioned his sidekick to stay before he grabbed hold of the ladder and descended.

The Soldier watched Calvin disappear, allowing him time enough to reach the bottom. Then, once Calvin yelled, "He ain't down here!" The Soldier jumped from the pile and took the half-blind boy by surprise. He slammed into Alexander with his good shoulder before he could have his gun whipped around. The young man was knocked down the hole. The Soldier gave no pause to see if Alexander had landed on top of Calvin as he had hoped. But once he closed the doors and slid the pitchfork between the two handles without a single bullet fired, he reckoned that's what had happened. By the time the gunfire did come, he had backed away from its trajectory.

Splinters burst from the doors like firecrackers. The Soldier twisted to the horses but found Silas blocking his path with a machete in his grip. The man inside the boy was struggling to come out, but The Soldier saw only a child as he observed his trembling hands and tear-drenched face. Werner had his rules about allowing his sons to enter the war before a certain age, but there had been more young boys, like the Yankee sniper, whom he had to fight and kill. It was the price they paid for choosing to do battle, such as Silas's price if he wanted the same.

"You threaten me further, boy, an' I will defend myself to yer act of aggression."

"Don't matta. You already killed the other half of me."

The boy had made his choice. The two opposing sides remained deadlocked while The Soldier listened to bullets ripping apart the shelter doors behind him. Time had become another competitor in this Mexican Standoff, but then Jeremiah's voice returned and offered, *You don't gotta kill 'im too.*

Sure, I do.

The Soldier took a step and Silas swung. He tucked the boy's flying arm under his then confiscated the weapon in a flash. He tripped Silas to the ground and pointed the machete's tip to his chest. The boy's face shivered with fear.

He's only a kid!

Who will be more difficult to kill when he becomes a man and seeks his revenge.

He's unarmed.

How many times I gotta remind you that this is war! Have you already forgotten or is you seekin' forgiveness when none is needed? Sins do not exist in battle.

The Soldier brought the blade down and stabbed it into the boy's neck. Then, as he pulled the machete back and gazed at the frozen look of terror on Silas' separated head, he could feel Jeremiah wanting to scream, but then The Soldier reminded, *He made his choice.*

Gimme back my body!

Not yet.

The shelter doors burst. The Soldier hustled to the two nearest horses and sent them running with a smack to their rears. He leaped onto the last and bellowed at the intense sting of pain the rib bone inflicted as he rode out of the barn. Gunfire chased him once Alexander and Calvin climbed topside.

Instinctively, the horse headed for the road, but The Soldier steered the animal around the barn and raced for the tree line that lay a half mile ahead.

The road would not be a wise choice. He would be exposed. The woods were a better alternative, providing added protection with its obstacles and shaded canopy. But there was one downside... rugged terrain.

Upon crossing the tree line, it was all The Soldier could do to not pass out from the excruciating pain. Keeping a firm grip on Werner's bone was doing more harm than good while jolted by the gallops. Decidedly, he let go but did not feel any less of the intensity. One way or the other, the price of his freedom would be unimaginable suffering.

The horse slowed, and as Jeremiah heard the babbling of a creek, he learned that The Soldier had relinquished control. He turned his head and listened for any sounds that might indicate Calvin and Alexander's approach, but so far, nothing was heard. Jeremiah felt a moment of safety.

Only for the moment, Dunderhead.

Thirsty, his ride drank from the creek as Jeremiah placed a hand on the rib bone, ready to fulfill the promise of yanking it out.

I wouldn't do that if I was you.

But you is me.

Then you'll kill us both if you uncork yerself and let us bleed out.

As uncomfortable and painful as it was having the thing stuck inside him, the bone would need to wait until he reached a doctor.

It was a struggle, but Jeremiah switched his

focus off the pain to concentrate on choosing where to go next. There were three options before him: continue over the creek, travel upstream, or downstream. Being that Calvin Hawte was a well-trained tracker, it would be all too easy for him to follow his trail on land. Water was the best route to take as his traces would be washed away.

He glanced in both directions. Even though it was too dark to see either, Jeremiah closed his eyes to listen to the rushing water. Having his reasons, he pulled on the reins and guided the horse downstream. The moment the animal took its first step into the water, Jeremiah realized he had not taken into account the rocky floor. The jerking motion was worse than before, and he was on the cusp of blacking out with each jolt.

Jeremiah patted the sides of the steed and discovered a lasso hooked to the saddle. He promptly removed it then wrapped it around his chest and the animal's neck to tie himself down. As unconsciousness took him, he leaned against the horse's mane and positioned his body in a way that would keep Werner's bone from pressing in deeper.

Jeremiah and The Soldier closed their eyes.

CHAPTER VI

Though sixteen and once a soldier, Alexander had proven to be less of a mindful man, and more like a brazen boy, when the careless, naïve hot-head had been hell-bent on chasing after Jeremiah without a horse. Once emerging from the storm shelter, both had captured a glimpse of the evildoer fleeing the scene of his most recent kill and charging towards the woods. Alexander did not stop to examine his decapitated brother, but rather, foolishly charged after Jeremiah without a mount to ride. Calvin had responded quick and tackled the boy to the ground, then proceeded to waste precious time persuading Alexander that the night was against them, and that they would be better equipped by waiting until sun-up. The boy did not want to listen, proclaiming that he knew these woods better than anyone, but Calvin had not been swayed. One error was all it would take to lose their quarry forever. Calvin saw no other choice but to use Alexander's heightened emotions against him. Eventually, he manipulated the boy into agreeing that his family needed burial before they started their hunt.

Even now, as morning's light illuminated Jeremiah's trail, Calvin was sympathetic to the kid's plight. In a matter of minutes, he had lost his entire family. Though it was not so uncommon for folks to lose many loved ones in wartime, this battle had not been against a nation, but by a lunatic previously thought of as a longtime friend. Still, Calvin feared for his safety by allowing Alexander to join the pursuit. The kid's fiery instints had demonstrated that he was now saddled with an immature and thoughtless boy for a partner, which proved dangerous.

Once Alexander had been convinced to bury his dead first, Calvin unpinned the boy from the floor then left him to attend to his undertaking in private while he rounded up their two lost ponies. Reclaiming the first had been the most difficult, but once finding her feeding on the side of the lane, he rode Alexander's mare and found the other more quickly. Calvin was elated to see Melville, his own horse of which he named after the author of *Moby-Dick*, Herman Melville, his favorite novelist. Though grossly misunderstood by his fellow countrymen-- those who could read--Calvin understood the pages of *Moby-Dick* to emulate morality, perception, and determination, qualities he struggled and often questioned about himself. However, having salvaged Melville and Alexander's horse, of which he did not know her name, Calvin deduced that Jeremiah now rode Werner's steed.

Hours later, he had returned to the Stebbins' homestead to find that Alexander had completed five of the eight graves. He did not offer his assistance, knowing Alexander would have refused. As foolish and erratic as the young man had shown to be, he had an air of honor and sanctity that would not be compromised. Werner had the same type of willfulness, and though Calvin never had the opportunity to find out, he was sure the other family members had had it, too.

In his few hours of solitude, Calvin utilized the moment to ponder the mind of the madman he had allowed to escape. He did the same for every man he hunted, and until this evening, it had aided in the impeccable success of his apprehension of each wrong-doer. However, in the case of Jeremiah Whiting, he had sorely underestimated this soldier. Calvin only scratched the surface of whom Jeremiah, the man, was without digging deep enough. But admittedly, he did not have much to go on. It was a miracle that he even had the information to come to McDonald County as it were. Jeremiah had thought it surprising, too, in the way he inquired how the Stebbinses knew the truth of Martin's death. In Calvin's questioning of the man, Robert Mitford, who had played dead for three days in the mud, hoping to escape a sniper's bullet, the soldier spilled all the information he knew about fellow Privates Whiting and Stebbins. He had stated that both men came from McDonald County, and it appeared that Jeremiah had premeditated his malicious plan to explode his friend with a grenade out of cowardice. But what Calvin should have also learned from Robert's account was that the army had strengthened a sociopath who would survive no matter the cost. Calvin had asked Robert if he had mistrusted Jeremiah prior to that incident, as he found it odd that Robert did not make his existence known to his two comrades when on the battlefield, but Mitford's response had been one of simplicity; stating that if he had called for their attention, he would have deonstrated his unobstructed position to the sniper. And that was the underlining information Calvin had missed when disclosed. Having time to think about it more, he now understood Jeremiah to be far more dangerous than any scoundrel he had pursued previously. This man was impulsive and showed more intelligence than any other he had brought to justice. Calvin could just kick himself. Had he solved the riddle of Jeremiah Whiting prior to tonight's events, perhaps he would be transporting the criminal to prison, or better yet, to a mortuary. But because of his error, he had watched a sixteen-year-old young man bury his two slaves and each and every loved one. He even fashioned a ninth cross and stuck it into the ground for Martin, which Calvin deemed honorable. It was that demonstration of virtue which had convinced Calvin to allow the kid to turn this pursuit into a two-man posse.

Jeremiah's trail ended at a creek. The two trackers halted briefly before Calvin reined his horse downstream.

"Why that way?" Alexander challenged.

"Because it's correct," replied Calvin, leaving no room for debate.

"How do you know that?"

Calvin stopped, beginning to regret his decision to allow the boy's company. Since the start of their journey, there had been many rifts between them, beginning with Calvin's affirmation that, given he was an experienced tracker who had maintained an exemplary record, he was the man in charge of this pursuit. However, Alexander had disagreed, reminding him that he not only knew these woods better, but the man whom they hunted as well. The quibble lasted but a minute, which was another minute Jeremiah had put further between them. To end the debate and shut the boy up, Calvin agreed he would listen to any input Alexander wished to contribute, but now, he was regretting that concession. He had no patience, nor time, to explain his every motive to the kid.

"Because I ain't never been wrong," continued Calvin.

"Well, I think you are now 'cuz Jeremiah's home is this way."

"He ain't goin' home anymore, an' he knows that courtesy of your momma tellin' him so."

"You shut up!" Alexander barked angrily. "Don't you speak ill of my momma!"

Again, hot-headed and naïve. He watched as Alexander gave his words some consideration, but the kid was slow to convince. Calvin suspected it would behoove them both if he were to take the boy under his wing and educate him in the business of human tracking. "If he heads upstream, he's gonna risk leaving traces that are gonna float back our way. It's safer for him to go downstream an' he knows it."

The kid continued his refusal to budge, which Calvin thought suited him just fine. He worked better alone anyway. Spinning his horse around, he headed downstream but then listened for the boy's horse to splash either towards him or away. It did neither. Calvin added stubbornness to the list of traits he had made for Alexander.

"Maybe I'll head up, jus' in case?"

The boy's voice had calmed; he had lost some confidence. No doubt, Alexander was beginning to question the reliability of his intuition under the bulk of his fatigue. Burying eight bodies had taken all night with only an hour left to spare before daybreak. He had gotten no sleep.

"Your choice," hollered Calvin, not giving a shit, exhausted as well.

The boy clicked his tongue, followed by the splashing of horse's hooves that trotted closer from behind.

◆ ◆ ◆

The running and sloshing of water from

beneath, along with the continuous melodies of wildlife all around, made the Ozark Mountains very much a living entity. Calvin found it relaxing. He never tired of it. As much as he appreciated his Kansas homestead, he often wondered where he and his family would be living had he not settled there before the war. Unfortunately, Calvin was never able to return to Kansas long enough for it to feel like home, but the war would be over one day and he had felt some uneasiness about going back. Not that he didn't miss his wife and son, he loved Jenny and Henry terribly; Calvin was unsure if he could return to farm life after spending the last three years as a hunter of men. In some ways, the farm sounded serene and orderly, but in others, it was dull and repetitious. It would take some adjusting to, but maybe Jenny and Henry would help make that transition into plains life easier. He sure did miss them. But for now, Calvin continued to enjoy the lively atmosphere of the forest, which felt more like home than anyplace else.

He was fortunate that Alexander had kept quiet the last handful of hours, as though he was no longer trailing behind. On more than one occasion, Calvin looked over his shoulder just to be sure Alexander still followed, maybe fallen asleep, but each time he looked, the kid was staring off into the world, wide-eyed. Calvin found it easy to empathize with his tragedy, having lost a mother to a crazed soldier as well; the only difference was that the man who killed his ma also happened to be his father.

He had been eight years old at the time, but Calvin had difficulties remembering the details of that gruesome night. Alexander did not have that same comfort, no doubt recalling every detail, especially that of his young brother Elias, whom Alexander had gunned down accidentally during the mass confusion. Calvin did not know how he might carry on if he were to lose Jenny or Henry, especially if it were by his own hand. As Calvin felt himself slip towards that atrocious wonderment, he shifted his concentration to the woods' harmonies, grateful for their calming distraction.

The creek expanded into a rivulet, and for the last two miles, Calvin had noticed blood drops on some of the larger rocks jutting from the water. However, the better discovery was the scraps of tree limbs they came across on the bank. Calvin motioned for Alexander to halt then studied the shavings from atop his horse.

"What do ya see?"

Alexander gaped at Calvin like peering at an old fool, but then answered the obvious, "Cuttings."

Clearly, the boy did not understand that he was being taught. "What else?"

Alexander studied the leftovers, dumbfounded. As he lingered in confused silence, Calvin decided it was best to supply him with the answer. "Jeremiah was here, but he didn't chop that wood."

"How do you know?"

"Those woodcuts were made clean and with precision by hands that were steady, not by a man in agony whose hands trembled."

The boy reflected on the explanation, which appeared to be sinking in, though he continued to be puzzled by a distraction. Eventually, he asked, "Who did then?"

The tracker gazed at the rustling trees caught in a mild breeze then looked ahead where the rivulet bent to the left. They had progressed further than expected; they were reaching the edge of the Oklahoma portion of the Ozarks.

"We've entered Indian Territory," he stated, matter-of-factly.

Alexander did not hesitate. He whipped out his pistol while scanning the forest. Not two seconds later, he fired into the trees. The thunderous clap rippled across the land as though it would carry on to Kansas.

Calvin looked to where Alexander had shot. There was no sign of any Indian or Jeremiah-- should either be Alexander's intended target. But if the boy had seen someone, the gunfire would have been returned, and there was none. Calvin looked at the kid with the wooden eye and amusingly asked, "Whach yer one good eye seein'?"

The boy scowled from the harassment, and his face reddened, but then answered the question. "Movement."

"Is that so?" Calvin continued to tease.

Alexander holstered his pistol, trying not to look a fool.

"We're in Cherokee Nation," appeased Calvin.

"They's friendlies, right?"

True, the Cherokee were civil to the white man when compared to the temperaments of tribes such as the Sioux, the Comanche, or the Osage. Yes, the Cherokee could be considered in a friendly way when compared to others.

"We're still trespassers on their land."

Calvin had about gathered all the information the wood shavings could give when he heard the stride of a heavy animal. Alexander heard the approach as well. Both men paused, weapons at the ready while staring at the bend just ahead. They continued to listen, certain it was a horse and only one. Calvin wondered who would be stupid enough to ride around these parts solo when a possible answer dawned on him... Jeremiah. He could be backtracking; a good sign that he was in disarray, which was why Calvin made it a point never to backtrack.

Alexander jerked his attention to the brush in front of the bend and fired again. Having seen nothing between the trees himself, Calvin suspected that he and the boy were going to need to have a good talking. Rash actions such as these could get them both killed. Fortunately for the kid, this fight would be two against one. No harm, no foul.

The approaching gallops were just out of sight. Both men had tensed before the horse sped around the turn. Calvin relaxed his tension while Alexander hung onto his. The boy's excitement amplified as he proclaimed, "That's my pa's hoss!"

Although Calvin could not be sure, he suspected it was Werner's horse that Alexander had shot at through the tree mesh. He would not praise the kid for nearly killing the family stallion, but Calvin was impressed that the boy had seen something out of his one good eye that even he could not see out of two. That was no small feat. Maybe there was hope for the boy yet.

The steed continued upstream. Alexander shifted his mount to block its path, but the rushing animal did not slow. Once within reach, Alexander clicked his tongue to grab the horses' attention, but the frightened beast ran past and stayed its course. Alexander turned to give chase when Calvin advised, "Let it be. You scared it when you shot your round."

"It's my pa's hoss!" He repeated.

"And when you return home, there he'll be. Some horses is smarter than humans. They know where to find home."

Alexander glanced back to the animal that was inching out of sight when a noise from the trees snapped his attention back. Familiar with the sounds of this forest, Calvin knew there was nothing to fear, but Alexander refused to be as complacent. It was a fact that all boys were trigger happy; however, Calvin had witnessed the first-hand dangers of an itchy finger when coupled with paranoia. He thought it best not to test the boy any further about tracking and just speak direct. "You can put that away now. He ain't tryin' to get the drop on us. He ain't here."

"I already told ya, ya don't know 'im like I do." The kid was not wrong about that, but they had reached a point in the search when Calvin knew his expertise outweighed Alexander's knowledge.

"Okay, you tell me what happened to him then."

The boy looked perplexed, as though constipated on the shitter.

"I don't know."

"Which is why you need ta listen to me."

"You got a theory?"

"I do," then paused to think, "but I ain't ready to tell you yet. I'll give you some time... see if ya can figure it out on yer own."

Calvin flogged Melville's flanks then guided his ride towards the bend. Alexander continued to follow his lead despite his outward frustration.

What Calvin had wanted to test the kid on was his ability to learn from the wood shavings. Jeremiah had, somehow, found some assistance. Help would have come from the locals, and there were only two types of people in the southwest parts of the Ozarks--Indians and the cavalry, with the closest fort being the Union-occupied Gibson, a full forty miles south. Not only was it far, but when soldiers roamed out of their fortifications, they would rarely stray from the trails. By Calvin's deduction, only the natives could have assisted their fugitive, though the unknown tribe continued the mystery. Knowing which would determine whether he was chasing a man who was dead already or still alive. As much as he would love to know Jeremiah Whiting was no longer walking upon the earth, it was not his right to kill a man; it was the law's... providing he could hold Alexander back long enough to see Jeremiah inside a courtroom. Unfortunately, the further west they traveled, the grimmer their prospects of finding the escapee became. They just couldn't go roaming into every native encampment during their search. Because of his mother, he was born half Blackfoot, and Calvin had too much respect for all natives to disrespect their communities. His nationality was a part of himself he always planned to keep a secret for fear of retaliation, concealing it from the military and any acquaintances. The only two people alive to know the truth were Jenny and Henry.

Calvin stopped abruptly--as did Alexander. He had been taking note of the rising water for some time. The levels had climbed fast and currently reached the soles of their boots. He peered ahead to another stream of water dumping into the rivulet, turning their path into a grand river, but more than that was the hidden threat that Calvin saw waiting beyond.

"We should not continue without escorts."

"Suit yerself," then Alexander stubbornly persisted on course.

It had not yet been twenty-four hours, but each hour had been long, and Calvin was disappointed to see that the kid had not learned a thing. Surprisingly, in some small way, he was grateful the boy made the decision to continue deeper into the territory. He, himself, had been on the fence about entering. There were new dangers ahead that only fools would walk into knowingly, but equivalent to the kid's caution was his determination not to let Jeremiah's trail go cold. Calvin appreciated the eagerness that kept him focused.

He steered towards land and was pleasantly surprised to learn that they had not been the first. New evidence awaited them on the shoreline. The time had come to see what the boy was made of.

"What are those?"

Alexander gazed at the parallel lines that continued down the dirt and pebble covered shoreline, surrounded by a posse of hoof prints.

"Summin' bein' dragged. Like two sticks."

So far, so good. "Go on."

"Horses. About six?"

"Eight," but close enough. "What else?"

Calvin watched the kid struggle, which promptly vaulted into frustration.

"Nuttin'!" The boy cried.

Calvin was not disappointed. The kid had been doing well; he just hit a small barrier was all and needed a little help over. "Look how deep those indentions run. Whatever was dragged was heavy... like the weight of a man by my calculations. Which means what?"

"He's still alive."

Correct. "An' there wunt no way he coulda cut that wood at the bivouac, 'cuz he wunt carryin' no tools."

Calvin kicked himself quietly. He had not given any consideration to Jeremiah needing to possess the tools for the woodwork. The boy had discovered an angle that he had missed. Though he would never admit to being outsmarted by the lucky amateur, Calvin covered his failure by pointing out something the boy had been wrong about... "You think that area was his bivouac?"

"Wunt it?"

"Shelters usually have a fire pit and what not. I didn't see no snuffed pit, did you?"

Alexander instantly went on the defensive. "Is that a crack about my sight?"

"Not at all."

"Oh, well, then I didn't see no fire pit neither," he agreed peacefully.

"What else?"

"Well, I know'd it was him though 'cuz of my pa's hoss bein' right there."

"So what then?"

"Someone helped him?" Before Calvin could ask who... "Injuns I s'pect, but I ain't rightly sure why the hell for."

That was all right because neither did he. "Which Indians?" Calvin asked, genuinely wanting to hear his opinion in hopes Alexander had a perception he didn't notice--just as he had with the tools. The boy was proving to be somewhat of a natural.

"Well, you said we wuz in Cherokee territory."

"It's their territory, but they ain't the only ones here."

"Who else?" He asked, genuinely nervous.

"Peoria. Shawnee. Osage. Choctaw. Creek."

Alexander had heard enough. What little safety he felt had diminished as he peered at their surroundings with fresh eyes then suggested, "Maybe we should go back fer that escort."

The kid's nervousness distracted him now and wouldn't be able to add any more thoughts on the investigation. Calvin attempted to reel him back in. "So, if it was Indians, why didn't they steal yer pa's horse?"

Alexander shrugged; nothing was going to distract his fear.

"He wasn't ridin' when they found him. I think he either got off or fell off near that clearing."

Alexander nodded in agreement even though he was not listening to a word.

"They either didn't see the horse or they couldn't catch it. Hell, you couldn't catch it either when it ran by ya, and you were familiar to it."

Some of his distress had vanished, and Alexander began to come back around. "They take 'im prisoner?"

Calvin was about to answer until his head perked up like a prairie dog peeking out of its burrow. Alexander's nervousness intensified at the sight of Calvin's worry. It was never a good sign when a man who did not demonstrate dread appeared anxious.

"Whachu hear?"

Calvin motioned for Alexander to keep quiet by pressing his forefinger to his lips. Though he concluded that the kid had thought he heard something discerning, it was not a noise that had put Calvin on alert, but an indigenous scent. When it came to body odors, white people had a contrasting stench to the natives. Their diets were different, and they took far fewer baths. Lugging pail after pail of water to a bathing tub was a chore so they typically relied on the use of aromatic fragrances to conceal their stink. The Indians did not use such perfumes or containers. They bathed in the nearest water source. For this reason alone, Calvin knew his present distress was legitimate.

The breeze came from the north. He sniffed the air again, hoping not to catch another whiff of what could be described as living a simpler life. Thankfully, the aroma had passed, but his concern did not alleviate. Calvin transferred every focus of his senses to his vision and peered like a hawk at the tree line across the rivulet. There he found six to seven natives shuffling from tree trunk to tree trunk. They were inching closer with spears and bows in their hands. He tried to see what clothing and markings they bore to determine their tribe, but the shadows concealed their details.

The option to go back the way they came had gone. Their only route to take was to continue onward. Thankfully, Alexander appeared to be unaware of their precarious situation as he still possessed some control over his angst. Without letting his partner in on his newfound discovery, Calvin calculated that their best course was to saunter into the covering of the southern woods as though they remained ignorant of the natives' presence. If not, the rushing water between them, a hundred feet wide and three feet deep at most, would slow their attackers, but only for a moment.

Unfortunately, that plan never came to fruition. A hostile battle cry suddenly boomed from the northern trees, followed by a barrage of slung spears and arrows. The first Indian vaulted from the woods, and Calvin understood why they had been so aggressive.

"Go!" He hollered while slapping the reins. The horse bounded south as Alexander kept less than a horse length behind.

The arrows and spears continued to come at them but fell short as the two men ducked into the region's covering.

Alexander glanced over his shoulder. They were still coming; on foot and by horseback, whooping, and hollering. "They don't look Cherokee!"

"Osage!" He replied, worriedly.

The warriors on horseback flung their weapons with deadly accuracy; they were gaining. Calvin zigzagged through the dense forest, dodging their projectiles when another sound of war cries came out of the west. At first, Calvin's impression was that their time had come, but he then experienced immense relief once he confirmed that the advancing newcomers were from a different tribe. They were Cherokee and could have cared less about the white men; it was the Osage trespassers they sought for battle.

Calvin and Alexander continued to flee as they left the eruption of a tribal war in the distance. Though the fading cries proved that they were no longer being pursued, Calvin did not let up on their speed. They were in the clear... and would try to remain so until they reached their destination.

"Where we goin'?" Alexander shouted.

"Ta get that escort!"

Both men continued to demand the most from their rides and would continue to do so for the next forty miles, only resting once they reached the Union-occupied Fort of Gibson.

CHAPTER VII

T he moon did not appear once night came. Without nature's lantern showing the way, it was all too easy to get lost in the immersive pitch black, but the two men were determined to reach Fort Gibson or ride their horses into the ground doing so. Calvin was worried, and had been for miles, once feeling Melville's wet coat, drenched with sweat. It was then that Calvin made the decision to slow from a run to a trot, but even at a curbed pace, they would not last much longer.

The freckled glow of torches, outlining the perimeter of a magnificent stronghold, couldn't have come out of nowhere sooner. Mostly single-leveled, the fortress lay at the center of a grassy knoll. Its walls, barracks, and other structures appeared to be wood and stone, but details of the fortification were still difficult to distinguish in its spotted torchlight. However, what needed no discernment was the sudden upheaval that emerged once noticed. Calvin had been concealing reservations about approaching a Union Cavalry for help, but since Alexander never questioned his plan, he never shared his concerns. No doubt, the boy did not see the color blue out of his one eye, but white, which he must have considered better than red, but should the men in blue coats with white skin capture them, torture them, and kill them, then it wouldn't matter what skin their assassins bore. Death could come in any color, even gray, as proven by their comrade in arms, Jeremiah Whiting.

The cavalry scattered about like cockroaches, apparently not used to keeping formation in the dead of night. Calvin continued to regulate his pacing; nice and slow. Alexander raised his hands in the air to show they were empty of any weapons once ordered to halt about twenty yards outside the gate. They were, then, forced to wait longer for whatever came next.

Calvin gazed at the four men on top of the wall and the double guards at the front gate, all training their rifles at the two intruders, when the guard, who had shouted the previous instruction to halt, then added, "You got no business here, graybacks!"

"I come to speak to your commander-in-charge on a matter of utmost national security."

There was silence, and it continued at length until the guard called for, "Becker!"

"Sir!" One of the men from atop the wall answered.

"Inform Colonel Phillips of the arrivals."

"Yes, sir!" He replied, and then scaled down

a ladder. His footsteps scraped across the parade ground until they faded.

The blue boys had kept them waiting for what felt like an eternity, but time would slow anything while constantly on alert. In truth, Calvin was quite surprised that this Colonel William A. Phillips had granted permission for them to enter... escorted, of course. And so far, the Union scum seemed an intelligent man.

Two guards were stationed just outside the opened front door as Calvin did most of the talking. Alexander occasionally interjected when he thought his partner was leaving out vital information. Those random annexations were starting to vex Calvin, however, he kept his grievances to himself when in the Colonel's presence. Any break he made when interrupted by the boy was made to look like a pause to recall the next part of his continuing story about Jeremiah.

"That is most unfortunate," confirmed Phillips as he kept the back two legs of his chair balanced with his feet propped on the top of his desk. The Colonel lifted the drink he had been nursing to his lips.

"Jeremiah Whiting is not only an enemy of the Union and Confederate armies, but the sum of our two great nations." Phillips lifted an eyebrow as though enjoying the words carefully chosen for the proposal. "I will bring this monstrous traitor to justice," concluded Calvin.

The Colonel took another sip as he mulled over Calvin's pitch. He prolonged his pause when removing a cigar from his coat in silence.

Calvin recognized the game the Colonel was playing. "So, ya gonna help us or not?" He asked impatiently.

Phillips broke off the tip of the cigar with his teeth then spat the end on the floor. He reached over and grabbed the candle from his desk to light the smoke. And just as Calvin saw no end to this game in sight...

"My heart goes out to you boy, truly," Phillips then shifted his undivided attention back onto Calvin, "but as you are well aware, we cannot extricate within these territories."

"I am not seeking extrication from you and your men, only safe passage to continue my investigation of his whereabouts. I am quite capable of seizing this underhanded criminal myself."

Alexander made a noise, or under-breath comment, which Calvin took as a signal of misinformation. He obliged the correction, "Ourselves."

The Colonel dropped the front two legs of the chair to the floor then leaned forward. It appeared the man was about to take him seriously, when instead, he reached back into his inner coat pocket and pulled out two new cigars, handing one each to Calvin and Alexander before inquiring,

"Whereabouts you from, brother?"

Calvin paused as though he did not see the relevance, but then took the offered smoke and answered, "Barber County... Kansas."

The Colonel's eyes grew wide; a pleasant surprise.

Calvin and Alexander lit their cigars using the same flame from the desk.

"Well, that's just a day's ride over the state line. Franklin County, myself. We are, indeed, closer brothers than suspected; separated only by a fistful of ideals and two rather drab colors."

Phillips stopped to regard Calvin. A faint smile formed as though he waited for appreciation to his splash of humor from the tracker but realized the loss of his attempt rather quickly. His grin faded. Phillips continued, "I admit, I am surprised by the kinship I feel towards you, more than any other gray... Confederate soldier."

"I am not a soldier. I am a tracker."

"Who once tracked lost Union boys... good soldiers, who may have been wandering injured and hungry after battle. But then you found them and saw to their executions."

A din of silence filled the room as Phillips waited for Calvin to concede to the charge, but once the Colonel realized there would be no confession, "Yes, I have heard of you, Calvin Hawte. Your reputation precedes you greatly, but that is not why I cannot offer aide in the apprehension of this vile..." Phillips paused, at a loss for words. "Well, I don't even know what to call him. Certainly not a man! I do find him that reprehensible." He wavered once again and returned to his leaning position with his chair steadying on two legs and his feet propped on the desk. Phillips puffed and puffed, deep in thought. "These are precarious times. The Indian Removal Act not only upset those from the 'Trail of Tears' but also those native to this territory. One might imagine that the Indians would not be at odds with one another, but hospitablely and warmly share their land with their brethren folk. Well, that's just simply not the case. They find it intrusive, and who could blame them? Thereby, it is not only my responsibility to preserve peace between the Union and the civilized tribes, but amongst all natives. That, sir, is no easy task. Surely, you can sympathize with my plight?"

For the first time, Calvin turned his attention to Alexander. By his apathetic expression, even the boy knew what bullshit the Colonel was spewing. He admired the kid a little more for his keen insight.

"Now, I could offer you two days of supplies..." resumed Phillips. "...if you choose to continue your hunt in these parts, but I highly recommend you do not do so."

Calvin stood. There was no point in suffering through this belittling charade and commented unappreciatively, "I believe you've already done too much."

Alexander followed his lead by extinguishing their cigars on the floor and then headed for the door when...

"Now, hold on. Don't be going all riled up. It's late, and although it's against our national crisis, I'm offering you to stay the night here as my guests."

Calvin paused just inside the door. He thought negotiation would be impossible, but still, he was exhausted. "Will you offer guided passage to Kansas state line come dawn?"

Though his eyes did not leave the Colonel, Calvin noticed through his peripheral that Alexander made no attempt to keep his perplexity off his face. He had never mentioned anything about Kansas. Surely, the boy would think that he was giving up and desired safe passage to home. Calvin hoped the kid would keep his mouth on his hot-head shut.

"I can offer you a small garrison to get you to the line, but once inside Kansas, you'll be on yer own."

Calvin gave a curt nod as a demonstration of his understanding, then the Colonel called for the guards outside the door to enter, instructing, "Take our brothers to the barracks and ensure that they are made comfortable and treated respectfully. They are my guests."

Silently, each guard acknowledged that they understood before beginning their escort.

No more words were spoken to the Colonel, only slight nods to show some form of gratitude for the very minor gesture of support. They exited Phillips' office, leaving the man to enjoy the remainder of his cigar while reclined in his chair.

As the two guards led them across the parade

grounds towards the opposite end of the fort, both he and the boy received many accusing glares and haughty scowls from the nearby cavalry. Under normal circumstances, Calvin expected that Alexander would have been distressed about being massively outnumbered by his enemy, but he understood that the kid had a more pressing concern that distracted him. "You ain't givin' up, is you?"

"No," stated Calvin, simply.

"Then what we goin' ta Kansas fer?"

Calvin halted, perturbed by the impudence of being questioned by a vastly under-ranked soldier in front of the opposing army. Through gritted teeth, he answered anyway, "Jeremiah is either in hidin' or a prisoner, an' I intend to seize him either way." He then resumed leading his apprentice after their Union escort grunted disapproval of their delay. "First, I will return home to organize a posse and equip ourselves proper before tracking the wretched bastard and bringing him to justice."

"You mean death," corrected Alexander.

"If that is what the law decides."

"It's what I decide!" He shouted.

Calvin continued following the guards, unintimidated by the rash aggressiveness displayed by Alexander, who kept only one small step behind him. He could sense the heat coming off the boy. He had an itch for a fight, and it did not matter to him that the Billy Boys were watching. The law, courts, judges, juries, none of it mattered to him. Only revenge. Calvin did not fault him for that; the kid had nothing left but hatred. Still, it was best to try to calm matters.

"Neither of us has slept in two days. This is a discussion better left for when we're rested."

Alexander didn't say anything in return; no quip or argument. The boy had retained some sensibilities though Calvin expected that the childish silence would continue well into the next day.

A mild breeze rolled across the plains. Calvin gazed at the large clouds of white fluff hovering over the plains. The tall blades of grass bowed under a wind's gentle force to create waves one would find in the ocean, and what hid below the surface was just as dangerous. Mounted high on Melville's back, Calvin could not help but compare himself to Captain Ahab on the hunt for his Moby-Dick. Upon further comparison to the likes of Jeremiah Whiting, his need for retaliation was just as fierce, but the similarities stopped there. Though his killer whale lurked beneath the waves of grass, so did other dangerous creatures with spearheads as sharp as shark's teeth. To most other men, like the squad of ten Union troopers who encircled him and the boy, no threat could be found, but to Calvin, what he saw kept him on edge.

He glanced to his left, curious whether he would

discover if Alexander also noted what was hiding in the fields, but the kid strode along without care or concern. Partly because he mistakenly felt safe in the company of their escort, and also partly because he was lost in thought, as he had been since they left Fort Gibson at daybreak, hours ago. It was another new day for mourning. Though devastating as losing family was, Calvin still felt uncomfortable by partnering with a boy who continued to allow his emotions to distract him. He decided to give the kid just one more day to finish his bereavement; otherwise, he would turn the boy loose and continue his search for the whale alone.

It was time to wake Alexander out of his stupor; it was time for another test. "Indians are keeping watch." The information meant for Alexander's ears had been overheard. Calvin noticed the escort tighten their grips on their rifles. He continued with his teachings. "Not being in immediate danger, and without letting on, tell me their position."

Alexander glanced in every direction--as did the squad--but nobody saw neither hide nor hair of an enemy. He nodded to the northwest.

He was correct but "Why?"

"'Cuz that's where you been gawkin' fer the last ten minutes."

Calvin could not help but grin a little at the clever cheat. Though the kid's perception did not make a good tracker, he had to give the kid kudos for maintaining awareness of another's concentration, especially while appearing so oblivious.

"You're observant for a blind man."

"I ain't blinded!" He hollered.

The kid was being aggressively defensive about his eyesight, again, and had been ever since the tumult at the farmhouse. Upon their first meeting, Alexander had caught him gawking at his right wooden eye. He then made a good-humored wisecrack, suggesting that if it looked odd, it was his father's fault because the eyepiece had been manufactured at his furniture factory. But now, all hilarity was a memory, and Calvin suspected why Alexander had become hostile; he blamed his poor sight, thus himself, for Elias's killing. Though mindful that the accident would have never occurred if Jeremiah hadn't gone on his murderous rampage, Calvin understood how easy it was to forget who the real culprit was sometimes. It dawned on Calvin right then where Alexander's mind had been all day; not on his entire family, just his brother. He wanted to empathize, but sympathy would not keep either of them safe. Calvin stood by his declaration to leave Alexander behind if he couldn't get his shit together. He had to; he had a family of his own who counted on him returning safely back home.

"I bet you can't even see that storm comin' either," prodded Calvin.

Alexander looked at the large white cotton balls in the blue horizon. "What storm?! I ain't seein' no storm comin'."

Calvin placed an expression of arrogance across

his face, and he would do so again when they became caught in wind and snow.

"Tell me where the natives are hidden."

Alexander looked northwest again but came back with no answer. "How am I s'pose ta see them when they's hidden?"

"'Cuz they don't wancha to see them. That's the point of being kept hidden." A few of the eavesdropping Yanks sniggered at the quip, which Calvin did not appreciate. His intention had never been to make the kid look foolish in front of the Blue Coats. "That's all right. You wouldn'ta been able to see them even if ya had two eyes."

"Then how can you see them?"

"'Cuz I know what to look for."

Once again, Calvin gazed across the land while Alexander mimicked. He waited for the northern breeze to rest before pointing out, "There. See the grass."

Alexander and the cavalrymen struggled to notice it at first, but once they let their eyes focus, it became apparent: small pockets of the tall grass did not resettle into place when the breeze relaxed. Though obvious there were bodies lying on top of the blades, which kept them folded down, nobody would have ever noticed without knowing what to look for.

The squad, as well as Alexander, made motions to raise their weapons when Calvin exclaimed, "Don't!" The men halted. He had their attention but only for a second. "They are just surveying us."

Of all the men, Alexander was the only one to listen. He relaxed his grip while the others showed no confidence in Calvin by keeping their tensions on high alert. Though knowing it wasn't his place, they needed to be ordered, "Turn away men. Do not aggravate them by letting them know we are aware of their presence."

Their leader--a captain whom Calvin could not recall the name of and who rode at the head of the pack--turned to nod curtly in favor of Calvin's assertion. The squad rested their weapons.

"So, who is they?"

"You tell me."

Alexander let out a frustrated sigh before glancing back to the patches, but the breeze had already returned to camouflage their whereabouts.

"They ain't attackin', so my guess is they's friendlies. An' we're still in Cherokee territory, so that's my guess too, I reckon."

Though he agreed with the kid's assessment, Calvin gave no reply, but could feel Alexander's stare digging into him.

"So? Is they Cherokee or not?"

"I ain't got no idea, but yer guess sounds as good as any."

The squadron let out another lighthearted chuckle. Calvin smirked. He had intended to play before an audience that time.

"So, why'd ya stop huntin' the enemy ta hunt yer own kind?"

The wind had suddenly shifted. It appeared

Alexander was not one for being the punch line of a joke and attempted to direct all attention onto Calvin by asking what had been clearly weighing heavily on his mind. The Yankees appeared to be just as intrigued.

"They were my orders, not my choice," Calvin explained and left it at that. Though honestly, he was not hiding much of anything else other than he had not been happy about the decision initially, but he did understand its importance... and orders were orders. Nine times out ten, the soldier had simply gone A.W.O.L. without committing additional crimes. Usually, they had either run scared or were desperate to get laid or be present for the birthing of their child. In cases such as those, minimal punishment would be given once returning to their squadrons. He did not have many Jeremiah Whiting types under his belt. It was only that other ten percent of the time when he felt more like a hunter than a chaser.

"My pa says you like the trophies; I says ya like being feared'd." Alexander must have been wise to see he was getting on his nerves because he continued to pressure, "Yeah, we heard of you long a'fore ya come to our home with news of Martin. Shit, I don't imagine there bein' many who ain't heard'a you. They say ya can smell men as good as a dog would, see farther and better than a hawk, and hear noises a rabbit couldn't hear."

"I ain't no animal. I just know how to hunt."

"So do I!" Alexander affirmed.

"For what? Fish?"

Although his question was meant to be serious, once again, the Yankees found their squabble entertaining.

"Elk... and deer!" Alexander spat.

"What about a man? You ever hunt a man?"

The boy paused, contemplating his decision first before boldly announcing, "Can't be much different."

Calvin raised an eyebrow. He could not determine if the kid was naïve or just plain cocky. "You think elk and deer are awares enough to squat in a field so as to hide from their predator? You think any animal has intelligence enough to track you while you track them? Don't be fooled, kid. Jeremiah certainly ain't no elk. If yer gonna stick with me, you need ta know how to hunt a man, and what to look for using more than just yer eye."

Although referring to his one eye was not intended to be an affront, he feared the erratic kid might consider it as such. Surprisingly, Alexander showed restraint when he didn't have a conniption though he did protest rather child-like, "I still say there ain't no storm comin'."

Their protection did as ordered, and turned around to head back to Fort Gibson once they reached the Kansas state line. Whether their accompaniment had deterred any attacks would never be known, but the trek was without incident, though he wasn't home yet. Until he did, there was still a chance that the storm he had warned Alexander about could delay their arrival. A dusting of snow and the wind chill factor had been concerning, but with the winter months advancing, they had been well equipped. Prior to leaving the Stebbins' homestead, he had suggested they prepare for frigid temperatures without knowing how long it would take them to catch Jeremiah. No two outlaws were the same.

Snow continued to trickle from the darkened sky that stretched beyond their vision. Surrounded by the endless dense grayish-white fog gave the sensation of being trapped inside a prison of clouds. Seeing more than twenty feet ahead was impossible. Despite the thin layer of snow that covered the road, Calvin still had every confidence they were traveling true. Alexander had made his doubts known earlier when he vocalized that he did not share the same assurance. At that moment, Calvin had shot Alexander the same haughty look he had given the kid the previous day.

Despite Calvin's confidence in his course, he did have trouble remembering how many feet ahead they had yet to travel. Thankfully, they soon came upon a tree. He did not recognize the tree at first, as the Red Lone Oak had grown so big in the time he'd been away, but then knew it had to be the one he planted for Henry because there were no other trees on this road for miles. His son had wanted it planted for climbing, and napping under its leaves during the warmer months. He could not help but marvel at its growth, immediately causing Calvin to wonder if Henry had grown just as radically.

A charge of excitement filled Calvin. His homestead lay only a few hundred feet ahead. He nudged his horse into a trot but then pulled back on the reins when his peripheral noticed a strange object. He had not seen it previously because the trunk had blocked his view of the two wood pieces nailed together in the form of a cross that stuck out of the ground. Calvin's breathing hastened as he rushed to the grave marker. He leaped down and wiped the snow off the wood, looking for any carvings or painted words that would have labeled whose burial he hovered over. There were none.

Calvin wanted to panic though suppressed his urge. Even in his agitated frame of mind, his observation pointed out that there was only one grave--not two--which meant that either his son or wife buried the other. One was still alive, but which?

He turned towards where his home lay hidden in the fog, and then charged on foot, calling, "Henry?! Jenny?!"

Where is it?! He silently shouted to himself, having expected to reach the farmhouse already. His yell of both names went unanswered. Finally, the front porch came into view... and then his barn, animal pens, and windmill that the low clouds chopped off at the head. He entered his house first.

The front door slammed against the inner wall and echoed a blast that resembled shotgun fire.

"Jenny?!"

He darted into the first of two rooms. Calvin felt strange and lost in his own home, perplexed why he could not find either his wife or son with all his superior tracking skills. He ran to the other room at the opposite side of the living space, but still, there was no sign of either.

A faint voice was heard coming from outside. Calvin dashed back the way he came, recognizing the urgency and excitement in Alexander's voice. He followed his partner's calls to the windmill where he pointed upward to a figure climbing down the ladder.

"Pa!" He heard his boy cry.

Calvin rushed across the clearing. He reached the windmill at the same moment Henry bypassed the last five rungs by jumping down. He grabbed his boy and pulled him close. His desire was to squeeze his son hard, but then resisted for fear he might squeeze too hard. Instead, Calvin lifted Henry to carry in his arms. He grunted as though lifting a heavy bag of sand.

"I guess you've gotten too big for this."

"It's good to see you back, Pa!"

The boy wrapped his arms around his father's neck. The affection was brief; too brief for Calvin's liking. He suspected Henry had restrained himself in front of the stranger, which reminded him... he glanced at Alexander, who failed to hide his jealousy. No doubt, the subject of family would be sensitive to the young man, who no longer had any.

"Is that your momma laid to rest?" Calvin asked, nudging his head towards the unseen tree.

"Yes, sir," answered Henry with a nod.

By the scarce emotion he showed, Calvin judged that her death had happened some time ago. His five-year-old son had been on his own ever since, possibly since he was four.

Neither Calvin nor Alexander had ever known such a miraculous boy of similar age. Calvin beamed with as much pride as a broken heart would allow. From what Henry had described, he was convinced Jeannette had died from a lethal case of tuberculosis. It was astounding that Henry did not fall victim to the same ailment. He imagined that was mostly Jenny's doing. The boy mentioned he could not care for his mother like he wanted because she would not let him near her. Even more perplexing was how Henry had avoided contracting the condition at inception. When he asked his son if they had received any visitors--thinking primarily of deserters stumbling upon his home--Henry claimed there had been none. The only other possibility of exposure he was aware of was from bad cow's milk, which made some sense. Henry did not drink milk; it made him sick in other ways: bloated and gaseous, so Calvin settled on one logical explanation and felt satisfied in his summarization.

However, it was not Henry's victory over

dodging the disease that made his son extraordinary. His survival instincts warranted accolades. In the eight months since his mother passed, Henry had not only tended to all the livestock, but harvested what he could of the fields, prepared his own meals, kept the house in order, and managed any unforeseen crisis that came with any of the aforementioned. One such task had needed attention that very day and was being taken care of at the time of his and Alexander's arrival. Like his pa, the boy's inherent knowledge informed him that a bad storm was approaching. He had been tying down the windmill blades as a proactive means to keep them from breaking free during the storm's strongest gusts, which...

A porch chair was heard being knocked over by a howling blast; subsequently knocking Calvin out of his deep thoughts. He gazed across the table at Alexander, who watched Henry sleep, despite the wind's vigor, just beyond the open bedroom door. Alexander could not stop staring; in a trance of his own.

Jealousy was Calvin's first summation, but as he examined Alexander more carefully, he saw his crinkled forehead and squinted eyes--they were tells of confusion. His immediate instinct had been wrong. The kid was not showing envy, but concern. Alexander turned to Calvin and looked him in the eye to ask, "Ya ain't gonna take 'im with us, is ya?"

Calvin would be lying if he were to say he had not given the matter some thought, and he would still be lying had he thought that the decision was easy to reach. But before he relayed his altered plan, "Indian territory's too dangerous for a white youngin."

"Then what?"

Calvin held Alexander's troubled gaze. He did not, for a single moment, want to look away when he told the kid that for him the journey was over. Breaking his perpetual stare would only provide Alexander with false hope: showing weakness in his resolve, and giving the impression that he had empathy, which he did, but not any more than he had for his own son. Henry was his reason for now becoming a deserter himself.

But Calvin did not need to utter a single word, expecting that his eyes had told Alexander all that was on his mind.

"But what about Jeremiah? What about what he done to my family?" The kid yelled as he jolted from his seat, swapping his confusion for rage.

"Get on with the life you still got. Go on home," advised Calvin. He was as equally surprised to hear those words as Alexander, but they felt right to say. He supposed that same guidance might have been nice to hear at the start of his career. Instead of being hell-bent on capturing soldiers who were nothing more than a prize, Calvin would have been here for his family and his wife in her time of need. Perhaps she would still be alive today. But that's not what happened. Like Captain Ahab, he had been lost in his ambition and twice granted the army's requests to extend bequeathing his services for "The

Cause." He asked himself if it had been worth the sacrifice, and then twisted to his bed where Jenny should be sleeping. The answer was "no." Unlike the sea captain, he would know when to stop.

Alexander wouldn't be able to comprehend this mentality. Its reasoning was something that needed to be experienced, not informed. The kid was still too driven by anger and proved so when he screamed, "What life?! What home? I ain't got nuttin' left, and you know'd that."

Calvin stood, and said with the most comfort in his tone he could offer, "Stay as long as you need," then walked towards his bedroom when he heard Alexander charge from behind. Calvin spun and blocked the boy's punch, then slammed the kid against the wall.

"Pa?"

Calvin glanced at Henry standing inside his bedroom's doorframe; alarmed. He kept exceedingly calm when he ordered, "Say goodbye to Mister Stebbins, Henry. He'll be sleeping in the barn then heading out come morning." He then turned to Alexander and with the same tone of serenity in his voice, "I imagine revenge is yer only family now. Try to remember what I taught ya."

Though the kid did not relax any, Calvin felt confident he would not make the same foolish attempt for another fight, so released him. Alexander gathered his coat then made a beeline for the door; humiliated.

The biting wind entered. Calvin sincerely hoped

the kid still had sense enough to take his offer to wait out the storm in the shelter. Granted, if he were the one fueled by the same hunger for a reckoning, Calvin was not so sure he would. Luckily, he came to his senses and rested his laurels on his newfound peace of mind. The whale was no longer his adversary. Calvin had trouble deciding if he ever was anything more than a poacher.

CHAPTER VIII

I am dead, and I have gone to heaven, believed Jeremiah as a beautiful melody awoke him from sleep. He could not understand the words of the song, but he could tell from the woman's soothing voice that the lyrics were of kindness and healing. No place other than heaven would treat him so well. Only in paradise would he feel comfort and warmth, and be free from the agonies he had suffered so recently. In the end, everything inside him had screamed, but now the screaming had been replaced with serenity.

Jeremiah lay on the shore of the watering hole on a warm summer's day. He turned his head to find Martin and Alice sunning themselves at his side. This spot was his favorite, during his favorite time of year, with his favorite two people, and that's when he knew it was all a lie. Jeremiah no longer believed he was in heaven. There was no need for the dead to carry memories with them into the afterlife.

Awareness that he had kept his eyes closed

struck him though he had no desire to open them. He did not care to see the world when dreaming made him so much happier. However, The Soldier did not agree.

Coward.

Jeremiah ignored the taunt but soon realized that he could not stay with Martin and Alice. They were dead. The Soldier had killed them.

Fully awake, Jeremiah continued to lie in darkness while he listened to the bird-like voice. She was not a part of his dream, but very real. Only one woman would sing such affection towards him, which meant that he was home and that his mother had forgiven him for his trespasses.

At the thought of her hovering near, Jeremiah gasped and wasted no more time. He opened his eyes to the disappointment of finding a hazy female figure outlined by the golden glow of sunlight coming through an arched entrance. He allowed a moment for his vision to stabilize, and once it settled, he focused on an unrecognizable savage woman. Instinct demanded that he bolt up in alarm, but he resisted the urge. Her smile kept him pinned in his supine position. Recalling that his first impression of her had been that of an angel, Jeremiah realized he might not have been mistaken. She was a lovely and joyous surprise, and every desire of his being demanded that he touch her skin.

The young squaw was startled when he grabbed her hand. She lurched back, but Jeremiah's grip was ironclad, and the momentum of her heave pulled him off the dried grass and wool blankets that covered his stone slab bed. The second he hit the floor, all his pain that had dissipated returned and shocked him back into unconsciousness, but not before he howled a piercing cry.

As Jeremiah awoke for his second time, the gentle singing had been replaced with chanting and beating drums from beyond the arched entrance. By his view, it was now night. He summoned the strength to lift his head, and then rested his gaze on the firelight that emphasized the edges of the open doorway. By what little light seeped inside, he could tell that his hospital room was nothing more than a hut made of mud.

We're injun prisoners.

Though he found his position worrying, Jeremiah did not feel entirely confident in The Soldier's summation. He thought back to what he could remember. There was pain; much pain and he had continued to drift in and out of consciousness while escaping Calvin and Alexander on horseback. He recalled having chosen to head west, but he could not remember having entered Indian Territory, though that did not come as a surprise being that his hometown was a half-day's ride from their land. Between then and his first awakening, every single moment escaped him. For all Jeremiah knew, he could have been asleep for a day or a month; or he might have been awake but just forgetful of everything that had transpired. What did appear evident was that the Indians had found him and taken him to their camp, but what remained a mystery was why he continued to live. The last people in the world he imagined sympathy from were the featherheads.

The more nothing made sense, the more fear filled him. He flung the covers off and spun his legs over the side to plant his feet on the dirt floor. He immediately slowed his movement to a snail's pace when a buildup of hurt exploded. He paused, needing to rest a moment, knowing that what came next would be more of a challenge.

Once prepared, he pushed off the bed and into a standing position. Only one groan escaped his lips, but it had been loud. Still, Jeremiah did not worry about being heard over the uproar of the prairie hoedown.

A breeze entered the hut as though warning him of his current condition. He gazed down to discover that the only cloth that covered his body was the bandage wrapped around his torso. He was, otherwise, naked. In ordinary circumstances, he would panic and find clothing, but tilting his head forward had created a torturous pain in his head. Jeremiah had no other choice but to sit back down.

The agony took its sweet time to subside. In the interim, he glanced over the small enclosure and found no sign of his tattered clothes. Jeremiah began to rethink his decision about an escape. Not only could a turtle out race him, but he was without attire, and he had no idea where his horse was--or if he even would be able to mount it if given the chance.

A surge of dread welled at the thought that The Soldier might have been right: he was their prisoner, whomever they were. If true, he would never be able to withstand the sensation of confinement again; the Yankee sniper had proven that. Unfortunately, there was only one way to know for sure.

Each step was slow and cautious. Jeremiah silently thanked the one who had bandaged his feet. The thin fabric did well to protect him from the terrain and the frigid climate, much like a pair of moccasins. He further appreciated the thickness of the wool blanket, which he draped over his bareskin, keeping him warm and decent. Jeremiah never had known such craftsmanship. A master had woven this tapestry.

He emerged from the hut and the music and chanting that filled the village came to a sudden halt. All eyes were upon him; at least fifty pairs of them. An impulse to turn and run sparked, but Jeremiah knew better than to make the attempt. Eagerly, he began to search for a kindly face; her face from somewhere within the crowd. As he gazed from one stern expression to the next, his eyes paused on a large elk hanging from two posts above a fire pit. Jeremiah's stomach grumbled, and he nearly fell over a second time when a pair of arms wrapped around his chest from behind. He gazed at the strong limbs that, no doubt, belonged to a man, shattering his hope that the lovely young lady, who sang like a bird, kept him upheld. Disappointment would have been a mild term for his sentiment.

Another injun approached. He was similar in age with long flowing black hair and carried a perplexed expression of disapproval. The unknown tribesman silently ordered the man behind him to halt. Jeremiah's mysterious crutch forced him to do as instructed.

The man before him then stared into Jeremiah's eyes as though searching for some hidden information. The redskin's glare lollygagged as Jeremiah felt the rest of the tribe bore into him with harsh scowls of their own. He was rendered frozen until the native turned, and the man from behind nudged him forward. Sandwiched between the two, Jeremiah resumed being escorted towards the masses.

Neither native said a word during their short walk. Even when they instructed their prisoner to sit in the dirt near the bonfire, they pushed down on his shoulder, giving the order silently. However, Jeremiah could not keep as quiet. He grunted and whimpered, discovering that the simple act of sitting on the ground did not come painlessly. It took every ounce of restraint to keep from bellowing out like a baby crying for his momma.

Jeremiah settled as the more authoritative of his two chaperones took a position next to two tribesmen opposite the flickering flames. All three glared at him from their higher position, similarly clad in leather skins and berating scowls framed by hair that stretched down to their backsides. The men, who sat on a log throne, were undoubtedly of importance. Both Jeremiah and The Soldier agreed that he had been presented to the chief and his most trusted advisor. By the looks of their consistently rigid and skeptical glowers, his presence was not welcomed.

At last, the unseen injun from behind showed himself. He looked younger than his counterpart, but only by a couple of years, and did not appear as confident because of his lack of intimidation. Jeremiah could tell already that he liked the less threatening one much better.

Together, they watched the leaders speak to eacth other in a language Jeremiah did not understand. The chief spoke the final word then beckoned for someone who kept hidden in the distance. The young Indian at his side sat beside him like a guard.

The one summoned by the chief had, in fact, been two. Both squaws appeared with plates of food, and of the two young ladies, one was the angel Jeremiah had longed to see again. Just as radiant as he remembered, he instantly thought of her only as his prairie princess. It was not until both girls stood directly in front of him that Jeremiah even noticed the other. She was pretty too; however, her appearance seemed like a thirteen-year-old shadow of his Savannah songstress. Most likely, the two were sisters.

Jeremiah and his sentry took the offerings. The girls walked away, but Jeremiah waited until they were out of sight before he peered down at the meat, softened grains, and a hunk of bread. His guard, however, wasted no time filling his mouth; unintentionally stirring an unsettling memory. The men from his squadron had been just as anxious when it came to dining in the dirt before a fire without saying grace. Just as memorable, Jeremiah had suffered silently through aches and pains then, too, while in constant fear for his life. If compared, all the running, humiliation, and deaths since absconding had been for naught. It was like he was back in the army.

"Eat," spoke the young buck at his side. "You need food. You almost died."

Jeremiah gawked at the injun. "Ya gots good English fer a savage."

"And you are unwise for a white man."

Jeremiah swapped his expression of surprise for appall, which the Indian found humorous.

"You should not insult the person who saved your life… especially when I am the only one who does not want you dead."

Jeremiah twisted his gaze to the glares that encompassed him. He knew they had disapproved of his presence, but upon closer inspection, there was a certain gleam of murder in their eyes unnoticed prior. Not knowing what else to do, he took a bite of food. It had been their cue. As though being instructed to let him be, they began to eat as well. Jeremiah was taken aback. Admittedly, he was unfamiliar with most native traditions. Never did he expect that he would share a common custom with these yahooers unless they were one of the Five Civilized Tribes influenced by the white man. But as he took in his primitive surroundings, he guessed not. That didn't bode well.

"What is your name?" The Indian asked.

"Jeremiah," he answered flatly.

"I have heard your name before."

Jeremiah froze, giving The Soldier ample time to advise, Leave now, without interruption from the Indian, who luckily stalled their conversation by taking another bite of his meal.

Sweat formed on Jeremiah's brow despite the chill that swept over him. He glanced anxiously for any idea of how to escape but saw nothing feasible.

I can't.

Then, somehow, even when burdened under the duress of panic, a realization clicked.

I only gave 'em my first name. How might they know me?

They healed your wounds, didn't they? Feedin' ya. They're prepping you for transport back ta Missouri. You don't think a reward ain't been offered fer ya, Dunderhead?

The injun then swallowed his food, allowing no time for Jeremiah to doubt him as he continued, "Your name is a popular white man name."

Jeremiah exhaled the heaviest breath he ever remembered letting loose. These Indians appeared to have no idea how important he was to his own kind. He tried not to laugh at his idiocy... wait, not his idiocy but someone else's.

You put the fear of the Devil in me fer no goddamn reason.

There was a reason, you Dunderhead. It's how ya need ta be thinkin' from now on if yer gonna live. Always keepin' yer wits. I ain't apologetic for that.

"My name is Yuma since you did not ask," the young buck indicated starkly.

"Yer Cherokee?"

"We are."

Jeremiah's gaze bounced from one mud hut to another, lit only by the bonfire they encircled. "I thought you civilized tribes was s'posed to be livin' in real homes, with churches, an' stores an' such?"

If Jeremiah did not know any better, he would have sworn Yuma's demeanor shifted from pride to shame as he explained, "This clan practices only the traditions of our people. We are ancient Keetoowah now."

"But you speak English."

Yuma ravaged the meat off the bone he held. He took the hint that the injun would rather eat than continue this conversation.

When Jeremiah turned his head, his intention had been to observe the details of the primitive village, but instead, his eyes rested on the one girl who had sung in his ear, sitting next to another.

"My sisters, Aponi and Salali. They treated your wounds."

The angel had a name and it was Aponi, the most beautiful name he ever heard.

More beautiful than Alice?

It's different.

'Cuz these savages are showin' ya more leg.

Yuma cleaned his elk bone then held it in front of Jeremiah's face, breaking his hypnotic gaze.

"Another man's bone was inside you."

Werner.

Yuma continued his introductions, not allowing Jeremiah time to recollect for long. "That is my father, Matolu. He is our chief and does not want you here. He does not like you."

A rush of anxiety interrupted his concentration of learning names and faces. Possessing the chief's disapproval had stamped out any sense of safety. The two men at Matolu's side appeared to extend his discontentment.

"Them too," explained Yuma, needlessly, and then motioned towards the injun Jeremiah was more familiar with first. "That is my elder brother, Kilwannee. He is a great warrior and hunter."

Jeremiah did not dispute that. Just looking at the man gave him the urge to flee like a stalked antelope.

"He don't like me neither?"

"Kilwannee does not agree with anybody but our father."

Silence. Jeremiah turned to Yuma and watched him glare at his brother. He could not tell which was more heated, the fire he bore through, or the animosity both brothers demonstrated towards each other.

Yuma's rancor was held for a brief moment before he switched his attention to the third leader, "And that is my uncle, Honovi. He is our medicine man and voice to the spirits. He was the one who called the great snake for you."

"Say what now? Great snake?!" Jeremiah choked, imagining a slithering reptile a hundred feet long with a mouth wide enough to swallow a cow.

"Do not fear. The Great Snake Spirit is a healer. You would be dead without its favors."

Jeremiah took a peek under his blanket. Perhaps he had been too discombobulated when standing naked in the hut to notice how well his wounds looked, but there they were; about two weeks healed.

"How long was I out fer?"

"Two days."

Jeremiah needed a moment to comprehend that his injuries were only two days fresh. It seemed impossible.

"Was you the one who found me?"

"And my brother while we hunted." Jeremiah glanced back to that brother who had not removed his stagnant glare. "You were in the river. You had fallen from your horse."

"What about you? Do you want me here?"

"Not really."

"Then why'd ya save me?"

"I believe the spirits whispered for me to do so.

They wanted you to be kept alive. That is why it was easy to convince the snake to help."

"The spirits like me?" Jeremiah asked with a sense of empowerment, but Yuma gave no reply. "They say why?"

"No," answered Yuma, perturbed.

"I thought you said yer uncle was the one who spoke to spirits."

"We are of the same blood. I speak as well."

Jeremiah could not find any evidence to contradict Yuma's stories. Had he not been living, breathing, walking proof, of what he was hearing, he would have had a difficult time accepting the tall tale of spirits with healing powers.

The subject had reached its end, but not the conversation. Jeremiah switched topics, interested in another matter mentioned previously, "Why don't nobody like me?"

"Your horse left you. It was nowhere to be found near your body."

"That's 'cuz it wun't my horse."

"It still would not have left you had liked you."

There's a good reason for that, he thought.

"You may stay until you are well enough to travel on your own."

On my own, Jeremiah replayed in his head, and then wondered just how deep he was inside Indian Territory. It would be a deadly walk to home with no horse, no boots, no clothes, and no weapon; that was if he were still to have a home.

"I ain't got nowheres to go."

Yuma gazed at him with a softened glare. The Indian continued to avoid showing any definitive emotion, but if Jeremiah were to hazard a guess, he would have put his money on pity. No doubt, exclusion and loneliness exuded from his character.

Jeremiah returned to his meal but froze his stare on Aponi when she and Salali sat at their father's side.

Yuma watched the man who demonstrated no composure.

"That is not the way to change my father's thinking."

Jeremiah shifted his observation to Matolu's glower. He heeded Yuma's warning that was more than just a warning, then looked beyond the cautionary advice and observed compassion as its shadow.

He wants me here, thought Jeremiah.

God only know why.

Maybe to be a friend. He speaks better than other injuns.

How'd you know that? Ya don't know no other featherheads, Dunderhead.

Yuma's gonna be the one who'll convince his chief to accept me. Jus' you wait.

Jeremiah glanced at Aponi. He smiled when it became evident that she was trying not to look back. He knew this coy game; white women played it too.

An' stayin' is jus' fine by me.

Oglin' his daughter ain't gonna make convincin' the chief any easier.

Jeremiah returned to his senses. He forced his attention to his plate, but considered what it might be like to live amongst the savages. Everything he could ever want was here: food, shelter, medicine, which defied all logic, and Aponi. This place was the perfect hideaway from anyone who desired his head at the end of a noose. Not even the great Calvin Hawte would dare scour the Indian Territory for him.

Jeremiah glanced at his newfound friend. Yuma looked back, and after a moment's hesitation, offered a simple smile.

CHAPTER IX

Hands down, Jeremiah never had a more remarkable experience. The speed at which he healed was truly amazing. His treatment had reminded him of those wagon peddlers who would roll into town with their claim of possessing a sensational elixir that cured all ailments and injuries. But not one of them had fixed what was alleged. For the last two weeks, Jeremiah had a mind to ask Yuma about venturing into a partnership where--for five dollars per conjure--he would call a snake spirit to come help those in need, though the best part of the con was... there wasn't a rub. The treatment actually would do as promised. He and Yuma would be beyond wealthy, but there was one drawback: Jeremiah was now, and always would be, a wanted man. The Soldier reminded him of that simple fact whenever inspiration began to flourish. The business was not ideal for somebody on the run. This complication was the very reason his buddy, Yuma, still had not heard a word of the proposal. While traveling from town to town, he would be discovered in no time. It was better to stay put, and Jeremiah knew that for a fact, even without The Soldier's persistent nagging.

Buck up and jus' get comfortable. Yer not goin' nowheres. We're here fer the long haul. We got a good thang goin' now.

However, life had not been good. Living with the Cherokee wasn't the blessing he had initially believed. Matolu had ordered that the untrustworthy white man not be allowed to take part in their culture. He was to be watched at every moment and treated as an unwelcomed visitor. Despite knowing that he could leave at any time, Jeremiah believed the village was his prison without being a prisoner. His cabin fever had worsened over the last few days, and he would have gone stir crazy if Yuma had not warmed up to him... just as planned.

The Indian sympathized with Jeremiah's rapid restlessness. He approached Matolu to ask permission for Jeremiah to join their hunt. Jeremiah also made a case for himself, but it was Yuma's persuasiveness that bent Matolu's will, despite Kilwannee's argument to the contrary. At that moment, Jeremiah's faith in Yuma was confident. The chief still had not granted him permission to live amongst their kind permanently, but this exception had been a ray of hope. Moreover, thanks to the snake spirit, he felt invigorated and ready to prove his worth. Unfortunately, the agreement came with a condition.

First, Yuma smeared a line of red paint from the top left corner of Jeremiah's forehead to his bottom right chin. Jeremiah did not mind the war paint, and even felt empowered by its application, but his courage vanished when presented with a deerskin loincloth. Then, to make matters worse, he was relieved of his gun and handed a cumbersome spear, and then forced to shave his beard. To hunt with the Cherokee was to hunt as a Cherokee.

Uncomfortable as he was being nearly naked while handling a weapon he had never used, Jeremiah did not protest to any of the conditions. Aside from his intention to win the chief's respect, the disguise would keep him camouflaged in the great wide open. And thanks to The Soldier, Jeremiah no longer felt safe behind these territory lines; always wanting to know what was transpiring in their old world. Most mornings, he would awaken unrested from a night of perpetual berating from The Soldier for thinking the law would just give up on him. *You ain't never gonna be safe. Not even here. Murder ain't the type of crime that's forgotten. Calvin's no fool. I bet he placed a price on yer head.*

He wouldn't do that, Jeremiah would argue. He wouldn't want another man to claim his prize.

What about Alex? He don't care who kills ya as long as he sees ya covered in maggot sauce.

However macabre, The Soldier's points were valid as always, but Jeremiah still believed the chances of any white man coming into Oklahoma to search for him were slim. They would be either greedy or a fool.

Nine people. They all didn't die by your hand, but theys all dead 'cuz of you.

Jeremiah was tired of the constant reminder. He didn't need that kind of distraction while on the hunt. For the first time since being in each other's company, Jeremiah ordered The Soldier to stay behind. Surprisingly, he had obeyed the order thus far. Even as Jeremiah crawled between the tall blades of grass that were being scratched at by a breeze and listened to the morning calls of a bald eagle high above, his head was full of silence.

Mukul stopped suddenly. Jeremiah did not see Kilwannee's signal to halt, but then he did not expect to while bringing up the rear of a line six men long. He lifted his head to take a gander when Mukul quickly yanked him back down. It had been difficult enough for Jeremiah to work closely with the man without adding spite to his swelling bitterness. Prior to their introduction, he did not think twice about the native who was visiting from a nearby clan, but then he noticed Mukul staring longingly at Aponi. He pressed Yuma for more information. "Mukul will marry Aponi," his newfound friend had answered. "In our custom, the husband comes from another village to live with his wife."

Aponi had been bequeathed. Back on United States soil, a man could merely challenge the would-be groom to a duel, and then claim the bride as his intended prize, should he be the victor. Though, even if a similar challenge was permitted, he did not feel confident that he would conquer such a brutish warrior.

Prior to departing the village, Jeremiah decided to let matters be. He would watch from afar and wait to see if Mukul might have a bad day. It was not uncommon for even the greatest warrior to meet an unfortunate fate, though regrettably, Jeremiah would not be the first choice to take Mukul's place as Aponi's intended. Matolu would not agree to the union; at least not yet. Until the hunt was over, Jeremiah's resolve would be tested as he did not much like being treated as an ignorant oaf by a feather-headed buffoon.

Fifty feet ahead of where they had stopped grazed a herd of antelope. Jeremiah jerked free from Mukul's grip. He reached into the back of his skin belt to produce his concealed pistol. No matter what the rules, a spear would never be a substitute for a gun. Jeremiah crawled to Kilwannee's position at the front of the line, interrupting his intense focus of the attack

"Won't shootin' it be easier?"

Kilwannee's stare bore into him. Even Yuma scowled at the suggestion. Though Jeremiah did not mean to offend either man, he regretted upsetting the only savage who had shown him decency.

He put his gun away and followed their cue to ready his spear. Then, as slowly as the rising sun, the party rose above the grass in unison. His pa had taught him always to focus on a single target.

Jeremiah did just that, but only he pulled back his weapon with the intention to launch.

"No," spat Yuma in a hard whisper. "Wait until you see its spirit, not its flesh."

Jeremiah gawked at him; confused. *Spirit? What spirit? Ain't they suppos'd ta be invisible?*

He returned his attention to the same beast. The antelope was alert and staring off towards the north. Jeremiah could see only one of its eyes, but what he saw was black and pearl-like, as though looking into a crystal ball.

The entire herd jutted their focus towards him, but Jeremiah's attention remained on the one. He could see it; the antelope's spirit as its eyes swelled with fear. What Yuma taught him had been true.

In his excitement, he launched. His spear was the first propelled in the barrage, but all had missed their mark. The herd escaped with their lives.

It was a disappointment, but Jeremiah did not find their failure as disconcerting as his fellow hunters; in particular Kilwannee who shouted, "You do not know hunting. Go home!" then stormed off. As Jeremiah began to question what he had done wrong, Kilwannee turned back to clarify, "Your home, not mine."

Every muscle in Jeremiah's body tensed; it was a mark The Soldier's return. He then withdrew his revolver and trained his weapon towards Kilwannee and fired.

A cougar collapsed as it cleared the thicket. Its weight collided into Kilwannee, and both toppled to the ground. The hunting party wasted no time in rushing to their cohort's aide, surprised to discover his cries were not of pain but fear. The predator had not perished instantly. In the moment of its death, its jaws stretched around the throat of its prey. The Soldier knew--as did Kilwannee--that the slightest spasm would tear into his throat.

Despite what Jeremiah thought, The Soldier had never left. He watched from his own patch of grass and paid attention to the herd. They had scattered before Jeremiah released his spear. Though it explained why there had been no kills made, it had not explained what had startled the antelope. While Jeremiah took the blame for the upset, The Soldier had suspected the herd sensed another predator. He kept a peripheral eye on the fields. Nobody else saw the wheat blades at Kilwannee's back bend against the breeze; not Yuma, Mukul, Jeremiah, or any other hunter. Only The Soldier.

Freed, Kilwannee rose to his feet. Blood streamed from a pair of puncture wounds in his neck. The injury was not severe, but there was no time to waste. Honovi ducked underneath one of Kilwannee's arms, allowing him to use his free hand to clasp his wounds.

They started their journey back to the village, looking at who they thought was Jeremiah with expressions of gratitude and respect as they passed. Although he was surprised by the reverence, The Soldier did not believe it came too soon.

Yuma and his brother warrior, Atohi, circled the

carcass. They gazed at the cougar with startled looks of interest then spoke in their native tongue until The Soldier interrupted, "What's you cherry niggers talkin' 'bout?"

The two Indians quieted. Yuma hesitated to respond while Atohi's baffled eyes never left the cadaver. The Soldier noted that the other tribesmen didn't understand what he had asked, having already picked up that most older injuns, including Matolu, did not understand a lick of English. Atohi, looking to be of similar age to the chief, was included. Jeremiah had been meaning to ask why, but The Soldier suspected the question might be delicate, which was why he told his counterpart to wait for the right moment.

"We should not have needed to bring pepper."

The Soldier kept silent. He did not know if he had heard the Indian right or not. *Pepper?* His expression must have spoken for him because Yuma went on to explain, "Ground chili peppers help when hunting."

"You gotta be fuckin' kiddin' me?"

Yuma paused. He looked at The Soldier like a man he did not recognize, but then proceeded, "The powder is used to scatter over our path. It hides our scent from predators. It can also be used to blind our prey and our enemies. However, the pepper only comes with us when we travel far and do not know the land, just as this cougar has done. He could not find food at his home. His search led him here."

"Whach yer meanin' is that his food is dyin' too

quickly?"

Yuma nodded. "Not only by your kind but the Osage. They, too, have been seen on our land."

"Trespassers get shot." The Soldier raised his pistol.

"Please. We have had enough gunshots for today."

Yuma walked away, and if The Soldier didn't know any better, he would have sworn that red cheeks was perturbed; a fine "thank you" for saving a brother he didn't even care much for would have sufficed. He thought to confront the matter, but as he watched the Indian squat with his brethren around the body then lift the cougar onto their shoulders, he considered the lack of appreciation was better left unsaid.

In the distance, the faint echo of Honovi's chants could be heard as he attended Kilwannee across the plains.

"We do not hunt cougar," spoke Yuma as they walked past.

The Soldier heard the perplexity behind his voice, as though he were at a loss for what to do with its meat.

"Well, since you didn't use yer pepper, I know a good chili."

◆ ◆ ◆

No longer needed, The Soldier returned to the subconscious world, allowing Jeremiah front and center, once again, to receive the scowls and glares from the villagers like any good subordinate. Jeremiah was beginning to sense a pattern to their relationship, always taking the fall for The Soldier's actions. He should be the one to stand here and endure their unjust and hateful glares. Though, for the life of him, he could not understand why their animosity had not waned. It was as though no one had cared to mention The Soldier's heroic feat... his heroic feat. The overall demeanor of the tribe provided an unpleasant remembrance of his pa--fitting since The Soldier did as well with his rustic and demeaning voice. Nathaniel Whiting had refused to show the slightest gratitude for any single virtuous effort, unlike his ma. If word of this day could reach her, Jeremiah knew she would fill his ears with praise. The woman always had supported his endeavors, which was why Betsy Stebbins' venomous words made no sense, *Ya think yer folks wancha, knowin' what you done? You brung shame upon their good name, Jerry!* However, his ma always forgave him, no matter what troubles he got into, and would so again. She had never turned her head away from him in shame; not once, and he had given her plenty of opportunities to do so during his upbringing.

Yuma sat next to him in the dirt. This section of the ground had become their usual spot; directly across the fire under the chief's watchful eye. Just as predictable were Kilwannee and Honovi at Matolu's side. It came as no surprise to see Kilwannee sitting at the fire instead of resting in his hut. When Jeremiah heard Honovi's chanting in the prairie, he knew the medicine man had been calling the Great Snake Spirit. Jeremiah did not know the depth of power these people had over the spirits, or how it worked, but the snake had accepted Honovi's call. With a wrapping of cloth around his neck, Kilwannee was on the mend, and glaring at Jeremiah with as much disdain as the day he arrived.

"A thank you mighta've been nice."

Jeremiah heard Yuma suppress a chuckle before replying, "Do not be discouraged. My brother is conflicted."

"He hates me fer savin' his life. Why? It don't make good sense."

"We believe we give back to the earth what we take. It was his time, which you interrupted. He is both grateful and ashamed."

"I don't think I'll ever understand you people."

"That is why you do not honor our ways."

"Well, you don't respect me none either."

"It is not us who wants something from you."

Jeremiah opened his mouth to reply, but there were no words of retort. Yuma's point was fairly made. Even The Soldier could not canter.

Jeremiah kept his gaze focused on Kilwannee, who glared back just as stubbornly.

"That snake spirit sho' seems ta be working some magic."

Movement at his side alerted Jeremiah. He twisted his neck, surprised to see Aponi and Salali hovering above him. They presented large clay bowls filled with the chili he had advised the women to make; at least, the best he could remember after watching his ma make it years' back. Then, as always, he ogled Aponi as she walked away, but this time, she happened to glance back and smile. That had never happened before. Jeremiah suspected it had something to do with saving her brother's life. She did not appear as conflicted as the others.

"You can never be with her. You know this already."

"When's she s'pose ta marry Mukul?"

Yuma stressed, not as an answer to Jeremiah's question, but as an extension of his decree, "Never."

When Jeremiah looked to Yuma, he did not see his friend but Aponi's brother. He gave Yuma a nod of understanding that there would be no recourse or further discussion on the matter. In fact, Jeremiah thought it best to distract Yuma from even dwelling on this conversation. He switched subjects rapidly. "What are these spirits anyway?"

The smile Yuma gave was wholly unexpected. Though grateful his distraction had worked, Jeremiah was not fond of being humored.

"What's so funny 'bout that?"

"Only that you do not understand the connection you possess with the spirits when you carry one with you." Jeremiah gazed at him peculiarly and somewhat unnerved. "I have seen him. Tell me about your spirit."

Jeremiah paused. He waited to hear if The

Soldier would say something to the contrary, but his voice remained muted. Taking the silence as approval, "Don't know what to tell really. Don't know much 'bout 'im. He ain't even got a name, but gots my daddy's voice. He's just a soldier though."

"Your Soldier Spirit is a great warrior. Better than you." Jeremiah scowled at Yuma for his insult and found a crooked smile on his face. He was making a joke, a funny one, too, once Jeremiah accepted it.

Yuma returned to his usual seriousness to proclaim, "He protects you."

"I s'pose," Jeremiah stated unassuredly before taking his first bite of the chili that reminded him of home.

"I did not know why the spirits whispered for me to save you at the river, but now I understand. They chose your Soldier Spirit to protect you."

"I ain't so sure 'bout that."

"That is because you do not understand the spirits." Jeremiah had stopped listening. Yuma searched for the simplest definition that made sense in English. "They are what binds the body to the earth."

"So they're like souls."

"Not like your souls," asserted Yuma, near defensive, but he calmed to explain further, "We believe all living things have a spirit, not just people. Once they die, they give their gifts to the land and people whose paths cross in life."

"Gifts?" Jeremiah repeated, intrigued. "Like

what?"

"Courage. War. Speed." Yuma paused and then emphasized, "Protection. The cougar your Soldier Spirit killed is sacred."

"How so?"

"The cougar gives strength and cunningness. He is a great leader."

Jeremiah mulled over the idea of these gifts when The Soldier interrupted greedily, *We could use a couple more of them gifts fer ourselves.*

"What 'bout that snake spirit. Is healing its only gift?"

Yuma shook his head. "Elusiveness is another."

Jeremiah scanned their immediate area. He spotted a lizard scurrying across one of the outer rocks of the fire pit. He set down his bowl then cupped his hands around the reptile. He held the lizard's head close to his own, as though looking at the critter for the first time with awe-inspiring interest.

"What 'bout this?"

Yuma looked upon the lizard with admiration as well, "Control and regeneration."

"Well, I'll be damned. Regeneration."

Jeremiah watched the reptile's tongue stretch from its mouth and then whip the air. A tinge of envy sparked from within--much like when he would watch a bird fly as a boy and think what a great thing it would be to have wings. An elongated tongue could be near as fun.

"Where they go after they die?" Jeremiah

followed Yuma's gaze up to the clear, starry night. "You mean heaven?"

"No. Not heaven," bit Yuma.

Jeremiah sensed his annoyance by comparing everything to his culture.

"They take their place in the sky to watch over us at night."

"You mean the stars?" Jeremiah teased at the incredibleness of the faith.

"It is what we believe, just as you believe in a white paradise hidden in clouds."

Though similar in some ways, their worlds were also very different. A few weeks back, Yuma had called themselves ancient Keetoowah... whatever that meant. At the time, he had not cared to learn more, but tonight was different; tonight he was intrigued by it all and desired to know. "Why ain't you like the other Cherokee? What's a Keetoowah?" Yuma grew solemn, just as The Soldier had anticipated. His prediction that this subject might be sensitive had been true.

"When your people forced mine from our land, some saw defeat. In hopes not to repeat another..." Yuma struggled to find the words that would match the meaning in his language, coming up with "... place where they cried."

"You mean, the 'Trail of Tears'?" He then chuckled, finding humor where Yuma found none. Yuma's face contorted with anger at Jeremiah's lightheartedness on the matter. He stopped his chortle. Yuma continued with his story. "Some believed that to survive was to adapt to the white man's laws. Matolu's father was one of those believers."

"He was yer chief?"

"I believe the wisest of all our leaders."

The gaze was brief, and if Jeremiah had not been eyeing Yuma steadily during the story, he would have missed him glaring through the flames at his father.

He despises him.

Jeremiah did not think The Soldier's estimation was as severe as that, but Yuma did demonstrate mistrust towards his father. It was the same contempt he showed his brother. These people, too, toted different emotions for their kin, much like the white men he knew and their families. Suddenly, they appeared more human than savage to Jeremiah, but only to Jeremiah. The Soldier did not need to utter a word of his disagreement.

"Our grandfather required my generation to learn English so we could communicate with the white man, learn politics to challenge him and govern ourselves, and to have no more tears. When your war started, grandfather made a deal with the Confederacy to send men to fight at their side. In exchange, our people would be provided with homes, a school, and a church. But when grandfather died, his wishes died too. My father took his place and blinded grandfather's visions. He wanted no part of a white world. We were forced out of the town with nowhere to return to but the land.

That is why we have gone back to Keetoowah. We are now the spirit of the principle people."

"I was wonderin' how you knew English so right."

"I can speak Spanish too."

"Yeah?" Jeremiah gasped, surprised. "Say summin'."

Yuma paused in thought then said, "Este guiso no es bueno."

Like a young boy about to see his first lady part, Jeremiah was all smiles and filled with anticipation. "Whadya say?"

"This stew is not good."

The smile vanished... not faded, but disappeared completely. It was Yuma's turn to laugh at him. Most likely payback, Jeremiah suspected, for his earlier chortles.

"How'd you learn Spanish when there ain't no Mexicans?"

"There was. A man needed a place to hide from the white men, just as you do."

The look Yuma gave while he paused made Jeremiah more uncomfortable than any he had received from the other tribe members.

He's figured it out.

Figured what? He can't know it all. It ain't possible.

I told you, boy, that ain't how to survive. Trust yer instinct. Trust me.

But Jeremiah couldn't. There was something about his newfound friend he... admired. Still, he did not like the attention he was receiving. He needed a diversion and asked the first question that came to mind. "This Mexican. What was his name?"

"And now you are trying to hide from me."

The Soldier laughed at him next to his ear. *Even I know this savage ain't that stupid ta fall fer yer trick.*

Jeremiah pondered what his next action would be. Having it figured out, he explained, "When I come back from war, I found that a man come and murdered my family while I was gone. He lef' me with no home."

"Then it is your father's spirit who has given you its gifts. You said they share the same voice. He is your Soldier Spirit."

That would make sense, thought Jeremiah, *if what I hadn't just told you wasn't a boldface lie.*

"The man who killed your family, does he hunt you now?"

"I don't know. Maybe." This time, Jeremiah told the truth.

Yuma continued to ogle him, heightening Jeremiah's uncomfortableness. He thought it was worth another try to pull the attention off him again. "Ain't you goin' against yer pa like he went against his by not wanting to be Keetoowah?"

His decoy had worked that time. Jeremiah could see Yuma's bemused expression by the comparison.

"I am not against my father," Yuma corrected, defensively. "Though I do not agree with all of what he does, I do agree with some. Besides, my father has not severed all connections with the white man. We continue to meet with your kind two times a year to keep peace."

Queasiness exploded in the pit of Jeremiah's stomach. The sensation of sanctuary fled in an instant. He could feel The Soldier wanting to spout a plethora of "I told you so's", but somehow managed to block him out. Difficult as that was to do, it was not nearly as ambitious as tempering his will to flee. Perhaps he had misheard Yuma, or perhaps there was more to the story. It was worth taking the time to discover. "Do they come here?"

Yuma looked at him quizzically. Jeremiah knew then that he hadn't done an adequate job of hiding his concern. If his friend had picked up on that much, he might have deduced that the man who stood before him was not wanted by just one white man, but all the nation.

Jeremiah exhaled a sigh of relief after Yuma shook his head and confirmed, "A Fort called Gibson. A day's ride."

Still, the situation was not ideal. However, knowing that the Americans did not come to the village settled Jeremiah's stomach enough for another bite of chili.

Aponi and Salali took the bowls of their father, uncle, and brother and carried them away. Jeremiah watched; he could not help himself. Once Aponi vanished in the dark, Jeremiah did not need to turn to his right to know that the disapproving eyes he felt burning into him were from Yuma, but he also felt the heat of another pair on his left. He glanced to the owner and was not surprised to find Mukul's condemnation.

If there ain't no changin' yer mind about Aponi, then he'll need to be dealt with.

Jeremiah stared back at Aponi's betrothed, and with The Soldier's help, he began to parlay some ideas of how to remove his soul, or spirit as it were, from the earth.

"Raul."

Jeremiah's preparation had been interrupted. He turned to Yuma. "Say what?"

"Did you forget? You asked the name of the man who taught Spanish to me. Raul."

Jeremiah was no fool. He knew precisely what Yuma just did. He had attempted the same rouse of distraction.

We need to be more careful when we're thinking, advised The Soldier. *This one's perceptive.*

You're right. Bes' come out only when needed.

When ya need me ta kill Mukul for you, I'll be ready.

CHAPTER X

Betsy Stebbins had cleverly deceived Jeremiah into thinking that the knife he had stabbed into her back had killer her. But when JoJo fell at her side a moment later and released the sickle from his grip, Betsy rose off the floor with the sickle poised high above her head. Ready to bring the blade down into Jeremiah head with the exploding power of cannon fire, Jeremiah heard the first cry for him to "Wake!" He turned, thinking the voice had come from somewhere inside the dark house. When he realized he was alone with Betsy, Jeremiah dismissed the warning he thought he come from The Soldier.

Betsy screeched like a banshee as she brought the sharp tip down towards his skull.

"Wake!" Jeremiah heard repeated before being ripped out of the Stebbins' house, as well as his dream. However, his terror did not end as he focused on a faceless silhouette that pinned him to his bed. It was dark, but Jeremiah was certain it was not The Soldier but Calvin. The tracker had found him.

Drenched in his sweat, he struggled inside his blanket that kept him netted as he whipped wildly to get free.

"Find your peace, brother."

Jeremiah knew that voice, it was not Calvin's. As the nightmare faded, reality filled its place. Jeremiah gasped long deep breaths in an effort to calm.

Yuma released his hold. "The first in many, many nights, but your dreams still trouble you."

A spring breeze entered the hut and cooled his clammy body. From previous experiences, Jeremiah knew there was no going back to sleep now, as did Yuma.

"Come. We'll fish."

Yuma exited the hut to wait outside. Sometime, within the year and a half of friendship, each man had become familiar with the other's habits. That was why Yuma exited the hut without uttering another word and waited outside, knowing that his friend required a moment to recover from the horror of his dream. Jeremiah reached into the woven basket beside his bed to find the comfort he desired. Though it was too dark to see, he knew of its location and pushed the lid aside. The fabric of his old clothes was much more abrasive compared to the soft leather he had grown accustomed to. Jeremiah did not know what power the material had over him that helped to relax his mind and body.

To look at the tattered and blood-stained wool in the light would be horrifying, but in the dark, they gave comfort. Perhaps the clothing reminded him that his old life was gone. Over time, Jeremiah had learned to despise that life.

No other area in the village's vicinity reminded Jeremiah more of his favorite parts of home. Tall trees created barrier walls along the snaking river that could pass for his favorite watering hole. The rolling plains beyond the tree line resembled the grain fields he farmed, and the stillness of the air mimicked the lazy days of his upbringing. These reminders could be the blame for his homesickness, but because of a single incident, this spot on the river was Jeremiah's most cherished place. This was where Mukul had died.

While in the company of others, Jeremiah used discretion when he smirked at the boulder that still had a blood-stain on its peak. Devising a plan to dispose of his competition had not occurred overnight as he initially expected. Months passed, and still no scheme had been realized. He bid his time in hopes that a plan would present itself that did not prove too convoluted. Killing Mukul would not have been as simple as luring him to a secluded location, and then stabbing him. Even if Jeremiah had been successful with such a simple plan, nobody in the tribe ever disappeared without a trace. The

Cherokee were keen trackers and would find his remains eventually--more likely sooner rather than later. Jeremiah had also considered planting a venomous creature, such as a scorpion or brown recluse spider, in his beddings but thought the idea terrible before he had it fully formed. Poison would have worked too slowly, and Mukul would not have died instantaneously. Honovi surely would have had enough time to call the snake spirit. The solution Jeremiah had ultimately chosen was a hunting accident, but even that idea had flaws. If successful at shooting an arrow or spearing Mukul through his heart, Jeremiah knew the reputation he had built, with the help of The Soldier, as a skilled hunter would be destroyed. He had long speculated that his hunting skills were the one reason Matolu had allowed him to stay so long. What Jeremiah hoped for was another cougar; only, he wouldn't be so quick to stop the attack next time.

Then, one day, his prayers had been answered. While the men bathed in the river, Mukul decided to scale the side of a rock wall. Nobody knew why, but as Jeremiah watched him, he assumed it was to pick the first flower of spring. It grew off a bush mounted on the tip of the wall's ledge twenty feet high. He further estimated that the flower had been meant for his bride-to-be since it also happened to be Mukul and Aponi's wedding day. However, before he could reach the bloom, he slipped. The root he struck that grew out of the wall twisted his body into a diving position, and he cracked his head open on a massive river rock. Jeremiah and The Soldier were not the only two who witnessed the young man's fall to his death, but they were the only two who knew the plot to see Mukul murdered. Thankfully, the Indian's timely accident made their strategy unnecessary. Ever since, when Jeremiah bathed or fished in the chilled river, he felt exceptionally warm. He needed only to be careful when someone watched him. If anybody were ever to be suspicious, the relationship he and Aponi had been allowed to kindle would be snuffed, and all his hard work these last eighteen months would have been for naught.

They had been the longest months he ever experienced, even more so than when a marching soldier. Although Aponi and Mukul did not marry, she had treated her mourning period as such. Jeremiah learned that it was her people's tradition for bereaving wives to keep unkempt and ragged for an undisclosed amount of time. This custom included no bathing to discourage men from wanting her. However, even soiled and foul smelling, Jeremiah would not be deterred. Finally, after one long year had passed, her friends and sister had concluded she mourned long enough. They bathed her and combed her hair, making her presentable for another man. Even by the end of that year, Jeremiah still had not yet convinced Matolu that he would make a worthy son-in-law. The chief employed too many advisors who whispered damaging words against him; Kilwannee especially. Conditions between Yuma and his brother had not mended either. In fact, their animosity towards each other only seemed to worsen as Yuma dedicated more time to his new brother. Jeremiah looked upon Yuma in the same light. He made a fine replacement for the friend he lost to a grenade in a war-battled field.

Then, just weeks ago, Aponi had been given permission to sit near him. The change of heart seemingly came out of nowhere. The Soldier had tried to warn Jeremiah of the tribe's hidden agenda, but since he did not know what that scheme entailed, Jeremiah chose to ignore him. He had settled on the conclusion that Yuma had whispered into his father's ear. Sometimes, his friend acted as though he would do anything for him; they had grown that close which, at times, was too close for Jeremiah's comfort. On these occasions, their bond was tested.

"Stop standin' so close. Yer scarin' 'em away," ordered Jeremiah.

Yuma always hung close. Even if he still was under orders to keep an eye on him, Jeremiah suspected it might also be a culture flaw to invade one's space. Whichever the reason, catching fish with Yuma was damn near impossible. The Indian kept his method of fishing by hand while Jeremiah insisted on using a pole. Each time Yuma struck the water like a viper, the splash would frighten all lurking fish.

"That is always your excuse for bad fishing,"

teased Yuma.

"I like my white traditions. Ya ain't never gonna talk me inta givin' up this pole."

Jeremiah followed Yuma's darted glance to the whereabouts of the sun that had risen only moments ago, but yet, could not be seen behind of a row of trees.

"Perhaps the fish are sleeping late today."

With no further consideration, Yuma exited the water to rest on the riverbank. Jeremiah sensed some distress. It was unlike Yuma to be defeated so easily, which promptly lead Jeremiah to consider that his friend had other reasons for suggesting their early morning outing. However, it was not until Yuma started making small talk that he knew for certain. "Tornado weather's returned."

Jeremiah gazed up at the violet sky. There wasn't a cloud in sight. Also, the cool night air still lingered, but a large twister did come close to their village a year ago last Spring, and that tornado had been prophesized as well. "Did the spirits tell you that?"

"They do not need to. It can be felt in the air."

As Yuma continued to examine the tempered sky, Jeremiah sensed he was about to learn the truth behind their excursion.

"You did not wake me with your loud dreams. I was already awake. I am to ask you to travel with Matolu to Fort Gibson this trip."

Though the war between the Cherokee and the Osage had been long over, there remained a lingering conflict, which did not make Jeremiah's hiding any easier. Their tension ignited, and to reconcile their differences more efficiently, the tribes now meet with Colonel Phillips monthly instead of bi-annually. Before each excursion, Jeremiah would be begged to accompany the chief. His presence was meant to demonstrate the support of another white man while continuing to reject the white man's civilization; although, Jeremiah had not been "white" for some time. Having had more exposure to the sun in the last two years than in his previous nineteen, Jeremiah's skin had turned the same shade as his tribe. Then, to add insult, he had allowed his hair to grow out. Though not the same length as Yuma's, or any other male injun's, it was at a length frowned upon by any American male. He doubted the Colonel would even recognize him as a white man.

Before he had the chance to decline, yet again, Yuma predicted, "I already know your answer."

Jeremiah pulled his lure out of the water and threw it to another section of the river, acting as though this conversation ever occurred.

"You cannot hide forever, brother. It is your Soldier Spirit that keeps you in darkness. He is what keeps you from my sister."

You think there's truth in that, boy? The Soldier challenged.

Jeremiah flinched. Though not gone--never gone--The Soldier had become scarce since Mukul's accident. He hadn't been needed nearly as much, so whenever he decided to shout orders inside his head or contest Jeremiah's position, it took him by surprise.

It looks pretty clear from here what they want from us.

It was a condition. To go to the fort with them was to prove his loyalty to the entire tribe, thus giving him permission to be with Aponi. That was why she had been allowed to primp her looks and associate with him. Matolu was fishing too; baiting Jeremiah by using his deepest desire as a lure.

He's a devious one that chief.

As usual, The Soldier appeared to be correct. He had tried to warn him before, but Jeremiah didn't want to listen. He would have rather believed that obtaining Aponi's love was a possibility.

The pit of his stomach swelled. He felt nauseous. If he did not agree to the chief's request, Matolu would not accept their union, but Jeremiah could never agree to his ultimatum.

No matter which choice you make, Aponi ain't never gonna be yours.

Jeremiah could feel a fury building at the deception, but before The Soldier claimed control and would force him to do something he would never approve, Jeremiah changed the subject in a panic.

"Well, that's my problem, ain't it? But what's yers? Why ain't you married yet?"

Yuma hesitated before answering, "I am not ready to leave my tribe." And that was all, but Jeremiah believed not all was said. He glared at his friend, waiting. Yuma finally added, "The women from other clans do not interest me."

Initially, Jeremiah did not understand why, but once realization struck he realized how naïve he had been.

"It's a white woman yer hankerin' fer, ain't it? It's why ya like goin' over to that fort. Hopin' maybe ya sees one of 'em there."

But Yuma did not confirm. Instead, he guided the topic back to its original purpose, "The Osage know when we will move. That is why many of us will go, including Aponi."

The fish weren't taking the bait, and neither was Jeremiah. He pulled in his line and sat next to his friend. "I see whacher all are doin'.

"Even though I do not like him, bring the Soldier Spirit, if you are afraid."

"I ain't afraid of nuttin'!" Jeremiah deflected.

An awkward silence fell between them, which only grew more unsettling when Yuma placed a hand on Jeremiah's knee to confirm, "You can never be with her until you go."

His friend was getting too close and touching again, making Jeremiah uncomfortable. Instinctually, he wanted to bolt and get more than an arm's length away, but with the declination to go to Fort Gibson, Jeremiah figured he already stood on unstable ground. He did not want to upset any member of the tribe further by insulting their habitual behavior, especially Yuma. Thankfully, Jeremiah did not have to endure the connection long before rustling and women's voices came from the meadow at their backs.

Yuma sprung to his feet first. He peered nervously at a dozen of their elderly tribeswomen emerging from the five-foot tall grass blades. Smiling as they passed, the women continued to the water while carrying a large pot of the red soap-like ointment Jeremiah had become accustomed to. He recalled using the liniment of puccoon, wild angelica, and buffalos' oil for the first time. Prior to settling amongst the redskins, if anyone had told him savages were cleaner than the white man, he would have shot them dead for being an ungodly liar, but truth be told, he had never lived so cleanly.

While the unreserved women stripped for their baths, Jeremiah's eyes caressed their skin.

"Come," he heard Yuma demand, but Jeremiah could not tear his gaze away. Suddenly, he felt his arm being tugged. Though he did not resist Yuma's physical force, Jeremiah refused to give the women their privacy until the stalks from the meadow covered their intimates.

The silence between the two men continued more than half the distance back to their settlement. If Jeremiah were to assume why Yuma had kept hushed, he would have assumed that his friend's disappointment concentrated heavily on his decision not to go to Fort Gibson, but Jeremiah made no such assumption while he could not stop thinking about the bathing women. Though the women were older, their age did not soften his erection. It had been too long since he had last been with a woman. The first thought that entered his mind was little Penny, but he shook her image out. He couldn't include the girl anyway as he never entered her. Before then, he had lived an abstinent life as a soldier. He had not had a proper lay since before the war when he and Martin traveled to Kansas City and paid two dollars for a night for some red-headed whore. She, too, had been of a riper age, which must have explained his tolerance for older women, though preferring them younger.

Jeremiah continued tailing Yuma when it suddenly--and pleasantly--dawned on him that he had to go back.

"My pole!" He exclaimed about the fishing rod. "I'll catch up." And before Yuma could utter a word of protest or accompaniment, Jeremiah rushed back.

He hustled to make it to the river in half the time but halted just inside the brush. He pulled the grass blades back and watched the women bathe while they gossiped and chattered. Their breasts were exposed just below the nipple in the shallow water. He reached into his breechcloth and pulled out his pecker. The first climax came after a few short strokes, but the second and third gave him time to enjoy the extraordinary sight.

◆ ◆ ◆

Images of the women would not leave his mind. Though they were not what he wanted most, they were enticing. What he physically desired had left. His time in the bushes took longer than planned, and during his prolonged absence, Matolu, Yuma, Kilwannee, and Aponi left for Fort Gibson with a small entourage of warriors. Guilt and shame consumed him for missing his chance to see Aponi off and to wish her safe travels. He had been too busy masturbating to her elders.

Jeremiah fed Martin a prickly pear. Although he ate the cactus leaf slowly, it was his favorite of all the greens. When Martin first came to him last summer, Jeremiah was ready to kill him and offer him to the women as the meat for another chili, but as the iguana's tongue flicked at him, he could not help but admire the spirit within. The large green lizard had come right up to him, as though daring Jeremiah to kill him. The habitually timid beast had acted strong and confident, qualities he did not customarily admire, but it seemed rather inhumane to cause harm to such a strange animal. As of that day, Jeremiah gave a corner space of his hut to Martin, the iguana, entrapping him behind a wall of stones as his new home. Jeremiah was just about to take his pet outside for fresh air when a crescendo of confusion suddenly stirred within the village, building into an uproar.

He had expected an attack for some time. The Osage were bound to take advantage of their weakened village when its leaders and best warriors were traveling. Yuma mentioned it had been a topic of discussion between himself, Matolu, Honovi, and

Kilwannee on several occasions, and during each of those conversations, the chief had stubbornly stood firm in his belief that attacks would not occur while their enemies best warriors were also at the peace discussions.

What a fool.

Jeremiah concurred. He nabbed his knife and spear before leaping outside. Ready to join the fight, he raced across the deserted settlement but slowed upon seeing the tribe: women, old men, children, and papooses, flocked to the village's nearest entry point. He relaxed. There was no reason for alarm, but still, something had stirred the hornet's nest.

He pushed closer to see what stood at the center of everybody's attention. Honovi and Salali were aiding an unfamiliar elder Indian towards the dormant fire pit. By crevassed wrinkles that cracked his face like the dry desert floor and the frailness of his brittle stamina, the elder looked to be no less than a hundred years old.

The crowd separated for an unobstructed path. Honovi and Salali attempted to steer the senior native to the nearest log, but he refused to sit until he reached the log used by Matolu and his family. Though the Indian sat wearily on the perch, he sat kingly.

The Cherokee continued to gawk in awe at the stranger though the ancient Indian did not return their curiosity. His eyes fixated on one man and one man only: Jeremiah. It was not uncommon, and nobody, including Jeremiah, had been put off by the incessant glare. He had come to expect it from all outside tribes--being the black sheep of the group--but as the elder continued to make threats with his eyes, uneasiness overcame him.

The Soldier cautioned that this elder might be a diversion tactic by the Osage, but Jeremiah disagreed. He had seen their markings and attire before when crossing paths on a hunt, and this elder did not wear the same.

Instead of gaping at the newcomer, Jeremiah watched his fellow clansmen.

They don't know where he comes from neither. They's just as confounded.

He looked closer and noticed the wonderment articulated in their, otherwise, apathetic expressions. The Cherokee were trying to determine his origin as well.

Salali brushed past Jeremiah with a chunk of bread and a cup filled with water. She handed the offerings to the visitor who removed his eyes from Jeremiah to accept.

Honovi sat next to the elder, then spoke in his native Iroquoian tongue. Jeremiah did not understand what Honovi had asked, and neither did the old-timer, but it became apparent that he had requested the man's name when Honovi placed his open palm against his bare chest and announced, "Honovi."

The elder mimicked the gesture and spoke, "Atraco," before he lifted his thin and trembling arm to point at Jeremiah, repeating the word

"Hobomock."

The tribe turned to Jeremiah. They gazed at him curiously, though not a single Cherokee could decipher the translation any better than Jeremiah. However, if they were able to pick up Atraco's malevolent demeanor and expression of contempt as well as he could, they too would understand his word to be some variation of evil.

The ancient Indian knew something; there was no mistaking that assumption, but not knowing what he knew or how he knew it unnerved Jeremiah and The Soldier.

Slowly, he backed away then ducked inside his hut, grateful to be greeted by Martin's blank stare. He needed to be alone to decide what to do next about the old man.

To hide while within the confines of the village had been impossible. Even after barricading himself inside the walls of his dwelling, Jeremiah still could hear Atraco shout the accusation, "Hobomock," over and over; the thought of listening to what could have been hours of incessant repetition set him on edge. He endured the torture for as long as could before managing to sneak away to the one place where he might find peace. But Jeremiah found no harmony at the river while The Soldier's loud lecture disrupted the tranquility of chirping birds and running water.

I warned ya not to let yer guard down. Now they've sent some injun ta come find us.

Him?! He's too old ta be a hunter.

Dunderhead! He knows who you are and what ya done. He singled you out.

There was no mistaking that bit of truth. Whatever allegation the old-timer strained to convey, he had been determined to make the Cherokee understand that Jeremiah was not who he pretended to be.

The water nearly lost all its glisten, and a bitter darkness crept over Jeremiah, which was not a result of the setting sun. Despite his uneasiness about the old man, he could not shake the despair of losing Aponi as well.

I s'pose I shoulda gone to the fort. I look like one of them now, wouldn't you say? Maybe nobody woulda recognized me. Then I woulda been able to keep her, and I woulda been gone when that old crow arrived. Maybe it's not too late, and I should ride out now.

Yer so fucking ignorant. How do you survive when I ain't aroun'? If they really was the ones who sent Atraco, then they're lookin' under every rock for ya. And if they didn't, you'd still need to introduce yerself to Colonel Phillips when you reach his fort.

I might not be a wanted man no more.

Jeremiah did not need to explain that rationale to The Solider. Both recalled the summer before last when Matolu came back from Gibson and reported that the American Civil War had ended, as well as President Lincoln's life, with the Union government prevailing. It occurred to Jeremiah then that with the Confederacy out of commission, there would be no army to desire his capture. Albeit, there was that other matter about the seven dead Stebbinses, but Jeremiah did not see how Calvin could consider that case relevant. He had been a soldier, not the law, and it hadn't been the tracker's family whom he killed. There was good reason to assume that Calvin just might have decided to give up his pursuit. It would explain why there had been no word or sight of him in all this time. Considering the idea a moment longer, Jeremiah supposed there was a good chance that he could be hiding from nobody.

The Soldier disagreed. *Murder was your crime above all others. The law's just biding its time, waitin' fer you to slip up and show your ignorant face.*

Jeremiah released all hope he had been clutching onto in a single long exhale. There was no arguing with The Soldier. Returning to his own people would be impossible, and the only way to be with his beloved was if Matolu's spirit soared with his ancestors. But after laying eyes on Atraco and witnessing a native who had lived beyond a century, there was a possibility that the chief could live just as long, if not longer. Jeremiah was not willing to wait indefinitely.

The assassination of Matolu would be different; far more complex than the plan he had imagined for Mukul, but Jeremiah was not deterred. Though the chief was considered native royalty, he still was nothing more than just a man.

Lost in his thoughts, Jeremiah continued to gaze beyond the water. The shiny specks of the sun's reflection fizzled in the river one by one. All kept calm and serene. Be it poetic nature or coincidence, Jeremiah thought it fitting that his desire for Matolu's death was at the same location where Mukul had died. Incidentally, this also happened to be the spot where the clan held services for their deceased.

As it dawned on him how bloody these waters were, splashing woke Jeremiah out of his trance. The dainty playfulness was close, but not within his line of sight. Hearing it again, he stood and peered over the brush of the bend to find Salali bathing alone, thigh deep in the water and showing off all her forbidden parts. He questioned whether he saw right at first. For any woman to bathe unescorted was anomaly, but then again, her usual partner did currently travel to the peace talks. Jeremiah listened for other voices or movement, just in case, but there was neither.

Maybe she come to be alone with me.

That ain't Aponi, reminded The Soldier.

As Jeremiah turned to leave, he stopped abruptly. His erection crushing into his breechcloth was an uncomfortable pain. More than he could bear, he freed his penis and allowed it room to breathe, but Jeremiah could not bring himself to let go. He only stroked twice before he had to stop; still too sensitive from the abuse he had put it through earlier. He needed something softer and gentler and wetter to release his buildup. Jeremiah turned back to Salali. He watched her caress her flesh then wring out her long hair.

You ain't never gonna have Aponi.

The chief had made sure of that when he had Yuma present his ultimatum. Just as Jeremiah had done for his tender erection, Matolu had done for him: they were both free now.

Matolu didn't say nuttin' 'bout Salali.

"A hundred months have passed, Lorena, since last I held that hand in mine, and felt the pulse beat fast, Lorena, though mine beat faster far than thine."

Salali was startled by the serenade. She dropped beneath the waterline and covered her body before she spotted Jeremiah's head floating towards her from around the bend, like a predator's fin.

"A hundred months, 'twas flowery May, when up the hilly slope we climbed, to watch the dying of the day, and hear the distant church bells chime."

Jeremiah paused his approach at the end of the verse. He stopped close enough to touch her, if he were inclined to reach his arm out but not yet. Though her expression was firm, Jeremiah had learned that to discover their emotions was to look into their eyes. Salali was alarmed.

"I reckon it's silly of me ta be singin' to you 'bout church bells, ain't it? Probably ain't never heard one." When Salali gave no response or indication, he changed his tune, "You hear'd that song a'for?"

Salali shook her head and released some of her

tension. She smiled weakly. Jeremiah enjoyed her naïvety to his seduction. He desired her all the more for it.

"We used ta sang it in the war," he chuckled. "Ain't sho' why. It only made the homesickness even more wretchin'. But it's a pretty song when sung well."

She shrugged.

"It ain't as pretty as you though." Her wan smile vanished. "I'm sorry. I didn't mean ta interrupt yer bathin'. I didn't folla ya here. Honest. I was over there, doin' some thinkin', mindin' my business when I heard ya. Ya didn't see me over thar?"

She shook her head.

Jeremiah studied their surroundings to reconfirm that they were still alone. "Why ain't the other women with ya?"

"They washed this morning."

But Jeremiah knew the true reason when he caught Salali glance towards her private area.

"Oh, I see. Ya comes to wash away yer monthly bleeds. Well, I apologize ag'in." Tired of being stagnant, he stepped forward. It came as no surprise when Salali recounted. He realized the error of his forwardness when he hadn't first clarified, "I ain't gonna hurt you. I jus' was hopin' for a favor, was all. Maybe you'd let me touch you so's I could see what yer sister feels like? If you look alike, you'll feel alike, right?"

Jeremiah reached again; Penelope jerked away again.

No. Not Penelope. Salali, he rectified.

Why his touch had repulsed them both was unclear... and hurtful.

Jeremiah's rage came without a warning. Salali was not prepared for his swift hand grabbing the back of her neck and pulling her close, but he had been just as unprepared for her screams and fighting back.

"I jus' wanna see," Jeremiah continued to explain while he muffled her with his other hand. He pressed his body against hers. She felt better than he had imagined: warm in the chilled water and supple, despite the rough goose bumps imposing her silky skin. He was confident that Aponi would feel just as pleasing.

Jeremiah's physical bliss came to an end when an unbearable agony burned his hand. Salali's teeth had sunk into the very same space of skin, between his thumb and forefinger that Penelope once bit through.

The shock of pain was overwhelming. Why he did not learn his lesson about covering a girl's mouth with his bare hand, he didn't know.

Jeremiah hauled back his fist and struck Salali square in the face then grabbed the back of her hair and dragged her out of the water. He would knock the fight out of her, and once he did, she would be as transportable as a child's doll.

He laid Salali on the shore then climbed on top. Her dazed look went through him. She teetered near the edge of consciousness until he entered her. Immediately, Salali awoke with a cry like being gutted alive.

Jeremiah covered her mouth with his good hand--his lesson still not learned--then hammered his pelvis against her. His thrusts were quick and short, and each lunge felt like his idea of heaven.

Salali refused to stop squirming, which Jeremiah did not mind as it heightened his pleasure. He bent over her, and then lovingly pressed his cheek against hers while he continued pounding again and again until a warm euphoric sensation engorged his midriff and fired ecstasy throughout his body. The mounting pressure took control of every part of him; his feet, his eyes, his mind, and his hands that pressed down harder on Salali's head.

Jeremiah's body had gone rigid for a flashing moment before he erupted into a series of powerful trembles, wailing and groaning as he climaxed. Then the high was over. Everything inside him: muscles, bones, blood... felt as though they had been sucked out of him.

He dropped the full weight of his body on Salali, but then jolted back up in shock. Sometime; somehow during their relations, her spirit had left her body, only to return after the blunt force of his falling weight discharged a mouthful of blood and phlegm into his hand.

She gagged on the spew that continued to shoot out of her nose and mouth as Jeremiah climbed off. Rolling onto her side, she inhaled mountainous breaths that filled her lungs with as much air as they would hold.

Jeremiah gawked at the convulsing girl, but his concern was for another matter. "You ain't gonna mention this, right?"

Though Salali's mouth opened, it was only to gasp for air. Jeremiah needed that answer. "Tell me ya ain't gonna say nuttin. I need ya ta swear it!" But her obstinacy continued.

He then considered explaining about what he saw--the images of Penelope that had flashed into his head. They had confused him. Along with his desperate desire for Aponi, she would be able to understand, maybe even sympathize with his behavior if she knew the whole truth.

"Salali," he called.

The Indian girl continued to quiver and wheeze. Overdramatic, she wailed and held onto her crotch, as though she forbade him to reenter her.

His anger rebounded. "Salali!"

Jeremiah grabbed her arms and pinned them next to her head. Once she realized he had no intention of forcing himself inside her again, she would listen. However, that chance never came as he gawked at her blood-covered hands.

There had been nothing theatrical about her agonizing performance. Her privates were wet with red, and his pecker looked to have been dipped the same fluid. But more horrifying than both was his breechcloth soaked with the blood.

"Oh Lord! Oh shit!" He panicked and yanked Salali off the ground. She continued to cough and writhe as he dragged her into the water. Jeremiah washed his penis then began to scrub the loincloth when he noticed Salali making no effort to wipe away the evidence.

"Rinse yerself! Do it real good!" But Salali could not, her body had shut down. She stood like a statue as the river streamed around her. "Go on! I ain't gonna do it fer ya!"

Still nothing. Jeremiah splashed water on her face but to no avail. He had no other choice and reached out to do it himself when his touch jolted her out of inertia. She cried out as though about to be raped again. In her desperate attempt to escape, she bit down on his injured hand.

Jeremiah screamed as her teeth sank to the bone. He punched her in the face with his free hand. Salali released her bite then scrambled out of the river.

He tackled her in the shallow water, but her cries continued to escape. He took no comfort in knowing that her voice could not travel the quarter mile to their settlement. Jeremiah rested on the idea that the others might be looking for Salali by now. Sometime, during the last five minutes, the plains had gone dark, and she had yet to return to the village.

Jeremiah covered her mouth with his good hand before remembering her teeth, and then moved his grasp to the back of her head. He dunked her underwater and muffled her screams to listen in silence for approaching voices or footsteps, but the resonances of the running river, as well as the splashing from Salali's flailing arms, made it impossible to hear what lay beyond.

He jerked his attention towards the tree line though knowing there was no point in looking. If they did not want to be seen, they wouldn't be.

Suddenly, he felt like the antelope of his first hunt; weaponless and vulnerable. But if any of his paranoia were true then they would be attacking to rescue their little squirrel. Instead, all was serene and calm... much too calm.

Panicked, he pulled Salali's limp head up from the water and then laid her motionless body on the shore. Jeremiah shook her and slapped her face, but his attempts to save her only grew more violent when she refused to awaken. She was gone.

Jeremiah fell beside her corpse and roared a cry of anguish that echoed throughout the passage.

You killed her. The Soldier confirmed the moment he returned.

"Where were ya?! Why didn't ya stop me?" Jeremiah hollered, which echoed down the river's corridor just as loudly.

Quiet! Talk ta me in here.

You coulda done summin'. Waked me up.

Ain't nuttin' but death could stop a bee from gettin' his nectar.

"I didn't mean to," whispered Jeremiah before his anguish had him in tears, sniffling like a five-year-old boy punished for sipping on his pa's moonshine.

Enraged by his adolescent behavior, The Soldier shouted the orders for him to... *Get up right now, boy!*

Ain't no time for wallowin'. We got work ta do.

Jeremiah looked to the twilight sky above, as though searching for some other world he could exist in other than this one.

Anyone coulda come upon her bathin' and had his way with her. We'll jus' send her floatin' down the river. No one would know otherwise.

Jeremiah cocked his head back towards the tree line.

There ain't nobody there, but a coward's paranoia. However, there was also the matter of the loincloth. Jeremiah gazed down at the stains that were beyond disguise.

Yer goddamn lucky it's dark. Jus' sneak back inta camp an' burn the evidence. No one ain't never gonna know no different.

What if someone noticed that me and Salali was gone at the same time?

Yer chances of that not happenin' are better with a lot of 'em gone to that meetin'.

The Soldier brought up a valid point. He always did.

Jeremiah gave into the plan. He dragged Salali back to the water by her feet. Ever so slowly, the river's current carried away the evidence. He watched and hoped, with any luck, that her course would continue to a place where her remains would never be discovered.

But what about Atraco?

CHAPTER XI

Jeremiah hurtled through the meadow though his panic was faster than his sprint. He had no assurance that there would not be a trap waiting for him once he reached the village. The Cherokee were very clever. The few times Jeremiah had witnessed the tribe bemused, Honovi used fire and magic to discover the answers they sought. However, to Jeremiah's advantage, the Cherokee did know not to disturb the spirit's respite until their situation was dire. Only once they reached wit's end did they solicit guidance. At least, that's how he had understood it after Yuma explained their tradition.

Jeremiah arrived then circled the perimeter of the settlement. He stopped a hundred feet behind his hut and analyzed his fellow clansmen from the darkened outskirts. Despite the fact that the leaders were meeting with the territory's presiding authority, their absence did not thin the tribe's numbers as much as Jeremiah would have liked. Deceiving them would not be simple. The day Jeremiah had been invited to stay, the accommodations Matolu assigned were to keep him close with the intention to always have the white man in plain sight. Jeremiah eyed his hut east of the crowded bonfire. If he could just slip inside unnoticed, nobody would be able to dispute his whereabouts if questioned. But if discovered outside, the ruse he would attempt to fabricate might not be believed.

All clear. Move now! Jeremiah did as ordered and bolted at a rabbit's pace until The Soldier ordered, *More natural, Dunderhead! You wanna call attention to yerself?* Jeremiah slowed. *Weave between the huts. An' fer fuck's sake, cover yer Johnson, will ya? Ya look like ya got yer goddamn monthly bleeds.*

Though it had been a struggle to saunter when all he wanted to do was run, Jeremiah reached the perimeter of the village unobserved. For the moment, he was safe, but only until any one of the many heads turned his way.

Thinking he might have a better chance of keeping his position unknown, Jeremiah took a chance and veered off course. He circled right, rather than left, around the nearest hut, and before The Soldier could call him a dunderhead for altering his plan, Jeremiah collided into Utina.

As luck would have it, she was alone; perhaps heading for the bushes. Jeremiah always liked Utina. She was one of the first women of the tribe to show him kindness, which explained why she smiled as she greeted him. However, her joyful expression faded in the next second when she noticed his blood-covered hands, as well as the stains on his loincloth he attempted to conceal. Her shocked eyes met his.

Snap her neck.

No!

Then I'll do it.

But before The Soldier could take over and reach for her neck, Utina took his injured hand into hers, and then examined the wound where Salali had bit him... twice. Blood that looked as black as oil in the night still dribbled from behind the dangling strip of flesh. It had not occurred to Jeremiah that the blood from his leaking wound could double as the reason for his rosy package. The Soldier must have come to a similar realization too because he no longer felt him attempting to take control.

Being an elder, Utina had not been required to learn English. She guided Jeremiah towards the center of the village, towards Honovi, in silence. The medicine man would surely call for the snake spirit, but when Jeremiah noticed who sat beside him, he was not surprised. Atraco glared at him directly, as intense as ever. This time, Jeremiah stared back. The old man knew something, but Jeremiah needed to know what. Despite the distance between them, he focused on Atraco's eyes. They appeared black like the antelope's, and Jeremiah caught a glimpse of evil just below the surface.

He yanked free from Utina's clutch, but the

obstinate old woman refused to let him be and reached to take back his hand. Jeremiah made his refusal clear by pushing the woman away and then ducked into his hut.

The old bastard knows. He's ruinin' everythin'! Jeremiah screamed in a tantrum. *It's over. We gotta go.*

The Soldier agreed with Jeremiah this time. Atraco would be attempting to communicate his knowledge to Honovi now. The language barrier would give Jeremiah only a minute to collect his things, but just the items he needed to survive when traveling to... he did not know, but that decision would need to wait; fleeing without attracting attention demanded all of his concentration. Hiding would be a dilemma for later, once he put some distance between himself and Atraco, Honovi, and any other tribesman who would soon learn what happened to Salali and call for his blood.

He gathered his spear, knife, bow, and quiver, but then after having an epiphany, dropped all but the knife. They were too big, and anyone who watched him leave with an arsenal would suspect something was wrong. Atraco's translation would no longer be necessary. Jeremiah needed to keep his baggage minimal.

He lifted the lid off the basket at his bedside and grabbed his old clothes. Removing his garments unveiled his Smith and Wesson Number Two Revolver at the bottom. Jeremiah buried his old boots, knife, and pistol inside the tattered material then tied it off with twine. Unfortunately, the gun would not be much use without bullets, which he had used the last of on a buffalo hunt a good year back, but he was not about to leave his piece behind. With nowhere on his exposed body to hide his rolled belongings, he tucked the bundle under his armpit, but then hindered his escape a moment longer to glance down at Martin. The lizard stared back, flicking his tongue as though waving goodbye.

"I don't wanna leave you neither, buddy, but it's time I gotta go."

What courage remained was crushed by Jeremiah's rising nervousness, and though he would have hesitated to step outside, The Soldier forced his legs to walk through the doorway.

Atraco had not uttered a single word. Jeremiah wanted to believe that perhaps his impression of the elder had been only his alarmed imagination, but as he paused outside beyond his door and met the old man's eyes again, he knew he had not been mistaken. Atraco had made the decision to keep silent. By drawing in the dirt with a stick, he had proven that he was capable of communicating with the others. He had chosen not to raise the alarm for a particular reason, which remained a mystery. That frightened Jeremiah all the more.

He surprised even himself by how calmly he strolled to the steeds. Because of Yuma's insatiable belief that horses still did not take too kindly to him, Jeremiah had never been given a mount. But that would not be a problem. After tonight's tragedy, he knew of one mare that that was now riderless.

Few noticed Jeremiah climb into Wahya's saddle, but for those who did, they did not try to stop him and question his actions. They were indifferent to his suspicious behavior, which devastated Jeremiah. Their lack of inquisitiveness was a sign that they had come to accept him as one of their own, now that he had no choice but to abandon them.

Jeremiah rode off, but before doing so, he glanced at Atraco one last time, although it was Honovi's confused gaze that captured his attention. The medicine man still did not know what Atraco knew, and it continued to trouble Jeremiah why the old timer wasn't shouting warnings as he had done earlier. Moreover, if Jeremiah did not know better, he would have sworn that the old man smiled as he galloped into the night.

The Spring night air was warm though Jeremiah shivered as a perpetual wind blew across his near-naked body. Splash back from hours of riding along the river's sandy shoreline was keeping him wet, but he had no other choice of route. The rushing water would erase the tracks Wahya left as they fled for the Missouri state line.

Dunderhead!

Jeremiah ignored The Soldier. His mind had been made up, convinced that life with the Indians had improved his character. Not only could he hunt and trap better than before, but he had also saved a man's life. Kilwannee may have been injun, but Jeremiah would retell his account of the day he killed a cougar to save a fellow hunter. The tale would not impress his father, but his mother, the more Christian of the two, would interpret Jeremiah's good deed from passages of the Bible. The scripture of Matthew 6:14 alone would be enough to absolve him of her penitence: *For if you forgive men when they sin against you, your heavenly Father will also forgive you. But if you do not forgive men their sins, your Father will not forgive your sins.* Jeremiah figured that with his ma's help, Nathaniel might come to accept that his son had been reborn, but neither needed to be made aware of Salali's tragic accident at the river, which was precisely that... an accident.

"Perhaps if I married and had children," considered Jeremiah, "would jar pa's approval posthaste?"

Having a child killer for a father... those lucky li'l darlin's.

When The Soldier demonstrated his rare sense of humor, it was often cruel, but straightforward. No woman would have anything to do with him. His name may return to good standing, but only in the eyes of his kin.

Now yer startin' ta think like a survivor.

"Maybe. But home is where we're still headed."

Then you best not delay changin' back into a white man 'cuz we've already crossed over.

Jeremiah hadn't noticed, but at some point during his respite, the river did narrow. The conversion to a rivulet commonly was recognized as the state line marker. He had reentered Missouri-- a land where natives were not welcome. He felt safe from his former tribesmen, but a new and hazardous risk would arise come dawn. Being seen by his fellow kind wearing nothing but an injun-made loincloth would get him killed quicker than the spark from a lit flint.

Don't take long, warned The Soldier.

A purplish pink hue blanched the night sky by the time Jeremiah tied his stolen mare to a nearby tree. He knelt on the shore then rolled out his apparel to uncover the pair of boots, pistol, and long blade he had tucked into the folds. His injured hand needed a good washing, but as he reached into the water, Jeremiah glimpsed a reflection that he did not recognize. The transition into one of them was truly remarkable, never appreciating the metamorphosis until it was time to change back.

He had dried his hands on the pant legs before he grabbed the knife with his sore hand. Wishing he had been born ambidextrous, Jeremiah bit through the pain of cutting his locks with the only hand that knew how to use. He tossed the plumage into the river and watched the water take away the residue of his brief, happier life. He then proceeded to chop his hair until it was short... as short as it was when he had been a soldier.

"Is that you or me? I can't tell."

Who do you want it to be?

Jeremiah wasn't sure. Seeing himself in such a state was unnerving, but putting a face to The Soldier would be just as unsettling.

I makes you uncomfortable, don't I?

Jeremiah paused first before he answered, "No."

Don't you lie to me, boy. You hear? Don't you ever lie to me 'cuz I'll always know the truth.

Jeremiah twisted his head away. It was difficult to look The Soldier in the eye when trapped in a lie. His sight rested on the pair of old boots. Getting dressed was one tactic to avoid The Soldier's reflection, as well as this conversation. Should The Soldier persist for the truth, Jeremiah would have to give it to him, and he might not like what he heard. That truth being that The Soldier did make him uncomfortable. When they spent those months apart after Mukul's death, when all was peaceful in the village, and Jeremiah had little to fear, he came to realize that much of The Soldier's killing had been unjustified. Maybe that was why The Soldier didn't like him harping on his regrets; he would come to learn that Silas, Alice, Martin... they all had died needlessly. The Soldier could have simply left Martin on the field instead of having him exploded. And in place of decapitation, Silas could have been detained with an injury to his leg while Alice... well, her death happened so fast, Jeremiah could hardly recall the incident. No, it was better to leave things unsaid at the moment, at least until they were in the clear.

Jeremiah readied his trousers, but first, he reached for the ties that upheld his red-stained breechcloth.

The Soldier protested. *You'll be leavin' a trail behind if you take that off an' toss it on the ground.*

He had been so concerned about discarding injun evidence from his body that Jeremiah failed to realize that it still would be evidence once off, unless the cloth was to be used in a different capacity. As such, he required a bandage for his wounded hand to avoid infection.

Jeremiah untied the breechcloth then covered Salali's bite marks with the bloody leather before stepping into his trousers and covering himself. The old wool scratched at his legs as he slid them up to his waist. They were as uncomfortable as hell, but then he remembered they were not his. Betsy had replaced his torn and bloody uniform for another man's threads while he bathed. Werner's? Alexander's? Maybe even Martin's? He never did ask; although, he remembered they had not been so painful to wear at the time. The Stebbinses clothes also brought back the pain of becoming Jeremiah Whiting once again; the other one, the Jeremiah, who knew that he was lost and lonesome, not the one who had lived thankfully as Cherokee.

The return of the old Jeremiah also brought doubt with him, and for the first time since leaving the village, he worried about returning home.

Yuma refused to participate in the staring contest with the Osage warriors while both chiefs attempted to work out their differences with Colonel Phillips as moderator. Validating their alpha egos proved exhausting, as well as distracting from the purpose of their visit.

Nobody wanted to be there; not the cavalry, not the Osage, and not Matolu's people, but all parties continued to glower a warning of retaliation should there be a betrayal of the temporary truce. However, if a battle were to commence, the natives would only be able to fight with passion as their weapon. Neither tribe had been allowed to carry once inside the fort. That rule began in the previous year when a meeting did not go as planned. Tempers rose, and threats were a breath away from war. Now, only Phillips' men were allowed to be armed. Upon entering the fort, every native was relieved of his weapon, which was then locked away in a storage room across the camp. Colonel Phillips would not risk the chance of another upheaval.

Despite the baleful glares that crisscrossed from troop to Indian to Indian to troop, not one could match the look of fury No-Pa-Wa-The Shinkah expressed. Yuma wondered if there was a time when the Osage chief did not appear murderous. It might have been that No-Pa-Wa-The acted differently with his own people, but while standing within the walls of Fort Gibson, the veins that webbed his cropped and roached head wiggled like trapped earthworms when his temper would flare.

No-Pa-Wa-The's warriors also wore similar faces beneath the red paint that amplified their ferocity. Strangely, they appeared more docile than usual this night. Yuma first considered that, they too, had grown tiresome of the continuous effort to be viewed menacing, but once he gazed to where their sights rested, he noticed that it was Aponi's presence that had calmed their hatred. Though she was his sister, Yuma wasn't blind to her possessive attraction. Not only had she mollified most of the men present, but Jeremiah also had been the victim of her lure. Only No-Pa-Wa-The appeared enraged by her appearance. The Osage chief's disapproval needed no explanation. Their culture did not think of women as equals as did the Cherokee. However, nobody, not even Colonel Phillips, blamed Aponi for No-Pa-Wa-The's temper. Even without her presence, the chief would have found something to ignite his rage.

Yuma snapped his attention back to Matolu. His mind had left the quarters for only a moment, but that had been long enough to not hear some of what required translation. Fortunately, it was easy to summarize what he had missed. Yuma blamed the earthworms for his distraction.

"The peace treaty has already been signed. They dishonor the treaty when attacking Cherokee."

Phillips continued to amplify his disinterest in the argument, not with words, but with his lethargic conduct. When they began to gather for negotiations, Yuma recalled the colonel stating that he saw these disputes reaching a settlement quickly, most likely underestimating the stubbornness of each tribe. Yuma was reasonably certain that Colonel Phillips saw one native the same as the next--red was red. However, once the first year passed without a satisfactory resolution, the Colonel had decided to double the number of assemblies each year thereafter, as it became apparent that they were not making progress. Moreover, what little was accomplished became lost or forgotten during their long breaks, as though what they had achieved on their issues had gone stale.

Wha'Kon translated Yuma's words to No-Pa-Wa-The, which then triggered more wiggles and squirms above the chief's brow, followed by shouting Yuma could not understand. He then interpreted his leader's response with equaled anger and passion.

"It is our food! It is our land! We will fight to keep it!"

Yuma relayed the words to Matolu in their own tongue but kept his voice low once Colonel Phillips finally decided to step in and moderate, "Now, the Cherokee can't help when buffalo or antelope or deer from your land decide to traipse on over boundary lines to graze. They become fair game."

Wha'Kon's glare switched from disdain to confusion as he questioned, "Traipse?"

"Walk! It means walk," hollered William Phillips, flustered.

Wha'Kon explained to No-Pa-Wa-The then immediately received his reply, which he repeated in English, "Move the line!"

"You don't look starvin' to me. There's still plenty to hunt on yer land. It's full-sized and filled with game. Maybe you should consider not huntin' so far from yer home?"

Yuma did not care for the colonel much, but he sure appreciated what he was saying, even if the words landed on deaf ears.

Wha'Kon continued to do his job, which made No-Pa-Wa-The's blood boil. The chief pounded his fist on the table. Then, as though No-Pa-Wa-The's anger was a call for action, his band of warriors pulled concealed blades from their sleeves and headdresses.

The colonel's army reacted instantly. They cocked and aimed their rifles at the Osage in the same moment the Cherokee armed themselves with hidden blades of their own.

Both tribes came equally prepared-- demonstrating why they did not achieve progress in their talks; they thought too much alike.

Aponi held a blade and a deadly glare that would make their father proud. Yuma was grateful that he had warned Aponi about his prediction of this impasse.

"You best tell those men to lower them knives," warned Phillips to all, though directing his focus onto No-Pa-Wa-The.

Wha'Kon interpreted, but submission did not

follow the order.

He and Yuma continued to translate the colonel's words, "You need ta be realistic here. Now there's plenty of this Godforsaken land for everyone ta live peacefully and without violence. I don't know how many times I need to tell ya ta make ya understand. I hear yer frustrations, but things is the way they is, an' killin' me ain't gonna change that one iota. All you'll accomplish is wagin' a war that you can't win. Our armies are better manned and better gunned, and they won't think twice about burnin' yer homes to the ground with yer wives and children inside. I guarantee it. They'll make sure every Osage is buried six feet under, or whatever it is you do with yer dead." Phillips composed himself as he gave Wha'Kon a moment to allow his translation catch up, then once ready, "Now if that's what ya want, you go right ahead, and take a stab at me. But if not, let's continue to sort things out."

All waited with their breath held for No-Pa-Wa-The to reach a conclusion. In the background, Yuma could hear a commotion at the front gate but ignored it while waiting for No-Pa-Wa-The to make a decision.

The Osage chief motioned for his men to put their weapons away.

"Hold on now," ordered Phillips, pointing at the table in front of him.

No-Pa-Wa-The's brutal expression returned as every Indian, including the Cherokee, began to relinquish their knives by resting them on the table.

"Pardon me, Colonel," interrupted a front gate guard. "Cherokee's come wantin' ta speak with their chief. They ain't bein' threatin' or nuttin', but they are actin' kinda wild."

Phillips glanced to Yuma, who gave an approving nod, but the guard did not budge until he received the sanction directly from his commander. "But only one."

The guard's stride lasted but a few steps before he stopped to holler, "Escort 'im in!"

Yuma filled in Matolu on the situation, after which he then matched Aponi and Kilwannee's curiosity. They did not wait long before seeing Honovi between two cavalry guards. He looked to have transported his angered and shocked face all the way from their village. Yuma knew to be concerned.

In their own language he spoke, "You must come home. There has been a terrible tragedy. It is Salali. She has been had by a man and killed."

Yuma had braced himself for bad news, but his expectation did not lessen his shock. It took every ounce of strength not to overact in present company; even Aponi, who was less familiar with these conferences, knew better than to show weakness.

Kilwannee demanded to know who while Yuma knew the answer already. Jeremiah's Soldier Spirit was darkness, and yet Yuma allowed him to stay. He had given The Soldier Spirit a home, fearing that if he had not, then the man he loved would be forced to leave with him.

"Jeremiah," answered Honovi.

His accent was harsh, but by Colonel Phillips' surprised reaction, not so strong as to disguise the familiar name. "Did you just say, Jeremiah?"

Honovi turned, aware that he was the one being addressed though distinctly confused. Phillips pivoted his attention to Yuma, "Is that who he said?"

Yuma nodded, stunned by the colonel's deep interest.

"That wouldn't be Jeremiah Whiting, now would it?"

Yuma knew better than to answer, as did Aponi, but Kilwannee was more than eager to reply. "Yes."

The colonel saw fit to come out from around the table in his flabbergasted state and continue his inquiries more directly. "Well, Holy shit. Have y'all been harboring a federal fugitive?"

When it came to English, Yuma was the best in their tribe, but even he did not understand the word "Fugitive?"

"That's what we call someone who runs from the law."

"We do not follow your laws," shouted Kilwannee as though being attacked.

Phillips chuckled his contempt. "That's yer response?! You don't even wanna know what the criminal's wanted fer?"

All three stared at him blank in the face though Yuma felt confident that he was the only one truly not ready to hear the truth.

"Desertion. Rape. Murder. He killed an entire family in cold blood. A family who helped raise him, including women and children."

Yuma could not ignore the horrendous accusations he was hearing; the similarities to what he had heard happened to Salali, though sparse, were too great to refute. His conscience had tried to warn him about The Soldier Spirit, but he refused to listen. Now, the punishment for his ignorance was reaped by the youngest, and most precious, of their blood. The only comfort he found was to know that Salali now soared with the spirits of their ancestors.

There were words Yuma needed to translate to his father that stuck in his throat. Kilwannee then did what his brother could not while watching his tormented face, as well as their sister's, with disdain. Yuma knew she shared his feeling of betrayal, but only he was to be blamed. He was the one who brought a murdering, raping white soldier into their homes and their lives. They would never accuse him outright, but they did not need to. He would be made to suffer by his own guilt.

Without reclaiming their weapons, Matolu darted towards the stables. The Cherokee entourage followed on his heels, leaving No-Pa-Wa-The simmering in what looked to be confused anger. But before the Osage screamed an outrage, Phillips beckoned the front gate guard over. Yuma had heard the Colonel whisper, "Fetch Mr. Stebbins from his holding cell, and take him to my quarters straight away," before falling out of ear shot.

The guard gave a curt nod then rushed across the parade grounds.

CHAPTER XII

C alvin recognized the rider, who stopped about a quarter mile back and waited next to the lone red oak that shaded his wife's grave. It may have been eighteen months, give or take, but he knew a stranger when he saw one, and this boy wasn't one. Aside from that, travelers did not just happen on the path that led to his farm; they only turned onto the dirt road with the intention of reaching Hawte Ranch.

"I remember him," noted Henry at his side. Like father, like son, also knowing a familiar figure when spotted.

Calvin had wondered if he would ever see Alexander Stebbins again. Part of him thought the kid might have died in the freezing storm that night. Come the next morning, after peering into the barn and discovering that the boy hadn't taken shelter as suggested, it's what would have made sense. However, Calvin also understood determination, the kind that possessed Alexander the same way it had once possessed him, and how resourceful willpower was when it came to survival.

Calvin beckoned Alexander to approach; it was the sign the kid had been waiting for. The boy kept his pace steady, nudging his mare forward, and then stopped where Calvin and Henry stood just off the front porch of their home.

"Tie up yer ride then come on in."

Calvin stepped inside his home while Henry silently offered to help Alexander.

Alexander, the kid who did not look like much of a kid anymore, sat in the same spot, perhaps even the same chair, as he did when the exchange of ugly words occurred before the rumpus of their final moment together. How naïve that boy had been. Calvin was curious to discover the kind of maturing Alexander might have done since last they met. By the appearance of his single weary eye, hasty reflexes, and three or four new scars, Calvin would venture to guess that he had put on about five years of experience in the one to two years that had actually passed.

Calvin gave them each a cup of coffee to show that he held no ill-will about that night though Alexander was the one who suffered the most. He then turned to Henry, who looked equally intrigued by their returning visitor, and instructed, "Go on outside and cook up some breakfast fer all of us while we talk."

"Yes, sir!" Henry stated enthusiastically though his body did not move out the door with the same gusto.

"Go on."

Once Henry was out the door, Calvin joined Alexander in a sip of coffee. The kid cringed. "Ain't you got nuttin' stronger?"

Calvin studied him for a moment before he rose and grabbed a bottle of likker off the shelf. He poured some into each of their coffees. Judging by Alexander's softened cringe after taking another sip, it was acceptable.

"I never thought I'd see you again."

"I wun't so sure 'bout that either."

"But you didn't come just to visit."

"I know where he is… kinda."

"Kinda? So he's still on the run after all this time?"

By the distraught expression that spread like a disease across Alexander's face, Calvin understood the boy to take his comment as a jab at his failure to capture Jeremiah, which was not the case. Some things hadn't changed, he reckoned.

"You was right. He's been hidin' with the injuns."

Calvin drank from his cup, and though he thought the likker was weak on the proof, he watched the boy wince after taking his next sip.

"How's the eye?" Calvin asked, changing the subject, once concluding where this conversation headed.

"Better than the other." Alexander had stated so while the tired eye and false eye both stared at him coolly. Then, wasting no time, "So, whaddya say?"

"To what?"

"You know the fuck what!" Alexander shouted while pounding the table.

"I told you ta let go of all that rage and move on with your life. Why would I aid you in doin' the opposite of what I advised?"

"'Cuz he done to a chief's daughter what he done to Penny, an' he'll keep doin' it over and over 'til we stop 'im."

Calvin struggled. He wanted to tell the boy that it was no longer his responsibility. He had become accustomed to farm life and loved it so much better; not only because of its structure and serenity, but because Henry was here too. Calvin had enjoyed teaching him about how to track, hunt, and shoot as well as read and write. The adjustment to a simpler life was not easy and came with its share of troubles, but in time he had accomplished what he set out to do and been happier for it. Still, there was a small part of him which would never bend to the luxuries of simplicity. That piece of him craved justice and lived inside the same heart reserved for his boy.

He took a moment and gazed out the window. Calvin did not intend to peer at Henry cooking their meals off the side of their house, but there he was. In a month, maybe less, he would have a small kitchen built where meals could be prepared under a covering. A collection of supplies for the construction already sat in piles behind the house. Of course, a kitchen only would be built if he were to stay.

"Those natives after him too?"

"Probably."

"Which tribe?"

"Cherokee."

"They'll find him quick."

Calvin heard an undertone of frustration in Alexander's voice. The boy could sense him stalling. "That's why I come. I need ta get 'im a'fore they do. What he done ta that girl, he done ta my family first."

"And?"

"It's my right ta serve Jeremiah his justice. Not theirs!"

"But natives ain't allowed back into Missouri."

Alexander contemplated Calvin's reasoning. "How you know he's headed back fer Missouri?"

"It's what makes sense," stated Calvin with unwavering confidence. "If he was in Cherokee Territory, Missouri would be the nearest state line he could cross, as well as being familiar to him.

"See. An' that's it right there. Yer good. That's why I needs yer help," he paused. "How did you git to be so good at things you do? How is that you jus' know things?"

Calvin tapped his fingers on the tabletop, deciding how much trust he should stake in the young man. But before he could settle on a conclusion, his mouth opened and ran like a runaway train.

"I don't jus' know things. I observe. I suppose I get it from the half of me that's native."

Alexander's calm and hardened disposition finally lightened. The boy raised an eyebrow out of shocked intrigue.

"My pa was a military man too. Him and a couple of other soldiers were tasked to relocate a tribe of Blackfoot. In doing so, I reckon he and those other men took it upon themselves to have their way with some of the young women and girls. Anyway, he got one of them pregnant, but never knew of it 'til years later when charged to report on the Blackfoot situation. He must've seen me and recognized my face as his own, but then didn't do squat about it 'til later that night, after he had time to gather a platoon of men. They raided the village, making it look like a nearby tribe had attacked. He killed my momma then took me."

"How old was you?"

Calvin turned to the window and watched Henry toast bread on top of a metal grate high above the fire. He was fighting with one slice, trying not to singe his hand as he attempted to free it from between two bars that captured it. "'Bout his age."

"Why'd he kill'em all? Why didn't he jus' take you?"

"He was angry, and he didn't think he was doing any wrong. I believe otherwise though, and he knew it. He tried to beat the Blackfoot outta me. He raised me in a military way, which was how I got involved in the war, while I kept my native roots and beliefs to myself. But to answer yer question, I suppose the combination of the two is what makes me good at my job."

"What kinda beliefs? Heaven?"

"No."

"So, native spirits then?"

He paused. "Sure."

Calvin didn't know if Alexander was trying to appear nonchalant about what he was being told, or if he truly was not affected by the tale as he sipped on his coffee. "Where's yer pa now?"

"Dead."

"You kill 'im?"

"I wanted to, but no, I did not. Without a trial, that would be murder."

Alexander paused at the objection, then his arrogance returned to defend his rite.

Calvin insisted, "Where you been all this time?"

"You mean when I ain't settin' in jail?"

Calvin raised an eyebrow, his interest piqued.

"I've been lookin' fer 'im."

"Where?"

"I'll tell you when we're on our way." Alexander slammed down his coffee mug. "We're wastin' time here!"

Calvin looked him calmly in the eye. "I ain't agreed yet to going."

"So you don't care no more? With everythin' I been through?!"

"And what has that entailed?"

Alexander rose. "Humiliation an' sufferin'!"

"Pa?"

Calvin looked through the window and saw his boy frozen at the fire pit, after hearing the commotion.

"It's alright, son. Keep on fixin'." He waited until Henry returned to his chore before addressing Alexander. "You frighten my boy like last time, you'll receive the same boot out the door, an' I'll make sure you never return this time."

The red in Alexander's face began to whiten when, without being told to, he sat back down, though Calvin could still see the fumes. "Hell an' back. That's where I been."

"What was you in jail for?"

"That nigger lovin' Colonel from the fort, Phillips, he was the one who done the humiliatin'. Jus' the other night he pulled me from my cell an' told me what he learned about Jeremiah Whiting from some injuns then released me jus' like that. The only thing he said afta that was, *It was fer yer own good.* No apology or nuttin'."

"What was you in for?"

"That's what I'm tryin ta tell ya!" Alexander hollered, back on his feet. "Nuttin'! Jus' bein' where I wasn't supposed ta be. Thaz all! I ain't gone mad or become a danger to anyone other than Jeremiah Whiting when I sees 'im."

This time, Calvin needed for Alexander to... "Sit down."

The boy did, and then took a large gulp from his

cup.

Henry entered with plates of scrambled eggs, toast, butter, and a jar of preserves. He set the meal on the table.

"Thank you, son," stated Calvin, continuing to educate the boy about being polite and well-mannered.

Alexander must have sensed that he was losing momentum with Calvin, so continued, "Is you a coward now? Is that it?" Calvin and Henry froze, awestruck. "'Cuz that's what ya are if you let some criminal continue ta traipse around in the nation you swore ta protect."

"Enough," warned Calvin.

"That no-good killer's gone keep doin' ta whoever he likes while you jus' set here on yer farm and teach yer boy how ta hide from problems."

"I said enough!" Calvin ordered. It was his turn to rise to his feet.

Alexander rose as well to meet him in the eye. "He raped a girl, and then killed her. Sound familiar?"

Calvin froze. The first image that came to his head was not of an Indian squaw lying bloodied and butchered, but the memory of his mother, laying bloodied and butchered. The horror kept him stone cold silent.

"I had a feelin' you was gonna be a waste of time."

Alexander headed for the front door, prideful, and had one foot outside when Calvin yelled for him to, "Wait." Alexander did.

Calvin peered at his son. The day his pa had died of a heart attack, he had sworn to be a better father than his own, but now it was like his father never departed; not when there was another man just as vile on the run. How he could be the best example for his son, knowing his pa's twin spirit ran free, was inconceivable. He would never be able to live in his own skin.

"We'll need to go on full stomachs first."

Calvin sat back down at the table, but before Alexander joined him, he could tell that the kid needed clarification. "Yer gonna go after 'im with me?"

"Go after who, Pa?"

"Moby-Dick."

Henry nodded his head. Calvin knew, having read that story to him as well as telling tales of the war, all he needed was to say the title for his son to understand.

"Am I goin' too?"

Although Calvin did give the matter a moment's consideration, he thought not. "No. I need ya here to tend to the farm, so we gots food and a roof for me to return to."

He saw the disappointment in his son's face, but Henry was smart. Calvin knew he understood his reasoning over his own passion.

Alexander sat down and joined the feast though all through breakfast, his tapping foot expressed his exploding eagerness to get on the road.

CHAPTER XIII

The spirits had done well this time. When they instructed Atraco to go help the Cherokee, he had reservations. This tribe was one of five who had sold their traditions and beliefs in exchange for treaties that did not benefit their native land and societies. Commonly, they were a type of people who did not possess a similar hatred towards the white man, but this clan's chief was not like the others. Not sharing the same language, he didn't know what had happened to cause Matolu's disdain, but the chief showed persuasiveness by being able to see beyond the settler's propaganda. Luckily for Atraco, Matolu did not demonstrate the intelligence to see beyond his conspiracy.

To Atraco, there was no such thing as Americans because America did not exist. Land could not be claimed by giving it a name. The settlers were nothing more than an infectious people who brought their decay and diseases. That was how they had been introduced to him centuries before, and that was who they still were today. The life he began was long ago, but no amount of time could make him forget the betrayal of not only the Europeans, but his own kind. Even his father, Squanto, had forsaken their heritage to travel with the white man across the water on their barges.

When Squanto returned years later, he returned to devastation. A deadly new curse had slaughtered his family, and he had been left to believe that none of his kind had survived. He would have believed to be the only remaining Patuxet, and Atraco allowed him to continue to believe that lie.

The year before his father's return, Atraco recalled seeing the signs of an approaching decimation. His people took ill and died as they screamed. He called to the spirits, who had been watching as well and blessed him with the ram's spirit of balance and prolonged life. With the ability to survive better than any man, he took to revenge and assassinated all he could, including the white man's most trusted ally... Squanto.

Atraco had been seventeen at the time he neared his old home in the land his father joined the settlers in calling Massachusetts. When he moved to slip poison into his father's drink, Squanto proved that he looked through white eyes when he could not recognize his own son standing so close. Atraco continued to let himself be unknown until the moment before his father gasped a final harsh breath. But his death was not exceptional. It gave no extra meaning and had been no more, or less, satisfying than any other.

For decades thereafter, Atraco continued his murderous quest for revenge until his body would allow no more. By the time he reached thirty-six, his movement had begun to reflect his years. With age came aches and pains he did not experience in his youth. The spirit of the ram had prolonged his life, but it did not keep his body from deteriorating over time. He had begged the spirits for the wolf or the bat to enter him. Their gift of rebirth would keep him looking young, but the spirits refused. They wouldn't allow Atraco to have more than one possession. A ploy to trick the spirits would have been planned right then if they had not already been aware of his greed, so a new idea was born that day.

He would see the intruders from far away worlds molested in much the same way as they had molested this land. They would come to know his suffering, but little did Atraco know that this one recipe for retribution would take generations to perfect. These Cherokee would not be the first tribe to perform his ritual. He had witnessed many failures over the centuries but not once was his conviction tested; always knowing that one day he would concoct a master plague.

The beginning proved the largest challenge. The mistake he had made was using wild animals as the host. Those creatures were pure of heart and did not possess the ability to coerce their brethren. The spirits, as though proving a point, did inhabit those initial few, but then turned them into monstrosities that did not survive the night. Some combusted from the overwhelming manifestations they contained, others threw their deformed bodies into fires and over cliffs while most ate their own flesh until they bled out. However, man was different; he was a master manipulator. What he lacked in carnal instincts he made up for with his capability to be scheming.

The first human possessor was a warrior from the Kiskiack tribe in an area the white man called Virginia. The Kiskiack had many reasons to have hatred in their hearts for the invaders and had been easy to convince to give their best warrior, Rowoco, to the spirits. But even with the gifts, Rowoco, and all the men who succeeded him, perished like common men would without affecting the world as Atraco had hoped. What he needed was immortality; a living curse.

He had sat on the idea that the ceremony needed an added ingredient for some years but hesitated for good reason. The final result would not be as perfect as what he desired. The consumption of human life had been added to the ritual some time ago. Its inclusion had given the creations greater strength and intelligence but remained too fragile for his liking. However, should the volunteer willingly mutilate himself then drink surplus amounts from his own veins during the sacrament, then the act would be a crime against nature that far exceeded what would be considered ordinary cannibalism. A curse would be born, and the transfer would be as simple as a bite or a scratch. Passing the possession would ensure that his plague would live on, if the carrier did not succumb to its one weakness.

Its teeth and claws would become the greatest weapon against itself. Living as long as he had, Atraco could not count how many times he injured his body--cutting his arm, face, or leg when he scratched too hard with his long nails or bit down on his tongue when eating. Any scratch or bite the creature caused to itself would spawn severe excruciation, or even death, for the body who held the curse could not be infected again. The result would be a conflict of extreme consequences, but exactly how extreme remained unknown until the animal could be born.

The time had come to stop delaying. Amongst these Cherokee people, one possessed more power over the others, and his youth made him easy to manipulate.

Atraco watched Kilwannee sleep as most of the village rested for the next day's ceremony. The sacrament to put Salali in the ground would continue throughout the week, but it was agreed that a new ritual would intercede for just one night.

Atraco's rite took much convincing. He and Matolu had only just met the day before when grief filled the chief. Typically, the Cherokee did not lament the deceased, but when innocence dies in warless violence, their roar could be heard like a sleuth of angry bears. The energy of Matolu's rage was primed.

Atraco had acted fast. He took the chief by the hand, and then connected with him through sorrowed eyes. Though he claimed Matolu's attention, he also attracted others, including the chief's eldest daughter and two sons. The one who answered to Kilwannee looked upon him with hope, but it was the one he heard called Yuma who appeared skeptical of Atraco's intrusion.

The chief allowed himself to be used as the elder's crutch while being led away from the others who surrounded Salali's remains. During the escort, he purposefully babbled on about the colors of peace in the sky, as well as the beauty of the land that was once unclaimed. Matolu seemed to have understood him without recognizing a word.

They entered the chief's hut then Atraco used his stick to draw a man that Matolu correctly depicted as Jeremiah. The visitor knew this because anger swelled and the passion for revenge burned in the chief's eyes, but Atraco waved his hand away. Then, in his own tongue, told Matolu that his way was not the way. The chief could not comprehend. His baffled expression told the old man that his interference with their customs was not needed. But in his persistence, Atraco pulled a large pig bone out of his interior vest. With it, he stabbed the sketch of Jeremiah repeatedly, and then waved "no" with stanch confidence.

Before the chief's continue was allowed to linger, Atraco drew the land and the sky then pointed to the clouds that hung above their heads. He continued his communication by using his hands to sign various animals. First, he spread his fingers over his head to signify the antelope. Next, he clasped his open palms together and then wiggled them to sign the fish. Then, he used each hand to extend his mouth and mimic his fingers as sharp teeth to define the wolf.

Matolu looked to have understood that much. However, before he could agree to the plan of asking for the spirits' aid, Yuma and Kilwannee interrupted. The younger son spoke foreign words that Atraco did not need to understand to know. The boy had given the advice not to believe this stranger's stories. What Atraco had done to attract Yuma's suspicion, he still did not know. His only thought was that the boy had a power the others did not. Atraco had found his mark.

Kilwannee did not share his brother's passion though he did appear apprehensive. Atraco invited him, and him only, to join their discussion. Not wanting Yuma to have knowledge of his plan, Atraco made a motion for the chief to dismiss his younger son from the hut.

That moment had been a crucial junction to their conference. Matolu's decision would determine whether Atraco could later sway the chief's agreement to his proposal. Unsurprisingly, Matolu had waved Yuma away.

Persuading the chief to accept the remainder of his great idea still did not come easy. Initially, he had objected to the drawings of a single man connected to the many animal spirits that encircled him, but Atraco found an accidental ally in the weak-minded Kilwannee. The angry son warmed to the proposal, and then advised his father to do the same. They were one step away from reaching an accord, but the step had a deep crevasse between them.

Kilwannee disagreed with Atraco's suggestion for Yuma to be the Great Spirit's provider. Thinking himself the greater warrior, he had been adamant about being its host, and Matolu agreed to the point of insistence. Try as Atraco did, he had failed to dissuade the men. He had no other choice but to concede. It was better that a lesser Great Spirit be born than none at all.

Atraco finished rubbing the white venom around the rim of Kilwannee's cup, courtesy of a friendly toad covered in red blots. Since killing his father, he had become quite adept in the art of poisoning. He walked away from Kilwannee and allowed him to sleep through the remainder of the night. He would get a head start for the river and prepare for the ceremony at next sundown. Though he had failed as many times as he had made attempts, Atraco was filled with confidence that he had not experienced before. The spirits would be misled into relinquishing their gifts just as simply as the Cherokee would be tricked into offering their most powerful asset. Atraco never doubted that the deception would come easy. The chief was just like his son, Kilwannee; simple.

Heard from across the village was the scraping of shuffling feet. Yuma peered up and spotted a hunched over silhouette with a walking stick hobbling in the night. He had no doubt where the mysterious old shaman headed. For him, traveling the quarter mile to the river would be a half days' journey. He took a head start.

Yuma returned to his responsibilities guarding Salali's body against any hungry wildlife. The majority of his misgivings towards Atraco changed once his Kilwannee explained how the Patuxet had come to aid in their retaliation against Jeremiah. When it came to anger over their young sister's passing, it was the one thing the brothers agreed upon. In a ceremony, Kilwannee would become host to a powerful Great Spirit. Though their customs were similar, the largest difference between the upcoming ritual and requesting the spirit's help, as they've done in the past, was the unification of many gifts endowing one embodiment. Atraco swore to have succeeded in this summoning many times before.

What little remained of Yuma's apprehension came from the old man's peculiar timing. From the other villagers, he had heard that Atraco arrived when Salali still lived. Somehow, he had known about the forthcoming tragedy. This elder native was either second-sighted or something else entirely.

The iguana, Jeremiah affectionately named Martin, flicked its long tongue at Yuma as he cradled the beast in his arms. The kindly creature made no attempt to escape. Jeremiah never did explain why he had turned to a reptile for friendship. True, he had not been welcomed by all the tribe and struggled to gain acceptance, but Yuma had offered his companionship since the beginning. Why that had not been enough for Jeremiah, Yuma never understood. The rejection always did sting, but not until Jeremiah stabbed him with betrayal was his heart gouged. Yuma did not forget that Jeremiah and his Soldier Spirit were not one and the same, but The Soldier needed to suffer and, unfortunately, the only way he could be made to pay was by accepting his connection to Jeremiah.

A wave of comfort washed over Yuma with the confidence that justice would prevail in the end. If there were one change he could make, it would be to convince the chief that it was his right to become a host to the spirits; not Kilwannee. He was the one who had brought The Soldier Spirit into their fold.

Yuma held Martin up to his face to look the ugly creature in the eye. Its long tongue flicked his nose and cheek, as though reminding his handler that Jeremiah had abandoned him as well. Yuma did not smile but felt a connection to the lizard he never thought possible.

"You, Martin, will have your revenge too. It is

promised."

Flick.

It was the dawn of sunset. For the six men carrying Salali, they raised the platform above their heads to transport her body safely across the river. The current was not raging, but Kilwannee had trouble keeping his balance. He didn't look well. Sweat covered his face while he found it difficult to breathe through an enlarged throat. Yuma had never seen such a strange illness. A sign or warning from the spirits first crossed his mind.

Atraco waited on the opposite side for the oncoming tribe. Difficult as it was to believe, the frail bag of bones somehow had managed to wade through the water without being pulled away. Yuma always thought his Uncle Honovi would be the finest mystic he would ever know until he met Atraco.

The other men and women followed close behind and carried what was needed for both ceremonies. Lavender and willow root to cleanse Salali for her journey beyond, and vases of blood for the ritual that would vindicate her death.

Once the bearers emerged from the river, they placed Salali in the spot where she struggled for her life. The area had not been difficult to recognize with its disturbed earth and red-stained ground.

Kilwannee rested on a nearby rock while Yuma

and Aponi stood next to their sister. Sad as they were, they did not cry; no one did. It was not the Cherokee way. Even when taken by the hands of a fierce predator, death remained a part of life. Once cleansed, passing into another land would be Salali's honor. But this time, they would not begin to purify the deceased right away. Anguish was a soiled emotion. To wash her could not be done while sorrowful, and an abundance of sorrow was required for Atraco's ritual. The Patuxet Indian had explained that to convince multiple spirits to offer their gifts, they would need to demonstrate their tormented grief.

Preparations continued until nightfall. A large bonfire roared to life beneath the lip of the high rock formation. Yuma recalled Mukul falling to his death from that same wall. Only now did he realize how many deaths this river had seen and wondered if a curse had befallen these shores.

Matolu approached Salali. He looked at her, and his face of sadness turned into rage.

Atraco sat too far away for his weak voice to be heard. Instead, he banged his stick against a rock to capture the chief's attention. The Pniese, then, swiped his hand across his face--a sign for Matolu to mask his anger. Unusual as it was to observe, the clan watched their chief obey another's order.

Atraco gave Matolu another moment to focus on his grief before he nodded that it was time.

"Go now," ordered the chief to his shivering elder son as he pointed him to the rock ledge over the fire.

Knowing he was expected to climb eighteen feet up the side, Kilwannee stood without dispute but then vomited a puddle of bile and blood.

Yuma rushed to Kilwannee with Aponi and Honovi at his side. They captured him before he collapsed, and then laid his body on the ground gently. Honovi began to sing upward to the sky.

Anger ignited Atraco. Again, he whacked his stick hard against the rock and then waved his disapproval with untamed passion. Though he could not vocally express his hysteria, he did not need to. His aversion became plain.

Honovi suspended his summoning promptly, understanding that the spirits should not be bothered before the ceremony... if there still could be a ceremony without Kilwannee.

Murmurs and rumblings from an uneasy people began to stir when Yuma unintentionally hushed them. "I will go," he offered in his native tongue.

Matolu had paused before he surmised, "You are conflicted by your love of the demon. You cannot give yourself."

Yuma froze in stunned silence. How his father could suggest that he had any love for Jeremiah was an outrage, and yet, he could not contest. However, to his defense came an unsuspecting ally in Atraco. The temperamental mystic thrust his stick towards Yuma, but Matolu waved the old man's indication away with a single gesture of disapproval. He then turned to his people, ignoring Atraco altogether.

"My warriors gather."

The chosen men did as instructed. Yuma joined his eight brethren in retrieving the jugs from the women Atraco deemed appropriate to handle. Yuma had been fortunate to have Aponi chosen as his bearer. The urn she carried contained very special blood that he would not have entrusted to anybody other than his sister.

Matolu stood as close to the fire as he could tolerate, and then withdrew a long knife from his robes. He turned both his head and the blade towards the stars. The ceremony had begun, but yet, Kilwannee's replacement still had not been chosen.

Despite appearing displeased, Atraco kept his walking stick sturdy at his side and watched with great attentiveness.

"Spirits, I beg for help. I shout for your wisdom by bringing our devastation to your attention. You are wise spirits. Please give your wisdom. Your gifts will better our world for all who walk here and soar the skies. I give gifts for yours."

Matolu slid the blade down the length of his palm. As told by the mighty current of blood that ran down the chief's arm, the incision had been deep.

No one moved. They had not been warned of this horror. With tempered awe, Matolu's people gawked at his self-mutilation until the sound of repetitive tapping snapped them out of perplexity.

Atraco stood then instructed the participants to move into position with jabs of his stick. The power of his repetitive motion articulated that there was no time to waste.

The eight warriors formed a line that ended with Yuma next to last; in front of Atohi. He watched his father approach Honovi at the front. The two brothers stood eye to eye when Honovi lifted his jar that contained the blood of a mighty creature who released its spirit upon death. Matolu's blood dripped into the jar. He then drank the mixture.

He moved to the next man, Waya, who held the blood of a creature he hunted. Each warrior had claimed his own. Some traveled to the forests and others searched in the deserts and rivers until he came back with the blood of his appointed beast. Matolu repeated his ceremonial drink and continued down the line, soon reaching Yuma.

The firelight illuminated only a small portion of his father, but Yuma still could see the paleness that had washed his face. The man had lost as much blood as he had swallowed. Yuma did not despair. He lifted his vase with great pride in his offering. For the blood of his spirit, Yuma didn't need to travel far. His came from an extraordinary beast. It had the gifts of regeneration and bravery, but most importantly, it had possessed Jeremiah's affection. When the chief drank, only Yuma was aware that the chief consumed the life of Jeremiah's beloved pet lizard, Martin.

Matolu left his side and approached the wall that a younger Mukul had unsuccessfully climbed when at full health. Only then was it made clear to the others that the chief had chosen himself as Kilwannee's replacement. Weakened by the loss of blood that kept his hands slick, Matolu's ascent should have proved impossible. He would not have the grip nor the strength to pull his body up, but somehow, he managed. Perhaps because there was one thing that the chief carried with him that Mukul had not, a heart that rejected defeat.

Not once did his father slip. Matolu stood on the edge of the lip and spread his arms as he peered into the fire below.

Yuma turned to Atraco unexpectedly. He did not know why at first, but then caught the old man staring at him instead of his father. His grin was unsettling and shuddered Yuma's body, awakening his previous misgivings about this ritual.

"Rattlesnake, I give blood for your wisdom," cried Matolu to the night.

Honovi stepped forward and tossed the blood from his jar into the fire.

The air became thick with anticipation from all who waited for the liquid to spark. If so, the blood had maintained its life-force and would be a suitable gift for spirits. If not, the offering would be rejected.

Crackling came from the flames, accompanied by tiny explosions of white light. The blood had lived, and the spirits were happy with the trade. An enormous black snake of smoke slithered out of the fire and rose towards the sky. All but Atraco and Matolu froze in fear by the dark magic.

The Chief readied for the creature's approach. He exhaled all the air from his lungs then took a deep breath as the smoke spirit reached his lips. Like the vacuum of space, Matolu sucked the gigantic monster into his body.

Yuma joined the others in gawking with disbelief, but he was alone in thinking there was evil at work. He twisted his attention back onto Atraco, who never looked livelier. The mystic beamed with pride at the man who had been blessed with the gifts of healing and elusiveness. The shaman, too, appeared possessed with the gift hope... until the ritual stalled. Atraco glared at the next man who had been captured by amazement. Angered, the elder whacked his stick and moaned incoherent words that mirrored those from a restless phantom.

Once jarred from his trance, Waya approached the fire. He mimicked Honovi's behavior when he tossed the blood into the flames.

"Grey Wolf, I give blood for your wisdom," the chief shouted from the peak.

Within moments, the fire popped and sparked before it released the smoke spirit of a charging wolf. Matolu took the beast inside him in a single breath.

The performance had been no less astounding a second time. Acquiring the gifts of two spirits rarely happened. In addition to the rattlesnake, Matolu had been given instinct and rebirth. Though still pleased with the progress, a part of Atraco's joy died once the chief accepted this spirit into him, as though the old man assumed the gifts of a jealous child.

"Prairie goat, I give blood for your wisdom."

The next warrior burned the contents from his jar, and once the blood finished sparkling like fireworks, the black cloud of a goat galloped towards Matolu. He inhaled the spirit and continued to do the same with each offering from the next four men until only two contributions remained. The first would come from his son, Yuma.

Matolu stumbled but caught himself before going over the edge. Yuma stepped towards the wall until his father held out a hand for him to stop. The chief rested on one knee. Once recovered enough to extend his neck over the side, he let it be known, "Lizard, I give blood for your wisdom."

Yuma turned to the fire and presented his vase, but then hesitated. Not only did his uncertainty mature as each spirit weakened his father, but no single man should hold so much power. In addition to the previous, Matolu's abilities had been enhanced by solitude and travel from the black bear, quick movement and energy from the spotted bass, vision and strength from the golden eagle, and cunning and balance from the cougar.

He felt the pressure of all eyes upon him as he struggled with his decision, and then looked to Aponi for guidance. She shook her head in uncertainty. The ceremony had disturbed her as well. Yuma struggled with the choice another moment before he decided to proceed. Seven of the nine spirits had manifested inside their father already. The ritual had progressed too far to abandon. The wiser choice would be to complete the ceremony in hopes that Martin's blood had died inside the vase, and the spirit of the lizard could be forced to deny his gifts of bravery and revival. He would find out soon enough, as would they all.

Yuma tossed his mixture into the flames. For a moment, he thought his prayers might have been answered when the fire remained silent, until an eruption of pops and crackles echoed inside the smoke that twisted into a giant iguana. As though it were racing up the side of the rock wall, the translucent beast scampered towards Matolu and was taken in to be with his kindred.

Atohi stood at the fire and was ready to dispense his contents when the chief collapsed and rolled onto his back. Many rushed, but Yuma was the first to reach the wall. He scaled the side without any hesitancy or remembrance that he never had been a good climber.

He reached his ailing father faster than expected. If not for his moans, Matolu would have appeared deceased. Yuma shook his body, unexpectedly releasing a small breath of black soot. It was a piece of the spirits. He imagined how they were leeching onto his father's insides and coiling around his spirit to squeeze the life out of him.

Matolu's eyes sprung open. Yuma pushed away with an overwhelming amount of fear. Never before had he seen red eyes, nor any color, glow with such astonishing brilliance.

His father reached out his hand and whispered, "Help."

Though the man still resembled his father, Yuma did not believe he was the same.

Moments had passed before Yuma mustered the will to continue with his assistance. He took his father's outstretched hand, but the demonic man slapped him away then nudged towards the ledge. He was making it clear that he did not want help to his feet but rolled over the side. Yuma gaped at the utter lunacy. The red eyes, the self-inflicted wound, the smoke spirits, all had been omitted from Atraco's description of the ceremony, and now, this suicide. He could not do what was asked of him.

The noise that came out of Matolu's mouth was unlike anything he had heard before, but Yuma heard it clearly when his father roared his disgrace that at the disobedience. Matolu climbed to his knees with no help from his son, but with the assistance of the spirits. Permitting only a moment's rest, he rebuilt the strength needed to rise to his feet though he hunched over like a man with no spine. Matolu tipped forward and allowed gravity to do the rest.

The clan watched their chief plummet into the fire. An explosion of burning embers erupted into the air then rained over their heads.

Atraco dropped to his knees and began to push dirt over the flames. Once he allowed the demonstration enough time to educate the others, he motioned for their help. All but one member of the tribe surrounded the bonfire and scooped the ground into the pit. Aponi had the insight to use the emptied jars to pull water from the river, but Atraco waved her idea away. It had to be the earth, and only the earth. Upon his clarification, she joined the others in dousing the flames with dirt and continued until their chief was buried in his own grave.

The moment after his father fell, Yuma had hung his head over the side to watch. Then allowing what he thought was an appropriate amount of time to pass, he concluded that the ritual had failed. The only accomplishment was in the success of killing his father, who now rested next to his dead daughter.

Following the will of a dark mystic turned his people into a mockery. Weakened by sorrow and their need for revenge, Atraco had smelled their vulnerability. The elder, appearing at the moment he was needed, had been no coincidence. His magic had shown him the way, but for a purpose that still had not been made clear.

Yuma looked for the old man with the moon's help. Once spotted, he would descend the cliff and make the Pniese reveal his secrets. But instead of finding the ancient soothsayer, he found impossibility. The man who could not walk faster than a baby taking his first steps was nowhere in sight. It was as though he had vanished. Yuma wondered if the elder might have fallen into the pit and been buried with his father. He cracked a smile at the thought but then deterred his wishful thinking and waited for the logical explanation to present itself. Until then, he climbed down the side of the wall and rejoined his people.

Yuma, along with and the help of others, hoisted Kilwannee onto their shoulders, and then carried him back to their village. Tomorrow they would cleanse their bodies of this evil before they gave Salali her proper burial and tried to forget the night they all had turned into vengeful monsters.

Atraco chuckled. Though the laughter was not hearty, he remembered the sensation of his chest convulsing as it pushed the air through his throat. It had been years... decades... centuries since he felt enough happiness to chortle. Atraco was glad to know that experiencing its pleasure was still possible.

Though this night had not gone as planned, he had never achieved better success. Being drawn to a chief with such weakness had been fortunate and a curse. Though easier to dupe than any previous leader he attempted to persuade, Matolu's weakness dominated the proceedings at the worst possible moment. Younger blood was needed to contain all nine spirits. If Yuma had been the one chosen, he would have been strong enough to host them all, perhaps more. It was a shame that the ninth spirit could not be summoned. Atraco would have very much liked to witness the bat add its gifts of camouflage and death to the creature. Still, the scourge that would soon be birthed would be a magnificent plague upon this land. The Cherokee were not the only people to embrace a good cleansing.

Atraco continued to walk through the brush. He could feel the power of the bat's gifts wearing, but thanked the spirit for the temporary camouflage that allowed his escape. He had not been surprised by the bat's generosity. The creature would have died in vain if Atraco hadn't swallowed the unused mixture. Still, he would have rather seen it used for its intended purpose.

As though the thought of his unmade creature had been its cue, the spirits of many roared as one rumble in the night.

The Great Spirit had been born. After two-hundred years, Atraco had succeeded... finally.

CHAPTER XIV

Smoke rose from the chimney, but there were no signs of the one who built the fire. He had waited fifteen minutes, maybe ten; time was difficult to tell when under the gun, which Jeremiah realized he could be quite literally. Perhaps his pa had spotted him coming through the forest and was now waiting for a clear shot. Betsy Stebbins once proclaimed he would do just that should he set foot back on their land. The Soldier did not need to whisper a warning into his ear to wait another five minutes, or more, before making his move.

He kept hidden in the shade of a tree that had overgrown since he had last seen it--the day he left to join Colonel Cooper's brigade. Its magnificent branches stretched over what remained of his parent's house, fenced in by unkempt growth. The small cottage was in shambles, but not more than how he remembered it. As much as he longed to be home again, he had not forgotten about his unbearable youth under its roof. Now that he could compare his upbringing to war, they each had their moments of being worse than the other. However, like Martin during combat, he had an ally with his momma. Jeremiah prayed that she would be the first image he'd see upon his return.

It's been five minutes, confirmed Jeremiah, returning to conversing silently in his head.

It's been one, corrected The Soldier.

But Jeremiah was tired of being eaten alive by anticipation.

With Wahya's reins in hand, he slinked out from under the trees' shadows and into the late afternoon sun. Fortunately, his mare made for an excellent shield but, unfortunately, he would not be able to make a quick escape on a dead mount.

The buildup of expectation for battle died a quiet death, for which Jeremiah was grateful. There was no gunshot or yelling, nor even stirring about the gloomy cabin.

Mind your cocky.

Jeremiah did, continuing his advance with unremitting caution.

He had crossed no more than fifty feet of the yard before he came upon the shack. Jeremiah circled around towards the back, peeking through each window as he passed. He spotted the aging fire in the hearth, but still, not a sign of his ma or pa. If they were not in hiding, then they had left and would be expected to return soon.

Jeremiah tied Wahya to the rear post, out of sight from the road that lead to the front of the house.

When his pa returned, he would rather the man not be tipped off to his presence immediately.

The surprise could be meant for you.

Jeremiah clutched the handle of his knife, in case The Soldier presumed correctly.

The front door's hinges creaked, and the wooden floor thundered as he walked inside. Though he had not forgotten about the hollow space beneath the boards, he did forget about the echo each footstep produced. The area underneath had been sanctuary from his father's many drunken fits of rage, just so long as he curled up into one of the corners; otherwise, a bullet might have nabbed him once it had gone through the floorboards. His pa did try to climb down after him once before, but then got himself stuck by being too big and too drunk. He never tried chasing after him again, so instead, fired his frustration into the floor. Thankfully, he always missed.

Jeremiah glanced at the bullet holes that reminded him of his childhood better than any Tintype picture. He then redirected his attention to the frameless mattress in the far corner of the room. The bed was his own and lay over the loose flooring that led below the house. Due to all his crimes, the idea that his pa might be huddled and afraid beneath his feet brought forth a smile. He would have shot a hole through the floor if he had the bullet to fire.

The grumbling of his stomach snapped Jeremiah out of his daydream. Having not had a bite in days, anything would have smelled good, but he did not need to be starving to salivate over his ma's cooking. The room had been too dark, and the windows too filthy to notice from the outside that a large black pot hung on a swivel arm over the fire. Jeremiah removed the lid and peered at a bean and corn succotash with far too much broth. He grabbed a bowl and spoon, and then helped himself.

Jeremiah sat at the table, but before taking his first bite, a bottle of clear liquid caught his attention. He uncorked the top and sniffed inside. The familiar contents made him anxious to take a gulp of the moonshine. Twice now since coming home, he smiled. A confidence filled Jeremiah that he had made the right choice to return.

Given a chance for the stew to cool, he picked up the spoon and took a bite. Though anything would taste delicious, Jeremiah knew it was not his momma's cooking. Suddenly, a fresh idea dawned on him. Neither he nor The Soldier had considered that his parents might no longer be the occupants of this cottage.

He made a beeline for the only other room of the house. The bedroom would be the place to find personal belongings such as clothes and keepsakes. He yanked open a dresser drawer and found no ladies' fashions of any kind, just men's hosiery that reeked of mold and manure. Continuing his search, he kept an eye out for any .22 short bullets but found only .44, which would not fit into his 1860 Smith and Wesson Number Two Revolver.

Piled in the corner lay a mound of men's apparel. The stench that came from the clothing did not smell any better than the socks, but he did recognize some of the aged and torn garments. They were, indeed, his father's.

The distant crackling of carriage wheels over a rocky terrain came from outside. Somebody was pulling up to the house.

Jeremiah rushed to the window but made sure to keep out of sight as he watched Nathaniel Whiting ride his horse-drawn wagon to the front door. His father did not look like a man of forty, but far older. He sported a beard, very familiar to the one Jeremiah bore during the war though Nathaniel's was coarse with gray hair.

Still clutching the moonshine bottle, Jeremiah made a dash for his old mattress. He didn't know what had possessed him to run like a frightened six-year-old boy, but he had no control over his feet.

You've been in battles, killed Stebbinses and armies wantin' you dead, and yer gonna retreat from this one old man?! The Soldier hollered in disgust.

He was. Jeremiah slid the mattress and jimmied the loose floorboards up, but then glanced back and spotted his bowl of soup still sitting on the table.

Well, if you're gonna run like a yella fool, take the evidence wit ya, Dunderhead.

Jeremiah raced back and grabbed his bowl then took it down with him into the pit.

The front door opened, and Nathaniel stepped inside with his '59 Sharps Confederate Carbine

Shotgun in one hand and a dead rabbit in the other. Through the cracks in the floor, Jeremiah observed his father rest his weapon near the door then slap the carcass onto the table. He wasted no time in skinning his meal.

While Jeremiah continued to watch in silence, he could not stop his mind from imagining the worst about his ma. Not one of her personals was here, the cooking wasn't hers, and she was nowhere to be found. All signs pointed to death, and Jeremiah had an immediate assumption as to who her killer had been.

The food smelled better with the rabbit added. Jeremiah had managed to eat what he brought down with him, and not make a sound in doing so, but he still was hungry. In retrospect, dishing his meal had been a smart move as his stomach surely would have growled by now and given away his position. However, he had been remiss in taking the moonshine. The bottle was in his hand, and he had not given it a moment's thought when panic overcame him. Certainly, his pa should have noticed its disappearance, but he gave no indication during the final preparations of his supper.

Nathaniel ladled himself a bowl then sat. Jeremiah wondered how much longer he would be able to keep still and silent. The underbelly of the house seemed a lot smaller than it used to be, and his body ached as he kept scrunched for the better part of an hour. The thought of rushing his pa, taking the knife he used on the rabbit, and killing him with it came to mind once or twice.

He'll kill you with that shotgun before you even get yerself above ground.

No doubt. The man may have aged, but he did not move like an old man.

Another idea, to crawl outside, came to mind. Luckily, Wahya hadn't made a peep and kept her presence unknown, but that plan only would be possible if he found a hole at the base large enough to squeeze through quietly. If heard, his father would have no other inkling but to think a wild animal had gotten itself stuck under the house. He would then start shooting. Firing into the floor was not anything new, but doing so while sober would be. In addition to having increased senses, he would have better aim.

Nathaniel did not take a bite of his meal. Instead, he placed his Colt 1860 Army Revolver on the table next to him, and even then, he refused to eat. He hollered instead, "Come out and eat, boy."

Jeremiah froze stiff. At first, he thought it was The Soldier talking, forgetting that the two men shared the voice, but then...

"Bes' not leave my hooch down there like a goddamn Dunderhead neither. An' bring that bowl with ya. There's plenty more."

Trapped with no firing arms to fight, he saw no point in continuing with this charade. The Soldier agreed, but then again, he would if he and his father happened to be one in the same. It would explain why Jeremiah had been more and more reluctant to trust The Soldier.

He turned around then pushed up on the mattress. Poking his head above the floor, the old man with a spoon gripped in one hand, came into view. His other rested next to the butt of the pistol.

Jeremiah climbed to the top then stood like a frightened child about to receive punishment. Silently, he asked for The Soldier's opinion of what to do next, but Jeremiah could sense his absence.

Coward.

Nathaniel beckoned him over.

Jeremiah did as ordered, and stopped at the table, half in the firelight. His father snatched the moonshine from his grip then took three swigs. He set the bottle down and bore his eyes into his well-tanned son.

"You look like a nigger."

Jeremiah remained silent. He would never tell his father about the last couple of years. Any mention of being civil with the Indians would be a bullet in his head.

"Well, dig it out yerself," offered Nathaniel as he motioned towards the hearth.

Apprehensive at first, Jeremiah decidedly turned his back on his pa. He scooped his supper into the bowl, but not one second had passed when he didn't expect to be shot from behind. Instinct had him ladle quickly, but with one hand injured, Jeremiah moved slowly; besides, it was best to take his time. More curious than scared, he needed to know if he would be deceived. Just as well, he didn't want to make any sudden moves that would demonstrate fear or guilt, or cause alarm.

The bowl was full. Jeremiah pivoted back and found his father's stoic glare from the table with the pistol still untouched.

"Sit yer ass down already, boy. I'm shit starved." Jeremiah did. "You still pray?" Jeremiah nodded. "Then do it in yer head. I don't want yer Lord gettin' all mixed up with mine." Nathaniel took his first bite but continued to speak at the same time. "You got demons comin' fer you, boy."

Reluctantly, Jeremiah closed his eyes. He did not want to give his father any provocation to shoot, like being caught in a lie, for instance. He kept his faux prayer short to open his eyes on the gun that continued to rest on the table.

"I ain't gonna ask where ya been. I knows you well 'nough, but I knew you was still livin'. Yer too fuckin' evil ta die easy."

Jeremiah gaped in awe. It was evil calling out another evil; much like that pot kettle saying.

"Yeah, I always knew you wuz ill with Satan in yer head. It was the price yer momma and me paid to God fer gettin' ta keep ya, I s'pose. She never believed it though. Only I knew."

No better segue would come to ask about his mother, but more than that, it was an opportunity to turn the tables on his father, and show who should be considered the bigger monster.

"An' momma? Wha' did ya do ta her?"

"You was always startin' fights an' disobeyin' like any other Dunderhead," he continued with every intention of ignoring the question. "An' you was mean as fuck to animals. I remember you liked torturin' 'em ta see how long they could scream before theyz dead. But the worst of it was when you killed yer momma."

Jeremiah slammed both fists on the table and leaped to his feet. Though the pain in his wounded hand exploded, he was still ready to launch over the table and take his father's throat into his hands for such an accusation, but then Nathaniel pulled his gun up and aimed.

"Sit yer ass down!"

Jeremiah could not stop his bottom lip from trembling, but he did as ordered and put his butt back in his seat. "Yer a goddamn liar! You killed her! You admit it, coward."

"It was the grief you caused her that done it. Whatcha did to those Stebbins an' that Alice girl. You caused her ta finally believe in what I'd been tryin' ta tell 'er fer years."

"I was protectin' myself! I survived like ya taught me ta do."

"Maybe. But there ain't no use fightin' God. There comes a time when every man gots ta give inta His will and stop sacrificing those around him so he can go on."

Now it was clear. More than just age had

matured his pa. The man had found Jesus though there could be no doubt that he continued to falter, as proven by his drink. Most likely, this occurred when he lost his wife, but Jeremiah believed rather firmly that he had not been the root of her demise. He kept his tongue calm and civil as he directed, "You do whatcha gotta."

Nathaniel cocked his pistol; the Colt was ready.

"What I gotta s'gonna depend on you, boy." Jeremiah looked baffled but kept silent. "I need ya ta give me a reason not ta shoot."

Again, the man who turned Christian was weak with his morals. He did not make a good disciple to fight against the evil he proclaimed to have brought into this world. Jeremiah studied his father briefly and witnessed an inner struggle. He stood a chance of survival as long as he told the man what he needed to hear. He chose his next words carefully.

"'Cuz I'm all you got."

Nathaniel uncocked his piece, then instead of placing it back on the table, holstered his weapon. Jeremiah did not express his relief, but gratitude did overwhelm him. He had garnered his father's acceptance, which could very well mean that the largest crisis of his life might have reached an end... finally.

"I wouldn'ta given you the chance a'for. It's a difficult thang ta live with knowin' the shame you brought upon us. We thought you was gonna be special bein' the only offspring ta survive yer momma's birthin'. We never thought you'd be our curse too."

His words were not pleasant to hear, but Jeremiah found them easy enough to ignore to eat in peace.

"Yer welcome ta stay, but ain't nobody can knows yer here. I don't get much visitation no more, so you'll help with chores outside, but no further than that. No church-goin', no huntin', and no goin' ta town."

All would be well between him and his pa, but even more miraculous, Jeremiah felt safer at home now than anywhere else. While hiding amongst the Cherokee, there always had been that lingering threat of capture, especially with those meetings going on at Fort Gibson. Detection seemed the least likely here, but before Jeremiah got too comfortable about living a good life, he needed to inquire about his one cancerous dark spot, "Calvin Hawte still lookin' fer me?"

"Don't think so. Ain't heard from 'im since that day you murdered them Stebbins."

The truth did stab him like a knife followed by a slow twist of the blade. He knew what he and The Soldier had done--each new day was a reminder--but hearing the accusation from someone else made it palpable. Still, there was one remaining Stebbins.

"An' Alex? What 'bout him?"

"He musta buried his dead that same night 'cuz there's a whole mess of graves there now."

"You went there?"

"Long time ago. I had ta see fer myself but ain't

been back since, and neither has he. I imagine he set off ta find you. Ain't seen hide nor hair since. Bes' guess is that if he ain't dead, he's still lookin'.

Jeremiah took another bite of stew. So did his pa. Without knowing what else to say, their conversation had ended as abruptly as that.

Evil, the word carried by his father's voice repeated in Jeremiah's head though he could not decipher whether it truly was Nathaniel's reflection or if The Soldier had returned and was playing mind games.

Was that you?

No response. Dripping sweat, Jeremiah leaned back in his chair and rested on the summation that it had been his pa. With a lantern at his side, he stared at the surrounding darkness. Thick clouds covered the moon's rays and kept all around him as black as the bottom of a skillet while trapping the heat that could be cooked with underneath its layer. It had been too damn hot to sleep. Jeremiah awoke drenched when the air leaped from comfortable to unbearable within hours. His pa did not seem to be bothered, which came as no surprise. The man would be used to these stifling conditions, having never left Missouri in all his life. Oklahoma's heat had been drier and easier to tolerate. It was incredible the effect sixty or so miles could have on the weather.

But Jeremiah did not grumble. Instead, he kicked back and enjoyed the serenity that was now his life. The only thing missing was some pipe tobacco or one of those rolled cigarettes he hadn't puffed on since the war. Or better yet, a cigar. That sounded even better.

Yuma said tornado weather was comin', Jeremiah offered in hopes of coaxing The Soldier into a conversation, but there would be no answer, not when a loud snap came from the tree. Jeremiah lurched to his feet.

The crackling noise had reverberated like thunder. The source was not something as meager as a twig breaking, but as voluminous as a thick branch--far too large to have been fractured by any squirrel, raccoon, or tiny creature. In no time, he recalled that panthers would sometimes wander into these woods.

Instinct had him reaching for his holstered pistol before he remembered its empty chamber. Though Jeremiah still kept his knife on him, the better idea was to retrieve his pa's shotgun. He stepped through the door and found that the Sharp no longer leaned against the wall, but his father's gunbelt did hang on a hook in its place. Jeremiah retrieved the Colt then stepped back out.

The silence had returned. He could not locate a target at which to aim his weapon.

Yer too calm, spoke The Soldier in his father's voice, marking his return. *Yer still a wanted man, ain'cha? Injuns coulda snuck onta yer land. You know better than anyone how crafty them savages is.*

Jeremiah did not jump to The Soldier's conclusions, but he had been given a bone to chew. He called out, "Who's there?" to appease The Soldier's curiosity.

No answer, and no surprise there. The Cherokee, nor any other culprit, would respond.

An' don't you discard Calvin or Alexander's resolve to see you dead.

The sound of rustling snatched his attention. Jeremiah peered up towards the limbs of the large oak tree that stretched over the house. Though he did not expect to see anything in the blackness, he did; a pair of red specks hovering in the branches. The glowing buds reminded him of that cigar he desired earlier, and he thought how curious it was to have his wish granted.

Maybe I'm seein' things?

Maybe not if I'm seein' them too, The Soldier confirmed.

The idea of Calvin and Alexander returning flashed across his mind again. Two men; two cigars, celebrating his forthcoming demise prematurely.

The dots moved, but even more intriguing than their reality was their unified movement, just like a pair of eyes. A panther's eyes would reflect off his lantern light in the dark, but they would not be red. No eyes he had ever seen before glowed red unless they belonged to a demon.

Like a slap to the face, Jeremiah's focus was lugged off the mysterious thing and onto the words of his pa, *You got demons comin' fer you, boy*, which replayed in his head.

Is that you or him talkin'? Jeremiah asked The Soldier.

Ain't me.

You wanna come take over now?

I only fight the enemy I know.

Jeremiah pulled the hammer back and trained the barrel as the specks brightened while they bounced. The leaves that surrounded the dots were disturbed by something much bigger, and Jeremiah glimpsed that something when it leaped and entered the lantern's light.

While he was knocked down and pinned to the porch, the thing remained a blur. As though under a spell, he stared into its two angry eyes. Jeremiah did not know what it was, but the eyes belonged to a creature that he could never have imagined. It was atrocious and covered in a thick fur that reminded him of a bear. But more disturbing than the red eyes and black fur was the snout attached to a familiar face. The disguise made it difficult to put a name to the resemblance, but whatever likeness it embodied came with tremendous aging.

Its mouth opened, flashing a row of spiked teeth. From the murky pit beyond shot a long, worm-like tongue. It dug into his neck and Jeremiah wailed. The onset of pain was astonishing as he felt his blood being pulled out of his veins.

The Soldier screamed for him to shoot the fucking thing, but Jeremiah's hand refused to move.

Whether it was the beast's hypnosis or his own fear, he felt paralyzed. Thankfully, his was not the only weapon nearby.

The explosive bang of a shotgun sounded from behind. The demon's head propelled back, and its tongue yanked out of his neck. The monster took a slug but did not die. Instead, it roared at his pa as though giving a warning it had switched targets.

The creature was swift. It vaulted into the air and had its serrated claws into position as Nathaniel struggled to reload the Sharp. The talons stabbed into him like twenty knives, accompanied by one tongue.

Jeremiah rolled onto his side and witnessed the beast hunched over his pa. When it had fed on him, Jeremiah could hear the horrific sounds it made while feeding. What blood he had left inside him curdled as he listened to it fed on his pa.

No longer crippled by his fear, Jeremiah took aim with his pa's pistol. It misfired. He tried again, and then again. Still nothing. He opened the chamber to discover it empty. Though Jeremiah had little time to cognize, he suspected that the chamber had been empty when aimed at him earlier. His pa never had any intention of killing him, which made the man's inevitable death all the more insufferable.

Nathaniel warbled a cry that should indignify any man. Jeremiah would have bet his bottom dollar that his pa had held out as long as he could before releasing the call of torture. Having experienced the same suffering, he could not think any less of the man.

The voice of his father told him to run. Whether it came from the man directly or from The Soldier, Jeremiah couldn't say, but he did not hesitate to obey. His pa had become the distraction he needed to race around the house and unwrap Wahya's reins from the hobble.

In the time it took him to mount the unsettled mare, a charging gallop replaced the disturbance of Nathaniel's struggle. The thing was coming. Jeremiah dug his heels into Wahya's sides, and the horse sped into the total darkness.

Yuma and his people had appreciated the moon for all its gifts, which Jeremiah never quite understood until this moment. Dashing through an unseen wilderness of trees, brush, and other obstacles at high speed terrified him nearly as much as the thing he hoped to have lost. A bright spot in the darkness was that the creature would have just as difficult of a time finding him... or so he thought.

Jeremiah peered over his shoulder and spotted the beady eyes rebounding when a barrage of twigs scraped at his arms and pulled his hair. He faced forward as Wahya dodged a large trunk. Her steering avoided her collision with the tree, but she failed to circumnavigate far enough for her rider. Jeremiah's leg brushed against the trunk and ripped open his pants. The bark had captured some skin, but luckily, it was nothing more than a scrape... this time.

Wahya whinnied and bolted forward with a

push of speed. Jeremiah was thrust back by the surge, knocking his shoulders against the creature's head. It had bounded onto the mare and dug its nails into her rump. Though panicked, he did not soon forget about the weapon that launched from its mouth and now expected it to pierce his spine at any second.

Jeremiah unsheathed his knife in a flash and swung it back. He stabbed the blade into the demon's side. Though he had hoped the creature would release its grip, it released a cry instead. He had done nothing but anger it even more.

It was now the beast's turn. Its mouth opened wide.

Quickly, Jeremiah yanked the steel out of its torso then swiped it across the creature's throat. The demon's neck split open, covering Jeremiah's face in blood. The thing retracted its claws from Wahya's hide, and then tumbled to the ground.

The night swallowed the beast. Jeremiah continued to watch for the red eyes' return, no longer minding the small branches that scratched at him. Once a handful of moments had passed, he silently rejoiced that he had done it; he had killed the demon.

If a bullet can't put it down, then no knife can, either.

It never failed. Jeremiah hated The Soldier for constantly interrupting his moments of success. The problem was, though; The Soldier proved correct when a screeching howl trembled through the night in the following moment.

It ain't never gonna let up 'til we kill it.

The Soldier made it sound easy, but Jeremiah recognized the challenge. Shooting it in the head and slicing its throat had only pissed the thing off more. And without knowing what type of demon he was fighting, he did not know what it would take to put it down.

Jeremiah slapped the reins. Wahya wanted to give in to her wounds, but he wouldn't allow that. She was not the only one who ached. Fatigue and chills overtook him when the adrenaline from immediate peril began to wane. The air had not cooled--it was still hot as hell--but he no longer sweltered in the mugginess. To any person who still possessed a body full of blood, it would be miserable, but to Jeremiah, his sweat felt as cold as ice. He needed food, rest, and shelter, but most importantly, he needed time to allow his body to regenerate what it had lost.

An' where do you think you'll be able to do any of that? The Soldier prodded. *Ain't no place for us to go.*

Ignoring him would have been easier if Jeremiah did not have the difficult decision of electing a direction to take once Wahya reached the main road. The Soldier was right; with no place he could go, left or right did not make any difference.

There's always San Francisco. You heard some nice stories about that place from some of the men in yer platoon, didncha?

Whichever choice they made, it would entail

starting over and what better place than hundreds of miles to the west, which might be to the left, he reckoned. It was too dark to make out specifics.

After turning, both he and The Soldier knew that part of their trail would lead them back to the Cherokee Nation, but should he make it to the other side, he would join the masses in a renewed life in California.

The woods behind him were disturbed, no doubt by the adamant beast. He kicked Wahya's flanks as hard as he could when a lightning strike illuminated the dirt road briefly. The distant thunder followed after seconds of silence had passed. The rain would not be far behind, and hopefully, that would be all. A good soaking would chill him to his core, but an intense storm might also wash away the scent of his trail. All the better now that Jeremiah had seen his position on the road during the quick flash. He was not too far from a place he knew where he could wait out the storm. Wahya just needed to get him there, and fast.

More lightning struck.

CHAPTER XV

The downpour arrived sooner than Jeremiah had expected, and stronger. Though the wind blowing against his drenched body was chilling, the water had been refreshing to drink. Dehydration had consumed him soon after he lost so much blood to the demon. The idea that he could drink a river was an exaggeration, but Jeremiah found his thirst unquenchable after gulping what his mouth could catch during the heavier torrents. He needed a cup desperately.

The thunderstorm's intensity had not been his only underestimation. Under normal circumstances, the scrape across his leg would have been minor, but as he fought unconsciousness, Jeremiah feared losing even a single drop more of his blood. Thankfully, he had as much going for him as he had against him. Not only was he approaching the place where he might find bandages and other necessities, but the demon-like dog had yet to catch up. With any amount of luck, an enormous storm could keep the monstrosity off his trail.

Wahya had lost steam a few hundred yards back. Her pacing dwindled to a stroll as she carried Jeremiah up the walk to the Stebbins's farmhouse. He had no fear of running into Alexander here, nor anyone else. His pa had stated that its only owner hadn't been seen nor heard from since that legendary day. Though he made no mention of the home being reoccupied, Jeremiah suspected nobody would want to live in a house that had beheld such horror.

And he assumed correctly. The farm was as desolate as a graveyard. The repeated lightning helped him locate the front porch in the, otherwise, blackness. Once Wahya was tied to the railing, Jeremiah used caution setting his foot down on the first of two steps. In addition to being difficult to see between flashes, the neglected structure would have weakened by time, weather, and termites. Stepping through a diseased piece of flooring would be probable, and could lead to another injury that his body couldn't afford to gain.

The front door screeched on its hinges. Jeremiah accompanied a torrent wind as it pushed inside the house. Glass crunched beneath his weight; remnants of the shattered bay window that lay on the floor. He paused inside the keeping room as the pounding rain and dense echo of waterfalls were surprising, but not as unexpected as the foreboding that filled the air in the room. In recent years, Jeremiah learned to believe in such things as spirits--desperately needing the gift of the snake to heal his fresh wounds--but there were other spirits, people's souls, with which he did not wish to cross paths. And if ever a place deserved to be haunted, it would be the Stebbins farmhouse.

Jeremiah waited for the next succession of flashes before venturing further. Rain water dripped between the small gaps in the roof while it gushed through the larger holes. He cupped his hands underneath the nearest flow to momentarily satisfy his stubborn thirst. When drinking, a notion of fixing this shambles came to mind. He saw himself living in this home he once envied, but that idea was quickly washed away through the cracks of the floor along with the rain. The work needed for repairs was just too much for a single man. Then, to add insult, The Soldier reminded that they would not have the fresh start they desired should they continue to live in Missouri or anywhere near.

Bes' get a move on.

The Soldier referred to finding the items they had made a mental list of while riding through the storm. Various objects comprised of what would be required for the long trek west. First and foremost were medical supplies. When Betsy had dressed his bullet wound, she did so in the bath as to keep his blood off her floor. He did not witness where the needle, thread, and bandaging had come from but suspected they were somewhere on the first floor as most household accidents occurred outside.

Check near the doors, offered The Soldier as though he were talking to a dunce.

During the lightning breaks, Jeremiah used his memories of the room as his guide. He did not recall any cabinets or drawers towards the front of the house, but remembered a large built-in off the side of the dining area near the rear door.

He took a step, kicking something metal. Jeremiah had a hunch that it was the sickle JoJo used in attempting to kill him. He did not need to wait long for the next sequence of flashes to prove that he was correct. The blade's rusted and dull edge would be an exceptional weapon once again after whetted. Jeremiah recalled how comfortable the swing had felt when he swung it into Bonnie's neck. The weapon would make an excellent start to the arsenal he would gather.

He hooked the edge to his belt then continued into the back room. Jeremiah brushed his hands against the wood cabinet that bowed outward from years of dousing. He gripped a knob then pulled; the drawer was stuck. After two more ineffective tugs, he stopped. Mustering the strength to yank harder than a seven-year-old girl was difficult in his condition, but The Soldier refused defeat and cursed, *Use yer goddamn knife, you fuckin' dunderhead.* Though the idea had been obvious, Jeremiah was having a terrible time thinking clearly. Being lethargic while disoriented from the strobing effects of the storm made him as dizzy as a goose.

He dug the blade into the crack between a

drawer and the casing and then twisted until the wet, rotted wood crumpled enough to shimmy the drawer loose. Before he could catch a glimpse of the material inside, Jeremiah knew it was a cloth and napkins for the table. Though they felt nice, the material was useless for the moment, but later, the larger piece would make a nice blanket when sleeping outdoors. Jeremiah tossed the tablecloth over his shoulder.

He pried open two more drawers, having no success before exhaustion overcame his motivation. The silverware from the first drawer would be of value, and money was an item on his checklist, but for the time being, he let it be. Silver was too heavy to drag in his current condition.

Matchsticks had been in the second drawer, drenched and unusable.

Jus' tie off yer leg with that tablecloth an' be done with it already, The Soldier griped, anxious to get moving.

Being that there were no other options available, Jeremiah rolled the covering into a tourniquet. Tying off his leg took more strength than what he had left, but The Soldier begrudgingly lent his muscle as well.

I gotta rest.

You damn fool! You rest now, you could be resting forever.

Then a drink, unless you got summin' against that too? Jeremiah sarcastically retaliated though not giving a shit if The Soldier contested or not. The urge to drink from a water barrel was greater than the desire for his next breath.

Jeremiah remembered seeing a row of decorative teacups on the cabinet that the lightning had revealed. He reached for where he was sure one would be and wrapped his rough hand around the flowered porcelain. From the back door, he captured the stream of water that ran off the roof. Jeremiah drank and drank some more until he no longer felt as sluggish, though he knew the rejuvenation would be temporary.

You'll need food now.

Though he had no inkling why, Jeremiah suspected The Soldier was goading him to check the kitchen. He did not believe it was for sustenance because any food would have either fed the local wildlife or been too old to eat.

There are other things, Dunderhead. Knives, spices, cooking irons. All would come in handy during our travels.

True enough.

Jeremiah sloshed through the muck and the pounding rain to the detached building. He stepped through the doorless entry and stood inside the structure that had withstood the test of time much better than the main quarters. Built to be flame resistant, the stone walls and slate roof helped keep the interior bone dry.

Again, lightning pierced the night, followed by an earth-shattering rumble. In that abrupt moment, Jeremiah's previous assumptions were confirmed. The kitchen had been ransacked. Burlap sacks lay torn, drained of their contents. The cooler doors hung wide open with the evidence of broken jars and dishes at the foot, but before darkness settled back into place, he caught sight of a lamp that sat on the counter, undisturbed.

A memory awoke of light beaming through the kitchen's orifices when last here. The matches would be somewhere near, and unlike the sticks inside the house, these would have remained dry. Patting the counter, Jeremiah found them in no time. He struck a flame and discovered a large ale barrel, untouched by time or wildlife. An overwhelming pungency of lime assaulted his sense once he removed the lid. He dipped his hand into the water then pulled out two eggs. They were two-years-old at best, but the solution of lime water would have kept them from rotting. He broke the tip and drank its slimy filling. Yep, still fresh, though citrusy, and could use a bit of spice.

Jeremiah rummaged through cupboards and soon discovered a shelf of airtight tin canisters. Inside the first was salt. The next was thyme, and then paprika, cayenne, and cumin. Thrilled by his findings, Jeremiah cracked the top of his other egg then sprinkled a pinch of salt and cayenne before he sucked it down.

By his own doing, Jeremiah's skin crawled. Though his feeding sounded similar to the demon's, the slurping was not what had reminded him of the beast. The pounding rain on the slate roof had masked the creature's arrival and, once again, he could feel the thing eating through the elongated leech attached to his neck.

Jeremiah twisted to the window where it perched and bore its beady eyes into him as intensely as its tongue, but unlike its previous attack, Jeremiah did not hesitate this time. He reached for his sickle against his hip and swung. The might behind his strike would have sliced the tongue in two had the blade been sharp, but the attack was not in vain. The curvature of the steel hooked around the appendage and yanked it from his neck.

The beast reeled in its tongue then bounded inside. Jeremiah gripped his knife when the thing knocked him against the counter. The blade fell to the floor, leaving no chance of slicing its throat a second time.

Face-to-face, once again, Jeremiah twisted his head, hoping the slimy projectile would miss entering his eye, when his focus rested on the set of spice canisters he pulled from the cabinet. He did not think of it himself, but when The Soldier shouted, *Pepper*, no more explanation was needed.

He reached for the tin of cayenne then closed his eyes and held his breath before flinging a wave of the spicy powder into the creature's face. After a short delay, the thing released its hold to shriek and flail throughout the confined enclosure. Keeping his eyes closed, Jeremiah slid into the protection beneath the counter and crawled towards the exit while the monster ripped through the kitchen. Its agony sounded severe. He had succeeded in getting away, but at the cost of pissing it off even more.

Jeremiah crawled outside and into the mud before opening his eyes or taking a breath. He glanced back into the kitchen for a mere second only to be continually surprised by the thing. Not only could it bounce from wall to wall to ceiling, but the beast had a ripple of spikes that stretched down its back to a tail that he had not yet observed. No doubt, this beast was like nothing he had ever seen or heard before. There was something special about this one-of-kind creature, and judging by its tenacity for him, Jeremiah had a feeling it wasn't acting of its own cognizance, but serving a master.

You can take over now. I gives you permission.

I do not require yer permission, Dunderhead. An' I told ya already, I only fights the enemy I know.

Jeremiah climbed to his feet, realizing that if he were to have a chance to survive, the time for being awestruck needed to end.

He tripped while racing around the outskirts of the house then fell face first in the mud. Pushing himself back to his feet, Jeremiah pressed down on the thing that had tripped him, feeling very much like a wooden cross. Suddenly, he was not in as much of a hurry. Though he suspected where he stood, he needed confirmation. The storm did not make him wait long before revealing the grave marker he held in his hand, and eight more just like it sticking out of the ground in a row. Nine graves.

Jeremiah dropped the cross then backed away.

Murderer, he heard muttered.

Jeremiah paused in momentary petrification before he resumed his flight more hastily than before. He did not know which terrified him more: the beast or the whisper that did not sound like The Soldier, but Martin. Either way, his only defense was to outrun them both.

What whisper? The Soldier inquired, not hearing the voice

Jeremiah did not understand how that was possible when it had been so prominent in his ear, but if The Soldier truly did not hear the harsh allegation uttered then perhaps it was all in his head, but his head alone. It would not be the first time his mind had deceived him. Jeremiah recounted the dead soldier in the clearing that often twitched and moved as corpses never should; not to mention The Soldier's existence and how he's been hauled up inside his head indefinitely. Or, he supposed, it could be that other thing he had thought about moments ago.

You think yer hearin' ghosts, laughed The Soldier uproariously. *You think yer hearin' Martin's spirit now?*

Ghost or not, I'd rather have him stuck in my head over you, blared Jeremiah as he rounded the corner and came upon Wahya's corpse. He looked away from the dead mare then turned towards the road. Jeremiah could think of no other alternative.

The Soldier blared, *Runnin's gonna get us killed!*

Stop yer cowardice and be a man. It's jus' another goddamn animal for fuck's sake. Take the upper hand, you snatchhat.

Usin' what? You got a weapon I don't know about?

You saw what that pepper did ta it. Though the idea had worked at that moment, the incapacitation would be fleeting. *But its got weaknesses, stupid. That's what I'm sayin'. It ain't unstoppable.*

The Soldier's boorish point was heard, and Jeremiah could not help but agree. The cayenne pepper had proven more efficient than he had anticipated, but he now needed a new plan, and fast, before the beast recovered its senses. However, though it did not improve his situation any, Jeremiah did find some relief in knowing that the creature was more animal than demon, and would no longer think of it as immortal.

The thought of going anywhere near that graveyard again was unbearable, but there were items left in the kitchen that he needed. Exactly what he would use them for, he did not yet know as he still hadn't formed a plan. He entered the house then raced towards the back, where the creature had been searching for him.

Jeremiah nearly collided into the beast in the dining area. No thanks to the lightning, the glow of its red eyes was what had alerted its presence. Luckily, the monster remained oblivious to their proximity--though the next flash would fix that.

Jeremiah held his breath as the storm decided it would expose him at that exact moment. He gazed into its old man face inches away from his, but the thing did not attack. Instead, it sniffed the air hard and heavy, trying to capture a scent; his scent. The effects of the cayenne were still at work.

The eyes bounced and jerked in the dark. The thing was attempting to shake off the pepper's mischievous ailments. Distracted, Jeremiah saw his opportunity to escape through the front doorway. Upon taking his first step backward, the floor creaked. The creature was alerted.

You dumb cuss! The pepper done nuttin' to its hearin'.

Every urge begged Jeremiah to flee, but he knew not to disobey The Soldier. The better idea of finding one of Werner's shotguns came to him instead.

Have you lost your senses? Did you inhale that pepper too? Guns don't do nuttin' to it but maybe slow it down but a second.

Precisely, Jeremiah argued back. *A second here and there could make the difference between life and death. Now who's the Dunderhead?*

Fighting back felt good, but even better when it had shut The Soldier up.

Though he did not know where, precisely, Werner would have kept his weapons, it was with some certainty that they would be in the den just beyond the staircase.

An' if they ain't? You think this thing's jus' gonna let you search every room?

I gots a better chance with it not seein' or smellin' me.

Though the sound of the cascading water that seeped through the cracks in the floor was resounding, Jeremiah did not doubt that the thing could hone its hearing as it could its smell. Gradually, he knelt with the quiet stamina of a cheetah, and then wiped his hand above the planks, in search of anything that he could toss to distract the beast's attention. He did feel something but feared it might be too small. Not yet able to peer at the object, it felt like a pebble, light-weight and solid. It then struck Jeremiah that what he held was one of the boy's knucklebone game pieces.

He threw hard and straight towards the china cabinet, hoping the bone would shatter the porcelain dishware to create a loud disruption... which it did.

The eyes darted towards the source, then the blinded creature collided into the cupboard and generated an explosion of crashing dishes.

Jeremiah hurried and made a mad dash for the den, forgetting the chair he once sat in while watching Elias and Silas play their game. He tripped and landed on top of the weathered furniture piece, shattering it.

The Soldier cursed him again for acting like a dunderhead; though he immediately shut the hell up when the bounding monster soared over his head not a second later. Jeremiah's ineptitude had saved him from being tackled by claws and teeth.

The creature landed on the adjacent wall.

Jeremiah panicked. The thing hovered above

and could drop on him at any second. He moved to escape its range but was stalled by the chair's fragments that captured and pinned him. Somehow, the bars of the back had entangled his leg. However, the creature didn't take the plunge; its eyes hung in mid-air above his head. Jeremiah's plight with the entrapment halted until lightning exposed the monster clinging to the wall like a giant lizard.

A fresh fear surged through him. The Soldier could not give the order to keep quiet fast enough before Jeremiah fought with the repressive chair. The creature spun around, lured by the sounds of struggle, and then froze in an upside down position. He had provided the beast a location to lock onto when its mouth stretched open.

Having the seat of the chair readily in his clutch, Jeremiah pulled it up to shield his chest. The needle-like appendage stretched the full length then knocked on the wood. Aggravated by the barrier, the beast unlatched from the wall and dove.

Jeremiah fell two feet beneath the house before he even realized that the corroded floor had collapsed under their combined weight. He splashed down into a lake of rainwater that had accumulated in the crawlspace.

The beast landed on the wooden seat that safeguarded his torso from its claws. Sometime between the pounce and the brief descent, all the air had been knocked out of him before the thing's bulk submerged him underwater.

In his desperation for air, Jeremiah lifted his

head to the surface and then banged his crown against the underside of the floor. There had been less than a foot of space between the water level and the ceiling. He breathed what he could before dropping his head back down.

Mother Nature struck again. Jeremiah could just make out the creature's feet standing on the chair seat against his chest during the flashes of light. Like a rung on a ladder, the beast was only a step below floor level. Without the aid of its other senses, he reckoned that the thing was confused as to his whereabouts, and might have stayed confused if Jeremiah hadn't choked. There was nothing he could do to stop his lungs from taking in water.

It attacked, but the flooring blocked its reach. The hole they created together had been made wide enough for Jeremiah's body and no more. Instead of biting into his head, the thing's teeth sank into the floor when it bent over, but the decayed wood crumbled like old cheese. The beast would have its prize claimed in seconds.

Jeremiah nudged the chair seat, testing how it would slide. The moment he slipped his wooden armor out from between them, the creature would either leap up top to find its balance or fall and sink the claws of all four feet into his chest. Had he been able to consider a better plan, he would, but he ran out of time when he ran out of air.

He jerked his shield and rolled. All but one of the creature's feet clung to the house's floor while the fourth dropped into the water, stabbing the muddy ground. The thing then crawled to the surface, but The Soldier would not allow Jeremiah the illusion that they were anywhere near safety.

Any halfwit should know why there's so much water built up down here.

Jeremiah did know. With nowhere for the water to escape, the walls of the crawlspace were sealed tight. The Stebbins had money enough to afford a brick foundation. When helping his pa, Lafayette, and the others build this house, they had laid the home's ground molding. There were, however, two small doors for entering when needed--or airing the heat trapped underneath during the hottest months--but in the rising water where the lightning flashes couldn't reach, Jeremiah became lost.

His coughs continued and would not let up anytime soon. The creature had roared a frustrated cry before chunks of the flooring began stripping away at an alarming rate, like being taken to by an ax. The thing was plowing through.

The house's undercarriage was not too dissimilar to the area beneath his old home, specifically its tight fit. Jeremiah half swam; half crawled, without knowing where he headed, though he prayed he might come across one of those two doors. However, with no horse to ride him out of here, he had no plan once he climbed out of the crawlspace. His current strategy only consisted of clambering for his life.

As though the house were caving in, floor pieces fell on top of him. His wild splashes and sporadic coughing left a trail that the beast had no difficulty following. More than once, it had torn through the floor and reached down like a bear fishing through the ice, snagging him each time but unable to latch on.

Hysteria continued to tempt Jeremiah into its consoling embrace with each dead end he reached. Difficult as it was to stay mindful, he exercised his resolute until a loud splash from behind startled him. Jeremiah pivoted in the pitch black and did the one thing he could in confined imprisonment... wait.

Seconds felt like minutes. It was as though the storm had stalled on purpose, not wanting to reveal the source of the exploding water. However, when the lightning did come, there would be more than enough holes in the floor to allow its flash entry. Any moment now.

But as Jeremiah continued to wait, he no longer needed the illumination to reveal what he already knew. Whether it jumped or fell, the creature was below the house with him. In its search, the glow of its eyes revealed what the lightning refused.

He coughed again; he had no choice.

The light from the storm shot through the gaps in the floor, revealing the creature as it dove into the water. Keeping under, the spikes on its back protruded above the surface. They scraped the underside of the floor as the thing writhed towards him as an advancing shark would. The fucking thing knew how to swim, too.

Jeremiah dove out of its course and then clambered to keep a safe distance, but the beast was not only faster on land, but in the water as well. He rolled onto his back then dug his feet into the cracks of the floor and pushed. Jeremiah propelled himself from the creature and then repeated the thrust again quickly. It was working. Though The Soldier did not say the words directly, Jeremiah still heard him prod, *It's about time you smartened up.*

Jeremiah found his escape and slinked up into the keeping room, but the creature was still faster, closing some of the gap Jeremiah had put between them. It would follow him to the surface unless something could be done.

Cough again! Over there!

With water still flooding his lungs, Jeremiah leaped towards the dining room, hacking and wheezing with ease. It worked. The Soldier's quick thinking had lured the thing away from any existing hole. The beast would drown with any luck; that was if it could be drowned.

Yer gonna try and fool yerself inta thinkin' that it can't dig upward while layin' on its back, aincha? This ain't the end, Dunderhead.

Very well, but Jeremiah hoped, at the very least, that it would not find its way out until he had reached a safe distance. In the meantime, he and The Soldier could strategize how they would achieve the upper hand in this war.

Jeremiah stepped out the rear door and back into the incessant storm. Knowing that the barn was a few hundred feet away, he headed towards it.

We don't need nuttin' from there.

There's weapons and such like you said, Jeremiah pointed out.

That was when we had a hoss to help carry them. Use yer noggin'! You can't be carryin' nuttin' weighin' you down.

Every part of Jeremiah wanted to be disobedient. When he steered away from the barn and headed towards the woods, it was while expending a great deal of willpower, though Jeremiah only covered a few hundred yards of ground before the blackness turned even blacker, and he collapsed. It did not matter which direction he chose; he couldn't outrun exhaustion.

CHAPTER XVI

The night had been brutal. Shelter would have been a welcome relief if available, but Calvin and Alexander endured until morning by staying under a plush linden tree until the storm passed. In most of that time spent, Calvin stared at Alexander in silence, knowing that he did not travel with the same kid as before. He had sensed something very different about the boy back on the farm but not realizing how different until they conversed, if only to pass the time. Though at first, getting the boy to talk was like digging out a nail without a head.

Originally, Calvin's only interest had been a mature conversation with somebody not prepubescent. Though Henry was beyond his years, there was only so much life experience a seven-year-old who had never been outside of Kansas could contribute to a discussion. However, the more Alexander insisted on keeping silent about his time spent in search of Jeremiah, the more Calvin was desperate to know the story. It took two days for the boy to let his guard down; or at least some of it. Even now, Calvin was unsure whether it was his tiresome badgering or the loneliness of silence that broke the kid's will, but his stories ended up being excellent material to pass the time on the last day of their three-day jaunt.

"I knew Jeremiah never gone off injun reservation," Alexander had expressed, which had been the start of his narration. "I started combing other parts, but I knew I was only wastin' time. I could feel it. You know that feelin'?"

"I do." Calvin had stated simply, not wanting the boy to stop his telling for too many questions. Alexander must have picked up on his subtlety because he continued right then.

"It's a different feelin' when you know yer huntin' fer prey an' when yer not. I tried to tell 'em boys at Gibson, but they wouldn't listen without you wit me. Though maybe it wasn't only you. I s'pose not many would hear the rants of a disgraced one-eyed derelict set on revenge. The first time I set foot back on that Union fort, they had received the official news of Jeremiah's rampage. I don't know how it was told to them, but it was told wrong. None but Phillips believed that I fought at yer side because it was only a single man we was fightin'. Bein' the sole survivin' Stebbins made me either incompetent or a coward in the eyes of others. But thank God you said summin' to that Colonel 'cuz he woulda never let me go otherwise."

"How'd you get back there?"

"What? The first or second time?"

"Start at the beginning."

"It was some months after you threw me off yer land…" At that moment, Calvin remembered having lost track of the conversation, distracted by his intention to correct the boy. Alexander seemed to forget that he had offered up his barn that night. Calvin had a desire to correct that distortion but then thought it better to keep his peace. He had rathered listen to the story than initiate a quarrel, curious to discover just how much of the boy's tales would be fabricated. "…then I come across the Santa Fe Trail an' headed west, 'cuz I figure if he was gonna leave Oklahoma, he was gonna go through. So I kept on 'til I almos' come to Colorado. Thaz where I stopped; in the panhandle. I knew there wun't no point goin' further 'cuz Jeremiah got injured real good. I remembered the blood. He'd be slow movin' so I waited. If I was righ' an' he was tryin' to head west, there wun't no other trail he coulda traveled. Land's too dangerous not be on the trail."

Calvin had been impressed with Alexander up until that moment. The boy had retained some of his teachings about tracking, which made Calvin proud, but when it came to inquiring about Jeremiah to the trail's passers-by in the panhandle, which Calvin also knew the nickname to be 'No Man's Land,' the kid did not demonstrate the needed tact.

By his own implication, Alexander had grown impatient with the failure of each new day.

Positioned in a spot he claimed, the kid flagged down caravans to warn them of Jeremiah Whiting and tell of his crimes with all the gory details. He had done this in hopes to be given permission to search their wagons and coaches for the man who might have secretly stowed away. At first, the travelers were said to be accommodating, but as caravan after caravan passed with no Jeremiah, the travelers became less so. Alexander claimed not to know why, but Calvin had a theory. Repeating a story time and time again would be grueling for any man, especially when telling a tale of such personal morbidity. With each retelling, his briefings would have shortened, and the people would not have understood his plot after receiving his frustrated and rushed version. If Calvin's notion was correct, then it could explain why Alexander had acted hesitantly about recapping his accounts, possibly tired of doing so, or perhaps it was shame for the choices he made thereafter. Alexander had ventured further, explaining that those who did not succumb to his request would then be motivated to change their minds with the threat of his firearms, and when those travelers were families, he did not care much about putting fear in the young ones. He then went on to brag about how he robbed those who gave him trouble, taking a few days' supply of food and water. Though Calvin kept his peace, he could not have been more disappointed in the boy. That was not how any man who sought to right a wrong should act; however, it did confirm that the boy's stories were not fabricated.

"Then there was this dry spell," Alexander had continued, "when no wagons came through, and I run out of supplies. Dehydration and starvation nearly took me, but then a hand reached out. I thought it was God liftin' me to Him, but it was the leader of these good Samaritans, Kit Carson. You know... from them dime store novels? The one and only!"

Though he never had read one, Calvin knew them to be grandiose adventures that would excite the ordinary reader. They were no Moby-Dick.

"He saved my life. Kit Carson is a true frontier hero an' I don't care what some say 'bout his stories, I says they's all true. Anyway, there was a lot them volunteers."

"Volunteers?"

"Dogooder's, 'bout two hundred of 'em. They was on a mission to raise up a new fort right off the trail, aimin' to keep any passin' wagon trains safe from Comanche and Kiowa. Anyway, I felt strong 'nough ta go back out in jus' a couple o' days, but when I almost died, my hoss did. They caught me tryin' to take one of theirs."

Calvin had asked, "That's what you were in jail for? That ain't the same as, *being where you wasn't supposed to be.*"

"That wun't why I was in jail. Sure, they held me prisoner after capture, but they didn't have no jail built yet, so they put me ta work instead, which was fine. I took my medicine like a man 'cuz of feelin' bad and all fer tryin' to steal from them after they saved me from my maker. I don't know what I was thankin'."

"You was thankin' 'bout Jeremiah."

"Yeah. I wanted 'im real bad. In the three months they kept me there, he was all I kept thinkin' 'bout each day, each hour. Even when I slept, I dreamed nightmares of 'im. It was hard, but they said I could go once it was all built. Well, actually, they'd run out of supplies. Didn't bring enough, I guess, 'cuz there were no barracks. We dug trenches ta sleep in, instead, an' then covered 'em up. Anyway, they sent me off with this hoss here and supplies fer my efforts, an' I headed East."

"Why East?"

"'Cuz one thing I knew fer sure while bein' there workin' beside the trail was that Jeremiah never passed by."

"Maybe he headed fer Mexico."

"Nah. Jeremiah was raised in the Ozarks with us. He wouldn't know how ta survive a big desert."

"He coulda gone north."

"In the land of the billy's!? He ain't suicidal. Nah. If anythin' he woulda head back east, but he wun't there either. He found 'imself a good home with the injuns. I knew I had been right 'bout that."

And he had been. At that moment, Calvin's favorable impression of the boy had returned some.

"You still ain't said how you ended up back at Gibson?"

"It wun't long after. I cut through the middle of

the state instead of keepin' on the trail. I thought it was a good idea at the time, but then them Cheyenne and Arapaho spotted me. I runned fer my life every day until Phillips' scouts found me. That was the first time. He let me go after a couple of weeks but gave me an earful a'fore doin' so. Told me I was goin' home an' never ta come back. An' he would make sure I did with an escort, like the one we had to yer home, an' jus' like that escort, they lef' me at the state line. But as soon as I stepped over, I stepped right back across once the coast was clear. What home did I have ta go to? There wun't nuttin' waitin' fer me in Missouri.

"Then what?"

"I spent 'bout six months or so goin' from village to village, but only to them civvy tribes. I didn't want no war, jus' information, but I guess my presence riled a few of them an' them bush niggers whet an' told on me to the Colonel."

"That was yer second time?" Alexander had nodded his affirmation. "Did ya learn anythin' from those natives?"

"Nah. They either didn't know, or they wasn't tellin' even though they blabbed about me quick enough."

From there, Calvin had to listen to about an hour of how unjust it was that the natives--though he had used other expletive, derogatory terms--could hide a fugitive but treat the man looking for him like the criminal. Next, he went on a tyrannical rampage about how Philips had mistreated him, though not while in lock up, but upon his release. The boy must have forgotten that while eating breakfast back the farm, he had already expressed his displeasure about how the Colonel never apologized or admitted guilt to holding him prisoner for the good part of a year; going on and on about how the man excused his actions by placating, "It was fer yer own good." Being ratted out by the injuns, the boy had understood, but being treated unfairly and dispassionately by his own kind twisted something inside him. Though it was the world they lived in, Calvin empathized; however, Alexander did make it difficult as he went on and on, and he would have continued going in circles if the monstrous storm hadn't cut him off. Calvin silently thanked the spirits for their compassion.

Come morning, they rode. In the hour, or so, since departing the tree, Alexander resumed his previous stupor. Not until they reached a familiar road did he speak once again, commanding, "We're goin' ta my home first," with the authority of law.

Whatever reason Alexander had to venture back to his house, he kept a mystery. Unfortunately, Calvin had every confidence that what they would find there would be nothing but more misery. Either Alexander was self-destructive, or he had some other motive, such as retrieving a keepsake or a favorite weapon. Calvin hoped for the latter and kept his mouth shut.

Alexander took the lead.

Nothing could have prepared the boy for the shock of seeing his home in its dilapidated condition. The wild vegetation dominated the fields, as well as all the structures. Weeds climbed the walls of the house, kitchen, and barn as though reclaiming their land. The outhouse was barely distinguishable as such. Just a couple of years of harsh weather without upkeep made the property look as though a decade had passed. Even Calvin could not deny his astonishment of the Stebbins' ranch.

Alexander continued to stroll towards the front door. The scraping of gravel from the hooves of their rides echoed in the loud silence. Calvin glanced up for signs of birds, missing their morning calls, but as the land, the sky had been abandoned too.

"You ever heard it this quiet here?"

Alexander's intense focus on the dead horse tied to the porch could not be pulled away. The saddleless corpse appeared to have been dead for months, by the way the thinned creature's flesh draped over its bones.

"You know that hoss?"

Alexander replied this time, but silently with a shake of his head. He studied the carcass a moment longer before he dismounted and darted into the house, as though expecting to discover the animal's owner still inside.

The boy was acting like his old self again when he did not use caution. Calvin yelled, "Hold up!" but his warning fell on deaf ears. Though he thought it a bad idea, he followed Alexander anyway.

Both stopped just inside the door to gape at the substantial holes in the floor. Calvin noted that the shredded pieces of wood encircling the openings were fresh and had been scratched out by something with large claws.

"What did ya come back for?"

"I come ta jus' see," snapped Alexander, "an' pay my respects to my family if you don't mind?" He peered through the holes to observe the rest of the damage.

"What's around here that would cause something like this? Panthers?"

"Looks like. It's what got that horse probably, but it don't seem like it got Jeremiah."

"Jeremiah?!" Calvin spouted, amazed.

"Well, sure. That's who was in here," stated Alexander as though it were as obvious as the hair on his head.

Calvin did not doubt that what they had found left plenty of room for suspicion, but how the boy could settle on his presumption with such confidence intrigued him. "And how do you figure?"

The one-time apprentice glared at his former master like a mindless oaf. "Whatchu mean, how do I figure? It's plain, ain't it? You tellin' me ya can't see it?"

If the evidence pointing to Jeremiah's presence

were there, Calvin, indeed, did not.

"He's only been on the run but a couple of days, an' that hoss ain't got no saddle on it. I betcha bottom dollar it's an injun hoss. How else you think an injun hoss could come around these parts?"

Alexander's point was valid. The typical white man rarely rode without a saddle whereas the natives had been more adept at riding bareback. Still, that was not enough to prove Jeremiah's return.

"Maybe somebody came upon the animal like we did and took the saddle?"

"When? Last night? It ain't been dead in the mud but a day."

Calvin truly did not know what to make of the preposterous account. "You think that corpse is fresh with its insides gone dry like that?"

"Well, I don't know what could explain that, but its fur still shines. No animal could lay exposed like that at this time o' year for days on end an' maintain such a healthy coat."

Calvin had been as dumb as a stick. Not only did the wisdom behind Alexander's rationale catch him off guard, but so did his own unexpected naivety. As much as he would have liked to have disputed Alexander's findings, he would have looked the fool in doing so.

From the moment he strolled off his land, Calvin never did feel the same as before. His thrill of the hunt had been displaced, and for good reason; Alexander had goaded him back into a life to which he had no intention of ever returning. Living on the farm with Henry was all that he had needed. Though, admittedly, the transition had not come easy, but he eventually learned to stop dissecting what he saw as evidence and learned to not be suspicious of everything. However, therein lay the problem. What Calvin originally had thought was nothing more than a lack of determination became a lack of exercise. Foolishly, he had expected to pick up where he left off years prior without practice, but reconnoitering required grit and heart, of which he did not possess like before. But the man who stood before him, he had the heart and fortitude of more than one tracker.

"An' these holes," Alexander held up a piece of the shaving to show its fresh cut, "they's new too. You tell me the timing don't add up good."

The timing did add up perfectly. Alexander was most likely correct in his assumption, but his notion did have a hole, and sometimes all it took was one to disprove a theory.

"So whatchu think dried up that horse so quick?"

Calvin reclaimed a portion of sovereignty by sideswiping Alexander and stumping the boy. It came as a comfort to know that he had not lost all of his powers of deduction. With rekindled confidence, he pushed, "And if Jeremiah was the one here, where would he have gone off?"

"Maybe he's dead."

"I don't see no blood or no corpse."

Stumped by speculation, Alexander huffed as he marched towards the back door--nearly falling into a new hole his foot created.

Calvin followed to where the boy stopped outside and scanned what he could see for any signs of Jeremiah. He searched for remnants on the ground, but the rain would have covered all traces with its mud.

Calvin continued to hang back. Alexander switched directions and stomped towards the kitchen. Upon entering, the probability of Jeremiah's presence increased when they discovered a knife on the floor that did not belong to the kitchen. The natives had constructed it, further proving where the horse had come from and the only logical person who could have ridden it this far into Missouri safely.

"You was right to come this way," offered Alexander, his voice containing a nuance of excitement; no doubt relieved that Jeremiah's trail had been reclaimed.

However, Calvin knew better than to jump to conclusions. "There's somewhere else we need to visit before we rest on our supposition."

Alexander nodded as though he understood which place was left unspoken.

"But first, you do right and go pay your respects."

The boy nodded again, but this time, his bottom lip quivered. Alexander pocketed the knife then stepped through the doorway. Calvin waited behind. The boy would need time alone with his family. Who knew the next time he would make it back.

When Jeremiah awoke, he climbed to his feet and expected that living to see a new morning would have been the biggest surprise of the day, but in the moments that followed, the astonishment of watching Calvin Hawte and Alexander Stebbins enter the old home was enough to knock him back on his ass.

The space in which he had lost consciousness and spent the night was not more than a few feet beyond the wood's tree line. Opening his eyes, they had focused on a large puddle. Jeremiah was not as concerned with how close he had come to drowning in the water; a greater fear had obsessed him. But there was no sign of the voracious beast.

He had clamored to his feet, and although he hadn't swallowed a drop of hooch since dinner with his pa, he suffered from hangover-like symptoms. Jeremiah scooped the soiled water from the puddle to quench his thirst before glancing over the shrubs. He spotted a rafter of wild turkeys and a family of raccoons, but nothing that glowed red captured his attention. However it happened, he had managed to lose the thing. Or perhaps the beast had discovered him and thought him dead already. Whichever was the truth, Jeremiah knew his safety was only for the interim, which ended sooner than expected when the echo of galloping came up the Stebbins footpath.

It had not been the monster, but someone just as

threatening, and after all this time, he continued to travel with the same companion.

It ain't possible, protested Jeremiah.

Like flies on dung, he fixated on both men until they disappeared inside the house. His gut told him to run, but then The Soldier piped, *Just hold on, crap-hat. If that thing's inside with them maybe, jus' maybe, no one will be alive ta walk out?*

But more than one did come out. Both Calvin and Alexander stepped through the back door minutes later, and once Jeremiah saw them mosey towards the kitchen, he knew the time had come to move.

The idea to steal one of their horses did cross his mind, but he abandoned that nonsense almost immediately. If seen, they would fire upon him. No horse could outrun a bullet, and he had no ammunition for his Smith and Wesson to fire back. Still, he needed a horse, amongst other things from his list. Jeremiah had not been able to check off one solitary item during his visit to the Stebbins homestead.

Best get a move on then. It won't take long 'til someone, or something, picks up yer stank.

Keeping under the natural cover of the woods was not only the smartest choice, but Jeremiah also recalled that the Mason farmhouse happened to be in the same direction. The twenty-or-so mile hike would take the day, but he should be able to persevere as long as there were no setbacks.

Though wet, the layer of dead leaves under

his feet continued to crackle. Jeremiah strolled as quietly as he could to the spot where he had seen the family of raccoons watching him carefully. The critters were long gone, but it wasn't them he was after. Jeremiah wanted what they had left behind.

He knelt on his hands and knees then sniffed the ground, delighted when his nose caught a whiff of the raccoon's pungent leavings, which meant that the excrement was fresh... all the better. He grabbed a handful of the filthy foliage then smeared it over his entire body. The hindering effects of the pepper would no longer handicap the beast. Without the rain to wash away his scent, Jeremiah suspected he smelled as attractive as clover to a bee in this forest; not only to the mysterious creature, but any predator. Without the possession of a knife, bullets for his gun, or sustenance to keep him moving, he would need all the help he could get to reach the Masons alive.

Calvin and Alexander paused with their weapons drawn outside the Whiting home. The claw marks on the floor of the porch had matched those scratches found at their previous location. They stood alarmed and dismayed, as they should, cautious to enter through the front door that had been left wide open. Darkness loomed in the interior with little light allowed through the caked glass windows and cracks in the walls.

"Nathaniel Whiting?! Agnes?!"

When his call was left unanswered, Calvin dismounted and cautiously approached. Three steps were taken before he paused. On the floor lay a pair of naked feet with the rest of the body cut off by the darkness.

"Whatcha see?" Alexander asked as his feet hit the ground.

Calvin entered the home. All but the boy's footsteps that followed remained silent.

The grotesque state of Nathaniel's corpse shocked both men. It was the Indian horse all over again with withered insides and crinkled flesh that hung off a skeleton frame.

"Jesus Crimmany!" Alexander spouted. "What the hell's goin' on aroun' here?"

Calvin knelt to investigate the remains, as procedure would dictate. Though there was residual blood, the miniscule amount was stained around the areas of his nightwear where his chest had twenty knives thrust into it.

"So it wun't no animal, after all. I ain't surprised the bastard kilt his own too."

"Jeremiah didn't do this."

Calvin continued his search for discovery when a blade stuck into the floor next to his hand. The resonant thump broke his examination. He peered at the knife Alexander had claimed from his family's kitchen.

"You tryin' ta convince me he didn't use that on his own pa? I can see all them stabbings. Just cuz

I ain't got but the one eye don't mean I'm a fuckin' dimwit."

Though rash, Alexander's point made the most sense. Still, Calvin could not agree with the boy's affirmation. The only thing that stood between him and reasonable logic was his gut. Without being able to pinpoint a motive, he decided to rely on his intuition rather than his eyesight.

He let the blade be and lifted Nathaniel's legs, then dragged his body outside and into the light. Although the skin got caught for a moment on a nail head and ripped, moving the dead weight should not have been so easy. The remains could not have been more than fifty pounds.

Immediately, the sunlight exposed a hole in the corpse's neck. To Alexander's immense disgust, Calvin stuck his finger inside and poked around, but the projectile he expected to find was not present. For a reason he could not explain, he was not surprised. Calvin relayed his lack of findings. "No bullet."

"So? What's that suppose ta mean?"

"There's a hole in his neck, but it wasn't from a gun."

Alexander kept silent while pondering, but what Calvin thought was deep consideration of the discovery turned out to be the boy's inability to look beyond his hatred for Jeremiah. "You still thank it was summin' else, doncha?" He wanted the man to be blamed for everything, even crimes he did not commit.

"Whatever did this was what did that horse in, and why would Jeremiah do such a thing to his only ride?"

"But the knife! An' the wounds!"

"That's right. There's twenty of them. How's a man gonna let himself be stabbed in the chest that many times without puttin' up a fight?"

Alexander hesitated, searching for an answer that wasn't there. In his panic, he settled on... "He died first then was stabbed out of anger. You know as good as me that Jeremiah's a mad loon."

"So what killed Nathaniel first?"

"Gunshot!"

"No bullet," Calvin reminded.

The boy was refusing to give. Calvin watched him think hard. It was as though he could see Alexander's brain squirm. It pained him to observe such desperation. Calvin continued his attempt to enlighten when he explained, "The body's still got some warmth. This was as recent as last night."

"So where's all his blood?"

"Exactly."

"This wun't no panther."

"I didn't say it was."

"Well..." but no other words followed. And it was there that both men came to an agreement in their dumbfounded silence.

Calvin climbed into the saddle while Alexander marched inside the house. Seconds had passed before he exited with the Indian knife, as well as Nathaniel's shotgun that he now claimed as his own.

Alexander had also found himself some calmness because when he asked, "Where we headed?" he did so without any aggression.

"West." Calvin had no doubt that was the direction Jeremiah now traveled; it was how the bodies lined up. The thing that hunted him came here first then followed him to the farm where it claimed his horse, further suggesting that Jeremiah was now on foot. Seeing what this thing could do--whatever it was--could mean that Jeremiah Whiting was dead as well, or soon would be unless he discovered a way to slay or outsmart this predator. Calvin made the mistake of underestimating the man's cleverness once before and would not do so again.

"What about Mrs. Whiting? Shouldn't we search for her?"

"The filth on those windows tells me she's been gone a while now," he stated with a degree of sadness that far outweighed what he carried for Nathaniel's passing. Calvin had only met Agnes the one time, and he liked her a hell of a lot more than her husband.

"What about Jeremiah? You thank this thing coulda killed 'im already?"

"What do you think?"

"I think if I ain't killed him, then he ain't dead."

Each had his own notion that led them both to the same conclusion.

CHAPTER XVII

Y ou missed somethin', blamed The Soldier.

Jeremiah did not know what though. He had covered his entire body with feces twice while en route to the Mason's farm, but he must have missed a spot because three trees over, the thing clung to a trunk and sniffed the air for him. Jeremiah stayed ducked behind a bush. Though he did not feel safe, no other covering would; not when the beast was capable of tracking him over a twenty-mile distance. However, somehow, for some reason, it lost his scent again.

Pushing his body to the limits to make good time was for naught. In the end, he had done precisely what he had hoped to avoid by luring it to the Mason's Farmhouse. Sitting on the outskirts of the property, Jeremiah had been waiting for old Peter Mason to finish his day and join his family inside the house. The trek had been exhausting, and Jeremiah brutalized his body when making the extra effort.

His new wounds screamed while he heaved and gasped for breath the entire distance.

That's it! Your breath, you Dunderhead! The Soldier exclaimed. *You was breathin' hard comin' here, but now you ain't.*

Of course. Jeremiah knew he should have known better. Yuma had taught him that certain animals, such as deer, had an exceptional sense of smell and could detect a nearby human from his breath alone. Though this thing was no docile deer, perhaps its nose was just as sensitive.

Jeremiah peered down and saw that he stood on a mound of pine needles. *Those'll work.*

He grabbed a clump of the plumage then shoved it into his mouth and chewed. He did not soon forget the bitter taste that reminded him of his days in the war. It was only too often that he and the other men had no means of brushing their teeth. They used what pine they could find to cleanse their mouths, as well as freshen their breath. Little did they know then that the pine oils masked their positions from local predators as well. He continued to chew cow-like while he kept his full attention on the beast that hunted him.

It sprung into the air then landed on the next trunk over. Its spiked tail coolly wagged as it stretched its nose towards the atmosphere and inhaled.

Keep chewin'.

Jeremiah did, but the creature wasn't leaving. Its sights had rested on the middle-aged man moving a portion of his livestock into the barn where they would be tucked in for the night.

Well, ain't we the lucky ones? That ol' man's jus' the distraction we need.

"What about his family?" Jeremiah whispered, but still, it was not soft enough for The Soldier's liking.

He scolded, *Ssh! Yer head voice, Dunderhead.*

That thing'll kill'em all.

The boys is already dead. Probably got themselves killed in the war.

Otherwise, they'd be helpin' their ol' man with the chores, agreed Jeremiah. *What about his wife and daughters?*

It'd be a favor we're doin' 'em.

Now, The Soldier was being downright cruel. Dying wasn't going to do the man, or his family, any favors. True, Peter Mason looked beyond his years, but he did not appear to be struggling in life. Clean and honest living had done him well. In fact, Jeremiah hoped to be just as lively when he reached his fifties... should he live to such a ripe age.

You want us ta get out West? There's only one way it's gonna happen.

We ain't gonna use those people as bait.

Don't think yerself nobler than ya are. Jus' let that thing take those Masons so we can take what we needs.

But they ain't the threat. The others we killed was 'cuz they wanted us harmed. This ain't the same. We should warn them.

Jeremiah began to stand when The Soldier yelled

so loud inside his head that he had no choice but to crouch and cover his ears. *You don't think he wouldn't trade you for that thing to save his own skin or his family!? Hell, he'd probably kill ya 'imself if he sees ya, knowin' who you are!*

By that notion, there was more truth than doubt. Should he attempt to warn them about what lurked nearby, Jeremiah did not stand a chance of even getting his words out. Peter would have him shot dead on the spot, most likely. But then again, adding kills that he could have prevented would be added weight on his conscience; even more, he did not much like how blithe The Soldier was with his guilt. In fact, ever since he and his pa had reached their understanding, he did not much like hearing what The Soldier had to say anymore, and not just because he used a voice that didn't belong to him; The Soldier cared for nothing but his own life.

Is that you thinkin' you wanna git rid of me, boy? The Soldier inquired, threateningly.

The creature was on the move before Jeremiah could respond. Antsy for something, it leaped-frogged across two trees towards the Mason Farm.

Jeremiah suspected he was the only one to notice that one of the lambs had snuck out the back of the barn because Peter did not chase after it, and The Soldier continued to rant, *You need me to survive.*

Jeremiah ignored him. Instead, he waited to see which victim the demon would choose to attack. While Peter began dragging farming equipment inside, the lamb did not travel far before stopping to graze at the opposite end of the barn. Both stood, unknowingly, equal distances from the beast that exchanged charging for prowling once entering the lush field. Keeping low, the thing stalked as quietly as a cougar.

The Soldier was watching now. Jeremiah could feel the added anticipation on top of his own while waiting.

It leaped, and took the lamb with it behind the barn, but the animal did not go quietly; it squealed loud enough to capture Peter's attention.

So the thing likes ta eat humans and animals alike. The Soldier confirmed. *Good ta know.*

But why not feed off of Peter? He's a bigger piece of meat than that small lamb.

Maybe it likes the taste of lamb better than a man.

Jeremiah then compared his likings of turkey and pork, always enjoying the taste of fowl better. The Soldier's estimation made some sense, but if correct, it was not to have Jeremiah rest easy. The outcome only confirmed what he had suspected. *It's been sent ta kill me.*

Animals filled the woods around them, and yet, for more than twenty miles, it only hunted him.

You still thinkin' you want me rid of now?

Peter heard another noise. He attempted to pinpoint its location, swerving to the side of the barn. Without discovering the source, he headed for the corner where he would find the indistinguishable monster feeding.

The rear door of the house opened. Martha

Mason stepped out and grabbed a small stick then used it to ring the dinner bell.

Peter paused to holler, "In a minute." His voice was far but legible.

"It'll be cold in a minute!" As was hers.

"I'll be right there."

"We're all waitin' on ya!"

"I'm checkin' that noise. Cancha hear it?"

"Yeah, I can hear it. It's jus' them cicadas. Let 'em be an' get inside."

He was too far to see, but Jeremiah was sure Peter looked baffled when he yelled, "Cicadas? You sure?"

"Only a few, but it's them. Now come on."

Martha's nagging had worked. After Peter hesitated a moment longer, he decided to obey his wife, closing the barn doors before entering the house.

Jeremiah rose from the bush.

Goin' into that barn ain't a good idea now. As soon as that thing's done with that lamb, you don't know if it'll go fer the others inside.

We can't leave without tryin'. It's what we came all this way for. There's things we need.

We need food too.

Jeremiah glanced at the two-story white farmhouse that the shadows of darkness slowly crept over. Lamplight illuminated one window, which would be the dining area.

How? Ya said so yerself; he'll shoot us dead when he sees me.

Not if ya take 'im by surprise.

With what? We don't even got the knife no more.

You got yer fists.

Only one fist right now.

Yer such a goddamn pussy. I'm takin' over.

You will not! Jeremiah shouted with finality. *Never again am I lettin' you control me like that. You only make the bad worse.*

You think you can stop me, boy?

Jeremiah gave The Soldier's challenge a moment's consideration then forlornly realized that he had no idea how to keep him from claiming control. Instead of antagonizing the arduous personality more, a better idea to reason with him formed.

An' then what? Them ladies is gonna scream bloody murder while you beat that man or strangle him. An' what if you ain't quick enough an' he fights back, or they do, or there's gunfire? Any of them noises is gonna call that thing to us jus' like that damn dinner bell she rung. We won't have suppa then, we'll be the suppa.

Jeremiah sensed The Soldier could not counter though he was quick to change the subject and remind, *We need food. We can't keep pushin' on like we're doin'.*

Jeremiah stumbled down a short incline, catching himself before falling from an onslaught of dizziness. Once it passed and he reached the fields, Jeremiah strode ever so quietly towards the barn, careful not to alert either the Masons or the creature of his position.

He lifted the guard rail on the barn doors gently then squeezed inside. So far, so good. Along with the bombardment of odors from the livestock, their noises walloped him over the head as well, drowning the sound of the creature's feeding just outside and, hopefully, any noises he might make inadvertently.

Jeremiah had seen a horse earlier and made finding him his top priority. He would, at least, be ready to ride out if discovered promptly, but the building was immense and disorganized; the sign of one man doing the job of two or more. Just as well, it was dark with only the light of dusk entering through the pinholes of the structure.

He used the wall of a pen to guide him towards the stables near the back. There he found three mounts to choose from, but just as extraordinary, a lantern hung on the post next to a convenient jar of matchsticks. He kept the flame low though it still shone bright enough to see a well-supplied barn.

Eureka. The Masons had procured enough items to open their own General Store, and seeing what items were available gave Jeremiah the idea of how he would be able to keep an upper hand on the creature, which reminded him...

He kept an open ear for any new, disturbing noises. Though he no longer could hear it feed on the lamb over the din of livestock, he would be able to recognize if the thing were digging through the walls to come inside, which he did not hear.

Keeping his cool, Jeremiah raced to fill two burlap sacks with rope, a hatchet, knives, and twine; everything he needed to set traps the way Lafayette Barlow had taught him. He tied the two bags together then tossed one end on each side of a restless stallion. He did not know the horse's name, but it was strong-willed and mean-tempered just like his pa. The other two were mares. Their mild nature would be unsuitable while attempting to outrun a determined predator. Jeremiah required speed and stamina above all else, so the bronco would be his first and only choice.

I ain't seein' no food yet.

Jeremiah's eyes darted to two large sacks of corn feed and oats that leaned against a workbench.

Dunderhead! We can't be carryin' nuttin' heavy like that. It'll weigh us down.

Fine. I don't need it anyway. I got the means to capture my own food.

We're starvin' now!

Jeremiah grabbed another item, a wool blanket reserved for the horses in the cooler months, when scraping came from the back. He had heard the digging only for a moment before the livestock turned restless with nervous excitement. It was coming.

He sealed his mouth tight and tried only to breathe through his nose. Of everything at his disposal, only two items could not be checked off his mental list: bullets for his Smith and Wesson, and a canister of cayenne powder.

Hastily, Jeremiah hung the lantern back on the post and was grabbing a handful of the matchsticks from the jar when a hat hanging on an adjacent pillar claimed his attention. He stole that too.

Jeremiah saddled up. The unsettled bronco squirmed and bucked, echoing words Yuma had once told him about how horses didn't like him. He began to wonder just how furious his old friend was with him.

Concentrate! The Soldier blared.

Jeremiah dug his heels into the stallion's flanks, gaining control. He rode to the doors then pushed one open, hoping not to find Peter Mason on the other side with a shotgun, reacting to the commotion inside his barn.

The coast was clear. He stormed out of the building undiscovered and unscathed.

Jeremiah continued to ride hard. Once he cleared the meadow, he looked back and saw no signs of being chased by the creature. Breathing through his nose and not his mouth had worked, as well as the dried excrement that clung to his arms, hair, and clothes.

Dumb luck from a dumb man, prodded The Soldier.

It wun't luck. Coverin' myself in feces was my idea, not yers. Then, as though poking a sleeping giant, *an' we gots what we needed without killin' no women and children.*

Ingrate. One day, yer thinkin's gonna get us both killed, but when that day inevitability comes, I knows watchin' ya suffer will make me happy as I die.

Jeremiah would not be provoked. If the Masons died tonight, it would not be by his hand or The Soldier's. He was free and clear of all disgrace, and his success had been achieved making decisions for himself while defying The Soldier. Even better.

Jeremiah pulled the stick out of the fire and took the piece of meat off its end. The opossum was lean, flavorless, and just about the best tasting creature he ever ate. It was his eighth, maybe ninth, bite and Jeremiah felt revitalized after swallowing each cut of flesh. He would continue to eat squirrel, opossum, raccoon--whatever the traps he had set would catch--until he felt like his old self or better. That's what it would take to survive the trek through the desert.

"A dog or wolf of sorts," stated Jeremiah, picking up where they left off in their conversation about the thing before he paused to eat.

Ain't even when it's got a snout like a bear.

Jeremiah jerked his head after hearing a clamor. He listened intently, but his hope that the traps had captured more food was a false alarm. The critter would be screaming, begging for its life. Jeremiah wrote off the noise to either the pop from his crackling fire or a splashing fish from Little Sugar

Creek just beyond a row of trees. The supplies taken from the Masons' had allowed him to set five traps in the vicinity of his camp: three spring snares, a feather spear, and a Paiute deadfall. The opossum had found misfortune when it triggered the deadfall, snapping its little neck instantly with a twenty-pound slab. His next victims would not be so fortunate as the traps still standing did not kill as quickly.

"What about them spikes and tail? Maybe it's some kinda giant lizard."

With a snout like a bear? The Soldier laughed. *Jesus Christmas, ya sure is a dolt, ain'cha? How you even survived before I came along is a goddamn miracle.*

"Is that yer reason fer not wantin' to leave my head?"

Maybe it's you who won't leave my head. How 'bout that?

"You must think I'm crazy to buy such nonsense."

Ain't you? How is it that you think you ain't crazy? There's no normalcy in talkin' ta people who ain't present.

"Lotsa folks talk to themselves," defended Jeremiah.

Maybe, but how many of them folk hear someone talk back? The Soldier paused before persisting, *An' from more than one voice?*

Jeremiah understood to whom The Soldier referred. Twenty-four hours hadn't even passed since Martin's voice declared him a, "*Murderer,*" just after encountering nine graves. In fact, something about that figure hadn't settled right with him at the time, which hadn't changed since. Using his fingers to keep a tally, he counted, "Werner, Betsy, the two girls, Alice and Penny, the twins..."

...an' them two niggers makes eight.

Having just seen Alexander walking and breathing that morning, Jeremiah suspected that the ninth marker belonged to Martin, whose body had been eviscerated and too difficult for the army to collect and bring home. "Maybe his spirit found its way back."

You can't really think his ghost was talkin' to ya? Why was it that you was the only one who heard it, if so?

Jeremiah didn't know, and it had been too long since experiencing good sense or reason to recognize its presence anymore. He considered that The Soldier might be right after all... he was crazy, and the only thing keeping him from falling apart was a line, thin as thread, separating his reality from delusions. However, that line felt tense and could snap at any moment. Retrieving some perspective, he thought it best to avoid a conclusion about Martin when the balance of his mental stability swayed so vigorously. But what he could believe to be factual was that he had heard him clear as a whistle.

It's only yer guilt yer hearin'. It'll suffocate you if ya let it.

"You suffocate me. Maybe guilt was what created

you." Jeremiah perked suddenly. He had given up his search for reason of The Soldier's existence, but then it came on its own. It was an epiphany, though Jeremiah suspected this revelation came with consequences, which The Soldier saw fit to take advantage.

Well, I'll be, he gloated. *That would mean that you was thinkin' of killin' Martin even before I arrived. Ain't that right?*

"Shut up."

That's why I come; you made me. You needed someone ta do yer dirty work for ya and keep ya rid of quilt. The Soldier howled with laughter. *How'd that work out? I mean, for fuck's sake, who names their pet lizard after the man he blew to pieces? A crazy bastard, that's who, I tell ya.*

Jeremiah rose to his feet to yell over the fire at The Soldier he imagined sitting across, "That wun't me who killed 'im, it was you! Jus' like you killed the rest of 'em."

Now, now, stated The Soldier, calmly. *I'll take the blame for Martin, Alice, and a few of them others, but I ain't about to be accused of stickin' it to them two young girls. They was all you 'cuz yer horniness. It's like you's a rabbit with four balls.*

"I'll kill you!"

Do it, you ungrateful sumbitch, The Soldier hollered back. *I gave you skills. I not only turned you inta a survivor, but I turned ya into a weapon too. Yer jus' too culpable and witless to appreciate what I gave. But if you wanna kill me, then do it, if you know how.*

Jeremiah didn't, though that did not stop him from threatening, "I'll find a way."

The snap of a branch from behind broke the standoff. The trigger of a trap had been released, skewering the monster with two spikes to its gut. The feather spear trap continued to work as planned when the injured creature stumbled backward into a lasso that triggered a second trap. The rope wrapped around the beast's ankle and flung its body into the air. It slammed against a tree trunk that pushed the two protruding stakes deeper into its side. The tiger-like roar it wailed was loud enough to wake snakes as the beast twisted and writhed upside down.

The stallion fought with the rope that bound him as Jeremiah approached the beast cautiously. With one hand resting on the handle of his new blade, he continued forward, no less amazed by the unnatural thing. Suddenly, he lurched back, tripping over his own feet, when its deadly tentacle lashed at him. Jeremiah had underestimated its range, and The Soldier laughed at his expense. Thankfully, the rope that upheld the beast saved Jeremiah's life, twisting the thing in circles that kept its fleshy spike out of reach.

Again with the luck. It's more than you deserve.

Jeremiah returned to his stance, no less determined to gut the thing, but he needed to get close; an impossibility as its tongue would not stop whooshing in the air like a lion tamer's whip. He stopped creeping forward just before it was no longer safe.

He watched and waited for an opportune moment to attempt his attack, but as he procrastinated, the rope's swinging began to dull and for the first time, Jeremiah got his first long hard look at the creature's face. Curiosity replaced his need for vengeance. The thing very well could be a type of wolf, as The Soldier had once suggested, or possibly a deformed big cat or an unknown breed of reptile. However, as the beast's face twirled into the glow of the campfire, its features were highlighted. What Jeremiah glimpsed reminded him of the familiarity he sensed after its first attack. He bent the upper half of his body down then crooked his head up to look at the fiend face-to-face.

Without expecting to calm the beast, he had done just that, as though he possessed hypnotic powers. The monster's tongue slithered into its mouth and stayed put while it gazed back. The answer did not come immediately, but once it did, Jeremiah became dizzy with shock and nearly fell over again. The thing wasn't only an animal, but it was part human, too, and not just any human, but Matolu.

Jeremiah backed away. The urge to run was powerful, but he knew better. Yuma had explained enough about the dark magic of a Pniese to know he could never escape on foot, horseback, or otherwise. But in all of Yuma's stories about the injun witches, not once did he describe anything that resembled what they sent to punish him.

Yer brain can't be so soft not to know who helped the

chief turn into this mutation.

Jeremiah did know. Everything fitted together and made sense. He knew Atraco's arrival had not been a coincidence. Somehow... someway... beyond what logic could comprehend, the elder knew what would happen to Salali. That was why he had smirked like the devil and kept Jeremiah's secret when he snuck away. Atraco came to the Cherokee with big plans.

He used them goddamn spirits. That's how come it looks like a bunch of other things.

Jeremiah stood straight then lifted his eyes to the thing's neck. The cut he had made not more than forty-eight hours ago had healed to a scar. If The Soldier was correct in his assumption--and Jeremiah had no reason to believe otherwise--then the demon Atraco created possessed the spirit of the snake... among others.

I'll tell you what else.

"You don't need to." The creature was no longer a mystery. Everything about it became as crystal clear as a cloudless sky.

Why aincha killin' it? Whatcha waitin' for?

Jeremiah had been hesitating without comprehension. He felt connected to the creature for some unexplained reason. Nonetheless, he tugged the Masons' hatchet from the wood it stuck out of then lifted it into attack position above his head. Still, he continued to pause. "What if they send another?"

What if? So the fuck what? The Soldier spat.

Jeremiah's attention was stolen away by the neigh of an unsettled horse in the near distance that did not come from his mount. Though the dark hid the intruding rider, Jeremiah glanced in its direction at the same moment his final spring snare trap sprung. By the roar of surprise, its quarry was a man.

"Calvin! Help me!" A young voice cried.

Even at a pitched shrill, Jeremiah recognized Alexander Stebbins calling for his companion. He did not wait for the famed tracker to appear but untied his ride immediately and bolted deeper into the woods. Even if Calvin hadn't spotted him in the open, the man would have been like a moth to a flame by the glow of his campfire, and he would perceive all the evidence left behind to indict his presence. The only items that remained in his possession were the knife and hatchet. All his extra rope, the burlap sacks, as well as the blanket, stayed at the camp with the... Jeremiah paused his thinking and smiled.

Well, all hope ain't lost, after all.

Indeed. There was every chance that the two manned posse would walk into a trap that he had not set intentionally. To trigger it would take a little curiosity and a step within its tongue's reach.

What if yer the only man it wants ta kill? The Soldier offered, attempting to burst his bubble.

Tell that ta my pa, Dunderhead.

Jeremiah continued to race for the trail as though the men remained only a breath behind.

Should one, or both, survive the creature, they would be on his tail again in the matter of a minute. The impossible idea to ride all the way to California non-stop did come to mind. Calvin would never let up, not while knowing his victim was within reach.

Gunshots fired into whatever thing he had left behind; followed by a distant cry seconds later.

CHAPTER XVIII

Calvin used the Indian-made knife Alexander had claimed from the kitchen of his old home to slice the rope. The boy fell a good three feet and crashed onto the thin bed of dead leaves that had concealed the foot trap he triggered. Calvin then rushed off, in a hurry. Having heard the pounding hooves of Jeremiah's escape, he raced back for his ride, but Alexander did not follow. The boy had ideas of his own, and like a daft fool, he fluttered like a moth towards the campfire's flames a few hundred feet ahead.

"Back this way!" Calvin hollered, only thinking that Alexander must not have heard Jeremiah high-tail it into the woods over his own caterwauling, but the boy insisted on disappearing behind the tree line instead of doing an about-face.

Gunfire exploded from the camp. Calvin rushed to his partner's aid, considering that Jeremiah's horse might have galloped off without him until wails of a ferocious beast reverberated from the trees. Calvin ran Alexander's path and followed his trail around the same group of trees to lay eyes on the boy fighting some unknown atrocity that dangled and writhed on a rope. It reached for Alexander, who did not cease firing at the ferocious thing until he ran out of ammunition. While the boy reloaded, Calvin drew his piece and trained his weapon on the barbaric beast.

"Shoot it for Christ's sake!"

But Calvin could not. Aside from being something vicious and unnatural, it was remarkable. No doubt, this was the thing that had been pursuing Jeremiah. He needed to know more, and it was his curiosity that kept Calvin hypnotized.

He stepped towards the monstrosity when a long, leathery rope shot out from behind rows of carnivorous teeth. Calvin felt a draft from its whipping tongue across his cheek. He leaped back, grateful that the appendage had reached its full extent.

Alexander locked the chamber of his pistol and resumed firing. Calvin watched amazed as bullet after bullet pierced through its bristly coat without any effect other than sending it into an absurd rage. At that moment, he foretold the danger of allowing something so unyielding to live, and then joined Alexander in trying to put the mysterious beast down.

Alexander emptied his chamber a second time, having weakened the thing only slightly. He reloaded again.

Calvin expected that they could use their entire reserve of ammunition in attempting to put this creature down with no guarantee of a positive outcome. Moreover, nothing would be left to take down the predator they actually hunted. Calvin allowed a bullet one more chance and took careful aim, firing directly into the space between the hellion's red eyes.

The thing's struggle ended as abruptly as a final breath. The motionless body swayed on the rope as though caught in the wind. However, when its eyelids did not close to conceal the tempered glow of red, Calvin knew he should have recognized it as a sign of its firm continuity. The time to warn Alexander to keep his distance had come and gone.

The boy had looked to him with a silent expression of confusion, most likely just as confused by the beast, when its tongue lashed again. Alexander did not react because he could not see the projectile coming towards his false eye. Not until it dug into his left socket did Alexander jerk back, but he could not leap far. The appendage's grip was cohesive. The boy grabbed ahold of the wet slimy rope and pulled like in a game of tug o' war.

A disturbing and garish sound of suction radiated from Alexander's skull. Calvin joined the pulling, but the slick slaver kept him from sustaining a grip.

He reached for the Indian knife and then stabbed the blade into the space where he thought its heart ought to be. Using both hands, he pulled down in a gutting motion. The thing's upper chest split open, spilling strings of entrails that dangled to the ground.

The creature released a deafening cry, but also its hold on Alexander. The boy launched backward and landed on the ground next to the fire that lit a trail of blood trickling out of the dark crevasse where his false eye once had been. Alexander covered the exposed pit with his hand and cried, "My eye! Where is it? Where's my eye?!"

Calvin scanned the ground covered with dead foliage, bark pieces, and timber. In the fire's limited illumination, it could take hours to discover where the ball might have rolled to while Jeremiah placed more distance between them with each passing second. To his contentment, the knob was gone for good.

"Can you ride?" Calvin inquired aggressively.

The boy gazed at him, as though bewildered by the question.

"Which is it? Jeremiah or yer eye?"

It took a moment, though brief, for Alexander to realize the more important of the two choices. He uncovered the cavity below his brow to use both hands as leverage when pushing off the ground. Though Calvin's next instinct had been to make a beeline for his horse, his plan was thwarted by the hypnotic lure of the cavernous hole in Alexander's head. He shivered under the boy's eyeless stare. It did not matter that Calvin could not see what rest beyond. The dark orifice of a skull was just as unsettling when covered with flesh.

Time was wasting. He sprinted back for his horse while Alexander had trouble bringing up the rear. Calvin could not comprehend why the boy staggered so blindly. His symmetry would not have been skewed by the loss of his eye because he hadn't been able to see with both for years. However, he did recall hearing a most gruesome sound very similar to slurping. Mosquitos and leeches fed on blood. It was not so impossible to believe that this unfamiliar creature could do the same. It also explained why a trickle of blood oozed out of Alexander's hollow.

Once mounted, the men shot past the camp and charged into the blackened forest, much too concentrated on catching up to their target to notice that the demon-like monstrosity had reopened its eyes.

None of his people had heard from nor seen Atraco since that day. Yuma sat on the outskirts of the village, just as he had done the previous two nights, and waited, but for what, he was unsure. He did not think the elder Pneise would return, nor his father, whatever thing he had become. Instead, he just watched the land and waited for any sign or signal from the spirits, hoping they would talk to his people once again.

For now, he stared at the moon and the stars as they shined over the land. Another storm was coming. Though the night deceived this fact, he knew better than to trust his sight. Its approach came in the breeze and was heard coming off the land. This next storm would be angrier than the last. Yuma feared many of his people would die from its devastation.

Others had also sensed what would come though they did not voice their reservations. Instead, they used the ordaining ceremony of Matolu's shaman brother, Honovi, as their new chief and the observance of Salali's final rest to mask their misgivings. However, they could not hide long from the truth. The great storm would tear down their barriers. And as Kilwannee shouted an alarm for Yuma to come quick, he feared that moment had arrived.

Kilwannee waited for him, using the doorway of Honovi's hut as his crutch. In their silence, the spirits had refused his brother the gift of the snake. Instead, Honovi used herbs and smoke, which had been working, however slowly. What remained unclear was whether the spirits had become aware of his people's deception. Other than their quietness, there had been no signs, but Yuma suspected that their silence spoke loudly.

Kilwannee led him inside to join Honovi and the other eight warriors who had aided in Matolu's transformation, as well as any man and woman who shared his blood. Their uncle never was expressive by nature; however, Yuma could see worry and shame in the lines of his face. He joined their circle around a small fire to listen to what Honovi had to tell.

"The spirits came to me in a vision. They have learned of our deception."

"How?" Kilwannee asked.

"Our chief has failed." Honovi paused to allow a moment of shame. "The Great Spirit returned to seek admittance back into its world, but the spirits did not recognize the unnatural thing that they bestowed their gifts upon. It was refused and sent back. Never to return."

"It will not be killed?" Atohi inquired.

Honovi did not answer.

Murmurs shuffled from one warrior to the next as Yuma and his siblings looked at each other knowingly. After their father's ritual, Yuma had spoken with Aponi and Kilwannee about being deceived by Atraco. Though his sister agreed to the betrayal, his brother's pride would not concede as hastily. However, now the spirits had made deniability impossible. If they could not ignore the evil they had assembled from their own gifts, then neither could Kilwannee nor any collaborator.

Honovi continued, "The spirits are outraged. They are to send warriors who will punish us for our wrong."

"When?" Yuma asked before the mumbling of speculation returned.

Honovi breathed in the smoke from the fire and closed his eyes to see what he could learn. When he opened them, he shocked everyone by announcing,

"Now."

The whinnies of the tribe's horses resounded outside in the same moment of Honovi's declaration. Their excitement was followed by a woman's scream, and then another with a child's. But before any single warrior could act upon the cries of distress, a rumba of rattlesnakes entered the hut from every orifice.

Aponi joined the other screams as the den of reptiles slinked through the door and windows. Each man and woman readied the weapon they had on hand, but the ground snakes had meant to be a diversion. More of their brethren wriggled through the straw roof and remained unnoticed until they landed on the heads of two men. Both warriors suffered multiple bites that brought them to the ground. The rumba amassed around them and engulfed their bodies. In seconds, the cries of the two great warriors were silenced.

A shrill of panic and suffering escalated outside, but as the barrage of rattling and hissing increased inside the hut, the other nearby assaults were camouflaged. Aponi squeezed next to her uncle as the men made a tight circle around their new chief. At his ear, Yuma could hear the old man mumble to the spirits, begging for their forgiveness, but at the vindictive rate the snakes continued to rain down, Yuma doubted they would grant0 clemency.

There were too many to kill, but that did not stop the others from swiping the air with their blades. However, Yuma had a different idea for a useful deterrent.

He grabbed the cool end of a log and pulled it out of the fire, then pitched the burning end from side to side. A chorus of outraged hissing exploded as the remaining warriors followed suit, choosing a fiery weapon of their own. Together, they moved as one, pushing back the angered creatures whose fangs glistened with dripping venom.

Yuma was caught off-guard by a single hiss heard above all others. He did not need to look to know there was one next to his ear, hanging from the ceiling. The sound of it readying to strike froze him, but then the breath of a swiping blade was felt on his neck, followed by a thump on his shoulder. Yuma peered out of the corner of his eye to see the decapitated snake's head land on the floor while Kilwannee's knife moved on to attack others.

The gathering reached the door. They squeezed through one by one, only to discover that what they had escaped into was a larger nightmare.

The village was overrun by large and small predators alike. Their aggression resembled nothing that Yuma had seen or heard about from any story. His eyes bounced in every direction, not knowing where to settle his concentration as one attack on his people distracted him from another.

Yuma stayed close to Honovi's side as he and Aponi pointed their torches at the door to keep the snakes from exiting. Three warriors tossed their torch logs onto the straw roof. Honovi's home ignited into a blaze as the remaining warriors joined the fray. In no time, the roof caved in and killed all the reptiles trapped inside.

Pained by their loss, Yuma could hear the whisper of Honovi's repetitive plea next to his ear. Their shaman chief was pointing out the many unnecessary deaths of their kind, but the angered spirits chose not to listen.

Tsiyi stopped in front of Yuma. The fifteen-year-old boy, who had the makings of a great fighter, positioned his long spear in the second before a Grey Wolf pounced, landing on the blade end. The beast had whimpered its last cry before the weight of its body snapped the weapon in two. But Tsiyi's predicament did not end with the wolf's sacrifice.

A massive Black Bear came from behind. It charged for the junior warrior who now was weaponless. Yuma took his knife and blared a cry of war as he leaped onto the distracted bear's back. He had managed one good stab into its breast before being thrown to the ground. The Black Bear turned and towered over him but then keeled over when two arrows punctured its neck. Once down, Tsiyi ran towards new screams that cried in the dark, eager to be their protector.

A pair of brother archers pulled back their next arrows and aimed for the cougar that was prepared to launch through the window of the next hut over. The younger brother released and hit his mark, but the elder's arrow flew rogue after a Golden Eagle dove and clawed his face with its talons. The first shooter reached for the bird of prey's legs but failed to pull it off when the eagle had a brother of its own to swoop down for the kill.

Aponi left her uncle's side and swung her torch like a club at the first of the two eagles. Sparks exploded when she made contact and knocked the beast to the ground. It clamored back onto its feet and spread its wings to fly until she stomped as hard as she could on its head. Aponi then reached for the second eagle when she had the wind knocked out of her. The attacking goat sped past as she fell to the ground, and then head-butted Utina into the fire pit. The woman flailed and screamed as the goat continued to charge into the thick of the battle in search of another victim to ram. Utina's shrieks continued from within the flames but soon lost in the panicked cries of the tethered steeds.

The horses did not attack like the other animals but became victims as well, stalked by an approaching cougar and another Grey Wolf working in tandem. Five warriors rushed in to protect their four-legged brothers when it dawned on Yuma that the invasion was by the animals whose spirits had been deceived in the ritual, and no others.

He broke Honovi's connection to their world and insisted that he tell the spirits, "We will make what is wrong, right again. It will be done. Promise them!"

As the shaman closed his eyes and appealed to the spirits with the vow, the aerie of Golden Eagles screeched their forthcoming attack. The birds dove for the fighters who had proven most skilled.

Though their bombardment came with the intent to kill, the assault was better suited as a diversion when a mess of iguanas scampered out of the darkness. The wave of reptiles leaped and clawed up their bodies as others chewed on the men's ankles, bringing down their victims to be devoured.

But then, the tide receded as swiftly as it rose. Just as well, the Golden Eagles lifted into the sky and dispersed while the goats and bears retreated into the brush. The cougars and wolf packs left last, but in their withdrawal, backed away slowly as to ensure that this battle ended with their victory.

No man or woman dared to retaliate.

The spirits had agreed to Honovi's bequest, but as Yuma evaluated the destruction of their village, he thought their acceptance had come too late. Only half his people remained, and for the few who had a chance of surviving their injuries, they still would be unable to participate in the proposed hunt. The warriors mauled by the iguanas bled profusely from the cuts of razored teeth and claws. A mother held her daughter, both crying from blinded eyes pecked out by the eagles, while Atohi's blood poured out of what remained of his left arm. Most wallowed and wailed from venomous snake bites, broken bones, and seared flesh, but not Yuma, and not Kilwannee or Aponi. Though wounded during the incursion, their injuries were insignificant compared to others. The children of Matolu had been spared from the onslaught, and their own people looked at them with accusing glares.

Honovi picked up a pouch from the ground and secretively disappeared into the brush. Yuma had no trouble deciphering that his uncle had gone to pick plants for medicine as the snake spirits would continue to reject their gifts to his people.

Aponi helped Kilwannee limp towards him. Yuma looked his sister in the eye and affirmed, "We will hunt our father. That is what was promised."

Both siblings nodded in their proverbial agreement. Kilwannee added, "Morning we'll go. Tonight, we heal our people."

Yuma switched his focus to his brother, "You will stay. You are still weak from the poison."

"We are of our father's blood. We will be the strongest," protested Kilwannee.

Yuma turned to the devastated remains of their village with heavy shame. Among the wounded, one stood out as having sustained only mild injuries from his encounter with the Grey Wolf. Perhaps the spirits had spared Tsiyi for a reason, or perhaps the young warrior was beyond his years in battle. Either way, Yuma took it as a sign.

"Tsiyi is stronger. He will go, and you will stay and heal."

Kilwannee's face contorted to disdain. He was prepared to demonstrate his strength by charging for his little brother when Aponi placed her hand on his chest to stop him.

"Our brother is right. Uncle will need help from you."

Kilwannee considered the words of his sister

first before he shed his anger and nodded his relinquishment.

Aponi turned to Yuma. "Father's trail has been washed by the rain. How will we begin?"

Yuma hesitated, his doubt infected his thoughts of hope. Nonetheless, he replied, "Perhaps the spirits will guide us if they truly wish for the Great Spirit to be stopped."

The three siblings nodded their agreement and then settled their minds of any further quandaries before parting ways to begin transitioning their, once peaceful, village into an infirmary.

"Matolu? It jus' can't be," Jeremiah repeated so many times, he had lost count, but not once did The Soldier take the bait. Since their roe, the voice had been silent. Jeremiah hated to admit it, but he could use The Soldier's thoughts on the matter; not to mention the lonesomeness he was feeling.

He did not want to take back what he had said. Jeremiah had meant every word, but he and The Soldier were like family members who didn't see eye-to-eye, yet lived together. They needed to overcome their differences. "Truce, then?"

He waited for The Soldier's response; if he should respond.

It won't matter if the thing looked like Matolu or a bear or a cougar if them two idiots done killed it fer us.

Jeremiah had listened to wailing roars spawned

by repeated gunfire. He did not see how Calvin and Alexander hadn't succeeded in killing that Matolu thing.

Don't be restin' on yer laurels, but unless yous plannin' on turnin' us around to go check, I'd quit wastin' what little concentration yer brain can handle on what we lef' behind. Bes' start thinkin' 'bout what's ahead. That sun's comin' up fast.

Jeremiah gazed at the horizon. The glow of dawn's light illuminated the crack between sky and earth. The Soldier was right; their time on the Elk River neared its end.

He twisted his head back for another look. All appeared as it should. The faint light of morning did not illuminate anyone, or anything, that pursued him. As far as Jeremiah could tell, he was not being followed. Perhaps the battle of Little Sugar Creek ended in such a way that was to his advantage. If he no longer needed to worry about Calvin, Alexander, or the creature, then it was with some relief that the Cherokee would be the last of his sworn enemies.

What makes you think them injuns won't jus' go an' make another? Maybe the nix one could wear Yuma's face on it, then he could slip his tongue inside ya like he always wanted.

Jeremiah had a notion of regret about the truce. Desperate for company, he had forgotten how much he loathed The Soldier's hateful badgering and ill-timed sense of humor. However, without his insufferable chatter as a diversion, exhaustion could take him down; only this time, Jeremiah didn't carry any rope to tie his body to the steed.

That's 'cuz ya pussied out when them dolts arrived an' ran like a spineless milksop. Now ya got nuttin' fer trappin', Dunderhead!

"You knew the plan. You helped make it. They was to end each other, an' by what I heard, it worked."

Jeremiah glanced down at the trail of hoof prints his horse left behind, just to be sure that the turbulent water erased them from the shallow shores. In the off chance that any one of his pursuers survived, he would not underestimate him, especially that four-legged one.

You ain't thinkin' we're in the clear yet, is you? Them Indians weren't a part of our plan. They're still lookin' fer ya and will see you better once that sun rises over the ridge.

The Soldier had never spoken truer words. Under the guise of night, the river was safe to travel. The towering cliffs to his right blocked the beams of moonlight while the choppy water obscured the splashes of the gallops of his mount. But once the sun cast its radiance, the curtain over the basin would be lifted while the woods to his left remained in shadows under a lush canopy. Any perpetrator who cast his eyes upon him would be allowed to do so without being seen.

The time to veer onto a new course had arrived. Jeremiah pinpointed a stretch of bedrock ahead. The layer of rocks was just what he had hoped to come across. Dirt and sand would mark his trail into the woods, but not stone. If he did happen to have a tail, Jeremiah could think of no better approach for ditching them. Then, without the pressure of being hunted, he would find a place to stretch out and catch up on some much overdue shut eye.

Was that a big plate of stupid you ate tonight? You ain't takin' that risk. Calvin Hawte's just as good of tracker as any animal.

I needs ta sleep. An' you ain't gonna stop me.

The Soldier began to sing, '*Oh, the years creep slowly by, Lorena, the snow is on the ground again. The sun's low down the sky, Lorena, the frost gleams where the flow'rs have been.*'

"Shut the fuck up!" Jeremiah shouted with powered rage. Immediately, he became sick with grief as he listened to his guilt-laden growl ricochet down the channel.

The Soldier scoffed at his idiocy. Jeremiah knew the voice had only meant to demonstrate how he planned to keep him awake, not realizing what pain that particular song would bring. Either way, he should have known better. No way would he be allowed to rest while The Soldier filled his head with warbling.

Upon reaching the bedrock, the stallion decided to buck up his hind legs, nearly succeeding in tossing Jeremiah off that time. He was unsure how many attempts the ornery steed had made to throw him, but they were becoming more random. Though nothing he could do about it now, Jeremiah wished he had changed his mind about not picking one of the mares.

He pulled back on the horse's reins until it settled. Though he did not want to reward the animal for misbehaving, there was a good chance they wouldn't see another drop of water for days.

What do you think yer doin', boy? We gots ta keep amovin'. Righ' now!

He waited for his ride to drink first before he hopped down. Ignoring The Soldier's order, he gulped mouthful after mouthful.

In the year and a half he spent with Yuma and his people, Jeremiah heard many stories about the other tribes. Friend or foe, they all had one thing in common; they kept their homes near the water. Because of this, he would have no choice but to cross the state furthest from any river, while praying for rain along the way. Being that it was prime storm season, he trusted that his chances were good for a positive outcome.

Jeremiah finished then splashed his face one last time. The cool water was invigorating and had awakened him some, but he carried too much fatigue to hold the sensation long.

We ain't got no more time for this bullshit! The Soldier shouted, enraged about being flouted.

I told you to shut up! Jeremiah shouted back, harried, but mounted his steed anyway. Then, against The Soldier's wishes, he took a moment to gaze at the sun that had stretched over the ridge in the last few minutes. There was not a storm cloud in the sky to obstruct his view, and the sun stared back at him as though promising it would make this day a scorcher. Suddenly, Jeremiah made another belated wish, kicking himself for not having the foresight to bring a wineskin pouch or a large flask from the Mason's barn to help carry some of this Elk River water.

You'd only lef' that behind at the campsite with the rest of it all.

Jeremiah tugged left on the reins gently, not wanting to upset the stallion further. The clopping of hooves on the stone headed towards the forest. He glanced down and noticed that his mount was leaving a trail after all, but should the sun keep its promise, the heat would have those dried in no time.

The Soldier had gone quiet again. This time, Jeremiah was not as desperate to have him come back, but during their prolonged silence, he had nearly fallen off his horse more times than his exhausted brain could recall. Thankfully, the rowdy buck had settled his dismay, at least for the time being.

Jeremiah's eyes drooped. They had rested for a minute, or an hour, before they sprang open and focused on the edge of the forest. Beyond the tree line lay nothing but endless desert.

He paused to observe and mentally prepare for the next stage of his lengthy journey west. Not only would this segment be the most arduous, but the moment he set foot in plain view, he would be an open target for anyone or anything, regardless if what they hunted was Jeremiah Whiting or just another intruder.

Gunshot!

Jeremiah twisted around. Two men on horseback charged towards him.

Another missed shot, but closer than the first.

Either his vision was still too hazy to make out their faces or they were too far, but Jeremiah did not need to see any details of their features to know the shooters were Calvin and Alexander.

Before either man could fire his next round, Jeremiah flogged the side of his mount, propelling the steed into the desert. The chase he dreaded most had begun.

CHAPTER XIX

The hot wind blew stronger when fifty feet above the basin. It banged against Jeremiah's eardrums as he stood at the edge of the crest with one boot on his foot and the other in his hand. Setting his bare foot on the gravel would burn like hot coals so, instead, he balanced himself flamingo-style with one leg hoisted until a gust of heat tipped him. Losing his balance, Jeremiah might have fallen over the ledge if he hadn't grabbed the horse's reins.

Step the fuck back a'fore ya kill us both.

I know what I'm doin'.

You've gone an' lost what little good sense you had lef'. Anyone can see you up here.

Jeremiah gazed west. Below the surface of a patch of dark gray sky, lay miles and miles of flat desolate terrain that rippled and waved in the intense heat. Any pools of water, like the one he happened to stumble across three days back, would be lost in the mirage. That puddle had been Godsent and provided much relief, though fleeting. Now, Jeremiah searched for his next miracle, thinking it might come from the clouds murky enough to produce rain.

You remember what happened las' time you got yer hopes up, don't ya?

Jeremiah did. He had seen clouds like these the day before, and the day before that. The results from those fronts had been nothing but dry electrical storms that detonated thunderous booms that quaked over the land like a tidal wave noise.

"You know what's better than takin' a bite of my favorite meal?" Jeremiah inquired. "Standin' in a monsoon. But I don't know what I would eat. How do I know which is my favorite when everythin' sounds too good?"

Although Jeremiah believed he had made perfect sense, he felt The Soldier's confusion. He supposed not everything said out loud was an accurate depiction of his thoughts, but that was expected from any man who had survived on nothing but piss for two days. First it had been his own, then once his recycled urine concentrated and fermented, he took what his buck expelled. However, now, the horse might as well be pissing dust. Still, succumbing to a body's discharge for hydration wouldn't be for naught. Jeremiah concentrated on better focusing his mind.

He licked his cracked lips that were sharp enough to cut his tongue while he pivoted east and followed the trail of hoof prints his ride left just that morning. The best he could tell, the tracks along the basin were his and his alone. Nobody else had strolled alongside them while he took shelter from the heat of the day in a nearby hollow though Jeremiah did not doubt that Calvin and Alexander were close. Since he had outraced the men five days back, he strained to devise a way to erase his trail. A suitable method would have been to drag a large piece of brush behind his horse, if only the rope he needed to tie it with weren't lying at the camp by Little Sugar Creek. Without the tools to make his mount's prints disappear, he would never lose his trackers. It was just more dumb luck that he had lost them for as long as he had.

But if ever asked what had happened on that day when Calvin and Alexander fell back after twenty minutes of hard riding, Jeremiah couldn't say for sure. He did have a theory, which pertained to water, or lack thereof. The men would not have taken advantage of the river before entering the woods. No doubt, they had spotted his trail on the bedrock, and because the stone was still wet, the expectation of being close enough to nab him trumped their intellect. With their pride cocked to full arrogance, they would not have speculated their pursuit to last beyond the day, and therefore, disregarded taking a moment to hydrate themselves and their rides, as Jeremiah had smartly done. The consequence of their negligence had resulted in their inability to capture him, or to even come close. If not for his forethought to ignore The Soldier's badgering about taking the time to drink from the river, the outcome would have been reversed.

There ain't no proof of that account. Their hosses might've been too old ta keep up, or maybe that Matolu thing caught up an' did'em in.

Jeremiah nearly lost his balance and blamed it on The Soldier for trying to daunt him unnecessarily. He hadn't thought about that creature because it had died.

The Soldier howled with laughter. *You thank that thing didn't survive Calvin and Alexander?*

"Of course it didn't. How else could they have walked away?"

Same way we did when it was still breathin'.

Though The Soldier's point was effective, Jeremiah refused to believe him. He couldn't.

Bullets and knives don't do nuttin' to stop it. You don't dare believe it's dead without seein' fer yerself.

"I do."

Then you always will be a dunderhead.

The heavenly sound of water patting the ground halted their conversation. Jeremiah looked up, but even the air seemed to gasp for hydration. Still, he could hear the dripping clearly, and it was coming from behind. He turned to his horse, whose urine had dwindled to a trickle. Immediately, Jeremiah thrust his boot beneath the horse's pecker to capture the last few drops. There was hardly enough for a swallow. Tilting the boot towards his mouth, he made the mistake of inhaling its fumes. The inside smelled more like sour piss than foot sweat. He would have puked right then if there had been any food to hurl. Before he swigged his one gulp, it had become apparent that he and his ride both would only survive like this for another day, if that.

You do know where we are, doncha Dunderhead? 'No Man's Land' means no man, which I reckon would include them injuns.

That was true.

An' ya insist that ya don't need me, scoffed The Soldier. *Any river you find won't be protected in these parts.*

"Why didn't I realize this sooner?"

'Cuz ya been drinkin' piss! Ya ain't thinkin' clear. We've only survived this long 'cuz of me.

Although there had been moments when The Soldier's help proved invaluable, Jeremiah knew the only reason they had survived the five-day trek across the state was because of his doing. He was the clever one, who chose to travel from dusk to dawn and rest in the shade during the day. This intuition not only ensured their endurance against the temperatures but kept them hidden from hostile tribes. They would never have made it to the Black Mesa in 'No Man's Land' otherwise. And as he recalled what little he did know of the panhandle, Beaver River was nearby... somewhere.

"Which direction?"

You was the one who listened to them savage's tales, not me.

"They ain't savages!" Jeremiah roared to their defense.

Well, it wun't good white Christian folk who called some kinda demon to come kill ya.

Two riders rode out of the east, obscuring his search. Too far to see in detail, both Jeremiah and The Soldier agreed that they were Calvin and Alexander, and no doubt, he had been spotted as well. Standing in front of the ominous clouds that would frame his presence in their point of view, he cursed himself for stupidly perching on top of a cliff.

There was no gunfire, not yet. Jeremiah mounted his horse who galloped down the side of the peak as fast as his exhaustion would take him. Jeremiah lost sight of both men, but just before rounding the basin, his trackers had closed in enough to see the trail of dust left by their charging mounts. To cover as much ground as they had, their mounts would have been in prime health. Somehow the trek across the state did not afflict them as severely. Outrunning his hunters a second time would be next to impossible.

The wind softened to a breeze as Jeremiah made a beeline over the long stretch of barren earth. Like a beacon of light in the dark, they would continue to follow his trail, and there wasn't a single thing he could do about that. Images of his riddled body lying in the dirt, or hanging from the end of a rope, raped his thoughts. He saw no way out of his predicament, and a part of him, shockingly, felt grateful.

You ain't thinkin' of givin' us up is you? We've come too far, boy. They can have us when we're dead. Not before!

As though the air had grown cold, Jeremiah shivered under the suggestion of death. The last few days of suffering under these extraneous circumstances were nothing compared to what would be in store for him once on the other side. However, despite all his transgressions, Jeremiah maintained that his fate was unclear. He had hoped that God would recognize the manipulative hold The Soldier had over him and take pity on his soul.

The arrogant voice laughed at him. *You think yer entitled to a plea of insanity? That ship has sailed, boy. Maybe, if ya didn't know you was crazy like a'fore, but now you know an' I'm still here. Time to face facts. You ain't never gettin' rid of me.*

Because he feared there was more truth than deceit to The Soldier's declaration, Jeremiah agreed the moment to voluntarily give himself over to his pursuers had not arrived, and never would.

He glanced over his shoulder, relieved to discover that Calvin and Alexander hadn't circled around the hill just yet when light flashed over the desolate land. Jeremiah turned back and faced a budding storm. The dark gray clouds took the shape of an anvil and swallowed the light like a snake would a rodent as it slithered southeast. The sky then changed its colors to a sickly green when a strong gust enveloped him.

It was twister weather, recognizing it well, but instead of trying to run as he would under normal circumstances, Jeremiah developed a notion that was madder than a March hare. By positioning himself in the right place at the right moment, he stood a chance of losing his trackers. The wind would wipe away all evidence of his trail like a magnificent brush. Then, just to be sure that they did not pick up his trace soon after, Jeremiah would alter his direction. The idea to continue west would not change. His diversion into Kansas, Nebraska, and possibly even the Dakotas, was meant to be only a prolonged detour.

No longer concerned with Calvin or Alexander, Jeremiah pasted his sights on the dark underbelly of clouds that had turned as black as soot. He endeavored to pinpoint where the tornado might touch down, and had guessed wrong. The roar of a passing freight train rumbled the sky as God extended his finger to a spot no more than a few miles ahead. The shock of the twister's vicinity not only panicked Jeremiah, but his horse as well. If not for the vacuum that continued to suck them towards the cyclone's vortex, Jeremiah would have lost the fight he had with his mount to keep their bearing true.

The shaft was not the largest he had seen, but this tempest was meant to be feared. Immediately, a circle of dust formed around the base of the funnel. It gave Jeremiah some much-needed perspective of its width, necessary for the success of this ridiculous idea. Though no less terrified, he watched it glide in his direction at an incredible speed. Jeremiah charged forwards.

Yer crazy as shit! The Soldier cried. *You'll kill us both.*

Jeremiah tuned him out. If the voice had continued whining about the dangers, he was kept unawares. Instead, he concentrated on the translucent dust ring, knowing the highest concentration of wind circled around the spout. He just needed to get close enough to be obscured from sight.

The wind strengthened and the wall of dirt grew taller the closer they came to colliding. The stallion's speed picked up despite his protest. Jeremiah imagined that the horse didn't need to exude any effort--not that he had any exertion to give.

They were close; maybe too close as Jeremiah could see the curtain of falling hailstones that the tornado left in its wake. He patted the mount's neck, as though the horse desired any affection from him, before he yanked the reins hard right.

The undercurrent continued to pull them as they struggled to cross out of its path, hoping that the unpredictable torrent didn't decide to veer off its current trajectory.

The whirlpool of dirt and debris was bearing down. Jeremiah dug his heels into the stallion's side, begging him to find the strength to run faster. Should the vortex's ring capture them, they would be lifted into the air and then tossed across the land like a stone skipping over water.

The clearing loomed ahead, but the tornado's

spiraling edge nipped at their heels with its intense force. Then, like two massive hands squeezing his ears together, Jeremiah's head felt as though it was being crushed by an incredible amount of pressure. He cried out as a means to release his pain. The extreme weight absconded once the twister blew past and continued its course towards the hill. They had done it. It was a close call, but they had survived.

I say it ag'in, yer too goddamn lucky for jus' one man.

Jeremiah stopped to watch the twister rip across the land and erase all evidence of his new chosen direction. Thankfully, if Calvin and Alexander did make it past the hill, they would not be able to see him just as he could no longer see the hill with the conduit blocking his view. Of course, in a perfect world, the deadly tornado would take care of both men once and for all, but even he wasn't that lucky.

A shot of pain ran up his leg after being struck, and then again on his shoulder. Though both slugs stung, they did not break his skin. Then, as though every angel in heaven was hurling stones, Jeremiah was doused with hail. He held out his hands then filled his mouth with the icy nuggets while the horse ate what he could off the land. Jeremiah chewed fast and hard to make room for more when the idea to catch the frozen pellets with his hat came to mind, but at the risk of being pummeled in the head by one of the larger stones, he thought better of it.

The cyclone blocked their path as it came towards them. Before the noise became too difficult to be heard over, Calvin yelled, "I see cover."

A stone shelf that jutted from a mound near a hill sat just ahead. They would make it in time if they hurried.

"We'll lose 'im!" Alexander protested.

"Better than our lives!" But the boy did not look convinced. Calvin watched his stubborn resolve getting in the way of good common sense. "You'll never catch him if yer dead."

Calvin swerved and made his way towards the overhang, leaving Alexander to make is own decision. Sure, there was a chance they could ride around the storm, but they only would make it to the other side if the funnel stayed on course. Of that, there was no guarantee. This way, they had a better chance of being protected from flying rocks, uprooted plants, and other hazardous debris.

The hot air washed over Calvin and grew stronger with each passing second as though he were the twister's toy at the end of a rope. Calvin did not look over his shoulder. If Alexander had decided to take his chances with the tornado, there was nothing he could do to help the boy anyhow. Instead, he kept his eyes on the approaching plateau while fighting against one of nature's most powerful armaments.

Only once Calvin reached the lip did he know that Alexander had taken his advice. Both men guided their mounts underneath then used their reins to tie both horses together as one. Quickly, Calvin unstrapped his lasso from the saddle, grateful to still have it on his person, and then looped it through the horse's reins before tying the end to a small protrusion from the wall. Once finished, he lifted the top of his shirt over his mouth. The boy did the same.

The outer band of wind blasted their hollow like a deadly weapon. A cloud of dirt swallowed them in one bite, and the rough wind scraped at their flesh like sandpaper. Calvin shielded his eyes and face as best he could, wondering if it were Alexander who screamed next to his ear or the horses who neighed in their pain. Either could be true. It was too difficult to make out any sound that competed with the thundering tornado.

Calvin dug his feet into the earth and hoped Alexander did the same. It was all they could do to keep from being dragged out into the open. The reins tightened in his grip. The horses were desperate to run, but the leashes kept them situated for their protection.

The twister's might intensified. The ferocity gave Calvin some relief as it was a sign that they were now on the backside of the funnel. They only needed to persevere a moment longer, but then he felt the lower half of his body lift into the air. Calvin dropped his full weight, and his body fluttered to the ground like a feather.

Alexander was not as heavy. Calvin feared the boy could be hauled away. He reached out a hand to investigate though it was against his better judgment. Alexander was not his son. Calvin couldn't understand why he gave a damn about this kid when his own blood would be the one to suffer should he lose his father to this twister. However, Calvin ignored his voice of reason and swiped his arm, despite not knowing when, where, or how this Stebbins had found a way into a heart reserved only for Henry. Calvin couldn't feel the boy in the place he last saw him.

The wind weakened fast, but the swirling dust took longer to settle. Even before it was safe to do so, Calvin opened his eyes and then uncovered his nose and mouth to shout, "Kid! Kid, where are ya?"

Not waiting for a response, he bolted out from under the overhang and glanced across the land. There was no sign of him, and the hail that had rained down soon after did not improve his vision. But as the tornado moved across the Black Mesa and took its rumble with it, Calvin heard coughing.

He turned back to the plateau, and then found Alexander sitting on top of his horse with both arms still wrapped around its neck for dear life. Calvin considered the boy's instinct to mount his ride that was more than ten times his weight an impressive maneuver. Of course, had the twister been mightier, then no amount of weight would have kept them down.

"You can let go now."

Alexander opened his mouth to answer, but his coughs wouldn't allow him to respond. He nodded instead. The boy then slid down the side of his horse when, like a waterfall, a stream of dirt poured out of his eye socket.

"The twister must have turned directions," he announced, explaining why they had received the brunt of the force.

"Maybe next time you'll let me make the decision," proposed Alexander as he held his hat out into the open to capture the falling hailstones.

"Maybe," mulled Calvin while doing the same.

They sucked on the ice pellets as their steeds ate the same off the floor. Then, once Calvin had his lasso fixed to his saddle, both men mounted their rides to charge around the hill.

It had been only minutes, but it might as well have been months. There was no trail and no sign of Jeremiah anywhere.

"Maybe the twister got 'im."

Calvin raised an eyebrow, surprised by the kid's composure. He was not upset or raving mad about losing sight of their man. Maybe the heat and fatigue of these last few days had drained Alexander of his gruff, or perhaps failure after failure was beginning to beat the boy down. Calvin hoped it wasn't the latter.

They used caution when strolling in the direction both expected Jeremiah to have traveled, careful that, if he had left a trail, they did not miss it.

But in no time at all, they realized their loss.

Calvin could think of no greater disappointment. He had miscalculated Jeremiah Whiting's skills again. It hadn't been enough to avoid underestimating him; he had needed to overestimate the criminal's abilities. That was why this chase continued on and on for days. No other time in the history of his occupation did Calvin show disarray by backtracking. It took nearly two days to pick up Jeremiah's trail again once returning to it after replenishing their water supply from Elk River. They had no other choice but to go back. Once Jeremiah scattered into the desert, both men were unsure what lay ahead.

Thankfully, Calvin knew how to talk to the natives though he could not speak their language. Although he did not understand the customs of those tribes whose land they trespassed on, he was not ignorant of their points of view and knew to show respect. It made the difference between being slaughtered and being saved. Though some, like the Creek, were more hospitable, all fed them and gave water before allowing them to rest in anticipation of their nightlong journey. That was how they had caught up to Jeremiah, and that was why losing him again had been such an overwhelming devastation.

"We'll keep West then."

"Sure. Why not?"

Jeremiah regained the upper hand, and Alexander knew it too. There was no better time for their target to change course, but the only two directions Jeremiah had to choose from were North and South. Guessing wrong would take them even further away from their quarry, while continuing in a straight line would ensure that they were distanced in any direction equally.

They traveled West under the heat of the sun and a miraculously blue sky.

CHAPTER XX

The road was, most likely, the infamous Santa Fe Trail he had happened upon, but Jeremiah hadn't a clue what to call the fortress that sat on an incline about a half kilometer yonder. Hiding in a shallow ravine-- a stone's throw away from the opposite side of the road--Jeremiah watched for movement, but all morning, the stronghold looked as tranquil as an abandoned graveyard. Without consulting The Soldier beforehand, Jeremiah crept to the surface with his mount in tow when the horse jerked his head in resistance.

It's a trap.

"How can it be a trap when no one knows we're comin'?"

That's what forts do. See them observation towers? They're observin' us, Dunderhead.

"Yeah, well I've been observin' too, an' I ain't seen nuttin'."

Well, no shit, boy. You couldn't see them dancin'

naked on the walls this far back.

Despite his own affirmation, Jeremiah did use caution in his advance. Between the gully and the front gate, only the random bush was available to hide behind; he didn't stand a chance in hell of sneaking up to the door. His best, and only tactic, should bullets start flying, was to turn and run. However, as Jeremiah crossed the halfway point of his jaunt, he came to trust that his own judgment had been correct... not The Soldier's. The fort was unoccupied.

The walls, though moderately damaged, continued to tower twelve feet into the air and looked to be in good condition. Remnants of shell casings, arrows, and burnt markings did suggest that at least one epic battle had commenced between the fort's occupants and the natives, but Jeremiah saw no bodies to prove his hypothesis; at least not yet. Even so, those corpses would have most likely been carted away by their surviving members or by the local wildlife.

Maybe a tornado came and cleaned house, mocked The Soldier.

Jeremiah halted near the entrance of a small stone structure. Thinking it might have been a guard house or welcoming post or both at one time, then dismounted to peek inside. Whatever it happened to be, it was now just an empty shed.

He glanced ahead at other stone buildings scattered just outside the front gate, but it was not until he was less than a hundred feet away from the main entrance that he noticed a manmade dugout with its dirt roof caved in. Once Jeremiah took a closer look, he counted seven more dugouts, each next to the other.

What do you expect to come from stoppin' here? We should go. We survived this long without shelter.

Ssh! Jeremiah hushed when hearing a familiar noise.

This ain't no place to hold up. We've gotta keep movin' North.

Quiet!

We stay too long in one spot, an' we'll git caught fo' sho'. Think about it, Dunderhead.

He should have known better. The Soldier would not allow him a moment's peace when needed. Jeremiah sauntered alongside the front wall regardless. The sound of babbling and trickling grew stronger the closer he ventured. It was water!

Jeremiah raced around the fort's corner to discover a conduit. It guided a current from a large creek about a few hundred yards due west towards the stronghold. Perched on a mound, the crick continued until it reached the incline then flowed into the ground beneath the fortress and disappeared.

The stallion's ill-manners returned. He pulled away to sprint to the canal and drink. Though shallow, Jeremiah leaped into the channel like he was a boy again at the swimming hole. He splashed and bathed and drank, but enforced his willpower to allow only one gulp. Though he felt life refreshed, he knew drinking his fill would make him violently ill. The same would be true for the horse. It took effort Jeremiah could not afford to exert, but he pulled the buck back with the promise of more to come later.

With his thirst mildly satisfied, his starvation stepped forward, front and center. Suddenly, the prospects of what might lie inside the fort were exaggerated.

The Soldier laughed again. *What the hell you expect ta find in there? Pheasant? Cheese and potatoes? Blueberry pie?*

Jeremiah would have settled for a plate of rat innards and mustard seed at that point. Multiple times during his trek, he had come across buffalo, but with a knife only suitable for carving and a gun with no bullets, he would get only one good stab in, maybe two, before the hulking beast charged off with superficial wounds. Prairie dog or rattlesnake would have made a sufficient meal if he still had possessed the proper tools for trapping. Those critters were too quick, and dangerous, for capturing by hand. Just as well, they had traveled in the night's darkness. Spotting something that required no capturing, such as a prickly pear, had been a bust.

Jeremiah came up with an idea to position his mount against the fortress wall then climb onto his back and peer over, but that insanity was short-lived. He would be handing over too much control to the animal who disliked him immensely. The horse that acted more like a stubborn ass would pull out from under his feet at first chance. Instead, he guided the steed to the front gate and then tied him to a post just inside the desert castle.

Though open, the front doors had been left intact, and from what Jeremiah could tell by his observation past the parade grounds, the entire stronghold was in adequate condition. This fort hadn't been conquered but abandoned, as though it had accomplished what it set out to do, and no longer served a purpose. The success of the inhabitants also explained why no Kiowa or Arapaho injuns had come out of hiding to attack a trespasser.

It also means that there ain't nuttin' of value. If they didn't flee, then they would have taken the time to pack their belongin's.

Still, it was worth investigating.

Not remembering when last he let his guard down, Jeremiah wasn't about to break his streak. He positioned his blade in front of him when approaching two adjoining structures just beyond the gate and to the right.

Inside the first, parlor-like room, a wood counter with one end slanted to the dirt floor with and two closed cabinets hanging from the wall above, were the only furnishings left behind. Hoping he might have entered the kitchen, he opened the cupboard doors. Instead of finding food or spices like he did at the Stebbins, he found only disappointment.

You was hopin' fer some cayenne, weren't ya? The

Soldier sniggered, amused.

"I wasn't."

You should have.

"Why?" Jeremiah grew suspicious. "You know summin' you ain't tellin' me?"

Maybe. Maybe not.

He pondered what it might be that The Soldier could know, when it dawned on him, "You don't know nuttin'." What The Soldier knew, he knew; just one of the few benefits of sharing the same mind. Having forgotten that fact briefly stressed just how desperate he was for rest. Sustenance just might have to wait.

If I don't keep remindin' ya about that monster, it'll catch up to us. That's why I'm lettin' it eats at ya. There was a brief pause before The Soldier howled at his own wordplay.

Jeremiah didn't find the humor amusing at all. At what point The Soldier had become a jokester, Jeremiah did not know. Already aware of his insanity, he never speculated that The Soldier could be just as much of a loon. Perhaps the conditions of their desert hike had damaged him as well.

"My trail's been erased, remember?" Jeremiah pointed out, attempting to bring some normalcy back to their conversation.

But that thing ain't like the other two. It won't be followin' yer footprints.

"Then where is it? Why ain't it found me yet?"

Why you askin' me questions you know I ain't got no answer to? Always the fuckin' dunderhead.

Jeremiah sauntered through an open doorway and into the next room with a large gathering of hay piled in one corner. Why both rooms were not conjoined as one, he could not decipher.

This was a hospital, informed The Soldier, surprisingly devoid of belittling.

"How would you know?"

This room was kept separate to give the injured privacy. An' the buildin's close to the fort's entrance fer quick access.

It did explain why there were cabinets, most assuredly used to house medical supplies. Though it infuriated him, Jeremiah knew better than to question The Soldier in all thing's military.

He purposefully kicked some long metal rods on the ground. They looked to be iron and possibly damaged parts from beds--hospital beds.

You see... ain't nuttin' but junk.

However, Jeremiah didn't see junk at all; what he had found was potential.

He strolled through the back exit; again, another door that was in fine condition and still hinged to the building. The doorway led to an open-framed structure that stood twelve feet away from the hospital. He did not need The Soldier's intellect to distinguish that this had been the stables. It further explained how the recovery room could capture a pile of hay in its corner from gusting winds.

In the far Northeast corner of the fort stood one of the two observation towers that he had seen from the trail. Upon closer inspection, he noted the crowned tops that were perfect supports for howitzer cannons, as well as the pulley system that would have been used to hoist them up top. Unfortunately, the pulley could also be used to lower them, which was how the occupants had taken those weapons back with them. Carved into the base was a doorless frame. Jeremiah poked his head inside and saw a ladder that stopped just beneath a trap door.

"We'll be able to see anyone coming now."

Or any thing.

Jeremiah exited, leaving the tower and the argument that would have ensued behind. He faced a long slender building that stretched parallel to the front wall on the opposite side of the gate.

The hike across the parade grounds was long. Jeremiah passed the time by eyeing more uninhabited dugouts between his position and the Northwest junction, taking note that not all four corners had been made into towers.

"They must've run out of supplies."

Well, anyone coulda figured that.

"But ya didn't"

He arrived at the building and used less caution than he did when entering the hospital, surprised when his peripheral captured sudden movement. He whipped his knife around and focused on a snake that slithered from this room to the next. The serpent had been too far to perceive its markings. The building's length stretched more than a hundred feet but considering the environment,

Jeremiah suspected it had been a rattler, and they were delicious.

He chased after his meal, running in-between two long tables that matched the distance of the structure. Jeremiah had prophesied that this might be a commissary. The tables that were clearly too long to transport would confirm his prediction; however, not a single chair or bench had been left behind.

Jeremiah followed the snake's crimped trail into the next room. Once walking through the archway, his pursuit ended at a hole in the wall. The Soldier scoffed but did not add to his mockery with a single word. Jeremiah shifted his attention to the den-like room, cramped in comparison to the commissary. He recognized the space as the kitchen by the rusted cast iron pot sitting on a cutting table below a row of cupboards, nearly identical to the hospitals. He would have been excited to search the cabinets for remains if the doors hadn't already been left wide open and visibly empty.

Jeremiah ran back outside through the room's single door. He had every intention to resume his pursuit of the snake when the glorious sight of a water well stopped him. He gazed down its cavernous chute. Though dark, glimmers of sunlight winked at him like a starry night, accompanied by the familiar sound of water trickling from the conduit. The underground stream continued to flow beneath this spot. Smelling the scent of the water coming up the stone chimney reminded Jeremiah of how incredibly thirsty he was still. He had waited long enough to take another sip.

The pail dropped into the pool and then was pulled back up by its rope. Jeremiah took a larger drink than he had intended; too difficult to resist.

The horse fought him each step of the way. Whoever had said you can lead a horse to water never met the Mason's bronco. However, once arriving at the bucket that Jeremiah had placed on the ground, it took no effort to make him drink. The horse would have gulped even more had Jeremiah allowed it, but like his own illness, rehydration needed to be tempered.

He let the animal be and crossed the parade grounds to explore the one building he had yet to investigate. The singular structure was about the size of his home back in the Ozarks, but unlike the other complexes of the fort, its foundation had been laid with wood that exhibited deep scratches covered with shattered glass and dried blood below an open window. Something ferocious had happened here; some form of brawl or scrimmage. Jeremiah looked closer at the markings. "You don't think that thing...?"

It can't be, interrupted The Soldier.

He rubbed his hand in the indentations then breathed some relief to know that they were not animal made. These marks came from something large and cumbersome, such as a desk or dresser. He picked up the largest of the glass shards. As in the river, the reflection he saw resembled his own, but he still could not identify who stared back. With eyes sunken into his skull and dark circles smearing the edges, Jeremiah assumed that this image had to be The Soldier because he could not appear so distorted.

So that really was you I saw in the river.

But then Jeremiah glimpsed a mattress next to a potbelly stove behind him in the reflection and pivoted to see if the mirror was playing another trick on his senses. There was no deception. Though the padding was soiled and black from the dirt--and whoever knew what else--it still was the softest thing he would have slept on in weeks, and those weeks would be prolonged even after he left...
If I leave.

I knew it.

"Shut up."

You can't live where you can't survive.

"I gave it no thought."

Bullshit, boy! We share the same fuckin' mind. I know what's yer thankin' when you thank it.

Caught in his lie, Jeremiah kept to himself, which he forgot was no different speaking directly to The Soldier.

We ain't got no food.

"Gots plenty o' water though."

Well, ain't that fuckin' dandy? But what about girls? There ain't none around, an' we both knows how much you like them girls.

"You keep it shut."

'Specially them youngsters.

"I told you to shut the fuck up!" He cried at the top of his lungs then dropped the mirror fragment and drew his blade. Jeremiah took his time and scanned the room. He knew The Soldier still had to be inside somewhere.

Their soft skin and their feminely ways. How could you resist? I might not have either... if I'd been there.

"You was there!"

What'd I tell ya about lyin' ta me, boy? Ya can't. He paused while Jeremiah thrust his blade into the air. *How'd ya like that wet hoo-hah? What'd it feel like when it was wrapped aroun' yer pecker? Like fuckin' a ripened melon, I'd imagine.*

Jeremiah turned and swung. Striking nothing again, he waited and watched, but the pain had crept into him. The tight grip he had on the knife handle reopened the wound Salali had given him. Blood dripped out like a spigot and dropped onto the fragmented mirror. Gazing down, Jeremiah saw him framed with a sadistic sneer.

Li'l pussies makes you feel like a big man, don't they? But you ain' gonna git none of that out here.

More blood gushed. Jeremiah gripped the handle even tighter. Soon, The Soldier's leer disappeared behind a sheet of crimson.

That be enough. Bes' go wash up that hand an' get some kinda bandage on it.

Of course! How he did not see it before was an enigma. After all this time, he finally had discovered a way to get rid of The Soldier, and the answer had been clearer than the reflection. The Soldier must have found a way to keep his mind closed to him. There had been lapses during the moments both had been too weak to control their thoughts. The most recent had been just before the tornado, when Jeremiah had toyed with the idea of death, and how it might solve this problem.

"I know hows ta git rid of you now."

Before The Soldier could protest, Jeremiah thrust the blade against his own throat, cutting his chin.

"Why wait for a tornado or Calvin or Alexander to be rid of you when I can jus' do it myself? Ain' this it? The only thang you fear?"

I die, you die, but you'll be the one livin' in hell. Not me.

"I'm already in hell 'cuz to you!"

Jeremiah burst with a cry from years of pent-up anguish. He dropped to his knees, not letting up on his incessant wailing.

"I shoulda jus' let you be the one to kill'em all yerself."

You is a thankless guttersnipe piece of trash who won't never be a real man!

The blade's tip penetrated his throat, but The Soldier stopped it from entering further. He grabbed hold of the handle and pulled the knife back slowly, but Jeremiah was stronger than expected. The Soldier had underestimated Jeremiah's strength; incapable of making the dunderhead let go of the blade. Instead, he reached into Jeremiah's brain and squeezed hard. The knife hit the floor.

But the struggle weakened The Soldier too, and he was unprepared when Jeremiah rebounded. He picked himself up off the ground while The Soldier's vice-like grip tried to keep him down.

"It's my mind!" Jeremiah yelled then bent over slightly. Knowing he would do whatever it took to be free, Jeremiah charged for the wall at full speed. His head had struck the stone before his body smacked the floor; unconscious.

CHAPTER XXI

The landscape started to change. The desert floor became rockier, which seemed apropos since they were merely a day or two away from the Colorado Rockies. Calvin had noted the shadow of the majestic range some miles back and pointed out the jagged purple hue against the horizon to Alexander, who cared nothing about the panorama. Calvin could not blame the boy. Without any indication that Jeremiah had taken this path, defeat was conditional. But Calvin could not admit to failure just yet. Acknowledgment of being beat would be his admittance that the conniving culprit had outwitted him. Though there might be a first for everything, Calvin would concede to anything but that.

"How much longer we gonna ride in the wrong direction?" Alexander asked with exaggerated irritation.

True, they persisted along a path different than

Jeremiah's, only because they didn't know which bearing was correct, and this matter had been explained to Alexander time and time again, but the boy could not be fully held accountable for his edginess. In addition to heat and fatigue, two years of continuous disappointment was mostly to blame. The tormenting combination was an ideal recipe for unpredictable intensities from an already hothead.

"We'll rest out the day soon then pick it up at night."

"I ain't fer restin', old man. Stop tryin' ta slow me down! I woulda had the fucker by now if it weren't for you an' the molasses in yer ass."

Alexander herded his horse in front of Calvin to cut in front of his path. Both men came to a stop. The boy was aiming to be confrontational. By the look of fury in his one eye, Calvin suspected he was ready to call it quits, and then, of course, hold Calvin accountable for allowing Jeremiah to get away with murder... quite literally. Alexander would have a case should he make such an accusation; perhaps it was more Calvin's fault than not. He was the one who had suggested they put more than a day between them to go back to the river for water, as well as his suggestion to brace for the tornado, rather than attempt to ride around it. Prior to his farming days, he might not have demonstrated such caution when mere feet away from a capture. Perhaps he had aged more than the two years that had passed.

"What is it you're hankerin' to do?"

Without meaning to, Calvin had stumped the boy. Alexander kept silent while he contemplated what to do with his newfound control, but then realized he had not planned beyond his mutiny. They were still hot, thirsty, hungry, and lacking any direction that would lead them to Jeremiah's position.

"Somethin' tells me you don't wanna hear any suggestions."

"There ain't nuttin' ta suggest!" He hollered at full volume.

"Then we're agreed."

Success. He had stumped the boy as planned, though an imperfect strategy. The result could go either of two ways. Calvin would exasperate Alexander's heat-stroked insanity, or the boy would cower under the realization of his ineptitude. As Calvin watched him settle on a choice, a chill ran up his spine. Dammit, if that hollow pit for an eye didn't spook him every time.

An explosion rattled the sky.

Calvin and Alexander spun to the northeast where a cloud of smoke ballooned into the atmosphere from behind a barricade of hills. The explosion meant there was life, and life in the middle of nowhere meant there was water.

Neither said another word to the other as they steered their mounts towards the disruption some three to five miles away.

◆ ◆ ◆

They had been in no condition to rush, and locating the inlet to the valley had taken more time than anticipated. In the two hours it took to enter the valley, there had been three more explosions, which helped to guide them. Their course inside the canyon swirled for another hour until the next eruption resounded around the upcoming bend. The ground shook, and both men eyed the valley walls nervously. Once reassured there would be no landslides, they sighed their relief; not only realizing they would not be crushed beneath a pile of rubble, but that they were closing in on their destination.

With each step they ambled around the curvature, their sense of caution heightened. Then, in the distance ahead, there sat a town amidst the hills. If Calvin and Alexander had not looked inside a deadly twister and battled a demon dog in the last few days, what they laid eyes on would be the strangest thing they had seen in recent memory.

The men continued to trot closer. Though there were some pine, oak, and walnut structures, most habitations were cloth tents. What buildings had been erected appeared to have been no more than a year old. There could be no argument that this town was one amongst many that was a recent product of post-war revitalization. Strange, though, that it was built up to be kept hidden.

No sooner than setting foot onto the town's thoroughfare, did a man, who looked to be in his early thirties, appear in the doorway of a building to their right. His deputy's badge did not come as any surprise to Calvin or Alexander since both noted that the structure he ambled out of was a jailhouse, as stated by the sign that hung above the lawman's head. He loitered in the door and kept his hand casually near his pistol when he greeted with a curious "Howdy."

Calvin and Alexander stopped then shuffled their rides to face the lawman, who nearly fell backward when peering at Alexander's face.

"Good Christ Almighty! What happened to you?"

"War," the boy answered simply.

Calvin glanced over his shoulder and took the town in with plausible consideration; not that he needed to, but he did so to demonstrate that he was a mindful man who used intellect before instinct. "What's this town?"

The deputy required another moment before he broke his stare of the boy, then twisted his glare from the empty eye-socket to Calvin and replied, "The town of Mumford. What's yer business?"

"Ain't sure yet. Who else came through?"

"When?"

"Last day."

"The two of you."

"No one else?"

"Nope."

"Ain't no surprise there," piped Alexander. "Don't no one can find this place."

The deputy smiled, as though only he knew the

punchline to a joke, and then explained, "Well, you come through the back way. Inlet's closer on the other side of town. Who you chasin' down?"

Calvin made a point to scrutinize the deputy's badge before he asked, "Sheriff near?"

The smirk the deputy sported was wiped clean off his face, but he had taken the insult in stride by offering, "I could have the answers yer wantin'."

Calvin had no more to say. He remained as quiet as a nightingale at noon while he locked eyes with the deputy. Thankfully, Alexander also had a mind to keep his mouth shut and stared at the lawman with his hollowed gaze. The inept deputy conceded in less than ten seconds from massive discomfort.

"Sheriff Mumford's the one settin' off the explosives. But if you insist in talkin' with him, you'll need ta wait."

"Where can we find comfort in doin' that?" Alexander injected anxiously. Calvin had to admit that comfort sounded welcoming, but he kept that notion to himself.

"Mum's the Word Saloon," offered the deputy as he nudged his head down the thoroughfare.

Calvin did not intend to chuckle. The deputy looked at him quizzically.

"Your sheriff must think highly of himself, namin' the town and saloon after him like they was his kin."

The deputy's smile warmed. "You'll git no argument from me," then offered his hand. "Name's Dillmore, Elam Dillmore."

Calvin hesitated a moment to look for sincerity in Deputy Dillmore's eyes. Once he found it, he shook. "Calvin Hawte."

Alexander did not offer his name but, funnily enough, the deputy didn't seem to be inclined to know the young man who easily could have been considered a sidekick himself. Of course, Alexander's missing eye might have played a part in Dillmore's neglect as well.

"Come on. Looks like you can use a drink."

The deputy closed the jailhouse door behind him while Calvin and Alexander dismounted. Dillmore met them in the street, but before he escorted the wanderers down Mumford's central lane, he turned to the boy, "We should look an' see what we can find ta cover up that hole in yer head first. These people here won't take kindly towards the uncomfortableness of yer ugliness."

As it were, Lester Thompson of Thompson's Mercantile had tied up his tent door early to aid Sheriff Mumford in the demolition of unstable boulders on the hillsides. To say that Deputy Dillmore demonstrated any appreciation or admiration for his superior would be a flat out lie. When explaining Mumford's plans to expand the town, the deputy scoffed as though it were a ridiculous idea. Beyond that, Calvin did not learn more, nor did he want to get sucked into any of this town's politics. He just wanted... well, he wasn't quite sure what he wanted exactly, but Calvin felt confident that he would know once it came. Fortunate for Alexander, Frye's Boots and Saddles, one of the few wooden structures, had been open, and Stan Frye obliged him by fashioning an eyepatch from the leather scraps he had lying about, and at no charge.

The girls liked the eyepatch and Alexander liked the girls; all three of them. The boy could not tear his gaze away from the railing of the catwalk above, where the flirtatious tramps allowed him glimpses up their skirts. Alexander gulped his whiskey but refused to budge. Making the first move on a professional woman made him nervous, which by Calvin's calculations, meant the boy had never had the pleasure of carnal sin.

Calvin gulped his third shot then set his empty glass next to the others before peering at Deputy Dillmore lingering at the bar. The lawman leaned against the counter while talking to the whore's sultry middle-aged madam in a voice too low to hear while the rotund bartender listened in and gave the occasional nod. Calvin did not need to hear to know that he and the boy were the topics of the trio's conversation.

At the opposite end of the long bar sat another local, who looked to have the world on his shoulders and drank methodically to numb his worries. The only other customer sat in the parlor at the next table over, passed out with his face planted on the top. In a standard setting, Calvin would have expected that this was the midday lull, but seeing as how this town wanted to be kept hidden in the hills, he didn't imagine it ever grew livelier.

Calvin had a chore for Alexander, and just as he leaned in to give the boy a distraction from the harlots, a very young girl, dressed in a yellow ruffled dress with a yellow bow in her hair, pushed in-between them. She looked to be no more than twelve and carried a basket full of matches under one arm.

"Matchstick, sir? Light yer pipe for one copper only?"

The lovely young thing, who seemingly came from nowhere, demonstrated her product by taking a wooden match out of the basket and holding it to his face.

"Sorry. Don't smoke, li'l one."

"Suzanne!" The madam hollered from the bar.

Both Calvin and Suzanne turned to the stomping of high-low boots coming their way. The madam reached for the girl's arm, twisted it, and dragged her off. Then, in the loudest voice Calvin ever heard as an attempted whisper, "How many times I gotta tell you ta wait 'til they pull out their smokes first? Now, don't that make more sense?"

"Yes, Miss Christie," skulked the little girl, trying not to cry out from the pain the madam put to her arm.

"Stupid, idiot girl!" She let Suzanne go to point a finger at the closed door under the L-shaped staircase. "Go try ta make yerself smarter by thinkin' about yer misdeeds."

Suzanne glanced at the door, but by the fear in her face, she could not move.

"Scat!" Miss Christie ordered then used the heel of her high-low boot to pound the little girl's butt rather than the floor.

Suzanne was jettisoned to the door. Then, at a monk's pace, she entered the basement and locked herself inside.

Alexander had not taken his eye off the ladies during the row; not once. And Calvin wasn't the only person who noticed.

"Well, if you boys ain't up fer a smoke, how 'bout some company?" Miss Christie presented as she motioned towards her girls.

"Company sounds nice," admitted Alexander.

The time to suggest that chore had returned. "We need supplies for when we pull out. And don't forget more ammo."

Alexander gawked at him as though every word he spoke had been in some unknown foreign language.

"Why me? Yer the one with the money." Calvin knew that the boy was referring to him paying for their drinks.

Like a dog spotting a squirrel, Miss Christie switched marks. "What about you then? Some pussy would put a smile on that grump face."

"Go on, Miss. We ain't here for none of that." Calvin then dismissed her with a wave of his hand.

Miss Christie arched her back as her disposition turned from shamefully sweet to aggressively sour instantly. "Well, then, what the fuck are ya here fer?!"

Just as he was ready to respond with "the sheriff," a tall and boisterous man entered the saloon through the batwing doors. Though covered in dust, the filth did not disguise the sheriff badge he bore on his uniform.

"Set me up with a couple, Paulie. It's hotter than Hades out there," spoke Mumford with a Northern accent... Boston, Calvin guessed.

Miss Christie turned from cold bitch to bitch in heat upon his entrance. She approached the sheriff with a zip in her step and stars in her eyes. Though not noticeable, Calvin also imagined there might be some perspiration between her thighs.

The sheriff did not appear to object to her aggressive welcoming, either. In fact, the moment she was close enough to take, Mumford grabbed her buttocks and pulled her in for a licentious kiss. Nothing could have torn Alexander's lustful attention away from the whores faster than the ravenous display of affection. When the time came to breathe, Miss Christie took the sheriff by the arm and escorted him into the parlor.

"We got us two newcomers."

Calvin stood to greet the sheriff on equal planes. Alexander started to follow suit; however, Calvin placed a hand on the boy's shoulder to keep him in his seat. He felt Alexander's anger rise when his shoulder tensed. The boy was perturbed, most likely under the assumption that his mentor still thought him a nescient kid. On the contrary, Calvin thought no such thing. He merely did not want the sheriff to get the wrong first impression when facing two capable soldiers. Having Alexander in his chair kept the mood relaxed.

"Sheriff," greeted Calvin.

"Who are you, and why've you come ta my town?"

"Name's Calvin Hawte, an' I'm lookin' for a man who might have passed through."

"Now, I already told 'im there weren't no man," barked Dillmore from the bar.

Mumford ignored his deputy to ponder.

"You lookin' for a bounty?"

"I'm a hunter, yes sir, but I ain't no bounty hunter. I am a man of justice and honor."

Miss Christie sniggered, but Mumford gave no such demonstration of doubt. "If that's so, who is it that you seek to bring to justice?"

"Jeremiah Whiting!" Alexander spat as he jumped to his feet. The roar of his loathing for the man boomed inside the parlor.

"Ain't never heard of him."

Calvin studied the sheriff's face in the search for signs of insincerity or deception. His examination was interrupted by a voice from behind, "But I have."

All eyes turned to the man who had been sleeping one off the next table over. Calvin squinted as he tried to put a name to the face that he had seen before. But it was not until the inebriate announced, "He murdered Martin Stebbins," that Calvin knew him to be Robert Mitford, the brave Confederate who had feigned death for three days in the mud at the Battle of Newtonia. Without this man's testimony, no one ever would have learned the truth of Jeremiah's guilt. Calvin felt immediate confliction. He didn't know whether to thank the man, again, for his service for seeking justice, or rap the soldier in the mouth for starting a two year interpersonal war that has only seen death and misery. In some ways, Calvin supposed he regretted ever knowing the truth. Had he, and the world, been kept naïve to Jeremiah's initial crime, he might still be at home tending farm... with Henry. It'd be just the two of them at this moment, and nothing else sounded better than that. But that was nothing but a daydream now. There was no turning back once you already left the past behind.

"Martin's my brother!" The boy announced as he rushed to the former soldier like an old friend.

"That must make you Alexander Stebbins."

"You hearda me?" He asked, surprised.

"Of course I hearda you. Any Southerner has."

Calvin took a moment to study the others. Nobody else appeared to be familiar with the name; except maybe Miss Christie, who stared at the floor. With a name like Miss Christie, Calvin did not doubt she had southern roots. But as for the others, they seemed unaware of the tale; probably Northerners who had come with Mumford.

Alexander took a seat across from Robert, but then the man yelled, "I didn't invite ya to sit with me, coward!"

The camaraderie Alexander had displayed for his former fellow rebel faded. Calvin kept his peace as he watched the boy's temper rise at the offense. An eruption loomed.

"Why don't you fill me in, Bobby?" Mumford demanded more than asked.

Robert was happy to. "This boy allowed his entire family murdered while he went on livin'. That tells me he deserted them to save 'imself."

Boom! Alexander pulled the pistol from his holster, but Calvin snatched it out of his hand before he could use it. The hothead leaped out of his chair, ready to fight for his weapon when he noticed that Mumford and Dillmore had their peacemakers trained on him. Calvin interceded quickly.

"True, this boy lost all who he held dear, but he ain't no coward. I can vouch for that 'cuz I was there when he tried saving them. Jeremiah Whiting is more demon than man, and that's the truth of him too. But this boy here," and placed a hand on Alexander's shoulder, "is a boy no more. He's a man, an' I have yet to meet one braver."

Alexander's eye grew twice their size, astounded by his mentor's admission, but the lawmen did not demonstrate the same impression. Their guns continued to hang in the air steadily, but then Robert raised his glass. "To yer kin then," and drank.

Dillmore had waited until Mumford lowered his

first and then proceeded to warn, "Either of you pull irons again, and I'll either lock you up or kill you. I ain't sure which yet."

Calvin gave the sheriff a nod to advocate his understanding and appreciation then waited for Alexander to do the same before returning the boy's weapon.

"Well, that was years ago, an' you still ain't gave up?"

"Never," promised Alexander.

"That is one helluva grudge, but I can'ts blame ya." Robert shook his head in disbelief then had himself another drink. He turned his focus to Calvin. "But you, sir. Mr. Hawte. Ain't you that tracker?"

"During the war I was."

Through inebriated eyes, Robert took a closer look. "Why have we met?"

"I paid a visit to you in your infirmary. I asked you questions about your account on the field."

Robert jerked his head as though the memory had smacked him upside it. His chuckle was raspy and weak, "A whole mess of questions if I remember righ'." He drank. "So, what's yer stake in this? War's over."

A good question; a damn good question. Calvin supposed he could go into a lengthy explanation which, as he looked around the room, most were curious to hear, but any reply would lead them further off topic, and he needed to keep this conversation on track. "Another time, maybe. I just need to know if you saw Jeremiah pass through or not."

"What? Here?!" Robert chuckled. "Don't no one jis' pass through Mumford. This place ain't nuttin', but a phony town fer deadbeats, vagrants, and criminals ta hide."

"You hush up now, Bobby!" The sheriff shouted and then motioned for Paulie to cut him off. The bartender nodded in agreement, reluctantly.

"We knows he's headed west," added Alexander. "Maybe he woulda come 'cross other nearby towns?"

Robert shook his head. "Excludin' present company, there ain't nobody and nuttin' way out here. No men, ladies, towns. None of it."

Calvin and Alexander shared a look of defeat. Their hopes for this town to give them some answers had been a bust until Deputy Dillmore piped up with "There is, however, a fort."

The interest of both men piqued though Alexander's was more so. "This fort got a name?"

"Nichols."

The boy... man twisted to Calvin with jaw-dropping awe. "I know that fort. That's the one I helped build. I betcha Kit Carson can help us find 'im."

"He ain't there no more. No one is."

Alexander took immediate offense and turned back to the deputy as though he had just insulted his dead mother. Thankfully, the deputy was too involved with being the center of attention to notice Alexander's fuming.

"They jus' up an' abandoned it some months back. I suspect they had no more work ta do after runnin' off all them savages. Killin' 'em all woulda been better if ya ask me. Dirty vermin always return if ya only chase 'em off." Dillmore then laughed at the thought.

It was Calvin's turn. He felt his blood rise, desperately wanting to reveal the other half of himself before he fired a bullet into the deputy's head, but Alexander didn't need his fuse relit. Calvin judged that it was best to lead by example. He satisfied his urge to see the vile man dead by knowing that men like him were not long for this world.

"It'd make a fine hideout now," concluded Dillmore.

"I could find it," affirmed Alexander. "It's jus' off the Santa Fe Trail."

"That's 'bout twenty miles back the way you came," offered Robert.

"Then the fort's another twenty miles northwest from there," concluded Mumford.

Alexander looked at Calvin. Both men shared the same notion, which was how Calvin knew what his partner would say before he came out with it... "That wun't far from the twister."

If these were pieces of a puzzle, they fit together nicely, which was how Calvin knew that they would find Jeremiah there; they had to.

Restless, Alexander nearly had both feet out the door when Calvin hollered after him. "We'll need those supplies first."

The young man turned and glared. Yes, he was delaying them yet again, but like the previous times, it was in their best interest. They may have failed to capture Jeremiah, but time and again, they always seemed to find him. And then maybe on one occasion, possibly not the next but some time soon, they would succeed. However, Calvin had a good feeling about today.

"Charles," shouted Mumford to the man who had remained silent at the opposite end of the bar. "Track Lester down and tell him to open shop for a couple of customers."

"It's Sunday!" The man rebutted.

"Just do it." Charles gulped what was left of his drink before he stammered out the door, but he did not leave fast enough to avoid Mumford's continued barking, "Then go check on those devil hounds you got for sons. Make sure Danny and Norman ain't messing where they ought not to be messing."

Calvin stepped outside with Alexander on his heel, but not before his cohort waved a good-bye to the girls on the catwalk. He paused on the planked walkway, and though he appeared to be taking in the sights, Calvin was admiring the overwhelming sensation of reaching an end to this hunt. And once it was over, he would return to Henry and continue the rest of his days living the life he had become accustomed to before Alexander reappeared.

Movement down the thoroughfare broke Calvin's concentration. He glimpsed a wild dog running across the street, searching for his next meal when a voice snuck up from behind. "I know where the fort is," expressed Robert through drunken breath. "I could shows you."

There was still some military in the man that the drink had failed to drown. Having witnessed the offense firsthand when in the field, he had a desire to see this mission through.

While Calvin gave the idea a moment's consideration, Robert Mitford took another swig.

CHAPTER XXII

The screaming and pounding in his head was what had waked him. The pain akin to being pummeled with by a rock hindered any recollection of what had happened or where he was, or who he was, but once the onset of his agonizing delirium faded, The Soldier smiled.

Jeremiah's plan to kill him had backfired. The spineless ingrate was gone... not dead gone, but gone, as though the Dunderhead had somehow gotten himself lost within the body they shared. Earlier, between bites of succulent rattlesnake, he had heard Jeremiah cry from the far, far recesses of his mind. His anguish sounded similar to a man who had been buried alive. The Soldier beamed, though he found no comfort in knowing that his incarcerated adjunct continued to lurk. As long as Jeremiah lived, there would be a chance for him to find his way back to the surface, and should that happen, The Soldier knew he better be prepared to fight to the death. He would not give up this body under any other condition.

He pulled his last bite of meat out of the fire and chewed. The feather spear he had set for the snake worked flawlessly though he was unsure it would have worked at all without Jeremiah's knowhow. If there was one thing that Dunderhead was more skilled at, it was trapping. However, with the worst half of himself unavailable for instruction, The Soldier had searched for any remnants or notes that Jeremiah may have tucked away in his memory... now The Soldier's memories. Unsuccessful in his findings, he had decided to attempt building the traps anyway, hoping that their shared subconscious would guide him. Swallowing his last bite, he stretched with the satisfaction of his filling meal though dinner was merely the beginning.

The Soldier picked up his knife and stick then whistled the upbeat *'Good OL' Rebel'* as he resumed whittling another spear. The fire from the open door of the potbelly glowed a warm orange on The Soldier's face as the setting sun fell behind the walls and cast an ominous shadow over the parade grounds. Moving the stove five-hundred yards towards the rows of dugouts would not have been any less cumbersome even if he had been at full strength, but sleeping indoors would not be acceptable, and these nights could grow cold. The best trap he could have set would have been for himself should he rest inside the confines of the building when knowing what was coming for him. He had dragged the potbelly, as well as the abandoned mattress, outside, and while moving his living quarters under the stars, discovered a steel canister left behind by the previous occupants. When opening the lid, there was no mistaking that the can contained kerosene. Unfortunately, there had been only enough petrol to ignite the stove and soak the rag end of a torch he fabricated.

"Can't imagine why someone would want to leave behind such a fine hob." As though waiting for a reply, The Soldier remained silent as he continued to whittle. "Maybe too hot to touch if those Dunderheads used it jus' before leavin'? I reckon that was most likely."

Still nothing. In some ways, it might take time to get used to not having Jeremiah around. For now, it was just him and the horse, who currently feasted on a small portion of hay he pulled from the corner of the hospital room.

The Soldier glanced towards the stable's unsound overhang, though not to watch the horse feed, but to inspect his earlier handiwork. The large feather spears trap, positioned between the hospital roof and the edge of the stable, appeared secure, as did the trigger stick rigged to the closed hospital door. Whoever walked through that door would never do so again.

"Whoever, or whatever."

The feather spear had been set for a man though it would work just as well on a beast, as would either of the other two traps he constructed. All day he had prepared and built, turning his temporary home into the deadly stronghold it once had been. The traps he laid from the junk left behind had become his army. He needed only to double his brigade to be battle ready, and then come tomorrow, his defenses would be complete. He and his mount could relax some and take the following few days to recover from the fair amount of damage and illness they had sustained before heading back out into the rough.

The Soldier twisted his head back around too fast and cringed, as though a rock had struck his skull again. No doubt, Jeremiah had given him a concussion. The Soldier fought through the pain to finish his project of whittling the wood stick into a weapon. He used the tip of his finger to test its point. The spear was ready.

The throbbing in his head returned as he lifted off the mattress. He paused to allow the pain to pass then lowered himself four feet down into the nearest dugout and planted the spike upward along with its brethren. Once finished, he climbed out of the dugout and dragged a faux wood roof, which he had previously cracked with the weight of the potbelly, over the hole. Now, whatever tried to sneak up on him while he slept would be in for an unpleasant surprise.

The Soldier reached for the next stick in his pile, but as the tip began to take form, a din from the stable halted construction. His obstinate cuss of a horse had become more frightened than at any previous moment. It tugged on the reins that kept it tied to the stable's structure. The log of the feather spear trap shifted. Though it still upheld, there was a good chance that it now might not work properly.

He rose with the intention of inspecting the trap when the stallion gave another powerful heave. The entire rigging trembled. The horse was desperate--determined--to pull loose. Something was approaching their compound.

"Shit!" The Soldier bellowed, not ready for an attack just yet. He dropped the partially formed spear then pocketed his knife before racing across the parade grounds to the observation tower. Scaling the stone pylon's concealed ladder, The Soldier ignored the painful pressure that squeezed his head, while desperate to see beyond the walls.

The lid of the trap door slammed against the roof. The Soldier climbed topside into the final rays of golden sunlight that radiated three approaching horsemen coming out of the east.

"What the... three?" He considered how that was possible when there had been only two the previous day. However, what could not be answered just yet was instantly replaced by the realization that these riders were still miles out, much too far for his steed to detect their approach. Something else had startled his horse, and he was unsure what that something else was until he spotted fresh animal tracks that the three horsemen followed.

The trail disappeared below the edge of the tower's crown. The Soldier stepped forward and peered over as the creature arrived at the base and leaped towards him.

The surprise had The Soldier launching backward. He tripped and collapsed while the beast clung to the tower's edge, struggling to pull itself over the lip. Scratching accompanied the creature's struggle; its hind claws had trouble gripping onto the stone structure. Before The Soldier had the good sense to leap back onto his feet, the thing slipped. The Soldier happened to glimpse an arrow protruding from its neck before it slipped out of his sight.

But the beast did not fall far. It recaptured its hold and then hoisted itself back to the crown.

The Soldier stepped down onto the ladder's top rung then slammed the trap door behind him. Within seconds, unremitting chopping began decimating the barrier. He hastened his pace as wood shavings and dust rained down around him. Once reaching the ground, he paused to analyze the distance between his position and the horse. The gap was far enough to be concerning, but as long as the creature concentrated its focus on the trap door, he stood a chance, but only if he moved right then.

The Soldier bolted. He did not clear half the distance needed before hearing the beast land on the dirt floor behind him. In the moment that followed, he had the breath knocked out of him when it slammed against his back. The tackle sent them both tumbling across the ground, but in the creature's charging speed, momentum catapulted off The Soldier and into the air. A loud snap echoed within the fortress's walls followed by a resounding howl of pain once the thing landed on its side.

The Soldier struggled to catch his breath, taking a moment to peer at the broken half of the arrow lying in the dirt; the other half lost inside the creature. Weakened, the thing wretched and stumbled. The Soldier recognized his opportunity at an offense and unpocketed his blade. Though nothing more than a carving dagger, he gripped the weapon like a hunter's knife, having every intention of using it as such. Without a head, the creature would not be able to see, smell, or bite; it would be left with no other choice but to die.

The Soldier came up behind the beast and grabbed its head. He then jabbed his blade into its neck, managing to hang on until its tail swiped his feet out from under him. He fell to the ground with the knife still wedged inside the creature's neck.

His plan had failed. In retreat, The Soldier scrambled to his feet then ran two steps towards his horse when he felt a pinch between his shoulder blades. His legs continued running as the rest of him had been halted.

No sooner had The Soldier's body slammed into the ground, did he feel his insides being pulled towards the notch in his upper back. The beast had him with that tongue thing, and it was strong enough to reel him in.

The Soldier clawed the earth that was as hard as rock. With nothing to latch onto, he reached for the broken half of the arrow and then spun around to jab its serrated edge into the creature's tongue.

Warm blood splattered in every direction. The Soldier crawled into a run, but then lost his balance and lunged back to the ground when every muscle in his body screamed with pain akin to leg cramps that would wake him out of a deep sleep. Instinctively, he wanted to cry out like a pansy but forbade himself.

The Soldier peered over his shoulder and was gobsmacked by the thing once again. The beast halted its attack to stand tall on two hind legs then use its top maulers to reach for the dagger's handle. Though the long nails of its claws hindered its attempt, the thing was desperate to grip the knife and pull it out as a human would, possibly achieving its goal at any moment. The Soldier's intrigue was temporary, and as though Jeremiah had walloped him upside the head with common sense, The Soldier awoke from his trance. He used what strength he had left to reach his panicked stallion.

At some point during the battle, twilight cast its sinister shadow over the world. Only a ghostly glow of the sun's light remained, which continued to dwindle with each passing minute. His shaking hands fought with a stubborn knot on the horse's reins. The Soldier glanced back to the creature's position and kept the sharpness of its red eyes in sight until they lowered just above the ground. The thing had dropped back onto all fours and now charged towards him. The time he wasted to free the horse was over, but The Soldier was not without options. He recalled how the monster had chosen the lamb over Peter Mason. Believing the thing was more animal than man, The Soldier wagered that its desire for food was greater than its need to feed its revenge.

The Soldier pivoted around the horse quickly then stood between both animals and waited. His attacker leaped. The Soldier ducked out of its trajectory in time for the thing to latch onto the steed with its outstretched claws. As predicted, the beast claimed its meal and fed.

Though the obstinate ass would have most likely died soon, The Soldier could not ignore the dread of knowing that he was now mountless.

Taking every advantage he had, The Soldier slipped away into the depths of the fort, and though premature, decided to put his plan into motion. There were other riders coming for him as well; three of them.

The demon still lived, and it had arrived, lurking somewhere beyond the entrance. Though the sound was faint, its feeding was no less grating than when it had slurped on his partner through his vacant eyehole. Calvin halted at the gate.

"It can't be. You kilt it!" Alexander assured.

Despair fed on Calvin's insides despite his partner's reassuring words. He did kill it, or so he had thought. Perhaps another had been sent in its place. He then attempted to hazard a guess from where it came. Until a few days ago, he had never seen one, and now there might be two. He shook his presumption out of his head. It had to be the same beast because whatever thing that had been sent to hunt Jeremiah had been unstoppable or damn near it, which also meant... "If that thing's here then so is he."

Calvin could sense Alexander's restlessness. The boy wanted to storm the fort, but instead, hesitated. He was learning restraint though Calvin wondered if the kid would have acted just as wisely had they been a posse of three. Robert Mitford wanted desperately to join their mission, but the drunk had been too sauced to ride, and time did not allow them to wait for his sobriety. Since the day they left the farm in Kansas, it was just the two of them, and that's how it continued.

Calvin returned his attention to the song of succulence. "Maybe that's Jeremiah it's eatin' on."

"Only one way to find out."

Calvin dismounted, and though his hesitancy persisted, Alexander followed. Both men had tied their rides to a hobble against a small structure before their weapons led them into the compound. Though before entering too far, Calvin glanced to the sky for any signs of a moon--not tonight.

Alexander startled the bejesus out of him with quick fire at a speck of orange light that glowed across the camp.

"Hold it," ordered Calvin. "Yer shootin' at a potbelly."

Baffled, Alexander paused to get a good look at

the stove. Calvin watched his partner struggle to see what he had declared then relaxed his weapon. Calvin doubted that Alexander could see the stove, having decided to believe his admission regardless. Good boy.

"Follow me. Ain't no one knows this place better than me," exaggerated Alexander. Since riding out of the town of Mumford, Fort Nichols was all the boy had talked about. For over a week, his partner had kept mostly quiet, but in the last day, he wouldn't shut up about the vital role he played in the stronghold's erection. And though he suspected there was some truth to Alexander's accounts, he was not in the mood to be led by a man who could not distinguish the difference between the monster's glowing eyes and the radiance of fire.

"It's better if we split."

"Suit yerself," huffed Alexander before he turned towards a long stone building that stretched the length of the south wall. Calvin watched him roam away. It did not take long for the night to engulf him.

He turned to his right, towards a much smaller structure. Then, continuing his cross to the entrance, Calvin caught sight of a silhouette. The mound lay just beyond the stone house. Calvin continued and did not pause until the dead horse became evident. He was certain that the animal had been the creature's feast from minutes before. He twisted back to the building and entered with renewed caution.

Dragging one hand across its surface, the wall guided him while he kept a sturdy grip on his iron with the other. Calvin came upon one of the four corners without incident, and then turned. Deciding to continue, he soon reached a doorway that opened into an adjoining room.

Calvin did not rush inside. Instead, he attempted to make sense of his situation by looking for two red pearls that glowed beside one another. Unfortunately, the same hint of presence would not work with Jeremiah. He had the capability of remaining unnoticed until it was too late.

Calvin took a chance and gambled with his life by entering. If someone or something were to lurch at him, he was as ready as he would be even in the light. But after taking no more than a dozen steps, he placed his hands on a backdoor and settled on the realization that he was alone. Calvin did not need to open the door to investigate where it led. He expected to find the same dead stallion on the other side. He walked through only as a quick means to exit the building.

A long slim piece of wood fell at his feet. It tap danced on the ground until it settled. As peculiar as the loose timber was to observe, Calvin became more unnerved by a loud scrape above his head. He gazed up at what looked like a beam that stretched from the building to the frame of a stable with spikes fastened to one end. Realizing the trap, he moved to jump out of the way, but the malfunctioning snare collapsed. The last thing

Calvin felt was the knock on his head and the eruption of pain before the dark night turned pitch black.

CHAPTER XXIII

The clamor Alexander heard had him leaping out of the commissary in the next moment. He called Calvin's name from the doorway, repeating his plea for a response, until a loud crack from the potbelly distracted him. The boy hollered, "When you gonna stop runnin' like a coward an' face me like a man!?"

The Soldier kept low in the dugout, peeking out just above ground. Breaking the stick had worked as planned. He had the boy's attention.

"You think callin' me out's gonna make you more of a man?" He chortled.

"I'm already a man, the same one who's gonna be judge an' jury for the murders of my momma, poppa, sisters, and brothers."

"Well, what about Elias? Who's gonna judge you for his murder? I could lay witness to you puttin' that boy down like a pig at slaughter. Ain't that the real reason you want me dead? You fear my testimony?"

"Fuck you!"

The resonance of Alexander's damnation was drowned out by the echo of his revolver. Wherever the rogue bullet had gone, it did not come close to its target. Alexander shuffled towards the pits as The Soldier laughed antagonistically. The dugout The Soldier hid inside had been carefully chosen for its position behind the stove that kept him blind to prying eyes; not only Alexander's but the lurking creature's as well. Where that thing had gone off to, he couldn't tell, but as though it were a ghost, he felt chilled by its continued presence.

"I'm gonna fuckin' kill you!"

But only the kid's words charged from across the parade ground and not the boy himself. He was being cautious; no doubt catching onto the deception.

He's re-strategizing, The Soldier explained to himself. He thought to continue exacerbating the boy with taunts of Elias's death, but he weighed the boy's guilt against another of his faults; one that would surely expedite results over the other. The Soldier perceived Alexander's greatest weakness to be his lust to see Jeremiah dead.

"So, you wanna be a killer like me."

And it was as simple as that. Coaxing a hungry wolf to a slab of meat would have been more of a challenge. Alexander stepped forward, but then stopped at the edge of the potbelly's firelight with his gun raised.

"I ain't nuttin' like you! I got righteousness on

my side!"

"What you got is vengeance, boy. Not countin' Elias, who else you kill?"

"P-plenty!" He hollered his stuttered lie.

"The war don't count, bein' in a situation of camaraderie an' all. It ain't the same. I'm talkin' 'bout cold-blooded murder caused by yer hate."

"It ain't murder when it's justice."

The boy's next two steps veered right when The Soldier needed him to steer left. He picked up another stick and snapped it in half. Alexander fired again, blowing up a puff of dirt next to The Soldier's head this time. Lucky shot. The kid shifted, and then lingered near the ridge of a concealed dugout. Just a touch more provocation was all The Soldier needed. "You ain't got it in ya ta be a killer. Yer jus' a Dunderhead like Jeremiah."

The Soldier did not realize he had made any error until the kid paused. The stove's light illuminated his dumbfounded confusion. "What the hell you sayin'?"

He could not retract his words even if he wanted to, which The Soldier didn't. Something about revealing his victory over Jeremiah felt invigorating. "I killed him jus' like I killed the rest of yer family, jus' like I killed Martin too. Jeremiah was an ungrateful bastard! I saved his life an' for that he wanted me dead."

Alexander stood still while his confusion turned to angst. "Well, who the fuck are ya then if ya ain't Jeremiah? Show yerself!"

Another snap was triggered, but The Soldier was just as confused as Alexander, who whipped around with his pistol and, in a panic, fired into the earth. Any man unaware of the hidden dugouts would have assumed he struck dirt, but The Soldier knew differently. An angered roar emerged.

The faux covering was ejected into the air and the creature hurled towards its shooter. Alexander managed another shot before tackled. Both stumbled backward then dropped below the surface after the board disguised as earth snapped under their combined weight. What The Soldier had intended to be a trap for the beast became so much more. He watched victoriously as two of his nemeses toppled into the pit of spikes.

Shrieking came from both, brought on by the wounds they suffered, but only the beast possessed the resilience to leap back out and retreat into the night. Alexander fired a bullet after it, but otherwise, he did not emerge. Instead, he wailed under stifled tears. Of the six spikes The Soldier carved, not one had been a killing blow to either boy or beast. The pride of accomplishment he upheld seconds earlier waned into shame in his lackluster construction. Though not complete failures, this was the second of three traps that had been botched, raising the question as to the stability of the third and how it would perform if sprung. Still, as the boy did not leap out of the hole, his wounds would be more severe than superficial.

The Soldier climbed topside but then used

caution when approaching Alexander's dugout. If the kid's six-shooter had been fully loaded, which he expected was true, then The Soldier was desperate to get his hands on that last round.

"Toss up your gun!"

"Fuck you!"

"Toss it up or I'll send this hot stove down to crush you."

There was a pause. No doubt, Alexander was giving consideration to his plight.

"Either way don't bode well for me."

"Then make yer choice, boy, an' be at peace with it."

"Answer me first. Who are you?"

"Ain't gotta name, but Jeremiah like ta call me his soldier."

The pistol landed near The Soldier's feet. He sniggered, "Dunderhead."

"Ain't gonna know no peace as long as yer alive."

The Soldier took the armament then sauntered to the dugout. The edge of the pit cut off the potbelly's light at the wall, keeping Alexander hidden in darkness, but that did not stop him from training his barrel to where he thought the kid lay.

"I knew you was still you. Crazy as flies on shit ya are."

Alexander gagged, and then spat. His own blood choked him.

"There was three of you. Where's the other one?"

"No one..." he coughed. "...else."

The Soldier made a threat by cocking his pistol.

"You sure 'bout that?"

"Jus' as sure as I know you don't got no bullets in that gun."

Alexander laughed heartily while The Soldier checked an empty carriage. The boy wasn't lying. "Come on down and take the bullet outta my hand, why doncha?"

The Soldier stewed in his spot while he considered his next move, but Alexander's incessant taunting did not provide the harmony necessary to concentrate. The very tone of his provocation grated The Soldier's very last nerve.

"So, wha'cha ya gonna do now, Jeremiah Whiting?"

"I told ya he's gone! I killed 'im!"

"You looks like 'im, an' talks like 'im, so I say you is him."

The boy choked again then expelled what clogged his throat.

"Who else rode with ya?"

Nothing. Alexander kept deathly silent to the point The Soldier expected that he might have finally died but then heard another spit. No more games.

He crossed to the potbelly with every intention of living up to his word about pushing the cast iron stove over the dugout's edge, when an abrupt impulse changed his mind. By the suffering sounds of his convulsions, Alexander might welcome death. Perhaps turning the boy's suffering into a thing of unbearableness was the way to procure the answer he desired. The idea was good.

He grabbed the torch that he had crafted earlier from a torn piece of the mattress, soaked in what was left of the kerosene, and poked it into the flames before swinging the lit end over the deadfall. Alexander sat upright on the pit's floor with a single spear protruding from his shoulder. In one hand, he held a spike, and in the other, the bullet The Soldier desperately required. The remaining spears sat in a puddle of the kid's blood. He was not long for this world.

"That's it. Come finish me off, Jeremiah Whiting."

"I ain't Jeremiah!"

"No, you're not," spoke a new but familiar voice. "Usted es el diablo."

There he was… the one whom The Soldier only could assume to be the third posse member. He had emerged, and the trackers could not have surprised him more by their choice of colleague.

"Yuma," he greeted as the stove's light basked the Indian's face, as well as a quiver strapped over his shoulder and an arrow aimed at his heart. "You didn't come all this way for me, did ya?"

"Where is Jeremiah?" Yuma interrogated sternly, yet calmly.

"He ain't never comin' back."

"Then you have made this choice easy."

The Soldier did not attempt to flee but rather, approached at a sluggish pace, careful not to disturb their momentary truce with any sudden movements. "Now, I did you a courtesy. We shouldn't be enemies, but allies, you an' me."

Yuma added more stress to the bow as he pulled back.

The Soldier believed the silent threat to be resolute and stopped. "I may not be an innocent man, but you ain't got a reason ta seek redemption on me. I ain't the one responsible for causin' grief to yer people."

"You are a coward not to admit your crimes!" Yuma yelled, his impassivity now miles away.

"I'm aware of the actions I am accountable for and own them. I ain't the one who can't admit to what is true."

"You killed Salali after you soiled her. Confess it!"

"I will not 'cuz I did no such thing. It wun't me."

"Don't listen to 'im! He's gone crazy."

Neither paid any mind to the boy. Instead, Yuma concentrated on The Soldier's emotionless plea. "I can understands why ya don't want ta put the blame on Jeremiah. He might have been naive to yer advances, but I weren't. Too bad too. Maybe we wouldn't have gotten inta so much damn trouble if he had. But Jeremiah liked the females... a little too much, I'd say. A real shame too 'cuz I think that Salali could've grown into a woman as fine as her sister, maybe more so."

The Soldier relaxed his icy stare on Yuma as he waited for the Indian to respond. After a moment's hesitation, the strain on the bowstring slackened.

"Goddamn! Kill 'im already ya stupid savage!" But the kid's senseless insult failed to penetrate Yuma's deep thought.

The galloping of four legs came from nearby. The Soldier looked for the red eyes in the exact location that Yuma flicked his weapon towards, but neither man saw what they had expected to find. The Soldier then pivoted his attention back onto the arrow that had already returned to threaten him. The situation had gone from tense to precarious. He had no choice but to take a risk, hoping that he wouldn't be pushing his luck when he added, "Can'cha tell yer daddy ta fall back?"

If not for the firelight, The Soldier would have missed Yuma's stunned surprise. But his revelation of knowledge about the creature's origin was not what had intrigued The Soldier. Humiliation dominated Yuma's astonishment.

"It cannot be controlled."

Something had happened; an occurrence of sorts, to warrant the Indian's change of heart.

"You ain't out here fer me, is you? You're huntin' yer father." Immediately, The Soldier was reminded of the projectile that had been lodged into the creature's neck. He then understood who had fired it.

Yuma let down his guard by lowering his weapon. "We were blinded by our rage."

"What are ya doin'?! Shoot the bastard, ya fuckin' bush nigger!"

The Soldier turned to Alexander, thunderstruck.

His words, though harsh, were commonplace, and not the catalyst for The Soldier's scrutiny. Instead, he considered the reason for the boy's presence, and it did not match Yuma's. Both Alexander and Calvin did not share the Indian's intentions for being here. Their objectives had been to kill Jeremiah; as Yuma's was to kill the creature. The injun never would have partnered with others who could be distracted by an alternative motive. Thereby, The Soldier thought it safe to conclude that Yuma was not the third posse member, but rather, the first member of a second posse that had spotted ride in from the east.

Upon his realization, fast approaching footsteps charged from behind. He pivoted as Tsiyi sprung out of the dark with his knife heaving forward. Instinct had The Soldier parry the thrust with his torch, but the force behind the Indian's attack knocked the light out of his grip. The two men latched onto one another's arms then wrestled for dominance as though performing in a match to the death from the glorious days of the Roman games. Tsiyi was younger and less experienced, but with his youth came greater strength. Both stared into the eyes of the other that swelled with determination and hatred. The Soldier wished for nothing more than to carve the Indian's pupils out with his own knife, which lay somewhere on the floor of the parade grounds... lost. He shifted his gaze to the weapon that hovered threateningly above his head, clasped in the hand of the connecting wrist he struggled to hold back. It would be impossible to take the blade without letting go--a mistake if there ever was one.

Without realizing what happened until it was too late, Tsiyi had him turned around and positioned with his back exposed to Yuma. The young combatant then shouted, "Now!"

As The Soldier listened to the tension on the bowstring being pulled, he forced Tsiyi to resume their dance. They paused once the light revealed Yuma's distressed expression, searching for a way to strike his target without injuring his brother warrior.

The creature was slick and cunning, and each man would have missed the thing slink into the pit if the corners of their eyes hadn't captured its brisk movement in the low light. No doubt, it had seen an opportunity to feed during the tumult and took advantage of the distraction.

Both Indians shifted their concerns immediately, switching to the grotesque feasting that emerged above Alexander's screams. Their reactions of horror informed The Soldier that neither had heard nor witnessed the thing's feeding habits before, noting that their astonishment gave him the perfect opportunity to steal Tsiyi's knife away. But the attempt failed; the injun had been prepared and swiped his leg across The Soldier's calves, knocking The Soldier onto his back.

Tsiyi dove forward with his blade, but The Soldier caught his wrists. Both men continued their foray as they had when vertical. The Soldier's focus froze on the tip that fell short of digging into his eye when he heard the zip of a flung arrow, followed by the howl of the beast. Tsiyi refused to be distracted a second time.

The Soldier felt a burning heat to his right. Noticing the torch, he reached for it with one hand, while the other continued to keep the knife from sinking into his skull. The Soldier fumbled for the torch before clasping his grip around the handle firmly, and then used its flame to burn Tsiyi off him like a tick.

The Indian launched backward, leaving himself open to attack. The Soldier took advantage of the opportunity and slammed the bottoms of both feet into his assailant's chest. Having drawn another arrow that was ready to fire, The Soldier prayed that Yuma's projectile would mistakenly strike Tsiyi as he ejected over the side and into the dugout. But Yuma's reflexes were sharp, and he retracted his bow.

Only the monster voiced its annoyance of being dropped upon with a discontented wail. Alexander kept his silence, which subjectively explained his death. And though Tsiyi did not share in the boy's demise, he kept remarkably quiet for a man fighting a voracious beast in cramped quarters.

Yuma shifted the arrow's tip back onto The Soldier, who froze. He was out of options or ideas for an escape, though death did not follow. Instead, the Indian appeared conflicted with his intentions, and The Soldier understood why. Sharing Jeremiah's body had been to his advantage, confirmed by Yuma when he lay down his weapon to reach out a helping hand to Tsiyi instead.

With the torch in hand, The Soldier scrambled to his feet and escaped into the night, leaving behind the frenzied uproar of bloodshed that grew softer the more distance he put between himself and the engagement of his enemies.

Calvin and Alexander would have tied their mounts to the convenient hobble against the shack just outside the front gate. The prospects of successfully retrieving a ride looked promising, but only after he made a quick detour first. When approaching the rear door of the hospital, The Soldier could not help but sense a hue of dissatisfaction. He wished he would be able to see the third and final trap sprung. Constructing it had been insanely difficult while in his beaten condition, more so than the other two snares combined. The deadfall had required energy and strength which he managed to pull from somewhere deep within. The Paiute would have crushed any living thing that stood beneath it... should it work correctly and not like its predecessors.

The Soldier approached Calvin's body, relieved to have had the forethought of bringing the torch with him. The light would make locating his gun infinitely easier.

The man, who had been more than just a thorn in his side for many, many years, leaked blood from a large gash in his head. The Soldier looked to see if he still breathed but could not tell while the heavy log pressed down against his chest. Though he thought to check for a pulse, the fading battle across the yard informed him that time needed to be spent wisely.

The pistol rested loosely in Calvin's hand. The Soldier claimed the weapon as easily as picking up a pebble when the fortress's walls echoed thundering gallops that charged towards him. Red specks, outlined by a dark silhouette in front of the stove's light, charged towards him. Also illuminated from behind was Yuma joining the chase, but no Tsiyi.

The Soldier's first instinct was to make a run for the horses, but once discerning he would not be fast enough, he reconsidered then searched for a better plan... too late, the thing was nearly upon him.

He lunged into the hospital through the back door that slammed shut at the same moment the creature hurled into it. The wood cracked at the center and the colliding force sent The Soldier flying half way across the room. He landed hard, knocking his head on the floor, and losing his grip on the torch. The hay in the corner ignited. The dried mound of grass that the wind had carried from the stable wasted no time spreading flames to the wooden structure that had become as arid as the desert climate.

The door defended two more attacks before having no choice but to break away and allow the thing inside.

The Soldier did manage to hold onto Calvin's pistol but refused to use it. There was no point. Instead, he retrieved his torch, hoping it would be the more powerful weapon against a creature that had demonstrated its ability to suffer. All living things that resented feeling pain would also fear fire.

The Soldier scrambled back to his feet as the beast vaulted towards him. He managed to clear the doorway to the front room when he thrust the torch like a sword at the thing. The creature halted then snarled its rage as it backed away from the flame.

The ceiling dropped fiery debris behind the beast. Sparks exploded and singed its tail. The monster whimpered like a harmless bear cub as the inferno gave The Soldier an idea. He ignited the doorway's frame with the torch. The arc of fire trapped the thing inside, allowing him to race out the front door, where he collided into Yuma.

Though seemingly out of nowhere, a ruse came to The Soldier, and in his best Jeremiah impersonation, he cried enthusiastically, "My friend! Yer safe!"

Yuma's face was stoic; unbelieving. He said nothing.

"This way!" The Soldier commanded as he made a beeline for the commissary that was clear as day in the flames' escalating radiance. However, once inside, the necessity for the torch returned. Its fire, though beginning to fade, pierced the black void of darkness enough to remove the shadows from the spacious hall.

As The Soldier had hoped, Yuma followed him inside. Both men ignored the howls of the tormented beast while The Soldier explained,

"Careful. A trap got rigged over there," motioning to the opposite end of the structure.

"Tell me your Soldier Spirit lies. Tell me you did not kill Salali?"

"Ya can't believe a word of what he's told ya. It was all him! You know me. We're brothers. That means Salali was a sister. He's the demon, not me." The Soldier then placed a comforting hand on Yuma's cheek. He nearly had the injun convinced "What we got between us is truth, right?"

The Soldier tried to read Yuma, spotting what he thought to be a suspicious glare. Even The Soldier feared he might have gone too far. He removed his hand then promised, "I can tell ya more later," then directed Yuma's attention across the lengthy room. "I'll be right back."

"How did you defeat your Soldier Spirit?"

"Later," repeated The Soldier. "After we kill it in my trap."

He paused, browbeating himself for having made such a simple error as stating "*my trap*." If Jeremiah had been the one who made such a slip of the tongue, The Soldier would have persecuted him for being such an incredible dunderhead.

Hoping that Yuma did not catch on, he attempted to cover his blunder by explaining, "I'll set next to the trigger, an' when that thing comes to you, you lure it towards me."

Allowing no time for Yuma to speculate any flaws in his plan, The Soldier raced across the long hall. He passed the Paiute, careful not to set it off in his haste, and then stopped where he had proposed the phantom trap to exist, next to the small storeroom.

He could just make out Yuma's position near the main entrance as they both waited for the monster. If not already, the thing would notice the window inside the room that trapped it then make its escape. But until it arrived, The Soldier allowed himself to be amused by the easiness of this subterfuge. He had grossly underestimated Yuma's affections for Jeremiah, realizing only then that no matter what type of man one was, adoration had the power to turn him into a pile of gullible mush.

The zing of Yuma arrows resounded within the walls and pulled The Soldier away from his thoughts. The creature was on approach.

Yuma hurtled towards The Soldier, but the beast did not enter the building immediately thereafter. The gap between the two was too large for the trap to claim both lives at once. The Soldier prayed that either the beast would gain speed or that Yuma would trip in the dark. He needed them closer together, but again, Jeremiah wasn't around, so neither was his good fortune. Shooting Yuma dead while the Paiute crushed the other was how the revised plan now.

The Soldier waited until the injun entered his torch light before lifting Calvin's gun. Ready to fire, he felt a compulsion to shout the same words he hollered to Martin, "I'm sorry, brother," before he pulled the trigger. However, Yuma did not die after hearing those same words. Instead, he dodged The Soldier's bullet; an indication that he had anticipated the attack, never fooled into thinking that Jeremiah had returned.

As though having been gifted a portion of Jeremiah's good fortune, the next stage of the plan came off without a hitch when the beast tripped the rope connected to the trigger stick. The entire section of the roof, plus more, crashed down on top of the thing. The thundering din of rock, sod, and debris was matched in intensity only by the wave of choking dust that followed--snuffing The Soldier's torch inadvertently. But before darkness reclaimed the room, he felt the satisfaction he feared he would miss. Watching the trap fulfill its purpose was a glorious moment. The Soldier could not have been more pleased with the performance. Though a giant slab of rock would have been a superior weight source, he had done well improvising with what the abandoned fortress offered. Using the water well's bucket and rope, he had hoisted the heaviest wood pieces, and the largest rocks, he could find to the rooftop where he piled them together.

The Soldier gazed blindly at the space where the creature would lie with its shattered neck and back and crushed skull, assured that not even a deformed demon cast by the spirits could have survived the barrage of dense rubble.

The tackle came out of nowhere. Yuma knocked the air, as well as his senses, out of him. The Soldier needed a moment to reclaim both, but the injun refused to let up. Yuma kept him pinned to the ground, pummeling his fists into The Soldier's face. Even when his target was on top of him, The Soldier knew better than to fire the pistol at a mark he could not see. Should he miss, he would be giving Yuma every chance to wrestle that weapon out of his possession. Instead, he used his free hand to feel for a piece of debris from the Paiute trap. Grabbing a rock, he then anticipated where the injun's head might be and swung his arm wide. It had taken three additional blows to the head before the Indian rolled off in retreat.

Crawling to his feet, The Soldier staggered into the small room. He skirted the wall until he came to the side door and stepped outside. Being in the pitch black of night was no less discombobulating. While the commissary blocked the burning hospital's light, the dwindling fire from the potbelly stove was too far out of reach. He continued to scuttle towards the water well until Yuma's annoying persistence rang in The Soldier's ear in the form of a war cry at his back.

Yuma tackled hard and the two men collided into the circular stone wall of the well. Not able to keep a firm grip on his gun a second time, The Soldier lost it to the night. His head was yanked back by the hair, in a prime position to be cut open by a knife when The Soldier relaxed his legs. The full density of his weight dropped, pulling Yuma over him. The Soldier heard the injun's head smack against the edge of the well then felt the Indian's hand brush against his shoulder as he attempted to reclaim his opponent. The Soldier wriggled out of the Indian's range then lifted his feet. The thrust was aimless though he struck Yuma in the gut and pushed him over the well's edge. The Indian made no sound during his descent, but the splash of his body echoed back up the flue.

The Soldier crawled around the well's mouth, in search of his lost pistol while listening to hear if Yuma had lived or died. Upon finding his weapon, a hollow gasp of air erupted from the shaft. Again, there would be no luck for The Soldier.

Damn you, Jeremiah.

He hoisted his body up the side of the well then aimed the pistol down the deep cavity, firing twice. The Soldier listened to the constant flow of the channel for a short moment before asking, "Yuma?! Is you dead?"

No reply came though The Soldier didn't expect one either way. But as to be sure, he placed his finger on the gun's trigger with every intention of emptying the barrel when an unprompted calculation enlightened him. He had lost count of those present. Calvin and Alexander made their own party, and as The Soldier figured earlier, Yuma and Tsiyi had been two members of a three-man posse that rode in from the east, which inclined him to believe that a third threat still lurked. Honovi, Atohi, even Atraco, were the first names that came to mind. The Soldier drew the pistol away from the well. Even if Yuma was still alive, he was detained.

These last three bullets were now earmarked for the man still to come for him.

Turning the corner to the front of the commissary, The Soldier was relieved to see that the hospital fire had not died completely. He reached for what was left of the structure and pulled out a thriving ember to carry towards the commissary. Within a minute, the building was set ablaze, and within another minute, it would engulf all that was inside. The Soldier did not leave immediately but took a moment to revel in his victory against the beast. The breath he exhaled was a mixture of fatigue and relief as he watched the flames take hold of the building and rip it apart like godly hands. But as remarkable as the destruction was to observe, nothing could eclipse the thrill of knowing that Matolu had failed to receive his revenge.

The commissary's firelight revealed the front gate while what lay beyond remained in darkness. It was then that The Soldier realized where the third Indian held his position. If it were him doing the stalking, that's where he would wait.

He had been correct in his summation. Both mounts from both posses were tied to the pair of hobbles outside the welcoming center. Of the five rides he had to choose from, only one had a lasso looped around its saddle horn. *That,* The Soldier thought, *would come in handy.*

He readied to climb in the saddle when a loud and high-pitched scream from behind thwarted him. Aponi had taken him by surprise before he had time to train his weapon. She leaped and brought down her knife with passionate fury. The Soldier blocked the attack, though by the amount of strength she put into her thrust, what love, if any, she may have ever carried for Jeremiah had turned sinister.

He pivoted around her next attack then swept his arm around the front of her chest, grabbing her from behind. Aponi fought with more power than expected from a woman of her stature. Continuing with her attack, she overshot her thrust. The Soldier used callous force in slamming her against the structure's wall.

"Why Salali?" She demanded.

"Wrong man, cherry pie."

"Yuma told me of the other spirit, but it is still you."

The Soldier spun her around violently. Though dark, he pulled her face close to his. With the help of the burning commissary, he had just enough light to see the glimmer in her eyes and knew she could see his just the same as he hollered, "Do I look like Jeremiah to you?"

"You spoke love to me."

"I tell you I ain't him!" He reached for his gun when the girl took advantage of his brief distraction and kissed his lips. The Soldier let it be. He relaxed his grip on the pistol once realizing that he was experiencing his first kiss. Though he did not share Jeremiah's feelings of Aponi, he admitted her beauty. Then, along with his first kiss, arose his first erection. Yearning and impulses tingled throughout his body. The Soldier began to understand what all the fuss was about, and how the urge growing in his pants had made Jeremiah do foolish things without thoughts of consequences. Something inside him had awoken; however, he was not Jeremiah.

The Soldier grabbed the back of Aponi's head and pulled her lips off his by her hair. She cried out from the pain he caused then had the barrel of his gun against her temple in the next moment. As he began to apply pressure on the trigger, a mighty roar erupted inside his head that was louder than any beast. The Soldier fell to his knees.

Leave her be! Jeremiah cried.

What he experienced was nothing short of his brain at war. Aponi's kiss had awoken his adversary from whatever state he had been in, and the man was willing to valiantly protect her to the death.

Distracted, The Soldier did not see the rock coming before it bashed into the side of his head. Aponi pulled her arm back, ready to make another attack when he focused on his external battle, rather than his internal, punching Aponi in the jugular. The red-faced harpy hit the ground, grabbing at her neck as though trying to pull it open for air. He then redirected his attention to Jeremiah, but this opponent would not be defeated as quickly. The Soldier needed to ride out, not knowing who might still live to come at him. He would stand no chance of being victorious in another fight while Jeremiah clawed for repossession.

I d'ruther it be anyone but you if I can't be the one in control of my own self.

The Soldier reached the mounts then untied four of the five horses from the hobble. He gave each a slap on its rear that sent them running. The fifth mount, the one with a lasso looped over the saddle horn, he unfastened last. The Soldier rolled one leg over its rear and settled into the saddle, but his action did not come without ramification. As he felt the inside of his head splitting in two, the scream that was meant to be kept internal rumbled over the land into non-existence. He inhaled short deep breaths to regain his endurance, but his gasps failed him. Unconsciousness was coming along for the ride.

"Not again," he mumbled.

Though he did not expect it so soon, the rope was about to come in handy. The Soldier mimicked Jeremiah's trick of wrapping one end around his waist several times before looping it around the saddle horn and securing the opposite end to the bridle.

Before he passed out, he hoped this horse, whoever it had once belonged to, knew to head west. Until he awoke, the animal would have total control.

God, I hope it don't take me back to them fuckin' featherheads.

CHAPTER XXIV

Keeping his eyes open was a struggle. The sun's intense rays felt like flaming arrows being thrust into his pupils, and once he managed to leave them cracked open, he saw why. The sky was as clear as anything he had gazed upon before, and though the sun seared, and the air breathed hot, its gentle wind chilled his face when it blew against his exposed sweat. The breeze felt like refreshing rain and had been the catalyst for pulling him out of oblivion, and not the boy who stared up blankly, clutching a lazily aimed rifle.

"You don't look righ', mister," stated the young kid, matter-of-factly, which did not come as any surprise judging by how his muscles ached and head screamed. "Where's yer hat?"

He wanted to reply to the boy and opened his mouth to talk, but the only noise that volunteered was a grunt. He felt foolish, as though the kid, who was seven, maybe eight at the most, was watching an infant trying to speak his first words.

"Wha'cha doin' on Melville? He's my daddy's hoss. An' why you got 'is gun too?"

"Yer daddy?" He asked, shocked that he had spoken so well so easily in the next breath. Perhaps the astonishment of the question had hauled him out of his incapacitation.

His eyes squinted at an unfamiliar barn surrounded by livestock next to an unfamiliar timber windmill, across from an unfamiliar sod and dirt-roofed homestead.

"Who are you?" The boy persisted.

Because his memories evaded him for the moment, the man did not respond right away. He hoped this environment would have loosened even a nugget of memory, but when nothing came to mind, he figured he might as well have been staring into the black of night.

Black of night, he repeated to himself. Something about those words struck a chord that felt more like a sour note. Desperate to realize more, he became overwhelmed by a small bout of panic when his mind and thoughts could not merge as one. Though knowledge felt within reach, something was keeping him from attaining his awareness.

The small hands holding the rifle's stock and chamber twitched. He was coming off suspicious by taking too long to respond. Quickly, he blurted, "Martin," though the name didn't sit comfortable with him. Even the boy did not look to be taken in, staring at him with the expectation of hearing something truthful. "Stebbins."

"You kin to Mister Alexander?"

Alexander? Stebbins? Something about that name rang true, not to mention the overwhelming sense of compassion that came with it, the same kind of love one might have for a cherished sibling. Martin considered that, perhaps, he had been truthful after all.

"Brothers. What about your name?"

"Henry Hawte, sir."

That name echoed familiarly as well, but unlike the other, Hawte made his skin itch, as though covered with spiders. Why the name of such a young boy put the fear in him was disconcerting.

"How come you tied to my daddy's hoss like that?"

He peered down at the rope that kept him secured to the mount. The sight seemed familiar, yet blurry like double vision, as though two memories from different times and different places crossed paths.

Once again, he could not truthfully answer though he didn't want to lie to the boy either. Martin Stebbins never committed such a crime, no matter how small the fib. Somehow he knew that, though not exactly sure how.

"I can't recollect."

"Is my daddy dead?"

He nodded curtly, yet sympathetically. Though he could not explain the haunting images of a man on the ground with a large piece of timber across his chest, his conscience let him know that he was good for his unspoken word.

The boy's intrepidity remained remarkably firm. "Who done it, Mr. Stebbins? Was it the bad man?"

Martin thought for a moment, trying to picture this bad man in his mind and then recalled such a scoundrel. He was of a vile nature, and to give him such a lenient epithet would be a wild distortion. *Evil personified* suited this villain more appropriately. "I ain't sure of his name."

"Jeremiah Whiting."

That sounded about right. "I reckon so."

"He dead too?"

The appearance of hope on the kid's face for a positive retort was almost too much to bear. He needed to know that his pa had been vindicated; he needed to know justice for his pa had been served. Martin nodded once, though briskly, and hoped it was the truth; not only for the boy's sake, but for the sake of justice. Henry's face fell regardless.

"What about Mister Alexander, Sir? He dead too?"

"Yep," he grieved with every part of his gut affirming it was gospel--still not understanding how.

"I thank you kindly fer educatin' me of my daddy's passin' an' bringin' back his iron an' hoss."

"She's a good girl," he commented while giving the mount a pat on the neck.

Henry smiled then chuckled. "Him. He's a boy."

"Aw, right. Him."

The boy continued to snigger loudly, no doubt

overcompensating from the news of his tragic loss but glad for the distraction all the same. Seeing the child humored was a pleasing sight, and Martin waited patiently for Henry to collect himself before he projected, "I could use a meal and some rest if you'd be willin' ta offer."

The kid did not respond instantly though his laughter did end. Suspicion still lurked within the boy. No doubt, Henry was used to being on his own and learned not to be so quick to trust. However, he must have perceived something kindly in the stranger because the kid took the horse by his bridle and led them to the barn.

Still tethered to the steed, Martin had no choice but to ride along. He started to untangle the rope, but the process was slow going. It hurt too damn much to move. Though his long sleeves had protected his arms, the tops of his hands were near black with pink splotches of raw skin from where his burnt flesh had peeled. The back of his neck felt just as scorched and crunched like dried parchment when twisted, but what hurt the most was his nose and forehead. He touched his exposures and felt his skin slide as easily as slipping on ice, and then the sting of fresh air breathing on his open wounds. With no hat, Martin thanked God for his full head of hair and the rebirth of his beard that had filled in nicely during the last two weeks.

Closing in on the barn, the many livestock that lingered around the byre greeted him with noisy enthusiasm. The best he could remember, animals always had shown keenness towards him.

Martin bolted into an upright position. Panic and sweat, synonymous with waking deliriously from an excruciating nightmare, saturated him. He directed his focus to the room, illuminated by daylight that poured through a single window, carrying with it the inviting scent of fresh-baked bread, as well as the uninviting clamor of pounding metal. An oval mirror sat stationed beyond the foot of his bed, supported by a waist-high dresser. And where lockboxes, perfume bottles, and other feminine trinkets would customarily sit in wait, this counter top was bare of any such knickknacks... not that Martin would have noticed.

The reflection that stared back was a devastating and alarming surprise. Prior to lying down, he recalled the kind boy bandaging and treating his hands, forehead, and nose with medicine. Even more than that, there had been a notion of deceit the moment he indicated his name to be Martin Stebbins. At the time, he could not put his finger on why he had considered that a crime, but while he stared at the man who stared back, the reasoning became clear. The mirror's reflection... his reflection... was an uncanny resemblance to that of one Jeremiah Whiting.

A deep rage swelled. The man rolled off the bed and grabbed a nearby chair by its backrest.

Ready to swing and shatter Jeremiah into hundreds of pieces, he froze, noting that Martin would not abide such destruction. Damaging another man's possessions, or a boy's, in this case, would alter nothing. He still would be who he was regardless, which was a man of compassion who understood the consequences of his actions. It did not matter how closely he resembled Jeremiah, what mattered was his denouncement of that foul monster.

And so that was what was decided, and that's how it would be until the end. He would not exist as Jeremiah, or that soldier-like persona, who had since gone missing, but as Martin. Whatever had transpired between those two rivals felt final, as though they fought the last battle of a victor-less war, leaving the spoils for Martin to receive.

He placed the chair back in its corner, expecting a rush of relief, but when no reprieve came, Martin heard why. The annoying clank of metal had stopped abruptly, replaced by the very vocal alarm of livestock. This bout of fear had awakened the perception of, yet, another monster, one that possessed anomalies such as red eyes, thorn-like spikes, and a serpent parasite that lashed out from its mouth. But that demon, for all intents and purposes, should be dead. The Soldier had watched an avalanche of rocks and timber crush it. Why he allowed himself to be overwrought by the dread of something that should be buried was puzzling. Perhaps Martin was more fearful than the other two personalities, *or more cautious*, he corrected.

Perhaps it was his distrust of The Soldier and Jeremiah that had him wanting only to believe what he could see with his own eyes. Not having faith in the others somehow felt right.

Slowly and cautiously, Martin exited the room. He skirted the central area of the house, noticing an untouched plate of chicken and corn as he passed to the front door, which had been left wide open. Upon seeing the boy scamper between the agitated cows, goats, pigs, and chickens, chasing down a red fox with his rifle, Martin's concern was appeased. In fact, watching the boy try to take aim at the thing that ducked behind the stampeding pigs was quite comical. He cracked a smile on his cracked lips, which stung like hell.

A growl resonated. His empty stomach wanted to join the barrage, surely awakened by the food on the table, but Martin chose to ignore the pangs of hunger just a moment longer; too entertained and curious to see how the hubbub would end. Henry's antics had Martin in stitches until the boy's aim locked on the fox. He held his breath; the suspense kept Martin on edge, waiting to see if the kid would succeed. He fired.

"Dang it!" The boy hollered in frustration.

Martin howled with laughter and wished there had been more, but the fox fled into the tall fields unscathed.

The show was over, and Martin's stomach rumbled again like thunder. It was time to eat. He sat in front of the plate he assumed was left for his consumption when not two bites in, the loud metal clanking returned.

He stretched his neck towards the door and cringed at the pain the motion inflicted, but he had to see what the hell the kid had been up to. Henry lay hunkered over a large hay rake sitting just below the windmill. The boy had the contraption turned upside down as he hammered on its monster-like teeth that pointed towards the sky. No doubt, the horse-pulled device had not been used for a while, but now that there were two steeds to pull the contraption, the machine could be utilized again, once fixed. But then, as quickly as the kid had picked up where he left off, he hopped off the hay rake.

The silence was soothing; the perfect side dish for an enjoyable meal. Martin delighted in both while they lasted, but not three bites in, the previous two decided to come back up. He leaned over the side and tossed his soupy chicken and corn onto the floor. It served him right; he hadn't been thinking. For having not eaten in days, he consumed too fast.

Martin heard Henry stir on the porch opposite the open door. The boy cringed at the puddle of chewed food covered in bile.

"I'll clean my own mess," declared Martin.

"You do that," agreed Henry then walked inside to pick up an oil can from the far corner before he turned and walked back out.

Following the boy out the door, Martin chose a rag lying next to the horse trough then dunked it. Before turning to head back inside to do what he promised, he continued to watch Henry, looking upon the boy with amplified admiration as the kid used the oil from the can to lubricate the hay rake's gnarled teeth. Then, once greased up, Henry used a wondrous amount of cunning and strength to position a tooth back into its rightful position.

A notion of pride came out of nowhere, and Henry wasn't even his blood. How proud Calvin must have been. After the war, Martin had hoped to have born a boy just as fine with his wife, Alice, but Jeremiah had stolen that life from him along with the lives of everyone else he loved. What a fool Calvin Hawte must have been for leaving such a fine son behind to chase a criminal who had done him no wrong, personally. If Henry had been a Stebbins, Martin surely would not have made the same stupid mistake.

And on that notion, an idea formed, or more of a proposal. Martin grinned at the prospect of his plan, and he would ask Henry what he thought of the idea when the time was right. But for now, he had a mess to clean up.

Yuma rooted his feet at the center of the village, keeping watch while listening to his people's suffering. The attack on their settlement, two weeks prior, had been only the beginning of the spirits' wrath. As expected, they hadn't been forgiving. Not only did they refuse to grant their favors, but the spirits exercised their ability to remove the gifts bestowed on them at birth. Nobody knew that the spirits were capable of such power, and yet warriors no longer fought. The spirits had succeeded in stealing their courage. Mothers did not care for their children. They refused to abandon their dwellings, choosing to sob all through the night and all through the day through blinded eyes and broken hearts instead. Even Atohi had lost his gift of resistance and submerged his woes in likker he had purchased from the Cherokee township of Tahlequah. The spirits were truly angered, and Yuma knew they had every right to be while their mutated brother continued to roam the desert.

Prior to arriving back at home, Yuma had been aware of their prolonged desertion when his pleas for assistance out of the well were ignored. Thankfully, Aponi had been there to help, and once freed from his cylindrical prison, Yuma raced to the smoking wreckage of the commissary immediately. The heavy stones were hot, and he had allowed no time to let them cool. Yuma paid for his impatience with burns to his hands and arms as he dug for the Great Spirit's remains that never were found. The beast had escaped. Yuma replayed the incident in his mind then, just as he had replayed it again, over and over, during the long journey home. True, it had been dark when the roof collapsed, and he had been under attack, but Yuma still believed that seeing the creature buried under hundreds of pounds of debris had been what he saw, and nothing different. And yet, somehow, the Great Spirit survived. Though the being continued to confuse him, he now understood his bewilderment was just. The beast Matolu had been deceived into creating was more than a host for the spirits, but something that should have been left unimaginable.

Even as he listened to his people's pain, Yuma did not disparage the spirits for their anger. They had every right to be enraged. He only wished that they did not act impulsively when terminating their influences while navigating him and his sister along the Great Spirit's path. If they truly wanted their malformed brother stopped, then they should continue to be a beacon in the night, no matter how many times it would take before his family succeeded.

Before leaving the compound, Yuma and Aponi had attempted to decipher their father's bearing without the spirit's aid, but the skirmish on the grounds of the fort had concealed its tracks well. However, Aponi did find something neither expected to discover, a man who continued to breathe.

Yuma turned to the hut that belonged to Jeremiah formerly. Inside, the white man coughed while Aponi attended to him. Curiosity egged Yuma to see how well the stranger was mending, but he thought better of it. His people, the ones who still had strength enough to scold, watched him. Even before they returned, Yuma knew they would not accept another white man into their home but neither he or his sister expected to receive so many threats of death for bringing him. Yuma could understand their outrage, and he tried to explain that this man was different, but they would not listen, not even their brother Kilwannee, whom Yuma had to fight back with a knife. Thankfully, their new chief, Honovi, spoke and they listened. He explained that the spirits had talked to him about the injured man, and he was to live. No more needed to be said thereafter because nobody dared anger the spirits further. But regardless of their wishes, the tribesmen did not stop watching with scrutiny, not only the white man, but the children of Matolu, too.

Aponi stuck her head through the hut door and waved Yuma to come. Once inside, he was astounded by what he saw. Despite the puddle of bloody mucus that pooled on the floor next to his bed, the patient looked remarkably well for a man who had nearly died from his wounds many, many times. This work was the compassion of the spirits. They had provided this man with the gifts they took from his people. It had been easy for Yuma to jump to this conclusion because he had seen the signs for days. Yuma had first suspected their intervention when the mounts had returned to the fort after being swatted away by Jeremiah--recounted Aponi. But what he initially thought was an act of mercy was not so. More clever than humans sometimes, horses knew how to find their masters in much the same way they knew how to find their homes. Their coming back had been for the sole purpose of retrieving this man to be healed, and their generosity continued many times over on the trail. Each time the man had very nearly perished, rain would come to revive him, keeping him alive until the next shower stormed through, which happened to provide drinking water for all. For a reason not yet made clear, the spirits honored this man. He began to awaken, unsettled to discover natives surrounding him. He did not panic.

Aponi returned to the simmering kettle perched above a small fire. She added herbs to the water and stirred as Yuma knelt down to the delirious man's level unthreateningly to explain, "You are safe here. You have come a long way to find your strength. My sister will continue to heal."

"Who is she?"

"Aponi, and I am Yuma."

Though Calvin did not let down his guard, he relaxed enough to give his name, and then take his eyes off Yuma to notice the wrappings of animal intestines around his chest. Before long, the fumigated air caught his attention and Calvin sniffed sharply, careful not to breathe in too deep. His chest would not have allowed that.

"Yarrow tea," he presumed.

"Your senses are strong."

"They've done me right," he mentioned, though not letting go of his suspicion.

"Then they should tell you we do not intend to cause harm."

Yuma followed Calvin's gaze past him, through

the door, and into the daylight. From his position, he saw the ravages of his village that his people have left alone as a reminder of their shame. But the picture painted must have given Calvin enough information to confirm, "You Cherokee then?"

Yuma nodded.

"I got some native blood inside me as well."

Yuma was not surprised. Calvin's bulbous nose and high cheekbones were common indigenous features, and the man had been able to detect the yarrow root by smell, but why he felt compelled to divulge this information was unclear. Yuma could only speculate that it was to let him and his sister know that they were amongst a friend, just as they had attempted to convey. However, all things considered, nothing explained why the spirits protected this man so diligently.

"My partner? Alex?"

Though Yuma never knew the boy's name, he did know about whom Calvin asked. His body had been found next to Tsiyi's at the bottom of a pit, and unless the animals had discovered his remains, he would be there still. Fortunately, Tsiyi's mount had returned with the others, along with a mare which did not belong to them. Using Tsiyi's steed to bring him home for burial, the unclaimed mount had carried Calvin. The choice to add the weight of another corpse to Tsiyi's horse before such a daring journey would have been unwise. But Yuma did not feel compelled to explain this to Calvin in detail. Instead, he shook his head solemnly.

Calvin allowed no more than a few seconds to grieve before he followed with... "An' what about Jeremiah?"

"We do not know."

"But you know to whom I refer?"

Yuma nodded, hesitantly. Calvin looked to be putting the pieces together, and it was all too clear by his attendance at the fort that he had been picking up those pieces for a while; along with that Alex boy. Soon, Calvin would learn of Yuma's part in hiding both men; Jeremiah and the spirit he called "soldier."

The tea was ready. Aponi poured a cup then held it to Calvin's lips.

"I got arms, li'l lady," rejected Calvin. He reached for the cup with his hand then pulled it back and squelched from the pain. "Yeah, all right. On second thought..."

Aponi held the cup steady as he drank. Calvin cringed at the tea's bitterness then hacked up more phlegm. He had spat red before he continued, "How'd you find me?"

"We arrived after you."

Calvin hesitated, working the details in his mind. Yuma suspected it wouldn't take long.

"You were the ones who was helpin' 'im, like yer helpin' me now."

His eyes returned to his surroundings with a fresh outlook, and though there was nothing left of Jeremiah to discern, by his repugnance, Calvin understood that the bed he lay in had once belonged to the man he sought.

"We did not know who he was or what he was capable of," stated Yuma, though not to justify his actions but in hopes that this knowledge would keep his spirit calm, and not interfere with his recovery.

"Then you saw what happened to Alex?"

Yuma nodded.

"What was it that got 'im? Was it Jeremiah or that thing?"

Yuma and Aponi exchanged glances. Their afflictive delay had inspired more questioning.

"You were the ones who sent it after him, weren't you?"

"You know the Great Spirit?" Aponi asked with bewildered excitement.

Yuma wished his sister hadn't spoken, but he could not condemn her. Because Calvin had expressed part of his heritage, he too had wondered if the man might have known about the creature. Atraco could have visited his people with the same offer to bear a corrupt abomination. Only, perhaps, they had turned down the Pniese's unearthly request, unlike his tribe. However, by the confusion expressed on Calvin's face, Yuma knew that to be untrue.

"Great Spirit?! That thing?!" Calvin exclaimed, aghast. "It ain't no spirit. How can it be? Spirits don't just walk around as they please..." then as though he could no longer be certain... "do they?"

Calvin coughed. There was more blood in his mucus than previously. His agitation was obstructing his health.

"You need more rest."

"Like hell!" Calvin shouted as he stood from the bed. His blanket dropped onto the floor, and the man bared all he had been born into this world with, with the exception of the intestines that kept his chest bandages in place. Aponi turned her head away as Calvin did not seem to be bothered by his exposure while his own temper distracted him. "Tell me honestly! How'd it get here?"

Calvin did have a right to know. He had seen it; seen what it could do, and even lost an ally because of the creation. Yuma told a short version of his story.

Calvin's legs had wobbled first before he sat upright on the bed. Either he had been awestruck by the tale, weakened by his poor condition, or any combination of both.

Yuma covered the man's privates with the blanket as to allow Aponi turn away from the wall, but Calvin's modesty had been short-lived. Once he asked how he had come to arrive at their village, and Yuma explained the situation with the horses, Calvin bolted to his feet again, though having the forethought to grab his clothes, boots, hat, and his empty holster.

"My gun?"

"Taken," assured Aponi.

Calvin gritted his teeth and fought to keep his pain silent as he bent down to raise his trousers. Covered enough to be considered chastely, he stormed out of the hut.

"You must wait," pleaded Yuma; following.

The man halted just outside the doorway to cover his eyes from the blinding light of midday.

"Where're the horses?" Calvin shouted. "Where's they kept?"

Reluctant to abet, Yuma did so anyway. His people were watching. Eyes peeked from around every corner and from the dwellings, including Kilwannee's. His brother would have regained some of his strength in the last few days. Yuma did not know if he would be able to protect Calvin from his brother's anger a second time. For the sake of their village, he thought it best to let the white man go.

Once guided to the pen, Calvin cracked his eyelids wide enough to look upon the horses.

"Where is he? Where's Melville? Why ain't he here?"

Yuma did not have a chance to respond before Kilwannee hollered "Thief!" from the center of the village. He then charged towards Calvin with a knife.

Aponi rushed to halt him, but their eldest brother swatted her back like an annoying fly. Murder, nearly the color red, burned in his eyes.

Though weaponless, Yuma intervened, giving Calvin a chance to make his escape in peace. He hurriedly climbed onto Alexander's horse and raced off.

Kilwannee raised his blade, ready to fling it into Calvin's back when the piercing screech of an eagle circling above evicted him from his madness. Its call had not been a distraction, but a warning not to interfere. Even more than that, Yuma heard it explain why the spirits shielded Calvin from harm. All made sense to him; he had been mistaken. The spirits had not relinquished their help in guiding them to their father as he had thought. With a clear understanding of their intentions, Yuma approached his brother whose anger continued to seethe. He waited until Aponi joined their tight circle before explaining, "The spirits have not abandoned us. That man is meant to lead us to father." He then looked to Kilwannee directly. "You are healed to ride?"

His brother affirmed his fortitude with a single nod.

"Then we will prepare for many nights. I suspect this journey to be long."

Both Aponi and Kilwannee looked to where Calvin was last seen before the brush took him from their sights.

"He is no longer our concern. We will keep our distance until our moment comes."

CHAPTER XXV

Henry had milked the cow. He then churned that milk into butter for the bread Martin smelled baking earlier that morning, butchered and prepared their meals, and now washed their dinnerware in the horse trough, and all the while he had tended to the farm, as well as worked on the hay rake, which needed a new part before it could be fixed. Remarkable.

"That was an excellent supper," Martin complimented as he rocked steadily in a chair on the porch, puffing on one of Henry's daddy's cigars. A strong breeze blew the tip and kept the burn constant, but should the wind pick up any more speed, Martin feared he might lose the cherry.

"Wun't nuttin'."

Most likely the largest understatement Martin ever heard uttered, though living as modestly as the boy had, Martin suspected the kid might not know what comfortable living was like.

"You run this farm all by yerself?"

"Usually. It's small 'nough. I think I'z bigger than it sometimes."

Martin smiled, but still, the boy's humbled wit could not deter the guilt that filled his conscience. Momma and Poppa Stebbins had not raised a freeloader--God rest their souls--and having his offer of assistance refused gnawed on his good morals. But as it were, Martin had trouble moving some of his parts without contending with tearful bouts of pain from his joints, muscles, and head. Once well enough, he would work his fair share of the farm's many, many chores as restitution.

Martin took another drag off the cigar while gazing at the wheat fields that swayed in the barn's shadow as dusk settled in. He conjectured that the time was as good as any to inquire about staying on to help with the farm, and maybe pick up where Calvin left off with his fathering. But then something about the idea felt off... rushed maybe. He figured, perhaps, he should discover more about this boy first before taking on a task he might be ill-prepared to accept. Making a few inquiries seemed a better idea; see what kind of situation he might be getting into should Henry accept the proposition.

He picked up a towel to help with the drying as the kid finished washing the last dish. "Where's yer momma?"

Henry pointed down the road towards a distant lone tree and what looked like a cross positioned in front of it. "There. Disease took her."

"She teach you to do that?"

"What? Dishes?" He laughed. "Nobody taught me dishes. They's easy."

"Easy 'nough that I can help dry?"

"No, thank you, sir. You needs ta help yer own health first."

The towel relaxed in Martin's grip though he had not set it down. He blew another billow of smoke into the breeze, which had strengthened in the last few moments. After watching the vapors disperse, his gaze rested on the cigar's hypnotizing red end that sent his mind adrift, becoming lost in thought. Before long, the cherry tip of the cigar transformed into the creature's red eye and the beast emerged to the forefront of his mind. He never had the displeasure of meeting the monster face to face, but that did not stop the images of two Indians fighting off the thing that they had a hand in creating. Yuma and Tsiyi were their names though he never had their displeasure, either. At first, Martin speculated that these images were more of Jeremiah's memories seeping into his thoughts but, by some mysterious means, he soon knew that to be untrue. The reflections belonged to that other one, this body's third member, who did not go by a proper name.

Are you there? He tested, hoping for no answer in return but needed to ask regardless; just like a child would reach into a fire after being warned that it would burn.

"Mr. Stebbins?"

Martin gasped softly, startled out of his reverie. He chuckled at his own embarrassment. Then, once the humor of his fright waned, he considered it would be better for the boy to acknowledge him less formally, should they become the next best thing to kin. "Call me Martin."

"How long was you ridin', Mister Martin?"

"Don't know. I wasn't quite myself when comin' here."

"You sure got beat up plenty bad."

"Well, like you said, he was a bad man."

"Still, how long?"

"I ain't sure. Where are we?"

"Barber County."

"Kansas?"

The boy nodded. Martin performed a quick calculation based only on what he could scarcely recall during his travel. On occasion, he had managed to open his eyes and gazed at a light that he had imagined being heaven at the time. But as for the remainder of the distance traveled, he remained unconscious during the stretch that had to be a good two-hundred miles from the panhandle to Barber. How he had survived such a trip astounded him to no end. There had to have been more to it that he couldn't recall. He might ponder more on that later, but for now, he responded to the boy with "Four, maybe five days."

"Was you chasin' Jeremiah too?"

Martin paused, thinking how he might answer truthfully. "No, he tried ta have me killed, but I survived him with the help of yer pa and my brother, plus some others. But I tell you what, I find great comfort knowin' that I'll never see 'im ag'in." And upon his own admittance, he truly did find great comfort in his words. Even the tension that he hadn't realized occupied his body, seemed to lift. Martin felt more relaxed than before and leaned against the backrest. He continued rocking at a much slower and lazier pace, supposing no better time to propose his intentions to the boy would come. Martin took a moment to gather his gumption when a strong gust filled the silence.

"Storms comin'," he announced instead, delaying his query. At first, Martin did not understand why he was so nervous to hear Henry's response. He would make a good father, he believed that much, and better yet, Henry already proved to be an exceptional son. Each needed the attention of the other, as did this farm. The proposal would be suitable for all involved. He could not make sense as to why the idea made him so damn edgy all of a sudden, but his confusion did not last long. His gaze returned to the cigar, as did the creature's eye. That was the reason for it. The beast's existence had been a reminder of the danger that surrounded him wherever he went. No matter who Martin considered himself to be, it did not deter from the fact that he was still perceived as Jeremiah, or The Soldier, externally. For any others who still might be on the hunt for either, they would observe them and not the man he had become on the inside. As long as Henry kept in his company, the boy would be at risk.

"Nah. It ain't no storm. Jus' some wind is all,"

Henry announced as he looked up to a cloudless twilight sky.

Smart boy. In truth, Henry didn't need him as much as he needed the kid. Henry had done an excellent job of living on his own already.

Then, as though the miraculous boy could read his mind, "Is you gonna stay on, Mister Martin?"

"I think not," he replied while looking away. If Henry's face was going to fall upon hearing the news, he'd rather not watch, and a good thing he did just that, otherwise, Martin might have missed the tops of the wheat blades that were being parted by something that charged through the field, heading their way.

Martin stood, ignoring the sharp pains brought on by his knee-jerk reaction. He tried to get a better look at what approached though still a few hundred yards out.

Henry had caught onto Martin's disquiet and stepped up onto the porch for a higher look himself. He asked worriedly, "What is it? Coyote? Cougar?"

While knowing what atrocities have lurked in this world, considering the boy's estimation was impossible. Martin may not have believed the creature to be dead, but he was not without hope that it had been. He knew The Soldier had seen it crushed. Martin's doubt was manifested by knowing that bullets could not stop it, so it seemed ridiculous to think that a rafter of rocks and lumber would fare better.

Martin had the right idea to leave; only it came

too late. He glanced at Henry, ready to make some form of advance apology for luring the thing to his home when instead, he yelled, "Run!"

Martin pushed the kid into the house ahead of him then slammed the door, catching his first glimpse of the beast as it sprung from the fields and charged towards them like a wolf that was the size of a bull.

Without being told to retrieve his weapon, Henry had the shotgun in his hands by the time splinters shot out of the door. Henry raised his firearm, but Martin pulled him into the master bedroom before the boy could fire. Closing them inside, Martin noticed the bedroom door was a lighter weight than the front. However long it would take the creature to burst into the house would seem like years compared to how fast it would burst into this room.

The window... it was their only escape. Martin used his foot to push the bed out of the way. He then took the shotgun and rested it against the wall. Henry would need both hands free to climb out the high window, just as Martin would need both hands to lift him, but before doing just that, he had instructions. As Martin looked the boy in the eye to give those orders, a faint voice infiltrated his mind. It commanded that he instruct the boy to get both mounts ready for the ride out. Martin refused, knowing it would be too dangerous for Henry. Instead, he ordered... "Get a horse an' go. Don't wait for me," then cupped his hands together, ready for the lift. Henry stepped down on them then was hoisted through the window as the bedroom door shattered like fragile glass.

There was no time; no time to leap out himself, no time to hand Henry's shotgun back to him, no time for anything but to grab the mattress from the bed and use it for his shield.

The beast vaulted onto the padding. The propulsion of force sent Martin flying into the wall beneath the window while he kept a sturdy grip on his spongy defense. The creature continued its relentless attack and swiped at the cushion. Feathers filled the room in an explosion of fluff as its claws shredded the fabric. The sharp nails ripped through to reveal the red bulbs that lurked on the opposite side.

Martin placed one foot against the wall, using the barrier to launch forward. He wrapped the mattress's cloth around the beast, pinning its razored nails to its side before tripping the thing to the floor, though having no intention of falling forward himself.

Like suffocating the monster with a bag, the fabric molded an image of its head when stretched. The material did well to block its bladed teeth from tearing chunks out of Martin's face, but the cloth could not contain the appendage that punched through.

The tongue thrashed the air, searching for him like a blind serpent. Martin turned to the shotgun, now on its side, when he noticed the mirror instead.

His actions were quick, springing to the dresser then tipping the heavy furniture piece on top of the creature as it struggled inside the fabric's hold.

Glass fragments doused the beast, allowing Martin the time he needed to retrieve the boy's shotgun. But in his panic, he had not thought clearly and pulled the trigger, unmindful of the dangerous situation he had just thrust into Henry's direction. Bullets and pellets were an infuriation, not a threat. Until that moment, he had the beast contained within these walls and distracted from chasing after the boy, but now it was desperate to flee and bounded through the window, stopping with half of its body outside, the other half restricted when Martin clinched its tail.

The creature's hind feet dug into the wall, scraping and pushing to complete its leap, but the scales that ran down its spine to the tail's tip, though sharp, made it easy for Martin to hang on. He balanced his feet against the same wall that took a shredding and tried his damnedest to keep from being flung by the muscular tail's wagging.

Martin repositioned his hand, only realizing his terrible mistake when the sharp edge of a scale dug into his palm. Just short of severing his hand, Martin let go and was propelled backward to the floor by his momentum, allowing the creature to scramble outside.

With the shotgun in tow, he scurried through the fragments of the front door and in a mad state, dashed towards the barn highlighted by the golden hour of the falling sun. But once inside, the shadows controlled all, permitting very little visibility.

Martin had no choice. He concentrated his attention on sound more than sight. From the far left corner, engulfed by darkness, he listened to the agitated stallions, no doubt terrified by the proximity of the ungodly thing they sensed. Towards the far right corner of the barn, Martin thought he might have heard the rustling of hay, but if so, it was soft and difficult to distinguish above the steeds' distress. Martin suspected it was Henry, and not the creature, burrowing into a hay pile to hide. His insight was confirmed when the digging noise of wood came from above. He trained the shotgun towards the rafters. Though his weapon was weak against the thing, Martin could not deny how affirming it still felt in his hands.

"Stay put, wherever ya be, Henry, an' don't move."

"Okay."

Martin hadn't expected an answer. Though muffled, he was surprised this bright boy had not had the foresight to keep his situation unknown. Now, he had to utilize valuable time to explain, "Don't speak any, Henry."

"Okay."

"I said don't speak! Jus' listen." He paused and made sure the kid now understood, which he did. "I'm gonna try and lure this demon out, an' after I do, I wancha ta mount up an' ride like hell to the nearest town an' wait fer me there. But only afta I chase it out."

Henry did not utter a word. He had learned well. Smart boy.

A smatter of tapping was heard shuffling near the ceiling. Martin gazed up and locked onto the brilliant red blemishes that gazed back. He did not fire; that had not been part of his plan. Instead, he backed out the doors in hopes of enticing the thing outside as he told Henry he would do. Unfortunately, the beast did not agree to that plan.

From the many times Jeremiah and The Soldier had watched it feed, Martin learned the monster had a special hankering for animal blood. That was how he figured maiming a goat would draw it outside. Positioned behind the hay rake, he fired a pellet into the goat's thigh. The decoy screeched in horrific pain and fell lame to the ground. Within moments, the creature bounded out of the barn to pounce on the suffering animal.

Martin's eyes bounced back and forth between the monster and the dim void beyond the open barn doors. As he gave Henry time to fumble out of hiding, untie his ride, and then mount it, Martin could not help but be drawn to the appalling sight of the thing feeding through the elastic hose that connected its mouth to the goat's neck. And while the animal's screams of being drained began to fade and the unearthly slurps of the suckling creature cultivated, Martin gaped at the goat's brown and white fleece draped over its ribs like the flutter of fresh linen settling on an unmade bed. He could watch no longer and returned his eyes to the barn where the boy continued to dawdle.

"Hurry, Henry," he hollered.

And no sooner had he yelled, did Henry bolt into the open on his daddy's horse. Martin not only recognized its coloring instantly, but the coiled lasso that had kept him from falling off as well, still looped around the saddle horn. Its placement did not come as a surprise, not after becoming aware of Henry's need to keep everything tidy and in its place.

But the boy had taken too long. The creature finished its meal and now searched for its next. Even on a full stomach, the horse could not outrun the charging beast. It leaped onto the mount's rear and brought the steed down just off the front porch.

Henry flew off his ride and tumbled across the dirt. The horse made for a good distraction as it whinnied its torment, but the boy pulled its attention back to him when he scampered to his feet then limped towards the windmill on an injured leg.

Martin pumped the shotgun, ready to shoot when nothing short of astonishment gave him pause. The beast, the thing, which had galloped on four legs like most other animals, showed that it was not like any animal when it stood on two legs as would a human. He continued to gawk, flabbergasted, becoming even more terrified by the thing than before. Spurred by his newfound panic, Martin pulled the trigger, but the shotgun refused to fire, as though petrified by the creature as well. He tried again, but the weapon had gone dry. He eyed the thing carefully, watching who its guttural instincts would choose: the lame boy or the lame horse.

It chose Henry.

The creature sprinted like a marathon runner, charging for the boy as he reached the windmill and began to climb. Racing past the ladder, Martin flipped his grip on the shotgun to the barrel end and then swung it like a baseball bat, connecting the stock with the monster's head. The hit could not have been more perfect, even with months of planning and practicing. The handle smashed the space between its eyes, stopping its head while its legs continued to run out from under it. The creature hit the dirt, flat on its back, but Martin was not satisfied, grateful that the rule about not kicking a man while he was down did not apply to this demonic man... animal... or whatever hell thing it was. He bashed the creature mercilessly with the stock of the empty shotgun, as though the weapon had always been meant to be used as a club. However, all he managed to do was upset the thing more.

The beast swung its tail and swiped Martin's legs out from under him. He joined the creature on the ground, and though he allowed a moment to see Henry positioned half up the ladder, he never would have outraced the creature back to his feet.

Even after all the pain he had caused the thing, it still had not been enough to deter its attention from the boy. Animals and children, both must have been a favorite meal.

The lasso from the saddle lay on the ground just out of reach. Martin knew the impossibility of catching up to the thing on foot, but he did perceive his chances of hooking it with the rope to be plausible.

He crawled to the lariat, jumped to his feet, and ran towards the thing that had begun its ascent up the tower's side. He needed to move faster. The creature scaled half the tower's height in the time it took for him to jog three steps. Luckily, Henry had reached the top already, but unluckily, he was now trapped on a small square platform next to the spinning blades caught by the budding wind; the same squall Martin needed to compensate for when making his toss with the hope that a surprising gust didn't throw off his aim. As the creature closed in on the boy, Martin knotted the lasso around the monster's neck on his first attempt.

He gave as hard a tug as he could muster. Unprepared for the wrench, the creature lost its grip on the crossbar and plummeted backward. In the forty-odd feet it had to descend, the beast wriggled its body around like a flailing cat and landed on all four of its feet, unscathed. It then stood erect on its hind legs, tall and mighty, while roaring a deafening growl that Martin recognized as a tactic. It was trying to weaken its prey with intimidation before it pounced.

Scuttling to secure his end of the rope to anything, Martin came up short. The hay rake was on the other side of the creature, the saddle horn on the injured stallion was too far, and the posts of the front porch were even further. And during his brief search, Henry reminded the beast of his presence when, in his squirming, he tripped on the platform and nearly fell. The boy caught the edge of the gearbox and, unintentionally ripping the covering off, flung the metal shield over the edge of the platform. More to the left and he might have put an end to this nightmare by embedding the steel guard into the creature's head.

The beast leaped back onto the windmill's crossbars, jerking Martin to the ground. He hung onto the rope for as long as he could while being dragged over the surface. He had no choice but to let go, the blood from his wounded palm forcing the rope to slip out of his grip.

"Hang on, Henry! I'm comin'!" Martin sprung to the fifty-foot ladder and began the climb.

The thing reached the platform. Henry ducked behind the exposed gear wheels that clanked and squeaked as they spun. He then absentmindedly placed his hand on the twirling pump pole that Martin thought must have burned the boy after he yelped and released the rod. Martin climbed faster.

Henry met the beast face to face, and the thing fired its tongue. The boy's reflexes were sharp. He used the uncovered gears for protection, but in doing so, stood with his back dangerously close to the spinning blades.

"Careful!" Martin cried, half up the ladder.

The monster countered Henry's position and spat its weapon again. Still quick on his feet, Henry dodged the appendage. It flew past his head and reached towards the blur of gyrating blades, striking a fin that knocked its tongue into the exposed gears. The beast cried pure agony as the rotating threads grabbed hold of its flesh and reeled.

The fan's rotation slowed but did not stop as the fierce wind proved stronger. Steadily, the monster's face was pulled towards the contraption. It whimpered with each hopeless tug it gave to be free then hollered mercilessly once the gears crushed its tongue between their metal teeth. The spinning shaft captured the deadly appendage, coiling it around the rod. Martin did not hear the tongue rip, but gore that poured from its mouth lubricated the twirling cylinder like crude oil.

Once its head and the pole connected, only then did the blades stop spinning. The wind kept the halted fins twitching, struggling to set them free.

It was now or never for the boy. Martin climbed to the top then reached out his hand. "Jump to me!"

Henry hesitated, watching the beast trapped between them swipe its claws every which way.

The windmill shuddered. Martin took his eyes off the boy to notice that the creature's dribbling blood had turned into a steady flow. It would be free once its tongue was ripped out of its head.

"Hurry!"

Henry made a motion for the ladder, but the ever-determined beast continued to swipe, blocking the boy's escape.

Use the rope around its neck, spoke a voice inside his head. It was Jeremiah.

Just as Martin had suspected; he hadn't been dead but in hiding. Martin wanted to ask why the hell he was still lurking, but he knew better than to start a conversation. Not only did he wish to avoid any dialog with a lunatic, but he simply had no time. And as much as he did not want to admit that Jeremiah's idea was good, it was.

Martin reached for the rope then tossed the free end around the hub of the jittery propellers. Hanging onto the rope tight, he jumped off the ladder, wrapping his arms around the creature's tail in his descent to the ground, but when the beast's body jolted, Martin lost his grip. Though a long fall, it was over in no time. Martin landed on his back and heard a loud crunch from deep within, followed immediately by a blast of pain, and then nothing. No agony, no tingling, just nothing.

Rain soaked him; thick and sludgy drops came from the thrashing creature dangling in a noose from above. The weight of his body, in addition to the creature's mass, had been enough to rip that fucking snake-like appendage right out.

The blades had been freed from suppression, and as they spun, they reeled the creature back towards the platform. It struggled against the windmill like a hooked fish would fight its captor until the propeller jammed again when the monster's head reached the hub, lifting the beast high enough to keep Henry out of its grasp. It had worked; the snare trap Jeremiah had whispered to him actually worked. Henry now had sufficient space to grab the ladder, and even with his injured leg, he reached the bottom in no time.

"You okay, Mister Martin?"

Martin attempted to lift a hand for help off the ground, but his arm refused to move. He tried to move his other, but it too disobeyed, as did both of his legs.

"No," he whispered in horror.

He tried again, willing some form of movement, but his energy was lost. Difficult as it was to admit, Martin knew he was not merely injured but paralyzed.

The beast continued to struggle on the swinging rope. The sight mimicked a similar moment in the woods from a memory he shared with the other two identities. Martin had no other option but to ask his old friend, *Are you there?*

Sure.

Got ideas?

I do, but first tell that boy to drag us back to the house, like Yuma did when he found me in the river. Same idea.

That's right. Though Martin hadn't been there personally, he knew the same as Jeremiah, and vice versa. He turned to the boy, "Get a long flat board from the barn. Is there one?"

Henry nodded.

"Good. Put a hole in the two corners of one end

and then loop some rope through and have yer hoss drag it behind him."

Henry motioned that he understood with a nod before he ran off.

"An' hurry!"

He shouldn't have done that. Yelling drew all the breath out of him, making it difficult to recapture. Martin took a moment to regain control of his breathing, which proved a challenge while panicked about the moans and creaks coming from the windmill. The thing insisted on jerking and pounding on the gears violently, attempting to regain its freedom. A diversion would help avert his worry while Henry constructed the gurney. Without pondering for one, Martin supposed he had the perfect distraction right in front of him... or inside him. Confronting Jeremiah would be plenty disruptive.

"Whachu doin' here, Jerry?"

Yous my friend. You was in trouble.

"We ain't friends no more. That's guilt yer feelin' for what ya done to me?"

It wun't me who killed you, an' you know that.

"I don't know that. Me and that soldier, we're both a part of you. Where is he anyway?"

I told 'im I'd kill 'im, an' that's jus what I done.

"Why?"

I didn't like what he turned me into, an' what he made me do to you.

"What he made you do?" Martin laughed, though it hurt, but then came to realize that his current suffering was not payment for his sins, but for the sins of those other two devilish characters. How he got dragged into their war was an enigma. Martin was dead; his fate sealed two years ago. Swearing to be Martin Stebbins from yesterday forward, he had forgotten to take into account that the real Martin was gone for good.

"I ain't supposed ta be here."

You goin'?! Jeremiah bellowed in alarm.

"This is yer providence, Jerry. Not mine ta face. This ain't no place for a dead man. I need ta be with my family. I needs ta rest in peace now, Jerry."

You can't go!

"You got crimes that ya need ta be present ta pay for. An' don't go puttin' the blame fer everythin' on that soldier like you do."

But I come back to help you.

"Then maybe you go on knowin' that ya paid back some of what you took."

Does that mean you forgive me?

"I could, but I ain't enough. You need forgiveness from more than jus' me, Jerry."

The list was long, and though communicating each name out loud would continue to distract him from the creature, he did not need to. Henry had completed his mission. At first, he wondered how the boy had managed to work as fast as he did in the dark, but on second thought, he supposed it wasn't so miraculous. The home he had been brought up in, that small rundown shanty in the woods, was kept in the dark most of the time. Just like a blind man, he knew where each furniture piece rested and could locate the position of each item with his eyes closed.

"My home? Not the farmhouse but the shack in the woods?" He questioned fearfully. But it had happened in a blink, Martin left him and returned to his resting place.

"Wait!" Jeremiah cried out loud.

"What for?" Henry asked, confused.

Jeremiah looked at the smaller, younger version of Calvin Hawte standing over him. Though he knew he could not feel his spine anymore, he was sure it shivered.

"Nuttin'. Get doin'."

"Doin' how? What I do next?"

Jeremiah went so far as to open his mouth and shout, "What the hell do you think?" but refrained from sounding irritable. Martin would not speak that way to him, and he did not want to risk confusing the kid when he needed to concentrate on this delicate matter. Jeremiah considered how Martin would respond before he calmly performed his best interpretation of his late friend. "Lay the wood flat then pull me on it. You strong 'nough ta do that?"

Henry hesitated, not replying until he had a moment to calculate what was expected of him though Jeremiah did not think the task difficult; it wasn't like he was heavy with weight. Skin and bones were the mass of his bulk after having starved for weeks.

The kid gave a nod of approval then lifted

Jeremiah's torso from under his arms. Had he not been awake, Jeremiah would have never known he was being dragged, unable to feel anything below his neck.

Once Henry had him on the stretcher, he grabbed the rope and tied its ends to the horse's gear when the windmill vibrated angrily. As the day transformed into night, the speed of the wind had strengthened. The propeller blades acted as though they were furious for not being allowed to perform their one and only duty with the creature's head jamming its machinery. One or the other was about to give soon. Either way, the creature would be free.

"Get that can of oil an' a lamp!"

"I almost got it hooked."

"Goddammit! Leave it, you dunderhead!" Jeremiah shouted, forgetting Martin's voice and startling the boy. "Do as I say! Now!"

Henry charged inside his home as ordered. In the time it took the boy to flame a lantern, retrieve the oil can, and return, Jeremiah feared the creature might realize all it had to do was slice through the rope with one of its ten blades. Thankfully, despite his bum leg, Henry did well in hustling and sprinted back in less than a minute's time.

Before the boy could ask what next, Jeremiah instructed, "Throw that oil on the tower then I wancha ta smash the lantern on it." And even as the boy wasted no time in doing as told, Jeremiah still ordered for him to... "Hurry!"

Burning glass burst in all directions as the

windmill's doused leg caught the exploding flame instantly. Just as well, the surrounding legs and crossbars were struck by a handful of the fiery shards that grew into blazes with the help of the fanning wind.

Jeremiah and Henry watched the flames climb when a strong gust nearly expelled the bonfire. Scorching embers were ripped from the structure and taken away. It could be miles before they landed, hopefully, snuffed by then. But the bigger concern was the tower. Though the gust dispersed, all the fire had been pushed to one side of the structure. It was burning unevenly, and another strong gust like the one before threatened the success of Jeremiah's plan.

A torched piece of the ladder broke off and landed across Jeremiah's body. He screamed for the boy, who kicked the ember away and then patted out the flames that had started to burn through Jeremiah's shirt.

"Pull me back!" He shouted, fearing the next blazing section to fall.

Not wasting his time with the horse, Henry slid Jeremiah towards the house himself. They reached the front porch's two steps then Henry pulled on the reins of the stretcher, lifting the head end of the bed and laying Jeremiah on a slant. He leaped to the foot end, ready to lift and push the rest of him onto the porch when Jeremiah instructed, "Wait."

The fiery tower was in perfect view. Though still lopsided, the flames had grown strong enough to withstand another gust and reached the platform in the time it took him to reach the house. In a few moments, the devil would be burnt at the stake, apropos since it was a method of witchcraft that had conjured it, and he, the intended victim, would be its executioner.

Jeremiah's lips slipped into a triumphant smile when hearing the windmill crack and splinter. The leg Henry had shattered the lantern against folded in on itself, initiating a chain reaction that had the other three legs crumble under the top-heavy weight. The windmill crashed straight down, taking the creature with it and erupting over the hay rake in a volcanic-sized explosion.

From somewhere inside the blazing turmoil, a roar, heated by pain and anger, singed the air with its cry. Then, once the chaos of fluttering embers and sparks settled, both Jeremiah and Henry discovered the reason for the creature's woeful affliction. More than being burned alive, four, possibly five, of the hay rake's teeth had skewered through the thing. The beast flailed and jerked, but its efforts were ineffective. The creature was going nowhere, but back to hell or heaven or from wherever it came.

The flames claimed more than the abomination. Just as the lantern had done when smashed against the tower, a fiery dome blew outward to birth infant fires that had the potential to grow to the size of their parent. Thanks to the large barn that shielded a majority of the embers from the wind, all Henry would need to worry about were the newborns. Unfortunately, there was no windmill to pull water from its deep well.

Henry continued to gaze at the thing he would know only as a monster made from nightmares while it thrashed inside the flames that peeled its skin and boiled the river of blood it emptied onto the ground. Then, like a wind-up toy slowing to an end, the beast died.

Intrigued beyond his other senses, Jeremiah shouted Henry's name twice before he turned his attention. Again, he felt out of breath. Jeremiah struggled to gather enough air to wheeze, "Bucket... trough... small fires... first."

Henry nodded then rushed to the nearest bucket next to the water trench. He dunked the pail then limped towards the blaze in the cow pen. Though some water splashed out as he hobbled, the small fire was doused by what remained. Henry rushed back to refill his bucket then headed for a larger flame near the barn entrance. It was then that Jeremiah heard strange tapping.

The noise was near his left ear. He rolled his head on the wooden plank from side to side but couldn't see a damn thing. Still, he heard it; he knew he did. Jeremiah kept looking then glanced at his left hand. His fingers... they were drumming the stretcher. They were moving!

"I ain't paralyzed," screeched Jeremiah ecstatically, though in his excitement, it did come across as odd that he still couldn't feel any part of his torso, legs, arms, or even the pressure of his fingers as they banged against the wood.

More tapping joined in the ceremony. He exchanged the sight of one thumping hand for the other, which acted like all possessed, and before he could inquire about this anomaly, both legs joined in followed by his entire body. Everything about him trembled.

"Wha... Wha..." was all Jeremiah could get out before a chorus of cracking bones and ripping flesh orchestrated over his dumbfounded gibberish. But the din of rupture could not hide The Soldier, as he clawed his way out of a crevasse in their mind to boast, *I told ya I'd be there ta watch ya die.*

Jeremiah had every intention of replying back when everything--each nerve and muscle and organ screamed all at once with searing pain.

Henry came running, as though answering Jeremiah's call for help, which the man never cried. He did not want the boy anywhere near him. Though Jeremiah could not understand what was happening, he knew that it was dangerous.

His head twisted to Henry and looked upon the boy with eyes glowing red and yelled ferociously, "Runaway! Now!"

CHAPTER XXVI

C alvin had every right to fear the worst. Something was wrong, terribly wrong. He dug his heels into his ride's flanks, jolting the horse from a trot to a run. On a clear day, such as this, the windmill should be seen from a mile's distance, but the landmark that had stood tall over his farm like a beacon was gone. Calvin felt his dread rise with each galloping step that brought him closer to home.

The ride back into Kansas had been difficult and relentless. From the moment he learned that Jeremiah Whiting had filched his horse at the fort, he suspected... no, he knew that his boy was in danger. How he could be so sure, he did not discern. Though Calvin no longer communicated with the spirits as he had when raised Blackfoot, the idea that they were sending him signals came to mind. The likelihood that his keen sense of tracking had returned was another possibility. But, of course, that wisdom only enlightened when imagination did not distract him with images of the torture his boy might endure when in the hands of a known child killer.

However, no amount of intuition could have prepared Calvin for the devastating sight of his home. The windmill not only collapsed, but it had been reduced to burnt rubble along with the barn and all of its contents, as well as the livestock that couldn't escape the flames in time. Among the fallen, lay his cherished steed, Melville, whom Calvin could not help but feel had betrayed him. Though once loved like his own offspring, Melville's deception coursed through him like poison. Melville was the one who had carried Jeremiah Whiting to his home, his sanctuary, his son.

"Henry?! Henry?!" There was no sign of him. He roared the boy's name once more before hurtling into the last structure left standing: his house, though no longer offering the comforts of home. A battle had occurred inside its walls. Shotgun shells and bullet casings littered the floor along with shredded pieces of wood that had once been his table, chairs, and doors. Nothing survived. The entrance to his bedroom mimicked the damage of Henry's bedroom door; taking the same beating, as though a stick of dynamite had been used to blow it open or... claw marks?

Calvin investigated the wild patterns on the wall. He touched, demanding physical confirmation of their existence, and then followed the gouges to where they ended at the edge of the empty door space.

He entered his son's room; a room that he would not have recognized otherwise. Nothing looked real. The bed and dresser matched his dining furniture by design while feathers blanketed the wreckage like a coop.

Calvin dug through the remnants, first wishing to find his son, and then not. He needed to know where his boy was, but not like this. He continued to flip-flop back and forth, changing his mind repeatedly until the decision was made for him. Buried beneath the debris, he uncovered Henry's frozen face. He stared up at him with his mouth hung open in mid-scream. Calvin crumpled to his knees. No words or tears would appropriately express the heartbreak that stabbed at his soul. Instead, he howled his bereft, but even his agonized cry of distress sounded weak and unworthy to his own ears. Perhaps no mortal sound could ever adequately convey the wounded rage he possessed.

Calvin had watched the light through the window glide slowly over the walls. It took the majority of the day to complete its short journey from the floor to ceiling. Once the luminescence vanished, Calvin awoke from his wide-eyed daze to peer at the indigo sky beyond, in search of something to fill the hole in his heart with a reason as to why he should move from his spot. Without his farm, his wife, or his son, he struggled to find purpose and, with twilight's help, Calvin settled on justice for his reason. It had proven a reliable motivator in the past. He only needed to decide who deserved their comeuppance. Many could be held accountable for his son's death. For instance, Alexander had been the one who pulled him from his home, half-cocked and rallying for support. If not for his return, Calvin would have never left his son to continue hunting Jeremiah. Melville also had a hand--or hoof--in Henry's demise, and should be judged for delivering the criminal to his front door. However, both man and horse would never satisfy his hunger for retribution because both were dead. He who was to be held accountable needed to be alive to take his medicine. And luckily for Calvin, such a man did continue to live, though Calvin was unsure for just how much longer. Had he had a pistol within reach to put to his head, he would have right then. Nobody else was to blame. Alexander did not put a gun to his back to order that he pick up where they had left off, and Melville only wanted to go home, not giving a shit about who rode on his back. Tempting as it was, he could not condemn another for his mistakes.

Calvin searched for any other kind of weapon, which he found on the floor in no time. Pieces of furniture shards surrounded him. Any jagged fragment could rip open his throat or slice open his wrists. Calvin selected the largest, most firm stake within reach, and then pressed it hard into his neck.

He felt no pain; he had gone numb. Die as he must, there was no point of killing himself if he could not feel the punishment. Calvin shifted the tip to the only part of him that he could feel aching... his heart. The idea of piercing that organ felt fitting.

With hands steady, Calvin gazed down at the shriveled remains of his boy, ready to declare their reunion posthaste, when he froze in his reproach. How he could depart from this world without giving his boy a proper burial was contemptible.

He set the stake down then reached under Henry's remains to gather him. Standing, the rubble that hid the rest of him fell to the floor, as did Calvin. It was not the added weight of his son that dropped him back to his knees, but the shudder he experienced when the skin on his son's weightless corpse drooped towards the floor like wet laundry. And his bones, Henry's bones, it was as though each and every one could be felt. Horrified, Calvin gaped at a body that more closely resembled a life-sized voodoo doll than his son, and yet, the sight did not take him completely by surprise. Grotesque as it was to behold, dread could not stop a recurring memory from distracting his attention away from Henry and onto Alexander. The image had haunted Calvin, off and on, since the incident when the demon-like creature had dug its eight-foot tongue into Alexander's eye socket at the camp, but what accompanied this recollection was a heinous sucking noise. No doubt, the thing had been feeding when it leeched onto the kid's skull, and it was trying to suck him dry, too, and would have if Calvin had not intervened.

Again, he had been protecting that boy instead of his own, but Calvin now understood he was not to take all the blame for Henry. Difficult as it was, Calvin gazed back down at Henry's terribly withered remains, thankful to know that he was not as responsible for killing his son as was that beast; as was those Cherokee bastards.

"Great Spirit," mumbled Calvin, repeating what Yuma had called it.

On his second attempt, he lifted Henry and stood upright. Calvin continued to the door cautiously, avoiding any debris. One clumsy slip and he could lose his grip and shatter Henry's delicate body like a porcelain doll. The slow pace also gave him time to consider how he would bury Henry. There would be no better place than under the tree next to his wife, but to do that, he needed a shovel, and something about the smoldering wreckage of the barn suggested that he no longer had one at his disposal. A Blackfoot burial it would be then which, upon further thought, was the most honorable tradition. Entombing Henry with just a few of the stones from behind the house would keep him protected from any hungry scavengers.

Once exiting through the front door, Calvin paused. There were three of them; Yuma, Aponi, and the angry one who had chased after him, all watching in eerie silence from atop their horses. His breathing hastened, and his eyes burned. Calvin had every inclination to set Henry down and charge after them with nothing but his bare hands as his weapon. Doing so, he would not be the victor, but that was not what stopped him from making a foolish errand. Henry mattered more than anything else at the moment. Still, that did not stop Calvin from threatening, "First I'm gonna bury my boy, and then I'm gonna kill yer pet."

"It is not a pet," affirmed Yuma.

"What the hell else is it then, cuz no spirit I know would do this!" Calvin held out his feather weighted son with ease. All three Indians guided their eyes away with shame. "Look at him! Look at my son! Tell me what did this!"

"We can help," expressed Yuma compassionately.

"I don't need any of yer fuckin' help! Stay away from me. Go home!"

Calvin steered towards the tree, spotting a trail of unusual animal tracks en route. They were familiar. He had seen this type once before at Jeremiah's camp in the woods. They belonged to that beast, the eater of his son, the thing he would now refer to as *Moby-Dick*.

Upon that notion, Calvin wondered what had happened to his previous whale, Jeremiah. From the moment he arrived at home, he could not remember if he had given that other monster a moment of thought. Had he gotten away, or did the creature finally get his man; something Calvin had failed to do himself.

Like a ripple in the calm water, the trail continued to the edge of the field before disappearing. Once he had Henry's remains laid to rest, he would pursue his new whale, steadfast, and this time, he would not stop until he either had the beast taken down, or he was killed in the process.

Yuma and his siblings hung back in silence, watching Calvin return to the house, hitch a flat wood pane to the mare he rode in on, then load up a pile of stones from behind the only standing structure. Watching the man work, Yuma could not help but be reminded of a similar experience, using a horse-drawn stretcher to transport an unfamiliar white man's wounded body to his village. Upon the thought of Jeremiah, Yuma skimmed his vision over the tops of the endless wheat, and as expected, he saw no signs.

In the hour Calvin took to complete his melancholy undertaking, he did so in silence. No more threats had been announced, and just as well, no words between Yuma and his siblings were communicated. Each kept silent, allowing only the land to speak because that was a part of the ritual. Nobody wanted to risk interrupting the whispers coming in from the fields, or the spirits that guided the boy's essence. Any disruption could confuse the child's spirit from finding his way, leaving it to wander where it would not be welcomed.

Calvin knelt in front of the formation and prayed. Then, once finished, he returned to his house and stepped inside. The man had disappeared for a mere moment before he returned with a rifle in one hand and a pistol in the other. Slung over his shoulder was a knapsack that he transferred to the base of the mare's neck, freeing himself from any obstructions to train his rifle on Yuma.

Kilwannee reached for his bow but halted once Yuma placed a hand on his brother's shoulder.

"He suffers because of us."

"Many suffer! Not just this man," Kilwannee disagreed, unwaveringly.

For once, in Yuma's opinion, his brother was correct, but then Calvin interrupted, "I'm warning you. I get one whiff of you followin' me, I'll hunt you next."

Upon his cautionary tale, Calvin relaxed his threat then mounted his mare, following the tracks into the field.

The Indians did as warned. Staying put, they turned back to the house, which Calvin had set ablaze before exiting. Clouds of smoke and billowing soot grew thicker and blacker with each passing second. The three backed away from the intensifying heat and continued watching as Calvin disappeared in the fields.

Yuma could sense the eyes of his siblings watching him for answers, not knowing what they were to do next. He, too, did not have a clear answer but dismounted anyway, considering a good start might be to examine the trail Calvin followed.

His two siblings followed suit and participated in investigations of their own; Kilwannee to the surrounding area of the burning home, and Aponi to the cooled remains of the barn and windmill.

The Great Spirit left tracks dusted with black soot, obscured only by Calvin's fresh hoof prints. He did not see what he had hoped to find--a man's footprints; Jeremiah's footprints.

"Yuma!" Aponi shouted. Kilwannee had heard the fear in her voice as well because he, too, sprinted to the large metal contraption where she stood. All three observed the remains, bewildered. The heat had been intense, damaging the machine beyond recognition, though it had not been hot enough to camouflage the spikes and tail of the charred remains of the Great Spirit, clenched in the mechanism's steel teeth.

"Our mission is over?" Aponi questioned.

"I do not understand," proclaimed Kilwannee, angry and confused. "Where is Jeremiah? Was he not here?"

"He was," confirmed Aponi and pointed to the dead stallion. "That is the horse that gave him escape," she then turned to Yuma directly. "Calvin must chase Jeremiah. Not our father."

"The tracks Calvin follows were not left by a man with two legs, but four. They belong to what we see before us."

"That is not possible!" Kilwannee shouted.

Yuma understood his brother's frustration.

There was something; something else that they did not understand about the Great Spirit, which Atraco had kept in confidence. Yuma was sure there would be even more surprising truths to discover than just the one.

"Do we follow?" Aponi inquired.

"Yes, but we must wait until we can understand better what it is we hunt."

"We can ask the spirits."

"We will not!" Kilwannee shouted. Yuma recognized the pain he felt towards them and all the grief they had caused.

"They will not help us. We must use what knowledge we have, and learn from the tracks it leaves behind."

"And what if there are others who see? Will they be blinded or killed?" confronted Kilwannee, though the challenge was warranted. At the moment, the Great Spirit did not exist to the rest of the world. With the exception of Calvin, and possibly Jeremiah, those who had seen it didn't live to tell about their account, but any cowboy, lawman, or traveler could stumble across the beast while it roamed. Should they be allowed to live, they very well might generate a panic, or worse, seek blame. Anyone would know that it was not of this earth by looking at it. Moreover, the white man loved to point his finger; it was the one thing he did better with it over pulling a trigger. Being that the native communities were already unpopular with the Colonies; Yuma could not abide having his people be the origin of more wars against his tribe or any other, even the Osage.

"No. We cannot hope to stop death by creating more death. We must dissuade those who see it then wish to tell others."

"How?"

In thought, Yuma gazed down at the remains of the Great Spirit then lifted his attention to the barn's wreckage where he spotted a drained goat at the base. Though it had a hole in its neck, Yuma spotted another in its leg that more closely resembled a bullet's. The animal had been wounded; most probably a decoy during the great battle.

"We will give it a name," proposed Aponi.

Yuma did not need to think to realize the cleverness of his sister's wit. Adding a name to anything weakened its mystery, and when the mystery weakened, so did fear of the thing.

"The Great Spirit, as it is already known," his sister recommended.

Yuma shook his head.

"Matolu," Kilwannee announced, holding onto some of the pride he once had for their father.

But Yuma disagreed, continuing his head motion. "They cannot know it comes from our people."

"Then we call it what it is... child killer."

Clearly not understanding, Yuma embellished his previous explanation, "They will be angry and afraid already. We do not want them to have more of either." However, Kilwannee's idiocy did give Yuma a notion that he thought smart. The name needed to sound non-threatening towards man though at the same time, not insult the intelligence of those being told. The point was to tell those who had seen the Great Spirit and witnessed its many gifts.

As suggested moments ago, Yuma glanced over the area to see more of what he could learn. His sight returned to the skeletal goat.

"Sucker of goats."

Yuma waited for the approval of his brother and sister. He watched them as they looked to one another in hopes that the other would be the first to either approve or deny. Then, when neither would demonstrate their verdict, both turned back to Yuma and shrugged their shoulders, unimpressed.

Yuma turned back to the fields. The sun had since set and cast a shadow on the quiet earth. Without the voice of the land speaking to him, he had an unsettling feeling that the journey ahead would not end anytime soon. Though, along the way, he would have many opportunities to think about the name more. Until then, he would learn to hone his skills in tracking without the spirit's help, attempt solidarity and peace with his ill-tempered brother, and practice the Spanish his long ago friend, Raul, had taught him.

Goat sucker.

Yuma turned to his siblings. "¿el Chupacabra?"

BOOK V

Return of the Chupacabra

ACKNOWLEDGEMENT

It's that time to acknowledge those who helped in the creation of something much less valuable than the priceless time they donated.

Sue McSorley
Richard Dickie
Chad Duncan
Casey Preston
Bobby Norman, author of Black Water
AJ Coonley, author of the Unforeseen Circumstances
Collection
Kandy Kay Scaramuzzo, author of Pie, An Old Brown
Horse (That Knows What He's Doing)

Thank you!

PRAISE FOR AUTHOR

A chilling tale with richly developed characters.

- THE BIBLIOPHILIC BOOK BLOG

The chupacabra is awesome, and so are the other characters. They live. They breathe. They bleed. Chilling and disturbing. Fascinating and addictive.

- FU ONLY KNEW BOOK BLOG

CHUPACABRA SERIES

Over the span of more than 100 years, 7 novels + 1 short story tells the tale of a cyptid beast starting in America's Old West to more recent times.

Night Of The Chupacabra: Chupacabra Series 1

Curse Of The Chupacabra: Chupacabra Series 2

Legend Of The Chupacabra: Chupacabra Series 3

Dawn Of The Chupacabra: Chupacabra Series 4

Return Of The Chupacabra: Chupacabra Series 5 (Coming In 2024)

Chupacabra Series 6 (Coming Soon)

Chupacabra Series 7 (Coming Soon)

Hunt For The Chupacabra, A Micro Story

BOOKS BY THIS AUTHOR

The Ghost Of Christmas Past, A Novella

**The Night After Christmas,
A Picture Book**

**(Coming In 2024) A Halloween
Tale Of Old, A Picture Book**

Rattlesnake, A Short Story

What Adam Wants, A Short Story

**(Coming In 2024) The Dead Diaries,
Short Horror Anthology**